THE WENTWORTHS

By the same author

Death of the Messenger of Joy. Compilation from the Bahá'í Scriptures on the subject of Life After Death. Bahá'í Publishing Trust 1980

Prayer: A Bahá'í Approach (with William Hellaby). George Ronald 1985

Education in the Bahá'í Family. George Ronald 1987

Sarah Ann Ridgway. First Bahá'í in the North of England. George Ronald 2003

O My Brother. The Story of a Search After Truth. George Ronald 2005

THE WENTWORTHS

Alias 'Un-Named'

Written and illustrated by
Madeline Hellaby

Book Guild Publishing
Sussex, England

First published in Great Britain in 2006 by
The Book Guild Ltd
25 High Street
Lewes, East Sussex
BN7 2LU

Typesetting in Baskerville by
MRM Graphics Ltd

Printed and bound in Singapore under the supervision of
MRM Graphics Ltd, Winslow, Bucks

A catalogue record for this book is available from
The British Library.

ISBN 1 84624 034 4

Acknowledgements

I should like to thank those friends who read the manuscript of this book for me in order to see if they thought the story was worthy of publication and for their kind comments and encouragement:

Miss Sylvia Beaghen, Miss Moragh Brooksbank, Mrs Ramona Cleasby, Miss Janet Fozzard, Mrs Wendy Lind, Miss Ann Parker, Miss Lorna Smith, Mrs Louise Turner, Mrs Zoë Turner and Mrs Rita Wright.

I should particularly like to thank Mrs Margaret Sharples and Miss Judith Oppenheimer; Margaret for happily accepting the unenviable task of correcting the manuscript and Judith for her invaluable help, because of her expertise with computers, in preparing it for the publisher.

About this Book

I cannot recall exactly when the Wentworth family and their friends and relations first made themselves known to me, because to begin with I did not write anything down but carried it all round in my head. I think I was about sixteen or seventeen when it started. The story only began to take concrete form when I wrote the first three chapters as a new serial in the Summer 1943 issue of *Story Club Magazine* (a magazine which a close friend and I ran from December 1939 to June 1944). At that stage I had no title for my story, nor, when I came to write it down, could I think of one, so I called it simply 'Un-named'.

I had no overall plan in my head when I began to write; I wrote as ideas came to me. In those days I did not realize that authors actually did research for their books; I thought they were knowledgeable people who wrote about what they knew. My knowledge of what went on in the world and how things worked was extremely limited and it never occurred to me to find out what I did not know. I wrote entirely from imagination, so the early chapters, particularly, show a certain degree of naïvety and ignorance. I wanted things the way I wanted them for the purposes of the story, so that was the way they were!

The story continued, in several exercise books, over a period of some three years. I recorded some landmarks in my diary: I had completed Chapters I to XVIII by April 9th 1944 (I was just nineteen), though only the first nine chapters appeared in the magazines. When I joined the WRNS in May 1944, magazines had to come to an end – I had completed the Summer 1944 issue before I left home. By August 7th 1945 I had reached what is now Chapter XXIV, but I recorded that 'This is not accurate as I have added a whole chapter earlier.' This chapter was written on sheets of paper and inserted into the exercise book in the right place. After that I do not give chapters or pages, merely that I wrote more, until I come to August 28th 1946, when I say 'Un-named has now come to a stop while I work out the next part in detail.' I had by this time got as far as the first paragraph of Chapter XLVI – I even stopped in the middle of a sentence – and the story was never finished. I was a few months over twenty-one.

It sounds as though I had at least a skeleton plan in my head as to what was going to happen next but I am quite sure I had not – I have no recollection of such a plan, anyway. The only thing I did know for certain was what would happen to the two main characters at the end (more or less) and so I wrote the first part of the present Chapter LI also, sometime before August 1946, again on sheets of paper; but what happened in between I had not thought up.

All the places in the story had prototypes in real life but only one *person* was based on anybody I had actually met; and he was only someone I met briefly in passing. It is strange, in a way, that an elderly rector should have left so lasting an impression on me that I based a character in my story on him! All the others, though, were entirely of my own creation.

I did a number of drawings of characters in the story – some several times – between 1943 and 1946; and each installment in *Story Club Magazine* had one or two illustrations of incidents as well.

I do not think I drew any more pictures after the August 1946 entry in my diary. It has always been a source of great joy to me that I could portray reasonably well all the characters who peopled my imaginary worlds in those days. I should perhaps explain at this point that I drew pictures on whatever paper was to hand and some of them were done on thin beige-coloured card. These latter appear a little mottled in reproduction.

Although I wrote the story during the War, the War itself is totally ignored. The only clue, perhaps, to the fact that it was written during that period is that the Oxford that features in this story is the Oxford I knew when I served there as a Wren from November 1944 to March 1946 – and wartime Oxford must have been very different from what it would have been like in peacetime. Also, my characters undertake a good many journeys by train or bus rather than in their cars. This must surely reflect the situation at the time I was writing, when petrol was rationed if not unobtainable for the ordinary citizen: we simply were not geared up to thinking in terms of cars.

In 1992 I unearthed the manuscript and read it through, as far as I had gone, expecting it to be quite awful, but I found it was not as bad as I was expecting. It was not great literature by any stretch of the imagination but I thought, perhaps, it was not entirely without merit. Anyway, I decided it was good enough to keep and finish if I could. When I came to a halt in August 1946 I think I was envisaging a huge great saga and I simply could not think what might happen next; but reading it through after a gap of forty-six years, I realized that it really did not need a great deal more adding to it to round it off. It was not necessary to write a lengthy saga; I did not need to cover more than one year in total. I thought up some incidents to bring it to a conclusion and during the second half of May and the first week of June in 1993 I sat down and finished it; so there is a gap of over forty-six years between the first half of Chapter XLVI and the last ten chapters. It was fun to try and finish the story in roughly the same style as that in which I began it so that the long break in composition should not be too noticeable. It must be fairly unusual to have a period of this length between the writing of the first forty-five-and-a-bit chapters of a book and the last ten! Since then I have tried it out on friends in various age groups, all of whom made favourable comments, so now, after another twelve years, having been busy writing other books in the meantime, I offer it to a wider public and hope they will have a similar reaction.

I can see that I put a great deal of my own experiences and thoughts into the story and it is full of the idealism of my adolescence and early twenties. The Wentworths and all the others were very real to me in those days – and indeed, still are! – and as I was writing the final chapters I saw them and the places they lived in as clearly as I did when I first began to write about them so long ago. Imagination is an amazing gift. I can see them all quite as clearly in my mind's eye as I can see things in my own life that actually happened.

I have very much enjoyed writing about the people in this story and this time it seems appropriate to give it a proper title, so I am calling it *The Wentworths*, with its original title underneath. I hope you will also enjoy their company in which to while away a passing hour.

Madeline Hellaby
2006

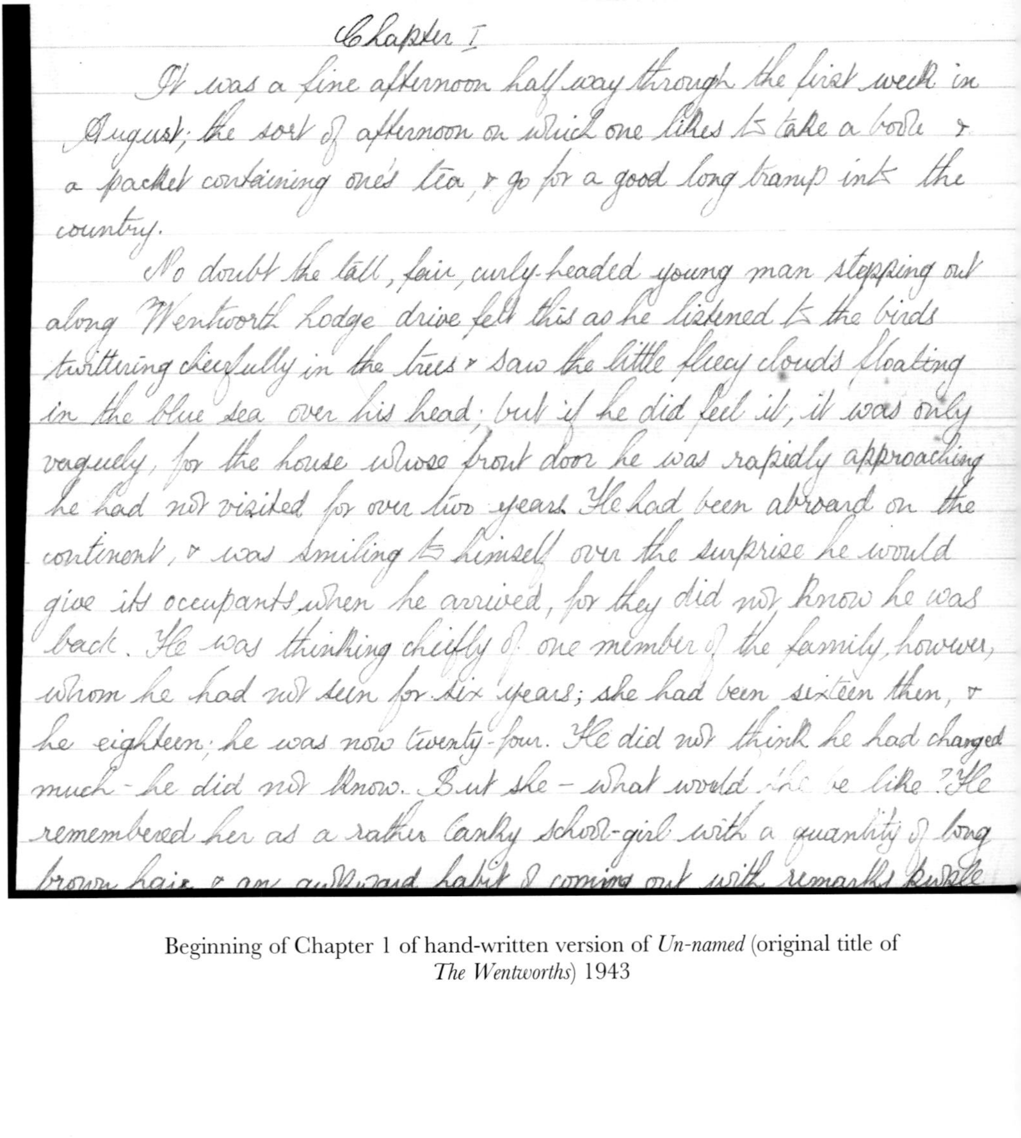

Chapter I

It was a fine afternoon half way through the first week in August; the sort of afternoon on which one likes to take a book & a packet containing one's tea, & go for a good long tramp into the country.

No doubt the tall, fair, curly-headed young man stepping out along Wentworth Lodge drive felt this as he listened to the birds twittering cheerfully in the trees & saw the little fleecy clouds floating in the blue sea over his head; but if he did feel it, it was only vaguely, for the house whose front door he was rapidly approaching he had not visited for over two years. He had been abroad on the continent, & was smiling to himself over the surprise he would give its occupants when he arrived, for they did not know he was back. He was thinking chiefly of one member of the family, however, whom he had not seen for six years; she had been sixteen then, & he eighteen; he was now twenty-four. He did not think he had changed much - he did not know. But she - what would she be like? He remembered her as a rather lanky school-girl with a quantity of long brown hair & an awkward habit of coming out with remarks

Beginning of Chapter 1 of hand-written version of *Un-named* (original title of *The Wentworths*) 1943

Chapter I

It was a fine afternoon halfway through August: the sort of afternoon on which one likes to take a book and a packet containing one's tea, and go for a good long tramp into the country.

No doubt the tall, fair, curly-headed young man stepping out along Wentworth Lodge drive felt this as he listened to the birds twittering cheerfully in the trees and saw the little fleecy clouds floating in the blue sea above his head; but if he did feel it, it was only vaguely. For the house whose front door he was rapidly approaching he had not visited for over two years. He had been abroad, on the Continent, and was smiling to himself over the surprise he would give its occupants when he arrived, for they did not know he was back. He was thinking chiefly of one member of the family, however, whom he had not seen for six years; she had been sixteen then and he eighteen; he was now twenty-four. He did not think he had changed much – he did not know. But she – what would she be like? He remembered her as a rather lanky schoolgirl with a quantity of long brown hair and an awkward habit of coming out with remarks that people would rather have left un-said. He expected she would have grown up very noticeably but he hoped she would not be too prim and proper. Then he laughed to himself as if the mere idea of her being so was quite ridiculous.

By the time he had thought all this out he had reached the bottom of half-a-dozen wide stone steps leading up to the front door. He shook himself, righted his tie, settled his breast-pocket handkerchief, and mounted the steps with an excited apprehension of what would follow the ringing of the bell.

A dog barked somewhere in the building and a voice cried 'Down Rex! Be quiet!' The next thing he knew was that the door was open and with a shout of 'Charlie!' a girl of about fourteen years had flung herself upon him and locked her arms round his neck.

'Hullo, Penny,' he laughed. 'Ow! Get down, you're strangling me!' He tried to undo her clasp, but the maiden would not release her hold until he had given her what she wanted – a hearty kiss. This received, she was willing to let go and allow him to hold her at arms' length and look at her.

'Taller and prettier than ever, by Jove!' he exclaimed gaily, paying her the compliments he knew she liked, for he did not reserve them only for those of his own age and older.

Penelope smiled, pleased, and replied,

'So are you – at least, I mean taller…' She stopped, confused.

'But not prettier, eh, Venus?' suggested Charles, in an amused tone.

'Oh yes! No – I mean…well, anyhow, come in. Helen will be very pleased to see you.'

'Helen? Are you alone, then?'

'Yes, the others are at the sea for six weeks – they've only been gone a week – and Helen and I are housekeeping.'

By this time he was inside and Penelope was shutting the door. Then she led him across the familiar hall and pushed open a door, saying,

'Go in, and I'll find Helen.'

He did as bid and stood once more in the room he knew so well. He had been in it often, for Charles Mainwaring was no stranger to this house. He had been one of its most frequent visitors ever since he could remember, and many things were recalled to his memory as he looked about him: the little chair he had always sat in when he came to tea, stowed away in its usual corner; the portrait of Helen's grandfather hanging over the mantelpiece whom he had once said was like a mixture of the Duke of Wellington and Henry VIII. One by one, incidents, temporarily forgotten, but revived when the causes of their happenings were seen again, came back to him with many quaint details to add to their enjoyment. As his eyes travelled from one object to another they were arrested by a family photograph standing on a beautifully inlaid cabinet. It was obviously a recent one and he moved towards it intending to examine it, as if to prepare himself for the meeting he could not help regarding in some measure awe-ful. His plan did not succeed, however, for he heard singing approaching the door, and the next minute it was opened, and a girl entered the room carrying a vase of mixed flowers, whom he thought the loveliest person he had ever seen.

Helen – for it was she – was watching her flowers and did not notice him at first; but as she was putting the vase down on a table in front of her, she caught sight of a pair of shoes which she knew did not belong to Penelope. She stopped dead and gradually raised her eyes from the shoes, up an extraordinarily long pair of grey pin-stripe trousers and light check sports jacket to the face, whose owner greeted her with a half-bewildered, half friendly smile. For a moment she was puzzled. Who could this be? Then a thought struck her. Could it possibly be? – no, surely not; he was abroad. He watched her expressions with amused interest, and smiled deeper. That left no doubt, and as recognition dawned, she cried, advancing with both hands outstretched,

'Charlie!'

'Helen!'

He took her hands and was about to greet her in the usual way, when he realized she was no longer a child; he paused, hesitating, and asked,

'May I? Do you mind?'

She smiled the way he always loved, and replied,

'I may be grown up in years, Charlie boy, but I still like old friends and old customs.'

With that permission he knew he need no longer doubt, and gave her a good, brotherly kiss – for he was almost a brother – just as he had done to Penelope.

Then she was plumping up the sofa cushions and telling him to sit down and let her look at him. That would not do – she must fetch him some tea. In vain he begged her not to bother; she would not hear of it. Just then Penelope came in.

'Oh, you're here! I've been looking all over for you!' she exclaimed, relieved, when she saw Helen. 'Where are you going?...Oh, let me get tea! I'll do it. Please let me.'

'Very well, only be careful with the best china, won't you?' answered Helen, returning to her seat.

'Don't worry, I'm OK,' came the reply from behind the closing door.

Helen turned to Charles.

'You dear old Charlie boy,' she said, 'I can hardly believe it's six years since I saw you last. You haven't changed in the least...What's the matter?' she added, for he was gazing at her as if he could not quite make out how the gauche schoolgirl of six years ago could possibly have grown into the tall, graceful young woman he saw before him.

'It's you, Helen – I can't understand you…you're sort of *different* somehow, and yet you're not…' For the life of him he could not explain what the change was.

It was a change too subtle for even Charles' keen perception to appreciate. For Helen was a woman, and delighted in many of the powers of attraction, the possession of pretty clothes and the intellectual accomplishments which most girls learn before they have left school. A generous degree of natural beauty was enhanced by a sense of colour and knowledge of tasteful dressing. She had lost the awkward gait of her middle teens, but the freedom of her youth had its reward in making her healthy, strong, yet graceful – 'a healthy mind in a healthy body' – which made all who knew her love her without knowing why.

No wonder, then, that Charles could not understand it; but he felt drawn to her because she was similar to himself. He was tall, fair, extremely handsome, loved the fresh air, yet was never happier than when studying his university subject – languages. They had always been good friends, ever since they could remember, even though Charles was two years older. Of course, the others had been his friends too, but Helen had come first in his affections. As he thought this, he saw the photograph and began,

'Helen, tell me –'

Unfortunately, Helen chose that moment to ask him a question and the result was that they both started to speak at once.

'Sorry!' laughed Helen. 'Go on.'

'My fault entirely,' responded Charles. 'No, you speak first.'

'Well, I was going to ask where you'd sprung up from, now I've time to listen.'

'Oh! Well, I've been home just ten days. I'd have been down sooner, but what with one thing and another – relations and whatnot, all wanting you to go and see them and tell them all about "*dear* Paris, I was there in the summer of 1900..." – you know – I just couldn't manage it.'

'Well, it's just wonderful to see you again. I can hardly believe it's you!'

'Dear Helen! Have I changed so very much then?'

'Oh no. You're just the same as I remember you, Charlie boy.'

'You know, Helen, if I hadn't known you any other way, I should have known you by that.'

'What, "Charlie boy"?'

'Yes. Nobody but you ever called me that. But now let me ask *you* some questions. How are the others? How are your father and mother, and all the rest? I'm longing to see everyone.'

'I'm afraid you won't this time – they won't be back till the end of September. Well, Father's the same as usual, but Mother was not quite up to scratch –'

'Oh, I hope –'

'Don't worry. She wanted a rest, and Phil was keen to get away, so after a lot of discussing and arranging, it was decided that Mother and Father and the boys were to go away and Penny and I were to stay and "keep house", as she puts it. She was terribly anxious to do it – she loves

Helen

Penelope

Charles

Illustration from *Story Club Magazine*, Summer 1943

housework, you know – so now she's revelling in greasy saucepans and baking powder!'

'She seems to enjoy it. I called her "Venus" just now. She *is* pretty, Helen. I hope it won't wear off when she grows up.'

'I don't think it will. She's a dear child, and she's a great help; and what's more, she's a great deal more sensitive to other people's feelings than I'm afraid I was at her age.'

'And Gerry and Alban, how are they?'

'Gerry's going to boarding school next term; he's thrilled! I hope it'll liven him up a bit. He's a quaint child, you know; always browsing over books. Perhaps Ilton will make him wake up a bit more. As for Alban – well, he's thoroughly enjoying himself at Dartmouth, as you can guess. If ever a lad was sea-struck, he is!'

Charles laughed. He well remembered Alban's nautical training when it was only a year old.

At this point Penelope entered with tea for two on a trolley, and proceeded to lay it out on little tables drawn up for the purpose. Charles exclaimed on her deftness but remarked on the fact that she had not provided for herself. She replied that she had had hers (which was not strictly true, for she had only smuggled a piece of cake about three o'clock) and had work to do in the kitchen. The real reason was that she realized she would be in the way, as Helen and Charles had not seen each other for six years and in consequence would have a great deal to talk about, and so considerately kept out of the way.

When she had gone Charles said in a queer voice, as if the interest were forced,

'What about Phil? Is he all right?'

Chapter II

Helen paused before she answered, guardedly,

'He's the same as usual.'

'I see.' Charles paused, as she did; then he said, seriously, 'Helen, I never could get you – or any of the others – to talk much about Phil. Why won't you? What is the matter with him?'

She looked up and began,

'Charles, I –'

'No, no, Helen, I want to know. You must tell me.'

'Well, if you insist. He never really got over that…'

'That murder which I didn't commit?'

'Yes. Oh, Charlie boy, I'm sorry. I know you don't like it –' This was added anxiously as Charles rose to his feet and went to the window. He played with the curtain cord, struggling with emotions which he found hard to control. He hated going over that month three years ago which he had spent in prison, suspected of a murder he had, as he said, never committed. But it must be done, so that he should understand the exact extent of Philip's hostility. That he firmly believed he had done it, Charles was perfectly well aware; he also knew that he had managed to persuade the rest of the family, with the exception of Helen, that he had done it, for had he not been present? When it was at last proved that he was not to blame, they had been the first to beg his pardon, and had not Helen, who had trusted in him from the first, been triumphant when she heard? But Philip never would apologize; for some reason best known to himself, Philip still chose to hold a grudge against him, even when his innocence had been proved beyond doubt. Why? What motive could he have had for such behaviour?. Was it jealousy, spite, or just his natural obstinacy? Whatever it was, Charles knew Philip disliked him, and accordingly, he avoided him on all possible occasions.

Having thought this out, he turned and said,

'Helen.'

'Yes?'

'Do you mind if I tell you all about it? I never have done, not even to Father, and I think I should feel easier with it off my chest.'

'Yes, do, if it would comfort you, Charlie boy.'

Charles returned to his seat, and having fortified himself with a piece of bread and butter, plunged into his story.

'Just over four years ago, you will remember, I spent my vacation helping to do office work in the family firm.

'There were about half-a-dozen of us working in this office, and the others hated me, because I worked hard and got on while they fooled about; I don't think your uncle knew what went on, or he never would have allowed it. I remember how they used to play up the foreman and "borrow" people's belongings to do some job or other (they were never returned). They tried to do it on me one time, but they didn't succeed. I was too quick for them! I tried to make them see that their behaviour was not cricket, but they wouldn't listen to me, considering me in the light of an upstart, and an object of ridicule because I wouldn't join in with their tricks. I know they wanted to get me into trouble, and this time they succeeded.

'One day, your uncle came round the works with some visitors, including Phil, who was interested in it. He stayed behind to speak to me, and as he was only sixteen at the time, naturally wanted to know all about everything, and would keep asking questions.

'Had it been at any other time I should have been only too pleased to answer them, but as it happened I had a job on hand which I particularly wanted to get finished; I suppose I must have been rather curt, for he remarked, "You *are* in a bad mood this morning!"

'I apologized and endeavoured to explain that I was extremely busy, when one of the fellows – a nasty, sly-faced, red-headed piece of work – cut in with, "Don't disturb mother's conscientious little darling on his duty, Mr Wentworth, he doesn't like it."

'That made me boil – I can see it as though it were yesterday – and I'm sure I blushed scarlet. I told him to hold his tongue. Then another, delighted at having an audience who would doubtless repeat all he had seen to those in authority, being of the family, added, "He even lets the foreman think he's done *our* work too." '

Charles began to get excited, and poured forth the next part of his tale as though he were reading parts in a play, without names, which made it rather difficult for Helen to follow; but she would not have stemmed his eagerness by interrupting for so trivial a matter for anything.

'At that I wasn't going to stand it any longer. I jumped to my feet' – he did so with clenched fists – 'and said, "Say that again, will you, you confounded liar, and I'll give you a hiding you won't soon forget."

'Did that make any difference? Not it. He said something else – I don't know what – can't remember now – and I went for him – the others just stood and looked on. We were in the space between his desk and the window. I had my back to it.

' "Now, you take back what you said, or I'll not promise what happens." He wouldn't, and I struck out. Just at that moment he tripped up and fell over backwards – I never touched him! He'd gone before my hand was anywhere near his lousy face – and he landed with his head on the corner of – and it was very sharp – the corner of another desk. He was killed! Killed! – but I never killed him. I never touched him! They wouldn't believe me – those fellows said I had – gave evidence that I had – although they knew as well as I did that I hadn't! It was a chance to make mischief, and I couldn't prove that I hadn't hit him. Phil couldn't see from where he was – he was behind him and it must have looked as though I had hit him, but I didn't!'

He calmed down then a little, and turning to Helen, cried,

'They sent me to prison, Helen, for suspected murder – me, Charles Mainwaring, suspected of killing a man!'

He sat down again, and Helen saw that great beads of perspiration were standing out on his forehead. That brought it home to her what all this meant to Charles – how he must have suffered with this weight on his mind, haunting him, haunting him, for more than three years.

'But you didn't do it, Charlie! I knew you didn't even though everybody else was convinced that you had. I trusted you; Phil couldn't make *me* believe it, though he tried to.'

'I know, Helen. I don't think I could have borne it if I hadn't had your faith to comfort me. And you were right – they had to admit it in the end.'

'How? How did the truth come out, Charlie?'

'One of the fellows who had a bit more conscience than the rest, confessed.'

'Confessed?'

'Yes – the truth. There, don't let's talk of that any more. I'm sorry to make you listen, but I had to get it out somehow.'

Charles thus relieved himself of a burden which had been secretly preying on him ever since that fatal day in the office. It never did so again, for it is amazing how confiding one's troubles to an understanding friend lessens them considerably. It is true, the saying that friends double our joys and halve our sorrows.

Helen discreetly changed the subject and soon had interested Charles in telling her about the past month, for she had had no letter from him during that time. He told her numerous stories of unlucky adventures in strange cities, enthralled her with descriptions of beautiful scenery and fascinated her with experiences among the people, streets and funny little old shops in the back alleys of Paris, Hamburg and other places he had visited. When Penelope came in to 'clear away the tea' he had quite forgotten his mood of half an hour before.

'Shall I take Rex for a walk, Helen?' she asked. 'He ought to go, because I hadn't time this morning and he hasn't had a good long walk since Monday.'

'Yes, and if Charlie likes, we'll all go,' replied Helen. 'We always take him on the down for his *long* walk,' she added. 'Would you like to come?'

'Very much. I haven't been for a proper tramp for ages. And I'd like to see Rex. Is he still as lively as ever?'

'Rather!' exclaimed Penelope. 'You can take him if you want to, till we get on the down. We have to keep him on the lead till we get there, because there're so many horrible dogs in the village and they all like to stop and talk. Rex doesn't generally take any notice of them, but he loves bicycles, I don't know why, and it's dangerous, you see, because you don't know what's coming down the road, and he might get run over.'

'Thank you,' said Charles, when this long explanation was finished. Penelope ran off to fetch her hat, leaving Helen and Charles to exchange amused looks and laugh over her speech.

'She's just the same,' said the latter. 'She always was one for lengthy explanations, if I remember rightly.'

'Yes,' laughed Helen, 'but she's not as bad as Gerry. You should hear him when he gets going – a regular Aristotle!'

She led the way to the door, saying as they passed into the light, spacious hall,

'Will you wait a minute while I just fetch my jacket?'

Charles obediently did so, and instinctively went towards the window and fresh air – for it was open. On the cill was another such vase of flowers as Helen had brought into the drawing room – a profusion of tiny-petalled flora, whose names he did not know, but whose delicate form he considered vastly beautiful. The whole vase reflected Helen: a complexity of separate units all joining to make one lovely ensemble.

He was disturbed from his reverie by Helen's return, followed a few seconds later by Penelope's abrupt entry from the passage leading to the kitchen with a large and lively King Charles spaniel, who rushed on the visitor with much yapping and wagging of tail, as if to say, 'Welcome! Welcome! I've not forgotten you.'

Charles allowed himself to be pawed, bending over him and slapping him vigorously.

'Hullo, Rex! Hullo, old chap! Glad to see me, are you? It's a fine dog! Oh, it's a fine doggy! – but don't do that please, old boy' – as Rex tried to kiss his face – 'You're a good old fellow but I don't like dog-lick!'

When Rex had at last suffered himself to be attached to his lead, they set off.

Helen (1945)

Penelope (1945)

Chapter III

They passed the Lodge gates and turning to the right, walked towards the quaint little Sussex village nestling in its hollow amongst the breezy, rolling downs. Taking a short cut down a 'twitt'n', as the narrow alley-ways are called in that part of the country, they came out into the main street, whose one triangular open space served as green, bus stop and general meeting-place, and which was overlooked by the most important shops in the village. There were not many people about, as it was the hour when shoppers return home to their tea and shop-keepers retire to their living-rooms for a brief respite, and hope nobody will come to disturb them.

A bus had just pulled up under the big shady oak tree in the middle of the triangle, and a few people were descending with the day's shopping from the neighbouring town; hardly anybody got on. A cyclist went by, two or three rather dirty children were gazing longingly at the mixed array displayed in the confectioner's window, and a dog barked somewhere in the distance. Having paused to take all this in, the three resumed their walk and, leaving the village behind them, emerged on to the open road.

It was a broad, sweeping road, let down between a wooded hill slope on the one side and windswept turf on the other. A white dotted line ran along the middle of it, for it was the main road. The fence – a string of poles with wire between – was some way up the high banks of long grass studded with the delicate mauve heads of nodding scabious and the tight acorns of the salad burnet.

Penelope clambered up and down, picking a flower here and a leaf there, until, by the time they reached the gate leading on to the down, she had quite a handful.

'Oh look!' she cried at one point, stopping to gather a long-stalked plantain. 'Here's a plantain with its Sunday hat on!' Ever since she could remember, that is what the family had called plantains in full bloom.

Having looked both ways to see no traffic was coming, they crossed the road, opened the gate (Penelope climbed over) and went through. There was a rough, pebbly track leading over the down, white with the chalk rock below it and strewn with flints, which Penelope picked up and cast aside in her efforts to find a pair capable of producing a spark. She gave it up after half-a-dozen fruitless attempts, agreeing with Charles that you had to have darkness if you wanted satisfactory results.

Rex, now released from his lead, darted here, there and everywhere, like a flash of autumn gold, bounding off in search of imaginary rats, rushing back to jump in excited circles round their feet. Charles threw him a stone and after that there was no peace until Penelope whistled to him to come exploring.

Charles and Helen walked on alone, recalling old memories and discussing the past six years.

'Why is it,' asked the former, 'that I never saw you? I called often enough.'

'I don't know, Charlie. I suppose you always managed to come when I was away, or out.'

'It seems strange, though. Anyway, it makes the meeting all the more pleasant now it has come.'

He smiled at her and she returned the compliment, both thinking how fine the other looked and how glad they were of each other's company. They were very good friends, these two.

By this time they had reached the top of the slope and paused to look round. Below lay the village in its mantle of trees, and all round spread undulating chalky downland, broken here and there by a cluster of trees or a patch of gorse bushes. The road gleamed white and ribbon-like, threading its way amongst the patchwork. A warm breeze was blowing, laden with the sweet fragrance of the thyme and the Sussex freshness, unimaginable to those who have not breathed it. The sun shone cheeringly and cloud shadows played tag across the grass.

'Isn't it just – just wonderful!' cried Helen. 'God has given us a very beautiful world!'

'Yes,' agreed Charles. 'Here we are, on top of the world, in the heart of all His glory and yet there are millions of poor beggars stuffing their heads off in offices, who never realize what miracles lie waiting for them just at the other side of their doorsteps if only they'll go and look.'

'I *couldn't* work in an office! – could you?'

'No, I couldn't. It's lucky we both like fresh air, Helen, or we should be having continual arguments as to whether or not we should go out.'

Charles (1945)

'Yes. You know, Charlie, I'm sure that's partly why we've always liked each other so much – we both seem to have similar tastes.'

'I'm sure it is. I certainly couldn't have borne you if you had been a bookworm.'

'Nor I you had you not appreciated nature as I do; and flowers, and houses, and pretty things. By the way, there's a lovely patch of rock roses along here. Shall we go and find them?'

'Yes. I expect Penny would like to pick some – I'll call her.'

He accordingly did so, but received no answer.

'I wonder where she is,' mused Helen.

'Oh, I expect she's burrowing with Rex and can't hear,' replied Charles. 'She'll be all right.'

'But the down has some dangerous places in it, and she may not bother to read notices. I don't like to leave her. Call again.'

'Penny!' shouted Charles, 'Pe-e-enny!'

There was still no answer, but he passed it off lightly, saying,

'Oh, she'll come when she wants to. Let's see your rock roses.'

'I sincerely hope she will,' responded Helen. However, she led the way off the track to the left, and soon a glorious patch of golden-starred rock roses set amongst a sheltering cirque of gorse bushes sent everything else out of their heads.

'I say!' exclaimed Charles when he saw them. 'How perfectly grand!'

They looked at them for a few minutes, then Charles said,

'It's very sunny and out-of-the-wind here, Helen. Let's sit down for a bit – it's quite dry.'

Choosing the sunniest spot, they seated themselves, and while Helen stretched out her legs in front of her and leaned on her hands, Charles clasped his knees in his arms and rested his chin on them.

After a few moments' silence, during which they had contemplated the view and taken in its beauty, Helen said,

'We've talked a lot about the past, Charlie boy; now let's talk about the future. What are your plans? Teaching?'

Charles made an exclamation of disgust.

'No jolly fear!' he replied. 'I couldn't sit at a desk all day, drumming French and German verbs into a lot of dull-heads who couldn't understand them. No, I want to get a job as a travelling agent for one of the big firms – an outdoor life for me! As I said before, I couldn't stuff in an office all day!'

'I should think not. That sounds frightfully interesting. Have you applied?'

'Yes, last week. I'm still waiting to hear the result.'

'Oh, I *do* hope you get the job! The very best of luck to you.'

'Thanks. But what about you? What are you doing?'

'At present I'm not doing anything – just playing the Lady Bountiful to the village children.'

'Do you call that nothing? Seems to me it involves many qualities which few people possess all at once – understanding, kindness, tact…And how does it go down? What do you do, exactly?'

'Well, I teach them sewing, music – some of them have talent if only it could be developed. Then there's gardening, and housework, and –'

'And you call that nothing? Well I'd like to know your idea of something. I think you're doing a fine piece of work, Helen, and I congratulate you on it.'

'Thank you. You'll have to come too.'

'I should be honoured. But do you have no holiday? – they must wear you out.'

'I'm on holiday at the moment; but I love the job. Don't think I don't get tired sometimes and feel I'm no earthly use – I do, especially when things go wrong. I shouldn't be human if I didn't, for nobody should ever be satisfied with what he does, except perhaps very occasionally. But so long as I succeed in making them happy, busy and useful, that's all I care about.'

'That's a very high standard, but with you to lead, I'd like to see the child who'd dare to fail or turn out a criminal!'

' "You pay a pretty compliment, Mr Gerrard",' laughed Helen. 'By the way, Alban will be very disappointed not to have seen you to say "Ahoy there, m'hearty!" to.'

It was Charles' turn to laugh, for Helen imitated her brother so well that he could almost see the sailor lad come rolling up the grass.

'When the others come back,' continued Helen, 'I'm going to spend a month with Margaret and Bernard.'

'Margaret? Bernard?' Charles sounded puzzled.

'Yes – you know, Margaret and Bernard Robertson.'

'Oh-h! yes; I know. Bernard and I were at Rugby together. How are they?'

'I thought you were. They're very well, thank you. I haven't seen Margaret since she was here last year and I haven't seen Bernard for about two years. I envy her, you know.'

'Oh? Why?'

'Well, because she has Bernard. I'm sometimes rather lonely, Charlie boy, because there's nobody at home to confide in. Phil's younger than I am. I wish *I* had an older brother.'

'Well, you've got an older friend, Helen.'

'I know, and you're almost a brother, Charlie dear, but you're not there always. Margaret is very lucky.'

Helen's jeremiads were cut short by the sudden arrival, from nowhere apparently, of a very excited Rex, who barked loudly and ran from bush to bush and then back to them, his eyes plainly telling them that something had happened.

'Hullo, Rex, old man,' said Helen when he first appeared. 'What's the matter?'

'I told you she'd come,' said Charles. 'Rex, where's Penny?'

Rex barked and ran to the edge of the gorse bushes, barked again and came back. Helen jumped up.

'Rex!' she cried. 'Where's Penny?'

The same process followed, only this time Rex did not come back. He dashed off up the slope, feeling sure they would see what he wanted. He was right, for Charles realized what Helen was fearing, and with one cry of 'Quick, Helen, after him!' ran up the hill in pursuit. There was no time to exchange words; both hurried as fast as they could, for Rex's behaviour showed quite obviously that something was amiss.

When they came to a fence with a notice saying there was a dangerous drop ahead, and Rex went through, Helen clutched Charles' arm with 'Penny! Good God!' Then they scrambled through the wire and carefully hastened to where Rex was barking up and down the edge of an old disused quarry.

They sank down on to their knees and looked over. About twelve feet below them was the rough, boulder-strewn floor, and lying with one leg crumpled up under her, motionless and white, was Penelope.

Helen gave a little shriek, and involuntarily put up her arm as if to shield herself from a blow. All the colour left her face and she cried out,

'Penny! Charlie! – oh, do something – quick!'

Chapter IV

'Hold on, I'll get her,' Charles said, stumbling to his feet. He made a rapid survey of the land and decided that the easiest descent was from the right, where there was a slope and not a cliff, and went towards it. He ventured slowly down, for it was nothing but scree and looked as if it might slide at the slightest touch. Once or twice he set some fragments rolling and had to pause till everything was still again, but he reached the bottom at last and made his way to where Penelope was lying. Helen, meantime, was watching him anxiously from above and when he bent down to pick Penelope up, she called,

'Is she hurt?'

'Can't tell yet. I hope not, but considering the height she fell from, I should think it's extremely likely.'

A sudden fear gripped Helen.

'Charlie! You don't think she's...*killed* herself, do you?'

'No, no. Don't think of such things,' Charles responded quickly. He lifted the little girl up as gently as he could but even so she uttered an indistinct groan.

'Penny, am I hurting you?' he asked.

There was no answer. If she had regained consciousness, it was only for a second, and now she remained a dead weight in his arms.

Assured that she could therefore feel nothing, Charles hoisted her on to one shoulder and retraced his steps to the bottom of the scree. Here was the difficulty. To come down was comparatively easy, but to go up again with an additional weight was quite a different matter. However, after some effort he managed it, and Penelope was lying between him and Helen on the grass several yards away from the edge of the precipice.

'Better not try to bring her round,' Charles was saying. 'She probably wouldn't thank us. The only thing to do is get her home as quickly as possible and send for the doctor.'

'But how do you propose to get her home?' asked Helen.

'Why, carry her, to be sure.'

'Carry her! But you can't!'

'Why not? I carried her up that slope, didn't I? Hard roads are much easier to walk on than loose boulders. Come; we're wasting time.'

So saying, he once more shouldered his burden, and they started off on the homeward journey, Helen holding on to whatever part of Penelope's person was available, fondly imagining that by so doing she was lessening the weight for Charles. She kept her eyes open for any possible transport, for she was sure Charles must be finding Penelope heavier than he would admit, but nothing appeared. The walk was therefore dreary; hardly a word was spoken, for each was busy with his own thoughts. Charles wished he had not agreed to go for the walk, or at least that he had kept his eye on Penelope and not allowed her to go wandering off by herself. Helen questioned herself alternately – what was the damage and oughtn't she to ask at one of the houses if they could borrow a cart. Periodically she asked, 'Isn't she too heavy? Hadn't I better ask them to lend us their wagon?' and 'No, it's quite all right, thanks, I can manage,' was the answer. Penelope, however, *was* heavy, and Charles was not sorry when they at last reached the Lodge and she was safely deposited on the sofa in the lounge. When she had been fairly settled, he asked,

'What's the doctor's telephone number?'

'Edmuston 7. But let me do something.'

'Edmuston 7? Thanks. You can do something by getting a couple of hot water bottles ready for Penny.'

'All right.'

Each departed to his task. Charles was finished first, and sought out Helen in the kitchen to demand smelling salts, water, sponge and a towel. These provided, he returned to the lounge and proceeded to bathe Penelope's face and hands. Then he applied the smelling salts, and after a few minutes, she began to show signs of life. She tried to turn over, but fell back with a groan and fainted again. Charles persisted with his treatment, and Helen returned to the room with the bottles just as Penelope came round once more. She put one at her feet and the other beside her. Penelope was still too dazed to understand what was going on, for everything seemed enveloped in a red mist, and Charles and Helen were merely indistinct shapes which moved in it. She heard a voice and realized that someone was speaking to her. What was he saying? She was only conscious of an acute pain in her right leg, and for some time could not concentrate on the words put to her.

'Where does it hurt, Penny?' the somebody asked for the second time.

She turned her eyes in the direction of the voice, and as her senses collected themselves, she found Charles leaning over her. In a minute she was fully conscious, though still feeling a little hazy. She made an effort to speak.

'In my right leg – below the knee,' she said, wondering why everything kept going round in circles. 'It hurts everywhere, but I think that's the worst.'

Charles looked at Helen, who was leaning over the back of the sofa. Though he said nothing, she knew what his glance meant: a broken, or at least a cracked bone somewhere.

'Can I have a glass of water?' asked Penelope faintly.

'Yes, dear, I'll fetch one,' said Helen. When she had gone, Charles pulled up a chair and sat down on it.

'There won't be much longer to wait,' he said to Penelope. 'The doctor will be here in a few minutes and he'll soon set you to rights. Does it hurt frightfully?'

'Well, rather.'

Helen returned with the water, and while Penelope was drinking it, Charles beckoned her over to the window and said, in a low voice,

'Helen, let us be quite clear from the start. This is my affair, as if I hadn't come this wouldn't have happened.'

'Oh, nonsense, Charlie!' interrupted Helen. 'We should probably have gone on the down anyway. We very often do.'

'But you would have been with Penny. Anyway, that's not the point. *I* am head nurse in this hospital, and Penny is *my* patient. We must have somebody to run the place, and if we both nurse her there won't be anyone to get the meals.'

'But Charlie –'

'No, Helen, I mean it. You can't run the house *and* look after Penny, so you leave her to me.'

'That's all very well, Charlie boy, today, but I shall have to manage by myself tomorrow, and the next day, and the next, till Penny's well, so why be so particular for one evening?'

'My dear, stupid Helen, do you honestly think I'm going to leave you *alone* to look after things? Surely you can't think that? As long as Penny's laid up I stay, whether you want me to or not.'

'Charlie, *really* there's no need, thank you very much –'

'Of course there's a need! Unless you want to see yourself worn to a shadow with all the extra work. Helen, *please*, it's my fault and I must do *something* to make up for it.'

'Let us be quite clear from the start.'
Illustration from *Story Club Magazine*, Christmas 1943

Helen saw he was serious even while denying heatedly that he was to blame, and she had to give in.

'You're a dear, kind boy, and I can't tell you how grateful I am,' she said when she had accepted his offer.

'Oh, that's all right. Only thing to do.'

The shrill call of the front door bell cut short their conversation and announced the arrival of the doctor. Helen went to let him in.

'Good afternoon, Helen,' Charles heard him say, as he walked into the hall. 'What's all this now?'

'It's Penelope,' Helen answered. 'I'm terribly afraid she's broken her leg. She says it hurts her.'

'Broken leg? Hm. Well, let's have a look at it.'

Helen ushered him into the room and introduced him to Charles.

'This is my friend Charles Mainwaring,' she said. 'Charlie, this is Doctor Kennedy.'

'How do you do, Sir?'

'Good afternoon, Mainwaring. I seem to know your face.'

'Oh yes, Sir, you probably do. I've been here often.'

Doctor Kennedy merely grunted and turned his attention to Penelope.

'Well,' he said, 'what do you think you've been doing breaking your legs and causing everybody a lot on unnecessary trouble?'

Doctor Kennedy had a way of making people feel exceedingly small sometimes, with his cutting remarks and the brusque tone in which he delivered them, but his 'bark was worse than his bite' and the shaggy eyebrows overshadowed a pair of kindly grey eyes, which, if keen, could also twinkle merrily when he wished. Penelope, however, was still too young to understand him, and if she did not actually fear him, she was never comfortable in his presence. Had she not been too much shaken up to bear moving, she would have wriggled uneasily under his gaze – he always made her feel guilty of at least doing things on purpose to annoy him; but as it was, she could do nothing but face him.

'I don't know,' she said, somewhat feebly.

'And I'm sure I don't,' responded the doctor. 'However, as you've done it, we shall have to mend the damage, I suppose. Now, where exactly is the pain?'

'In my right leg, below the knee,' said Penelope, with studied deliberateness. The doctor started to feel it, saying,

'Tell me when I come to it.'

Penelope set her teeth and clutched the side and seat of the sofa during the operation, for it was very painful and she did not wish to show it.

She watched him with fixed eyes till his thumbs pressed on the tender spot.

'There!' she cried and tears came into her eyes.

'M-hm,' said Doctor Kennedy, rising, 'Well, I can't be quite sure whether it's a break or only a crack until I have an X-ray of it. Probably you don't feel like coming to the surgery do you, eh, wounded soldier?'

'I don't feel as if I could move an inch at present.'

'No, I daresay you don't; but I'm afaid you must. I have to see what the extent of the damage is. We'll be very careful.'

Penelope realized now that she hurt all over and she really did not feel like moving just then. But she knew that there was no arguing with Doctor Kennedy and she had to go through with it. The sooner it was over and done with the better. She therefore accepted the inevitable with a reasonably good grace and merely said,

'Oh all right.'

She submitted to Charles lifting her from the sofa and carrying her to the doctor's car. She was laid very carefully on the back seat and the three of them drove off.

The X-ray was taken and Penelope was brought back and laid once more on her sofa, glad to be able to lie down again and relax. It had been rather an ordeal although she had been brave and had not complained.

As the doctor was leaving, he turned to Charles and said,

'By the way, young man, you might call for some medicine in an hour or so.'

When they came back into the lounge, Helen stood in front of Charles and said firmly,

'Now, Charlie boy, it's my turn. You've done quite enough for one afternoon. I insist on your sitting down and letting me get you a cup of tea.'

'Well, it certainly would be a good idea, but,' he added, raising a finger and wagging it at her, 'only on one condition.'

'What's that?'

'That you have one too.'

Helen laughed.

'All right, you silly boy, if that's the only way to make you have it.'

Penelope begged to be allowed to partake also, so the three of them relaxed over what was for all a very welcome drink.

Chapter V

The X-ray revealed nothing more than a cracked fibula, which was soon dealt with; it was a pity that the cure was not also as speedy, but Doctor Kennedy ordered six weeks' rest at least if it were to set properly. Penelope groaned when she heard the verdict, for of all people to be 'cooped up indoors' – to use her own expression – she was the worst, being a particularly fresh air type of person.

However, orders were orders and she had to submit. Charles and Helen rearranged the lounge so that the sofa was by the window, and she was established there. She had the windows open as much as she was allowed, but the confinement tried her sorely, and she longed to be outside. She did not know how much she loved the downs until she could no longer go on them; then she caught a cold with lying in a draught and this, on top of the restriction of the sofa, contrived to make her utterly miserable.

Charles was untiring in his efforts to amuse her. While Helen – at his command – was busy about the house, he would spend the time sitting beside her, reading, playing games, or telling her about his travels on the Continent. He was patient with her moods, and when she was feeling particularly sorry for herself, he would tease her and tell her funny stories until she was forced to laugh and forget her misfortunes.

Helen had decided not to tell her mother and father what had happened. As she said to Charles, it would only upset her mother and make her holiday unbearable with worrying about Penelope. She would, in all probability, have insisted on coming home, and Helen would not have that, as she had not been well and a change and a rest were necessary. Charles agreed and they both bound Penelope to secrecy. Helen wrote that Charles had called in and was staying with them, and she would try and persuade him to remain until they came back so that they could see him.

Unfortunately, Penelope's cold did not get better; in fact it grew worse and she had to be transported to her bed. She became feverish and wanted attention at all hours of the night as well as the day. Charles slept lightly and was ready at the slightest call to fetch her a drink or smooth

Charles was tireless in his efforts to amuse her.
Illustration from *Story Club Magazine*, Christmas 1943

out her pillows. In vain Helen begged him to let her take a turn, or he would wear himself out. He only laughed and said he was quite all right. Besides, he added, when she went to sleep, thunderstorms, let alone feeble cries, could not wake her. Reluctantly she had to admit that it was so, but she was anxious for him, all the same, and wished he would not do so much.

Doctor Kennedy came every few days and when the fever was at its height he came every day. She was thoroughly shaken up by the fall, he said, which made her more susceptible to illness than she would have been otherwise, but he did not consider there was any danger; she just needed great care, which he was satisfied to notice she was receiving. Charles, he observed, was beginning to look tired and he fancied he knew the reason why, but he wisely said nothing – to Charles, at least – for he knew that he was of the type who, once having undertaken a job, would carry it through to the end whatever the consequences. To Helen he did make some remark on his observations.

'Young Mainwaring,' he said one day as he was leaving, 'he's looking pretty washed out. What's he been up to?'

'He insists on looking after Penny entirely by himself, Doctor. He won't let me do any more than help. Can't *you* make him stop?'

'No, my dear,' with a pat on the shoulder, 'I think we'd better leave him. He wouldn't appreciate an interference and it can't do him any harm.'

'Really?'

'Yes, really. There, child, don't worry. Let your friend handle this in his own way. He'll thank you in the end.'

'Well, if you think it's best...But Penny? – she *is* better, isn't she, Doctor?'

'Yes, yes. She'll mend now. She slept soundly last night, so we'll soon have her on her pins again.'

'But her leg? All this tossing about hasn't hurt that, has it?'

'No, there's no harm done. Now you go and have a good rest, Helen. You need it.'

With that he departed, leaving Helen with two feelings – one of gladness because Penelope was better, and the other of anxiety, in spite of Doctor Kennedy's reassuring words, for Charles.

By the time Penelope was well enough to be brought downstairs again, it was well into September. The family were to return at the end of the month, and there were a lot of preparations to be made for their return, which kept Helen busy. Once again, Charles acted as companion to the invalid and read and talked as much as she wished. He even made up pieces of poetry for her and to her, which amused her greatly and with which she was duly delighted. But there was a more frequent tendency on Charles' part to yawn and to lapse into silence. He did what he could to prevent it and would not complain, and as Penelope did not seem to notice it, he struggled on to the best of his ability.

The time drew on, and it was within a week of the family's expected return. Helen and Penelope began to get very excited and Charles experienced the same feeling of throbbing apprehension he had had when he first came nearly six weeks ago. They talked of them quite frequently and Charles found himself looking forward to seeing them all again, even Philip, whom of the family he least wished to meet.

One evening, while Helen was seeing Penelope to bed, he stood by the window in the lounge, wondering to himself whether he ought not to go. He had come with the intention of going the same evening, and had stayed practically six weeks. Had he not already outspent his welcome? They would not want to be bothered with a visitor when they had just come back from a holiday. He knew himself what it was like and what a great deal of work had to be done to make up for the time spent in 'pleasuring'. After all, he could call again when they were more ready to receive him. He came to the conclusion he should depart and told Helen so when she came downstairs for their evening chat.

Helen would not hear of it. He had stayed all this time working like a Trojan and he was not going to run away at the last moment.

'How shall I face Mother and Father about Penny if you're not there to stand by me?' she said.

'As if you're not perfectly capable of defending yourself,' laughed Charles. 'Besides, you won't want me hanging around at a home-coming and a family affair.'

'But Charlie boy, you know you're almost one of the family.' A roguish look came into her eyes and she wagged her head, saying, 'I know! You don't want to see Phil. You're avoiding Phil. That's what it is.'

'In that case, I most certainly will stay, just to show you that I don't care a brass farthing for Phil,' replied Charles, yielding, which was exactly what she wanted him to do. She laughed and said,

'I thought that would get you. But anyway, do sit down and I'll fetch you a cup of tea – *please*' as Charles showed signs of remonstrance. 'Lie down on the sofa – it's the most comfortable.'

'Thanks, I will.' Charles threw himself on to it and relaxed for the first time since he had been there. He was more tired than he knew, and what with the warmth of the fire which had been lit for Penelope and his own weariness, he closed his eyes and gradually forgot everything else but how pleasant it was to be comfortable…

Helen returned with the tray, and placing it on a nearby table, said,

'Here we are, Charlie boy. This ought to be welcome.'

There was no answer. Helen looked at him and saw that he was fast asleep.

'Poor old Charlie!' she whispered. 'He's completely worn out. Oh, if only I'd known! He shouldn't have done so much.'

She tiptoed to the chair where Penelope's rugs were kept and, taking the top one, unfolded it and softly and carefully spread it over him. He never moved, so she ventured to raise the arm which was hanging over the edge of the seat and place it gently under the rug. She fetched a hot water bottle and set it at his feet, then paused to study him.

He was just the same as she remembered him, only now it was a man's face and not a boy's she was looking at; he was taller and broader than when she had seen him last but in every other respect he was exactly the same. She was so pleased to have him with her again that she wanted to hug him, and probably would have done so had she not thought he would wake and be scandalized. She had had so little time to reflect on Charles as Charles, so different had his visit been from what they both expected, so now all her feelings seemed to come with a rush and it was only by a great effort that she restrained herself from following her instincts. The next minute she was reproaching herself for having thought of such a thing.

'Don't be an idiot,' she said to herself. 'Now is not the time to indulge in sentimental romanticisms. If you stand there staring at him much longer, he will probably wake up. You don't know you haven't got the power of the Evil Eye!'

Resolutely she turned her back on the sofa, put the guard in front of the fire, drew the curtains so that the light should not wake him in the morning before he was ready, and crept out of the room.

She looked in on her way to bed but Charles was still asleep, so she left him undisturbed. Penelope had been slumbering for two hours, and the house was very still. Helen went upstairs but she did not go into her bedroom. Instead, she pushed open the door of her study, which was next to it. Slowly, and in deep thought, she entered the room and automatically switched on the light. The curtains were not drawn, so she moved across the room to effect the operation, and as she approached the window she saw that there were one or two stars. The light inside prevented her from seeing whether or not there were more, so she opened the French doors and went out on to the verandah. Now, in the darkness she could see that the sky was sprinkled with myriads of stars.

' "Sit, Jessica. Look how the floor of heaven is thick inlaid with patines of pure gold",' Helen whispered, thinking her thoughts aloud. She spent quite a few minutes gazing at the splendour of the firmament before she remembered what she really had to think about.

She knew that Penelope's leg would not be right for some time yet and she also knew that she was not fully recovered from her illness. She was still pale – she must get out of doors tomorrow; Doctor Kennedy said she might – and thinner than she had been. This could not be concealed, and if she, who had seen her every day, noticed it, would not her mother, who had not seen her for six weeks? Wouldn't it be better, as she would have to know soon anyway, to write and tell her what had happened, so that she should not have a shock? It was so near the end of her holiday now that she could not disturb her rest by the news. True, she had agreed with Charles not to mention it, but she decided it was time to speak. Charles would understand, she knew, and she was sure he would second her opinion. Yes, it was best. She would write now, although it was late; there would be no time tomorrow.

Accordingly, she returned to the room, and having locked the doors and drawn the curtains, took out her notepaper and began her letter. As she wrote quickly, she soon finished. She read it through, addressed and stamped the envelope and licked it up. Having satisfied herself that all was well, she went to bed.

Chapter VI

Next morning she was up early, and had all the household jobs done by eight o'clock. Charles was still asleep and she had not the heart to wake him. Better let him sleep it off, she thought. Penelope, however, was wide awake when Helen came in to see to her washing and ask what she wanted for breakfast, and working herself into a 'fret', as Helen called it, because she could hear Rex barking outside and could not go and join him. *Why* did Helen take such an awful age to come? She'd been awake for hours! Who has not experienced that feeling when he has been ill or for some reason unable to get up? Surely there can be hardly anybody who has not. The first thing she said after bidding her sister 'Good morning' was,

'You *have* been a long time. I was beginning to wonder if you were ever coming.'

'Which is a sure sign that you're better,' replied Helen, as she threw back the curtains. 'Let's have some air in here. It's terribly stuffy.'

'Yes, please, open them all, as wide as they'll go.'

'No, we mustn't have too much wind, or you'll be catching another cold, and then what would Mother say?'

'She doesn't know.'

'She will do tomorrow.'

'Why? Have you told her?'

'Yes, I posted the letter this morning.'

'But I thought you said –'

'I know, dear, but I've decided it's best Mother should know. She would get an awful shock if she came home and found you like this. It'll be bad enough as it is. You want some colour. As soon as Charlie's ready, we'll take you outside.'

'Will you? Oh, good! But I'm frightfully hungry, Helen. *Do* let's have my breakfast, please; and I say, have you had yours yet?'

'No.'

'Well, bring it up here and have it with me, will you?'

'Very well.'

Helen brought water and the wherewithal for washing, and leaving Penelope to look after herself and clean her teeth, she departed to prepare the meal.

It was pleasant in Penelope's room. The morning sun streamed in through the window, giving everything a cheerful atmosphere, which in some measure compensated for the invalid's hatred of her bed. How she longed to be free and out of doors in the fresh air! She sadly missed her before-breakfast run with Rex, exercise she had been used to. Rex, too, felt the lack of exercise, and had to content himself with chasing butterflies, real and imaginary, in the garden.

'Where's Charlie?' asked Penelope halfway through her breakfast. 'He's not gone, has he?'

'No, he's not gone,' replied Helen with a smile. 'On the contrary, he's very firmly fixed. He's asleep on the sofa in the lounge.'

Penelope leant back on her pillows and laughed.

'Hush! Not so loud, you may wake him!' cried Helen hurriedly. 'But really, Penny, you need not laugh. The poor boy's quite worn out; and you are to blame, Miss Wentworth.'

'I'm sorry, but I couldn't help it. I never saw any notices about it being dangerous, so I naturally went to look – you know I always like to examine things – I suppose I went too near the edge, because the land slipped and I with it. That's all I can remember.'

'Well, you've learnt not to go poking about near precipices again, which is one good thing. Of course, another good thing which has come out of the accident, though I'd rather not go to such drastic lengths in future, is that you've kept Charlie here to see the family, which he wouldn't otherwise have done.'

Just then the back door bell rang and Helen got up and collected her tray, saying,

'There's the milkman; I must go. Hurry up and finish. I'll fetch your tray in a few minutes.'

Penelope had to stay in bed that morning, because Helen could not bring her downstairs alone, and she would not wake Charles for so trivial a matter. To Penelope it was not so trivial, but being a considerate child, she resigned herself to her fate and tried to amuse herself with a book, for Helen was too busy to be with her.

There was much for Helen to do. Beds had to be aired, rooms got ready, baking to be done and things bought, and she could not help feeling rather glad that she could get on with her work undisturbed. The morning flew before she knew where she was and she had to prepare lunch. For this it was necessary to know whether or not Charles would be partaking of it, for she did not wish to have anything left over. She therefore peeped into the lounge to see if its occupant showed any sign of life.

Charles turned over. Helen took that to mean that he was awake, or at least waking, so she crossed the room and stood at the foot of the sofa, watching him.

After a few minutes, Charles freed an arm and rubbed his eyes to remove the sleepies; then he became almost awake and saw Helen.

'Hullo,' he said, 'I appear to have had a doze.'

'Yes,' replied Helen, laughing.

'By the way,' went on Charles, 'I seem to remember your saying something about a cup of tea. Didn't you?'

'Yes, a mere sixteen hours ago!'

'What!'

'Don't start so, Charlie boy. Yes, it's nearly lunch-time. I came to see if you wanted any.'

'You bet I do!' responded Charles. 'I'm starving!'

Helen began to tease.

'Well, suppose, instead of spending your time idling on other people's sofas, you go and do a little work for a change and earn your dinner.'

'Well, I like that!' replied Charles, rising to his feet. 'What do you think I've been doing for the past six weeks but work, Miss Helen?'

'You silly boy, I didn't mean it.'

'I know. Anyway' – he struck an attitude – 'at your service, Modom. What do you want me to do?'

'Take a bowl out of the pantry and see how many strawberries you can find in the garden. If you bring me fifty or more, I *might* give you one as a reward.'

'How do you know I shan't eat them on the way?'

'You won't have any lunch if you do. Now go on, there's a dear boy, and let me tidy up.'

Helen almost pushed him out of the room, he protesting the whole time that she should let him tidy up. They both talked at once and as they were both more or less laughing, it was several minutes before he had finally gone.

He went into the pantry, and having selected the bowl with the least number of cracks, chips and blemishes, he let himself out of the back door and proceeded to look for strawberries. The cultivated ones were long over but there were still wild ones, red and white, to be found all over the garden.

The house was built on the side of the down, and the garden sloped gently down to the front gate. It was a lovely garden, well laid out in no particular pattern. There were borders and rockeries and lawns, an orchard and a kitchen garden, and the strawberries grew all over everywhere.

Charles searched diligently and soon collected fifty. He paused to admire the next door garden. The path which led up to the front door was bordered by beds of brilliant carnations of many different colours. He was used to red, pink and white ones, but these were much more varied, some even were streaked and striped in various hues. When he went in he asked Helen about them.

'Oh, that's old Mr Honeydew,' she explained. 'He cultivates them. They're his speciality. He's always experimenting with them – crossing colours and all that sort of thing. He's been trying to get blue ones, but I don't think he's succeeded yet.'

'Well, they make a jolly good show. Oh, here are your strawberries.'

'How many did you pick?' – with a scrutinizing look.

'Fifty. I haven't eaten any, honestly.'

'Good boy. Here's one for a prize.'

'Thanks.'

'Can you help me down with Penny? Lunch won't be ready yet, so you can amuse her till I ring, if you like.'

'Yes, I will. Dear me, what else can I think of to do? I've about run dry of ideas.'

'Tell her about Europe. She likes that.'

'Does she? Then here goes.'

Charles found that Helen was right. Penelope was never tired of hearing about his travels. He got her established on her sofa and she was very sorry when lunchtime came and he had to stop.

She had only just finished her pudding (Helen and Charles had not finished) when Doctor Kennedy arrived. He had an annoying habit of coming in the middle of lunch. Helen hastily covered her plate and put it on the kitchen range to keep warm, then hurried to let him in. He, of course, was blissfully unaware of the trouble he caused, and imagined he fitted in nicely, as nobody ever complained. Not that complaining would have had any effect: he was too fixed in his ways.

Penelope suffered an uncomfortable ten minutes while he was in the room, but he said she might have a chair in the garden, for which she inwardly blessed him, though aloud she only said, 'Good.'

Half an hour later she was settled comfortably in a wicker chair on the lawn, extremely glad to be out-of-doors once more.

'Now,' said Helen, 'you've got three days to get brown in so that you won't look so much like a snow-drift when Mother comes back. Mind you do it.'

'Don't worry,' responded Penelope, 'I will.'

Mr Wentworth (55)

Mrs Wentworth (52)

Philip (20)

Alban (17)

Gerald (12)

Illustration from *Story Club Magazine*, Summer 1944

Chapter VII

Penelope was as good as her word. She was of the type who get brown very easily, and as she spent the next three days as much out of doors as possible, she soon lost her pallid look and became more like herself. Doctor Kennedy said she might begin to use her leg again, provided she did it gently and did not try to do acrobatics on it. At first it seemed strange to be walking, but she soon grew accustomed to it, and but for the fact that she was not quite so lively as before, nobody would have known there was anything wrong with her.

And now the time drew very near: Mrs Wentworth wrote to say, after much motherly anxiety over Penelope, that they would be arriving at Mereford next day at 3.15 p.m. and would take a taxi to Edmuston. Helen was not to trouble to go and meet them. They would, she hoped, be home by four.

Accordingly, on the afternoon of the following day, Charles, Helen and Penelope were sitting in the garden, trying not to look excited and all pretending that, when they gazed intently in the direction of the road if a car went by or something stirred, they knew it was nothing really, and did not imagine that the taxi would arrive half an hour before its appointed time.

At half past three Penelope walked down the drive and opened the front gates, 'so they wouldn't have to stop'.

At a quarter to four she walked down to the gates to see if they were coming and walked back again disappointed, deciding to wait until they *did* come. This she repeated three times, and was returning from the third, when the long-expected taxi at last turned in and drove up to the front door. There was much 'hullo-ing' as they hurried to welcome the wanderers and much shaking of hands as the latter tumbled out of the taxi and began to collect their luggage.

Everybody knows what a home-coming is like and how everybody talks at once and starts to tell stories of the holiday before anybody is ready to listen; but this one was rather different, for there was an accident to be lamented over and a visitor to be greeted cordially by all except one, in whose heart there nestled a bitter enmity which he did not try to conceal. Charles, having been warmly hailed by Alban, who, strong upholder as he was of everything which is meant by the term 'gentleman', considered him as the finest one he knew, found himself face to face with Philip. His first reaction was one of aversion, but he quickly smothered it, determined that he, at least, would not show what he felt. He held out his hand and said cheerfully,

'Hullo, Phil, old man, how are you?'

Philip gazed at him with hatred in his eyes, and not deigning to take the proffered hand, replied,

'As well as possible under the circumstances.'

Charles felt damped and his hand dropped to his side. What was the good of trying to be pleasant and overlook past wrongs if the other person were not willing to meet you halfway?

'Oh,' he said, and there was a marked difference in his tone of voice, 'I'm sorry to hear that. I had hoped you would have benefited from your holiday.'

'Fat lot you know about it,' grunted Philip, and turned to carry some of the cases indoors.

Helen had heard what passed and was grieved; she saw Charles' eyes flash and his lips set in a hard line as if trying to suppress the rush of anger that swept through him. Feeling that an apology was due she advanced towards him, but she was saved from a difficult task (and as she told herself the next minute, a foolish one, as it would be better to ignore it) by her father seizing him, shaking him warmly by the hand, for he was very fond of his 'other son', and saying,

'Well, Charlie my boy, it's very nice to have you back again. How are you?'

'Thank you, Sir, I'm fine. You look very well; I hope you've had a good time?'

'Yes, we have, we have.'

Their conversation was here interrupted by Mrs Wentworth, who, having seen to the luggage and given orders all round, could now give her attention to Charles.

'Well, Charles ' – Mrs Wentworth never called him anything but that – 'I hear we have a lot to be thankful for.'

Charles felt the difference in her manner, but he was not going to make any difference in his, for he knew it was only her way. She was very fond of him really; so he replied,

'Hullo, Mrs Wentworth. If you mean Penny, yes.'

'I do. We can never thank you enough. I don't know what might have happened if you had not been there.'

Charles hated this kind of thing and tried to turn the conversation by saying,

'Oh well, she's all right now, so you have nothing to worry about. I hope *you* are quite recovered?'

'Oh yes, thank you. The sea air does me good. I get so *cramped* here, you know. Helen!' – Helen came up – 'is tea ready?'

'Very nearly, Mother. I've put the kettle on.'

'Good. Well, suppose we go indoors and get ready.'

Everybody decided it would be a good idea and followed her into the house. Helen went into the kitchen to make the tea and Charles, with Penelope's help, carried the garden tea-table and chairs out on to the lawn.

When everybody had settled down, tongues flew fast and the food was disposed of to the tune of 'Did we tell you about...?' or 'Oh, Helen, there was *such* a funny man on the train!' and so on.

Charles sat between Helen and Gerald and gradually got the latter to talk about his holiday; for Gerald was very shy and hardly spoke a word when there was company. He had grown used to Charles and had not minded his presence, but a gap of two years is a long time to a sensitive child, and he felt restrained and unnatural; but it did not take long for Charles to put him at his ease by his friendliness and sympathy, and he was soon chattering away as if he were afraid of no man.

Philip sat on the other side of Helen and maintained a sulky silence except when spoken to. He hated company, especially that of Charles and Alban. He had never got over his defeat with Charles and he knew that Alban, at least, despised him. Alban could not understand how anybody of the name of Wentworth could be like Philip. He himself was as honest and upright as the best of men, and could not tolerate anything the least bit 'shady'. Philip, on the other hand, was selfish and moody, and did not care what he did. He had been used to suppression and spoiling by turns. To his father, who was a retiring, inoffensive, gentlemanly little man, wrapped up in his books, he was a puzzle. His mother, from whom he inherited his obstinate temper and his desire for superiority, had petted and indulged him until he began to get out of hand, when she had had violent struggles to make him do things. Usually it had ended in Philip's getting his own way. At the age when he should have felt the paternal firmness, it had not been given, for Mr Wentworth did not know how to manage his unruly son. His mother had tried bribes and promises as a reward for unpleasant labours, but if Master Philip had not wished to do a thing he had not done it. Yet he could be friendly enough if he thought he could get something for it.

His nursery days had been one continual string of quarrels. Alban, who had been his exact opposite right from his cradle, rebelled under the domineering attitude of his brother and mistrusted him. Penelope had avoided him and Gerald was frightened of him; and this was the atmosphere in which he had grown up.

Only Helen really understood him. There was something in her affectionate and sympathetic nature which told her that, different as he was from the rest of them, it was partly because they never tried to see any good in him. He had been spoiled by indulgence and embittered by suppression and it was this, added to their antipathy, which made him what he was. Philip felt Helen was his only friend and he was grateful, though he did not often show it. As he grew older and the others drew further and further away from him, he learnt to appreciate it more and returned her affection by letting her know his troubles. Somehow, Helen had a way of finding the right spot in other people's hearts, and she had certainly found it in his. She never quarrelled with him but was always tolerant of his faults and ready to be his confidante. When he went away to Cambridge a year ago, she wrote long letters to him, full of the love and friendship he missed elsewhere – Philip did not get on with anybody but Helen and one or two young men of similar temperament at the university. He wrote home, but his letters were short and unsatisfactory. Only to Helen did he tell in full his experiences, knowing she would not tell anybody his secrets. It was the complete trust he had in Helen which reassured him. He had never known her to be anything but loyal to him, and he would listen to her counsel without feeling that she was trying to 'preach'. He would do things for Helen that he would do for nobody else and he would obey her when he would have spurned requests from the others.

This was only in private. In public he would have scorned to admit that he allowed his sister to 'order him about', as was proved by the usual rupture between him and Alban which took place at tea.

Alban and Charles were kept busy serving the company, while Philip merely sat still and did nothing; the reason being that he did not wish to help either his brother or their visitor in being what he termed 'polite little gentlemen'. Alban resented his inaction and said, jokingly,

'Ahoy, you landlubber! Show a leg, will you?'

Philip ignored him as he had not been addressed by name, and went on with his cake. Alban tried again, dropping into ordinary English.

The usual rupture.
Illustration from *Story Club Magazine*, Christmas 1944

'Look, Helen wants something to eat. Suppose you do a spot of work for a change. We've hardly had time to have anything ourselves, keeping you supplied.'

'I can fetch what I want,' said Helen, hoping to avert the impending storm.

'No, you sit down and let him fetch it,' replied Alban. 'He should have enough manners to look after you.'

'Of course,' sneered Philip, 'you're a model of politeness, aren't you? Well, if you preach so much about good manners, why don't you fetch her something yourself, instead of ordering people about as if you were a dictator?'

'If *you* had any manners you'd have seen to her yourself a long while ago. Why should Charlie have to do it?' (He had passed her what she wanted while this had been going on.) 'Especially when he's a visitor.'

'If the Navy is full of such polite little gentlemen as you, it must be a hopeless place,' said Philip sarcastically.

Now quick as Alban was to uphold the right, he could restrain himself fairly well as long as the Navy was not brought into it; but as soon as anyone started to decry his beloved Service he lost his temper completely; and when that person was Philip, he could say some very biting things.

'Yes,' he said, and his eye gleamed with suppressed fire, 'yes, the Navy is a Service for gentlemen, and nobody like *you* could ever enter it!'

'Don't worry. There's no likelihood of my being so daft as to try. I've not grown so soft that I want to be cringingly polite to everyone I meet.'

'No, that's the trouble. It would do you good to go to sea, instead of wasting time and Father's money gambling at the university.'

'You're a liar!'

'I'm not. It's the truth and you know it!' (Alban had long had his suspicions and had waited for a chance to see if he was right.)

'Say that again, will you?'

'Yes! It's true – isn't it?'

'Liar!'

'I'll fight you for it!'

They would have done so, had not Charles intervened and parted them.

'Leave me alone!' cried Alban. 'He called me a liar, and I'll jolly well tan him for it!'

'You are over-excited, old chap,' said Charles gently. 'There's no need for these violent demonstrations. After all,' he added in an undertone,

Tea in the garden, 1943

'true gentlemen don't lose their tempers and fight when anybody annoys them.'

Alban saw that he was right and stopped looking fierce. He glared once more at Philip, who was gradually being soothed by Helen, and sat down. Helen was not so rapidly successful and had great difficulty in calming down her infuriated brother.

'Phil, Phil, do be reasonable. You shouldn't quarrel like this.'

'Who cares whether we quarrel?' cried Philip. 'Gentleman Alban?'

'I care, Phil.'

He looked her in the eyes but he could not meet the earnest gaze expressed there; it pierced him right to the soul, making him admit inwardly that she had 'caught' him. On the surface he glared, as Alban had done, at his opponent for several seconds before he relaxed, and muttering, 'Oh, all right,' sat down.

Later that evening, when he had had time to think about it, Alban realized that he 'should not let the sun go down upon his wrath'. But how could he beg pardon of Philip? It was impossible. Pride would not let him, although he knew he had started the quarrel. To anyone but Philip – Charles, or even Gerald – he would not mind apologizing; but then they would not have behaved like that and would have taken his joking in the right way. He was not sorry for anything he had said, for it was all true, but perhaps...if it had been Helen...but he was not Helen and anyway, it was over, so what was the use of worrying?

Philip had no idea of repentance. He stumped up and down his bedroom fuming inwardly at what he considered Alban's 'deuced impertinence'. Helen left him to cool down before attempting to reason with him, and only ventured to knock on her way to bed. At first he did not hear her, so she tried again, louder.

'Who's that?'

'Helen.'

'What do you want?'

'You. Mayn't I come in?'

'I suppose so. Hang on a tick.' He strode over to the door, unlocked it and let her in.

She began by asking questions about his holiday, and worked him into a good mood, then judged her time to open the painful subject. She seized the opportunity of a pause in the conversation to say, gently,

'Phil, must you and Alban always quarrel like this?'

'I thought you'd get on to that before very long.' The black look was returning to his face – 'Why can't you leave me alone?'

'Phil!'

Helen sounded so hurt that her brother could have bitten his tongue off.

'If that's how you feel,' went on Helen, 'perhaps I'd better not say any more. I'm sorry to have disturbed you.' She rose and went towards the door.

'Helen, don't go!' cried Philip, realizing he had not meant what he said. 'I'm sorry – only I was feeling angry. Please don't go – you're the only friend I've got in this place. I'm sorry.'

Helen was won by his sincerity and returned to her seat.

'It was your mentioning Alban,' explained Philip. 'I hate him! Conceited prig!'

'No, Phil, he is not,' contradicted Helen gently (you could not cross him with any degree of violence); 'it's just that he doesn't understand you. You are so different. He is used to a life where everybody does things for people; you are used to one where everybody does for himself. There is something to be said for both sides.'

'If he would just practise and not preach I shouldn't mind so much,' responded Philip. 'It's when he starts ordering a fellow about that I get annoyed. I can't stand that kind of thing.'

'But don't you think he had as much right to be annoyed as you, Phil? After all, you called him a liar, you know.'

'Well, and what if I did?'

'I think you might apologize, don't you?'

'Apologize? To him? My dear Helen!'

'Why shouldn't you?'

'I couldn't. Impossible.'

'I understand.' Helen knew it was pride which prevented him; pride, and the fact that it was Alban to whom he must apologize.

'Well, anyway,' she added, 'do try not to lose your temper again. It grieves me so to hear you always going at each other's throats.'

'It depends on what he does. I don't guarantee anything if he starts getting cocky.'

Helen knew from experience that this was as much as she would get in the way of a promise, for any task which was unpleasant to him, so she was satisfied, and rose to her feet.

'Goodnight, Phil, have a good sleep,' she said, shaking hands, for Philip would not have let her kiss him had he been offered a thousand pounds.

On the way across the landing she met Charles.

Philip (1943)

Penelope (1945)

Gerald (1945)

'Hullo,' said the latter. 'I was wondering where you were. Going to bed?'

'Yes. Are you?'

'Yes.'

'Well, goodnight, Charlie dear. Sleep well.'

'Thanks – and you. Goodnight.'

He saluted her in the old way of a kiss on the forehead and they departed to their respective rooms.

Helen's thoughts as she climbed into bed were very mixed. Philip was becoming an ever-increasing problem to her, and if what Alban had accused him of were true, she did not know what would happen. Alban would soon be getting his commission, though, and then he would go to sea and perhaps they would forget their enmity. It was a vain hope, but it cheered her. They certainly all looked very well after their holiday – Gerald was as brown as a berry – and she was glad to see her mother was so much better. She had got over Penelope's accident remarkably well, and half her worries had been set at naught by her healthy appearance. The accident – she could never think of it without remembering Charles. She owed him – in fact they all did – a bigger debt than could ever be repaid; and he had told her at tea that he must go the next day. How she would miss him! He had grown so much part of their life during the past six weeks that she could not imagine what it would be like without him. Well, she would be going to Margaret's in a few days and perhaps that would compensate for the loss; but even while thinking this she knew that it would not…

Charles' thoughts were much more simple.

'Dearest Helen,' he said to himself. 'How long will it be before I can see you again?'

‘Can’t *you* break a leg or something?’
Illustration from *Story Club Magazine*, Summer 1944.

Chapter VIII

Breakfast next morning was spent in alternately discussing the holiday and lamenting that Charles was to depart that afternoon. They were all sorry except Philip. He, as usual, was rude.

'I wish you weren't going, Charlie,' moaned Penelope, gazing wistfully at him. 'Can't *you* break your leg or something, and have to stay for another six weeks?'

Before Charles had time to reply, Philip cut in,

'Why you can't let a fellow leave in peace without all this fuss, I don't know.'

Alban cocked an eye at his brother.

'Well,' he said, 'perhaps if it were *you* who was going, nobody would make any objection.'

This nearly started another quarrel, for Philip could not bear being teased, but Helen coughed and saved the situation by saying,

'Phil, have some more bread?'

When he turned to answer her she gave him a warning look, and the incident passed over.

Charles was determined, before he left, to have it out with Philip and discover what was the matter with him. He made several attempts to speak to him but they all failed. Finally, he caught him in the library, where he had gone to replace some books he had borrowed. He was at the top of the ladder when Philip came in to find something to read. When he saw Charles he stopped and would have walked out again, but the latter called him back.

'Phil, don't go.'

'What do you want?' demanded Philip, pausing.

'Come in and shut the door,' responded Charles, descending from his perch. Philip did so. Then he walked over to where Charles was standing, and stood with his hands in his pockets.

'Well?'

'Don't look so fierce, old man, I'm not going to eat you.'

'I wish you'd stop "old manning" me,' snapped Philip. 'If anyone should be old, it's you.'

Charles ignored the latter half of the remark.

'Phil,' he said, 'Why can't we be friends?'

Philip said nothing.

'You treat me,' went on Charles, ' as if I were a dog, kicking me with your tongue instead of your feet. If I've done anything wrong, do let me know what it is, so that I can make amends for it.'

'It's no good trying that on me,' grunted Philip, 'because it won't work.'

'I'm not trying anything on you. I only want to know why you behave like this towards me.'

There was no reason. Philip felt he was inferior and was therefore malicious. He had tried to create mischief once and had never forgiven Charles for having been acquitted. He knew he could never be like him, and bore a grudge in consequence. The spitefulness which goes with inferiority was the real trouble, and of course, he could not explain that to Charles. So all he said was,

'How should I know?'

'Oh come, you must have a reason.'

'Well, what's it to you?'

'It's a lot to me, Phil, because it clears up all our difficulties.'

'Does it? You're hopeful.'

'Yes, I am.'

'Well, "live in hope if you die in despair",' sarcastically.

Charles saw it was no use trying to pursue the matter further, and gave it up.

'If this is all the encouragement I get, I don't think there's much good in going on,' he said. 'I, at least, am sorry we should have to part enemies, but please don't imagine I bear you any ill-will. I believe you'll be out for lunch.' (Philip had carefully arranged it so that he would not have to be present when Charles left). 'Well, even if we can't be friends, perhaps you won't mind saying "cheerio" as if we were.' He held out his hand.

'Cheerio,' mumbled Philip, ignoring it.

'Come, do shake hands with a chap,' begged Charles. Philip reluctantly did so.

'I warn you,' he said, 'don't come moralizing near me again, or there'll be trouble.'

'No, I won't,' responded Charles. 'Goodbye, Phil.'

Philip did not deign him any further reply, so Charles turned and walked out of the room, feeling dissatisfied with the knowledge that he had failed and almost wishing he had not attempted a reconciliation.

Helen saw him come out and, by the expression on his face, guessed he had been talking to her brother. The dissatisfied look faded when he saw her, and he relieved her of the tray she was carrying, saying laughingly,

'You won't have a butler to do things for you after today, so you'd better make the most of him while he's still available.'

Helen smiled and said sadly.

'I wish you weren't going, Charlie boy. How soon can you come and see us again?'

Charles would like to have replied, 'As soon as you want me, Helen,' but he realized that was too sentimental and changed it to,

'As soon as you have recovered enough from this visit to be able to stand another.'

'Yes, it was rather strong-minded of me to put up with you for so long. I don't think my nerves will stand another visit just yet.'

'I thought not. By the way' – they had reached the kitchen door by this time – 'where am I supposed to be taking this to?'

'Well, it was originally intended for the dining room, but of course, if you'd rather eat your lunch in the kitchen, I've no objection.'

Charles made an exclamation of disgust and returned to the dining room.

'Are you going to have cocoa?' he asked as he put the tray down on the sideboard, 'because I'm really expert at making it. Bristles can vouch for that.'

'Not at lunch,' answered Helen, 'and whoever is Bristles?'

'Oh, he's the chap I met abroad I told you about. His real name is Benjamin Brisley, but we always called him Bristles. I think you've met him, haven't you?'

'I seem to know the name.' She began to put the things on the table. 'Wasn't he that awfully nice boy we met at Margaret's once – at a tennis party – with a sister who was brilliant?'

'Yes, that's the one. He's a jolly decent chap. Now let me help you.'

'Thank you.'

Lunch was even more miserable than breakfast.

'I always think,' said Alban, cutting up his meat into accurate squares, 'that it would be a much better plan if when visitors left, they left in the middle of the night, or before anybody was up, so that there wouldn't be any of this dismal waiting.'

'All right,' laughed Charles, 'I'll remember that next time you come and see me.'

'I don't wish to speed the parting guest and all that, but I do think it would be a good idea. Don't you, Helen?'

'Nobody would want to send Helen away quickly,' put in Gerald, then blushed, surprised at his own daring. Alban got up and went round to pat him on the back.

'Well done, small fry,' he said condescendingly, 'you're coming on! Just get rid of the self-consciousness and you'll be perfect.'

Everybody laughed and Gerald blushed even more. Alban sat down again.

'Poor Gerry,' said Helen, 'it's not fair to tease him. It's very nice to have him say that. Thank you.'

Gerald smiled in gratitude and squeezed Helen's hand under the table.

'You must come again and have a proper visit, Charlie,' said Mr Wentworth when the mirth had subsided. 'We've hardly had time even to say hullo; and we've been so full of our own travels that we haven't heard anything of yours, and they must be far more interesting.'

'Thank you, Sir, I always look forward to coming here. As for my travels, I don't expect they are much more spectacular than yours. I think, if you really enjoy yourself, it doesn't matter where you go, and holidays in your own country can be just as interesting as in any other.'

'Well, there's something in that, certainly,' replied Mr Wentworth.

The bus from Edmuston to Mereford on which Charles was to travel was due to leave at half past two. The final adieux took place at the front door, but Helen and Penelope set out with him along the drive. When they reached the gate Helen turned to her sister and said,

'I think you'd better not come any further, Penny.'

'Oh, mayn't I?' asked Penelope mournfully.

'No dear, I don't want any more accidents.'

To Penelope Helen's word was law.

'Oh, all right,' she said, and there was no tone of resentment. 'Goodbye, Charlie, come again soon, won't you?'

'Certainly, if I may. Goodbye, Penny. Take care of that leg.'

'Yes. Goodbye.' Charles submitted to being kissed, and with one final goodbye, Penelope left them.

When she had gone and they could no longer wave, Helen became serious.

'Charlie,' she said, 'I must apologize for Phil. I couldn't help overhearing what he said to you yesterday, and I saw you come out of the library this morning and thought you must have been talking to him. He doesn't know what he says. Please forgive him.'

'I do, Helen. I understand now why he hates me but I can't explain it; he has no *reason*, exactly.'

'Yes, I know...I wish you could get on together. It must make it so miserable always to have this feeling of animosity in the air. I wish something could be done about it.'

'My dear Helen, I don't care a brass farthing for Phil, as I believe I said before. Please don't worry. I don't bear malice.'

'Really?'

'Yes, really.'

'Well, it's a great relief to hear you say that. I was so afraid you wouldn't forgive him for being rude.'

'All the kindness and friendship I receive from the rest of you more than compensate for any amount of rudeness from Phil, and anyway, I'm used to it now.' He looked at his watch. 'I must go. It's twenty past now.'

'Wait a minute, Charlie. I know I can't express it adequately in words but perhaps you will understand. I can never thank you enough for what you have done for us. You saved Penny's life, and nothing I could say or do could ever repay the debt we owe you.'

Charles was rather at a loss for words; he wanted to deny it, but could not think of a suitable way to do so. He was therefore silent and let his eyes speak for him. If Helen could have read what was written there she would have been surprised. To a more experienced person their expression would say quite plainly that Charles would have considered himself amply repaid if Helen had consented to marry him; but she had not yet learned to read that message, and took his silence to mean that he did understand.

'I know this sounds very weak and story-bookish,' she went on, 'but if, in the future, you ever want anything, you have only to come and ask, and if it is in my power to give, you shall have it.'

Charles saw that he could not refuse, as Helen was so very much in earnest. He grasped both her hands in his and said with feeling,

'Thank you. I will remember. Goodbye.'

He bent down as if to kiss her in the usual way, then stopped, for no apparent reason, and just looked at her instead. Helen was puzzled. This was very unusual; what had happened? She did not say anything, however. Charles gave her hands a final squeeze, and having said 'Goodbye, Helen' once more, turned abruptly and walked away.

She waved until he had gone round the corner, then walked slowly back to the house, wondering what had come over him. He was quite different. She cast her mind back over the past eight weeks but could discover nothing extraordinary in his behaviour, and was forced to admit that, although she thought she knew his character inside out, for once she had been beaten.

The Wentworth family (1943)

Chapter IX

The house was very strange that evening and for Helen and Penelope, very lonely. Alban cracked jokes and told funny stories, but they seemed out of place, and instead of lessening the gloom, only added to it. They were sitting in the lounge after tea. Mr Wentworth was deep in the newspaper and oblivious to anything else. Mrs Wentworth was knitting from a very tricky pattern and kept pausing to count the stitches. Helen was playing a game with Penelope, Philip had not yet returned from his outing and Gerald was reading a book. Alban's yarns fell on unappreciative ears.

'You are a mouldy crew,' he said, after his best and funniest story had been received in silence except for a half-hearted laugh from Mrs Wentworth. 'What's the matter with everyone tonight?'

Nobody answered. Having wandered aimlessly round the room for a few minutes, Alban suddenly had an idea and left the room. Nobody noticed his departure. Mrs Wentworth went on with her knitting, Helen and Penelope continued playing halma and Gerald turned a page in his book. Mr Wentworth put down his paper and closed his eyes…

Suddenly there was an ear-splitting crack. Everybody jumped, with suitable exclamations.

'What on earth…?' said Penelope, bending down to pick up the halma man she had dropped on the floor.

Alban appeared from behind the screen clutching his chest and staggered across the room.

'Alban! My boy!' cried Mrs Wentworth, rising in alarm.

'Oh! Oh! I've been shot!' gurgled her son, rolling his eyes. He collapsed into a chair, still with his hand to his heart, and emitted some blood-curdling groans. Gerald stared as if his eyes would drop out and turned quite white. For a few minutes even Penelope was deceived; then she had a brainwave and looked behind the screen. Philip's air-rifle lay on the floor. She emerged, waving it triumphantly.

'Fake! Fake!' she called. 'Look what I've found!'

Alban saw his trick was discovered, and relaxed.

'Cad,' he said, 'spoiling the fun.'

'Alban, Alban, what did you do it for?' asked Mrs Wentworth. 'I really thought you'd been hurt.'

'Well,' responded Alban, 'I had to do *something*. It was like a blinking prison-house in here; everyone so silent and miserable. Look at Gerry,' he added, pointing to his brother, who was still keeping at a safe distance, not quite reassured even by Alban's returned cheerfulness. They turned in the direction of his finger and all started to laugh. Alban advanced and stroked him on the head.

'Poor ickle Gerry-werry! Did 'e fink a nasty man had shot his ickle bruvver? Did 'e?'

'Shut up!' said Gerald, diving away from him.

When they had settled down again, Helen said she must write letters, and went upstairs to her study. Before getting out her pad, she stood in front of the fireplace and examined three portraits hanging over the mantelpiece.

In the middle, in a simple gold frame, was a very life-like oil painting of Charles, done about three years ago by an artist friend of hers and given to her as a Christmas present. It was an excellent painting; the expression, half-serious, half-laughing, was caught perfectly, and his merry blue eyes twinkled with fun, just as they always did when he was in that mood. She had not realized before what a fine painting it was, but now she had seen him again she could tell it was exactly like him.

The other two portraits, photographs this time, hung on either side of it. They were of Bernard and Margaret, and had been coloured, so they were not out of place against Charles.

There could hardly be a greater contrast than there was between Charles and Bernard. Both were fair, but whereas Charles' hair was curly, Bernard's was perfectly straight, and was darker below the surface. The one had a strong, well-shaped face; the other's was thin and tapered towards the chin. One could cover his feelings so that no one might know what he was thinking; the other's face was a book in which one might read without difficulty every emotion that was passing. One was full of fun and yet knew how to be serious; the other was mobile, highly strung and intensely musical; Bernard played the piano, and lived for his music. You had only to listen to him to know what he was feeling, and he composed his own pieces as well as playing those of others. Bernard would have been quite good-looking but for one thing; he had a broad, high forehead, fine nose and sensitive mouth, and his eyes were always eager

Margaret (1945)

and full of expression. The one thing that spoilt him was his remarkably thick eyelids. They seemed incongruous in such a face and but for the fire in his eyes would have made him look half asleep. There seemed to be no reason for it; neither of his parents had them and they did not appear in his sister. To people who knew him well they soon ceased to be a distraction, for every other line in his face was so full of ardour that one forgot the details in contemplation of the whole.

Margaret, in Helen's opinion, was the only person she had ever seen whom she could describe as 'beautiful'. She had seen many people whom she considered pretty, but nobody could in any way equal Margaret. She was fair, like her brother, and resembled him in a way, but she had not that passionate sensitiveness which he possessed. She was extremely dignified (this to Helen was an indispensable part of beauty) and the fire in Bernard's eyes was softened to an expression of deep sincerity in hers. When Bernard smiled it was an impulsive, fleeting movement; when Margaret smiled her face seemed to Helen to assume the look she might expect to find on the face of an angel.

She gazed at them a few minutes longer, before tearing herself away from the delightful occupation of reminiscence, then fetched her writing materials, and sitting down at the table, pulled the lamp towards her. She wrote the address, and having sat thinking for a few minutes, set to work:

'My dear Margaret...'

Margaret (1943)

Bernard (1945)

Chapter X

Had Helen not had plenty to keep her busy during the next few days, she would have found them to drag as if they would never pass. Luckily for her, her mind was too occupied with her coming visit to have time to think much about missing Charles. Deciding what to take and what not to take and handing over the affairs of the house to her mother and the maids, who returned from their holidays the day after Charles left, kept her from being miserable.

Alban went back to Dartmouth a few days before Helen was to go to Margaret's; Penelope was allowed to go to school again, with a letter to say she must not do games or gym for the rest of the term. This, naturally, was a terrible situation for her, as she loved anything athletic and she was afraid it might mean her losing her place as centre forward in the hockey team. Nothing could be done about that and as Helen said, 'Time will show.'

Gerald was not starting at his new school until half-term. In the meantime his father looked after his lessons so that he should not miss anything. He also made him play games with the boys at the village school, which Gerald, shy as he was, hated. Any form of sport was distasteful to the book-loving lad, and he would far rather have remained curled up in a chair with a big volume of Carlyle's *The French Revolution* than exert himself on the football pitch. But Mr Wentworth, much as he loved books himself, knew that it was not wise to let Gerald become a bookworm and develop his brain at the expense of his body. At least one hour every afternoon had to be spent out of doors, and no amount of pleading would make Mr Wentworth relax his orders for one second.

At last the day came on which Helen was to depart. For some unaccountable reason Philip went with her as far as Mereford. The explanation he gave was that he wished to see that she got safely on to the train and did not leave any luggage behind, but Helen could not help wondering whether there were not a more deep-seated motive for his actions. It was so unusual for Philip to play escort; perhaps – though it seemed doubtful, as he hardly ever showed any feeling of repentance – perhaps he was trying to make up for the bad behaviour of several evenings ago. She soon ceased to worry about it, however, and gave her mind to talking to him.

They reached Mereford in half an hour. The bus stopped outside the station, and having hailed a porter and given him instructions as to what to do with the luggage, they bought tickets and went on to the platform. The London train was due to depart at 9.56 and had not yet come in. Helen provided herself with *Punch* and the *Daily Telegraph*, then they stood and waited for it. It should arrive in ten minutes, the porter told them.

'Is it Wednesday or Thursday you go back to Cambridge?' asked Helen.

'Wednesday.'

'Oh, well, good luck for the new session.'

'Thanks.' There was a pause; then, 'Helen.'

'Yes?'

'You'll write me pretty often, won't you?'

'Of course. I always do.'

'I know, but I thought you might get tired of it. Anyway, please do.'

'Yes, indeed I will; and mind you answer.'

'Well, you won't mind if I *don't* write an awful lot, will you? You see, I shall probably be very busy.'

'Oh...no, I won't mind, so long as you *do* write. I like to know how you're getting on, you know.'

'I know you do, and you're about the only person in this hole who does.'

'Oh, Phil, you shouldn't say things like that!' cried Helen in a reproachful tone of voice.

'Well it's true. I'm fed up with living in that mouldy little village. Who cares about me there besides you? Father hardly ever speaks to me, Mother treats me as though I were a kid, and the others certainly don't care a hang what happens to me – especially Alban.'

Helen was much upset by this outburst, which only served to prove further how little they understood him, or he them. She felt that to try to explain their behaviour would only make matters worse, so all she said was,

'I'm sure you're very much mistaken, Phil.'

'Would to God I were!' Philip frowned. He did not understand that it was largely his own fault that he did not find his family congenial. There was neither time nor place just then for further confidences, as the bell rang and a few minutes later the train screamed into the station and gradually stopped. Doors were flung open and people began to descend, some hurrying off to catch another train, some shouting for porters and others loudly embracing friends who had come to meet them. Those on the platform hastened forward, to find, if possible, a carriage to themselves. This was quite easy, as it was not a busy time of year. Philip had soon secured a corner seat in an empty carriage for his sister and she climbed in. He put the few belongings she was carrying with her into the rack and then went along to see that the luggage they had left in the hands of the porter was being dealt with to his satisfaction. Helen leant out of the window in the corridor to wait for him, thinking over what he had said on the seat. He had never gone so far before and she wondered if at last she was going to get to the bottom of the trouble; he had not said much, but having once begun, he might be persuaded to go on. It was enough to set her thinking. It seemed that what was necessary was that they should all learn to know not only themselves, as the old Greek proverb said, but each other. Would it not be a good idea for her to try to bring this about? It would be a delicate and tricky task, she well foresaw, requiring a great deal of tact; but there was no harm in trying, and anyway, in describing their various characters to them she would get to know them even better herself.

They stood talking for several minutes before the guard came along banging doors which were still open and making sure that those which were shut were shut properly. Helen shook hands with her brother and last hasty requests and instructions were passed as they started to draw away. Helen waved until she could no longer see Philip and then went back to her carriage and shut the door. She found another person had entered while she had been gone and was now occupying the seat opposite her own. She looked up from her book when Helen came in and her face seemed vaguely familiar. Helen sat down in the corner seat facing the engine and opened *Punch*. Every now and then she stole a glance at her companion and tried to think where she could have seen her. Apparently her companion had been doing the same thing, for after about the fifth glance they both looked up together.

Helen laughed and said,

'You must think me awfully rude to keep staring at you like this, but I can't help feeling I've seen you before somewhere.'

'Do you know, I was thinking exactly the same thing about you,' cried the other girl. 'Where could we have met?'

'I don't know. What is your name – if it's not rude to ask?'

'Not at all. I should have asked you the next minute if you hadn't got it in first. My name is Helen Brisley.'

'Of course!' exclaimed Helen. 'Why didn't I remember? I'm Helen Wentworth; we last met at tennis at Bernard Robertson's about six or seven years ago.'

'Why yes, of course! How silly not to have thought; but six years is a long time, and people change so much. Didn't you have plaits in those days?'

'Yes, terrific ones that I could sit on. But I've had them off since then.'

'So I see! Well, isn't this funny? Fancy meeting you in a railway carriage, of all places.'

'Yes, the world's a small place, as an aunt of mine always says when she meets anyone she hasn't seen for a long time.' They both laughed, and Miss Brisley went on,

'I remember that tennis party very well. I got dragged into playing a single with a frightfully brilliant friend of yours – what was his name? – he met Ben abroad.'

'Oh, you mean Charlie. Yes, and you won, if I remember rightly. I was disgusted!'

'Were you? One thing I remember particularly well was going completely crazy over Bernard and his music. Isn't it silly the things one will do when one is a giggling schoolgirl?'

'Yes, utterly ridiculous. I never got that far, though. Charlie and I were always good pals, and that was enough for me – no hero worship on either side. We both told each other quite candidly if we didn't like anything about each other.'

'Yes, there was no "Your best friend can't tell you" about you two. By the way, how is he? Have you seen him lately?'

'Yes. As a matter of fact, he's just been staying with us. In fact, he only left a few days ago.'

'How lovely!'

'Yes, and you'll never guess where I'm going now.'

'No, where?'

'To spend a month with Bernard and Margaret.'

'Oh, you're not? *How* funny. I haven't seen them for ages.'

The time passed rapidly with such a lot to talk about and old associations to pick up, and neither of them read much of the literature they had brought in order not to be bored. It passed so rapidly, in fact, that they were both surprised when the buildings of south London suddenly started to flash past the window.

Helen and Penelope (1945)

'Good heavens!' cried Miss Brisley. 'We're nearly there! I'd no idea we'd got so far. We'd better collect our things.'

'Yes,' replied Helen, 'but the time does fly when you're interested.' She took down her things from the rack. 'I suppose you're not coming to King's Cross by any chance?'

'No, I'm afraid I'm going west.'

Helen looked at her and laughed.

'*Are* you?' she exclaimed. 'I'm sorry to hear that!'

Miss Brisley realized what she had said and laughed too.

'Well, not in that sense, unless you call going with Ben going west. He's meeting me – under the clock.'

'That's where everyone meets people,' said Helen.

'Yes. Will you have time to come and say hullo, or will you have to dash off?'

'I'm afraid I'll have to dash. You see, my next train leaves in three quarters of an hour and I've got to find a taxi and drive across London yet. I'm sorry, because I'd love to have seen him but I don't really think I should, thank you all the same.'

'Oh...Well, I don't want to make you miss your train. We'll have to meet some other time.'

'Yes, we will. This looks like Waterloo. Now to find a speedy, obedient and intelligent porter. Well, I'm awfully glad to have seen you,' she added as the dirtiness of Waterloo station engulfed them. 'We'd better say goodbye now.'

'Yes – goodbye. Give my love to Bernard and Margaret.' She opened the door and they jumped out.

'Yes.' They shook hands, and having said 'Goodbye' once more, hurried to secure a porter. The last Helen saw of Miss Brisley was standing under the clock with a young man whom she presumed was Ben, but they did not see her and she had no time to wait. She walked as quickly as she could in the direction of the taxi-stand. The porter had got there before her and was helping the driver to put her cases into the taxi.

'Whereyergoin?' he demanded.

'King's Cross,' responded Helen, 'and I'm in a hurry, as my train goes in just under three quarters of an hour.'

'Right mum,' said the taxi driver with a strong Cockney accent, springing into his seat. 'We'll get yer ter King's Crorss in 'alf a jiffy.'

Helen tipped the porter and got inside. She was soon being rushed through all the back streets of the capital, for the driver obviously knew he could proceed with fewer interruptions if he kept away from the main roads.

King's Cross was eventually reached and she was securely in possession of a comfortable seat. This time, she was alone and able to read and eat her lunch undisturbed. It was a through train to Grantham, where Margaret had arranged to meet her. The journey was not particularly interesting and she was glad she had provided herself with something to pass the time.

Chapter XI

When nearly two hours had passed she folded up her paper and watched out for Corby...Between there and Great Ponton she put on her gloves and hoisted her belongings down from the rack over her head. When the latter village had flown by she went out into the corridor and walked along to the door. The window was up, so she lowered it. Her heart began to beat excitedly and she found it difficult to maintain a calm exterior.

The rails doubled and trebled; sheds appeared and with a final shriek the train rushed into Grantham station. Helen leant on the window and looked out for Margaret. There were not many people about and she did not take long to spot Margaret's tall, dignified figure standing by the steps. Bernard was with her, which Helen was very pleased to see, for she did not expect him. She waved; they saw her and waved back. The train gradually slowed down and stopped. They came forward and arrived at the door just as she was getting out.

Greetings accomplished, Bernard went after the luggage while Margaret and Helen crossed over the bridge, talking all the way.

Outside, Bernard's car was waiting for them. They got into the back seat and conversed until the owner appeared with a porter. The luggage was hidden away on the grid and they drove off towards the centre of the town.

'Terribly dull road, this,' said Bernard. 'Don't you think so?'

'Yes, I do,' replied Helen, 'but there's better to come, if I remember rightly.'

'Oh yes, there is.'

'Doesn't the church look beautiful?' said Margaret, as they turned into Westgate and the tall, graceful spire of St Wulfram's appeared above the red roofs of the houses.

'Yes, it's a wonderful landmark. What's it like inside? I've never been into it.'

'Haven't you? We must take you, then,' said Margaret, while her brother went on,

'It's not bad – smells fusty, you know, but then I've yet to find a church of that type which doesn't.'

Helen could not help smiling at his brief description, but she did not contradict him, for it was true.

'I suppose it's the stone,' she said.

'Yes,' responded Bernard, 'you get the same kind of smell in any old stone building which isn't often aired. I wish they'd do something about giving churches a good blow through every day. I hate trying to sing hymns in an atmosphere of fungus and prison cells.'

Bernard felt strongly on this subject, as Helen well knew, and she also knew that it was largely owing to his efforts that the church in his own village was the fresh, airy place it was. She had been in it several times and had been much impressed with it. Besides its airiness, the carpets and cushions always looked clean and new. Margaret's influence was felt in this quarter; on the first day of each season they were changed. In spring the church was green; in summer, heat was removed by cool blue; in autumn it flamed gold and in the winter it was made cheerful by the warmth of crimson. There was no elaborate painting on the ceiling. A few tasteful pictures hung on the walls. The old and beautiful carving on the seats and choir stalls gave it a unique appearance, and it had its effect on the villagers. The church was always full on Sundays, partly because it was blessed with a very energetic and broad-minded vicar, but also because it was a place to which it was a joy to come and worship. Helen looked forward to seeing it again.

They left the town behind them and drove on into the country. The hedges and trees were putting on all their glorious autumn colours, their leaves burning in the afternoon sun.

'People say Lincolnshire is a dull and uninteresting county,' said Margaret, 'but I think it has almost more variety than any other.'

'People who say that annoy me,' put in Bernard before Helen had time to reply. 'I'm sure they've never been here, and only read it out of third-rate books. In either case, they don't know what they're talking about.'

'Exactly,' said Margaret. 'I love Lincolnshire. There are hills for those that like them and flats in the fens; there are woods and meadows and cornfields and some most quaint and picturesque towns and villages.'

'Yes,' agreed Helen. 'Next to Sussex, I think it's the nicest county in England.'

'Is that a compliment or only politeness?' asked Margaret.

'No, I mean it!' cried Helen. 'I should have said "almost as nice as Sussex" if I was only being polite.'

'I'm glad you like it,' put in Bernard. 'It would be unfortunate if you didn't, considering you are going to spend a whole month here.'

Half an hour's driving brought them to the small country town of Strowsby, one of many in Lincolnshire which had outgrown the village stage but had not decided whether to become proper towns or merely to stay as they were.

The Robertsons' house was roughly a mile beyond Strowsby, set back from the road amongst a shelter of trees, which, however, were not too close to it to block out the light. Only glimpses of it could be seen from a passing car, except at the gate, whence the front door was visible at right angles to the road.

The house, though not all that old, was extensive and stood in its own grounds. It seemed much too big for Bernard and Margaret and the few staff they kept, but it belonged to their parents, who were out in India. Sir Arthur Robertson had been knighted several years ago for his invaluable work in the Civil Service. The children had been born in England before their father was sent abroad, which happened when Bernard was ten and Margaret eight-and-a-half. Fifteen years had elapsed since then, during eleven of which they had lived with an aunt and uncle and gone to boarding school, Bernard proceeding to the Royal Academy of Music and Margaret to university. When Bernard reached his twenty-first birthday, Sir Arthur had expressed a wish that they return to the family home, which had been occupied by a friend while not required, and keep it for him and his wife to come back to when he retired; so brother and sister once more set foot in their old home and both set about redecorating it and installing modern equipment almost before they had had time to examine all the old haunts of their childhood and make sure nothing was missing which should be there. Bernard dealt with such things as refitting the bathroom and kitchen and any constructional alterations which had to be attended to, and Margaret, with the same taste and discretion which she later exhibited in connection with the church, looked after colour schemes and what kind of curtains to hang in the drawing room; but no decision was made and no order given until each had consulted the other and discovered any difference of opinion. In this way much trouble was saved at the beginning, and instead of having to waste time and money by realteration later when it might have been very awkward, when one room was finished they could feel satisfied with it and know it need not be touched again.

Bernard pulled up outside the porch and opened the door of the car. He unwrapped his long, thin figure from the driving seat and helped

Bernard with some music

Helen and his sister to descend. The luggage was carried indoors, and Margaret escorted her friend upstairs and showed her into her bedroom.

'This is my favourite room,' she said, and there was the slightest tone of pride in her voice. 'I don't think you've been in here before, have you? We call it the Bridal Chamber.'

'Well!' exclaimed Helen, laughing. 'I've heard of White Rooms and Blue Rooms and Green Rooms, but I've never before heard of one called a *Bridal Chamber!*'

'It used to be called the White Room once,' explained Margaret, 'and we christened it the Bridal Chamber when we were children; but it was so dirty and looked so cold when we came back to it that we changed it completely. The china figures which used to be called the bridesmaids are still there, though.'

'What about the bridegroom?' asked Helen.

'We never got as far as that,' responded Margaret. 'Perhaps you will be able to provide him.'

'I don't think I brought my top hat,' said Helen with a twinkle in her eye and not at all disturbed by Margaret's jest, 'but I can always ask Mother to send it on to me. What kind would you like – tall, dark and handsome or fair, fat and forty?'

'Whichever suits you best; after all, you are to sleep here, I'm not.'

With that she opened the door and Helen crossed the threshold. The room in which she now stood was no more like a bridal chamber as she imagined it than she was. 'Autumn Chamber' would have suited it much better. The wallpaper had an unobtrusive pattern of subdued colours on a pale yellow base; the woodwork and furniture were dark oak; the carpet was a mingling of autumn hues – browns, reds and golds, with a touch of green to relieve it; these colours were repeated in the curtains and upholstery; the counterpane, toilet covers and towels were old gold; the washstand in its own little recess gleamed spotless with its shining fittings; the ornaments were of highly polished copper and brass; and crowning all, a magnificent bowl of chrysanthemums of many different shades and varieties stood in the hearth in front of the empty fireplace.

Helen stood and gazed enraptured for several seconds, taking it all in; then she said,

'Oh, Margaret, it's truly beautiful! I *do* like it. Thanks awfully – *and* a four-poster bed!'

'I'm so glad. Yes, I thought you'd like that. We have a particular weakness for four-poster beds.'

Helen was still exclaiming over the room, much of whose needlework

Margaret in evening dress (1945)

and craftsmanship she later discovered had been done by her friend, when Bernard appeared with her cases. He put them down and shook his hands.

'What on earth have you brought with you, Helen?' he asked 'It feels like lead.'

'You forget I'm staying for a month,' answered Helen, after thanking him. 'Just a minute, where's the hat box?'

'Is there something else? Sorry, I didn't see it. I'll fetch it.'

Bernard hurried away and soon reappeared with the missing piece of luggage.

'Here you are, Madam,' he said, throwing it on to the bed.

'Oh, please be careful!' cried Helen in alarm. 'I've got a new hat in there.'

'Oh, I'm sorry,' apologized Bernard, 'but if you ladies *will* have hats that won't bear a little rough treatment, what is one to do?'

'You wait till you see me in it,' responded Helen. 'I look quite ravishing, I assure you. Really though,' she added, turning to Margaret, 'it's a perfectly ridiculous affair, but I just couldn't resist it.'

'I know,' sympathized Margaret, for she was very particular about her headgear. 'I can't wear silly hats, though. They don't suit me.'

'No, you want something dignified, like yourself,' said Helen.

'Shall I order tea?' asked Bernard, who was rather bored by all this feminine talk.

'Oh, poor Bernard! I'm sorry,' replied his sister. 'Yes, please do.'

Bernard sped away on his errand and Margaret shut the door after him. She turned to Helen, who had taken off her hat and coat and was now washing her hands, and said with an anxious expression in her eyes,

'Helen, I want to warn you about Bernard.'

Helen shook as much water as possible off her hands and began to dry them on the hand towel.

'Bernard? Why? What's happened?'

'Nothing has *happened*, exactly; it's what he *is*. You probably know that he is very highly strung and extremely sensitive.'

'Yes, I remember that.'

'He used to be terribly nervous and excitable when he was a child,' went on Margaret, 'and his love of music has not done much to lessen it. Of course, he has outgrown many of his fears, like the dark and seeing horrible shapes in it, but he is very easily hurt, and I'm so afraid that if anything happens which upsets him more than usual, he will do something which he would be very sorry for afterwards.'

Helen folded up the towel and hung it on the rail. She walked over to the dressing table and proceeded to comb her hair.

'I knew he was highly strung,' she said, 'but I didn't know it was as bad as that. I haven't seen him for two years and a lot may happen in that time, but I didn't think he was like that then. Perhaps my memory is bad, though.'

'Yes, I'm afraid he was. I'm used to it and know how to manage him, but other people – even friends – cannot always understand him and sometimes use the wrong words. Do you see what I mean?'

Helen put down the comb and turned to face her friend, who was leaning against the end of the bed.

'I know what you mean,' she said gently, 'and I'll try not to do anything to annoy him.'

'You're not offended, I hope. It's not that I imagine you *would* do anything rash, but…'

'Of course I'm not offended. Why should I be? I'm glad you've told me.'

'Some people might be.'

Helen advanced and grasped her hands.

'Margaret, dear, you can trust me,' she said. 'I know how concerned you are about Bernard and I won't be the cause of any upheaval if I can help it.'

'Thank you. I'm much relieved. I thought I had better tell you at once rather than leave it, when it might be too late. Now, if you're ready, we'll go down.'

Chapter XII

That first evening was spent in bringing family history up to date. Helen told them about her unexpected meeting with Miss Brisley and gave them her message.

'Oh, "Bristles",' laughed Margaret. 'I well remember him; a small boy with a flair for model aeroplanes. He used to bring them with him when he came to tea and he and Bernard used to fly them all over the garden.'

'That was years ago, though,' continued Bernard. 'Before we went away. What fun we used to have! Do you remember the time when his helicopter got caught in the beech tree, and the job we had getting it down?'

'Yes, and Ben tore a large hole in his shorts climbing up after it. I always remember that because they were a new pair, and he was so upset about it that Mother took pity on him and did one of her marvellous invisible darns over it so that it wouldn't show and he wouldn't have to tell his mother what he'd done.'

Helen laughed at this and asked,

'Did she ever find out?'

'I believe Mother told her about it later, when the newness had had time to wear off. Anyway, nothing was ever said.'

'We'll have to ask him over one day with his sister,' said Bernard, 'and Margaret, how about asking Geoffrey to come over one day and stay for lunch?'

'Yes,' replied Margaret, 'we must have him over to meet Helen. I don't think you've met him, have you?' she added, turning to Helen.

'No, I don't think so. Who is he?'

'Geoffrey Lyndon. He writes books.'

'Does he? I'd love to meet a real author; but I don't seem to know the name. Is he famous?'

'Very. But he doesn't use his own name.'

'Oh, I see. Well, what does he call himself? Have I read any of his books, do you think?'

'You must have. Everybody reads them,' said Bernard. 'Actually, he

Bernard Robertson 25, Margaret Roberston 23 (1943)

doesn't wish himself to be known, but I don't think he'd mind us telling you, do you, Margaret?'

'I'm sure he wouldn't; and think how embarrassing it would be for poor Helen to have a "real author" in the house and not know what he had written!'

'The situation would be a little delicate, certainly,' said Bernard, and Helen chipped in,

'I won't repeat it if he doesn't wish it to go any further.'

'Well,' said Margaret, 'have you read *The House of Pride* or *Christ's Country* or –'

'Or *Strange Adventure* or *The Orientalist*,' interrupted her brother. 'Oh, we could go on for years!'

'Yes, rather!' exclaimed Helen eagerly. 'Did he write those?'

'Yes, and I don't know how many more besides. Now do you know?'

'Indeed I do! I love his books. Whatever is the author's name?...Why, it's Lyndon Jeffries. What an awfully good way of doing it!'

'Isn't it clever?' said Margaret, delighted with Helen's enthusiasm. 'He's only twenty-six, too.'

'*Is* he? Good heavens, I thought he was much older than that! He must have been all over the world to gain the experience and knowledge he possesses; and his themes are so varied! I read every new book of his that comes out, and I've got them all at home. I'd no idea he was so young.'

'It is surprising,' said Margaret, 'and his stories are so wonderfully told. He teaches without seeming to do so.'

'Yes, I've learnt a lot from reading his books. Fancy his being a friend of yours! *Do* ask him over! I've always wanted to meet him, but I never thought I'd have such a chance as this. When can he come? I can hardly wait!'

Margaret laughed at her excitement and Bernard, with a twinkle in his eye, said,

'We shall have to keep a tight hold on her, or poor Geoffrey will get no peace!'

'You are as excited as a child!' cried Margaret, but she was glad that Helen was too thrilled herself to notice an unusual heightening of colour in her face and a certain unexplained expression in her eyes. 'We will certainly have him over. When shall it be, Bernard? Have you any concerts in the near future?'

'No, not for another fortnight – you know, the one in Ilton – but there will be plenty of rehearsals, though, next week. Any day this week suits me; the sooner the better, I think, for Helen's sake. How about tomorrow?'

'Tomorrow wouldn't be too convenient, as it happens. Say Thursday.'

'All right, I'll ring now and see if it suits him. It's Strowsby 217, isn't it?'

'Yes.'

'Thank you. To lunch on Thursday. What time shall I ask him to come?'

'Oh, about eleven; then we can have a good long talk beforehand. And he'd better stay for tea as well.'

While Bernard was ringing up, Helen asked how they had become acquainted with Mr Jeffries?

'It was rather strange, really,' Margaret told her. 'One day about a year ago I was busy in the house, when the front door bell rang, and there was a perfectly strange young man enquiring for Bernard. I showed him into the music room. Bernard was practising and I made to tell him he had a visitor, but this young man wouldn't let me disturb him. "Wait till he's finished his piece," he said. Luckily, it wasn't a long one, and I left them together. It turned out that Geoffrey had heard him play and had been attracted by his face – he has an eye for faces, especially interesting ones, and you must admit that Bernard's is interesting – and with the boldness which belongs to most of his type, decided to find out what lay behind it. To cut a long story short, he soon became a very great friend, and as he only lives in Strowsby, we see quite a lot of him when he isn't abroad.'

'Oh, I see,' said Helen, who had listened with interest to the story. 'How awfully nice for you.'

'Yes, it is.'

Bernard here appeared, to say it was perfectly all right and Geoffrey would arrive about eleven o'clock on Thursday.

'Good, said Margaret. 'Now, Bernard, will you play for us?'

'Certainly, if you would like.'

'Oh yes!' cried Helen. 'Please do!'

Bernard went through to the music room and sat down at the piano. Helen leant back on the sofa cushions to enjoy herself.

Chapter XIII

Helen was glad Margaret had warned her to be careful with Bernard, for she found him a great deal more sensitive than she remembered. He spent most of the time, when he was not required for anything else, practising the piano, and once he was established at the instrument it was useless to try and talk to him.

He had passed his LRAM exam several years ago, followed by GRSM at the Royal Academy, and was now making his name in the musical world as a rising young pianist with no small degree of skill. Many eminent musicians who had heard people talk of him and had said to themselves 'just another of these fussed-over prodigies with no real talent', were surprised when they heard him play and were pleased to admit they were wrong. The name of Bernard Robertson began to be circulated in society as denoting a good performance, and people flocked to any concert where he was to play.

He was now having a well-earned holiday after a series of concerts and hard work, but he did not practise any the less on that account and Beethoven's sonatas and Bach's fugues could be heard at all hours of the day. The music room was a light, airy apartment adjoining the drawing room, which opened out on to the terrace, for the ground behind the house was lower than it was in front. When the French doors were open one could see right down the garden from the arch between the two rooms. Helen liked to lean against this arch and listen to him. He could not see her, for he faced the opposite way, and he would not have minded if he could, because once he had begun to play he was blind to everything else but the imaginary world the music created for him. Sometimes, indeed, she stole round to the front of the piano to watch him. If the music were of a quiet, gentle type, his expression was calm and far away, for he played without music and often composed as he went along. If it were loud and energetic, his face worked, his eyes flashed and his hair flew about almost as fast as his fingers. At first Helen thought it merely affectation but she soon learned to cast that idea aside. Bernard was far

Charles
(1945)

Bernard
(1945)

too sincere to allow even the faintest shadow of hypocrisy to enter his manner.

Helen played the piano herself but her performances were nothing compared to Bernard's. She had talent but he had genius, and she never tired of listening to him.

Thursday came at last and Helen began to be very excited at the thought of meeting one of her favourite authors. She wondered what he would be like. Her picture of him was rather vague, but it was clear enough for her not to want it to be shattered. What she could see of him in her mind's eye was a small man with a great deal of curly red hair. She was sure he had red hair, but beyond that she could not be certain of anything. She would not ask Margaret to describe him, for she knew she would have a shock when she saw him – people were never how you imagined them – and with true conservatism she intended to hold on to her idea as long as she possibly could.

They were examining a piece of Margaret's embroidery on the seat of a stool in the drawing room when Geoffrey arrived and rang the bell.

'Here he is,' said Margaret.

Bernard restored the stool to its proper place and they waited for the visitor to be shown into the room. They waited with very different feelings. Margaret's were the strongest, but she managed to conceal them and Helen, who was almost too excited to keep still, did not notice anything unusual in her expression. Bernard's were merely those of somebody waiting to welcome a friend.

The door opened and 'Mr Lyndon' was announced. He entered and advanced to greet them, and before Helen knew what was happening, he was being introduced to her.

'How do you do?' he murmured, shaking hands.

Helen could hardly have had a greater shock – was this the much-talked-of Lyndon Jeffries? This the red-headed genius she admired so much? Why, he was tall and broad and his hair was dark – almost black. No, this was not the author of her imagination; true, he had a pair of observant dark eyes, a pleasant, sympathetic expression, and he was the sort of person one would expect Margaret and Bernard to like, but he was not Lyndon Jeffries. He was nothing more than an ordinary young man going under the name of Geoffrey Lyndon.

It certainly was a shock, and Helen took several minutes to recover

Geoffrey Lyndon 26 (1943)

from it. When at last she became aware of exterior sounds, she realized Margaret was speaking.

'It's far too lovely a day to sit indoors,' she was saying. 'Let's go outside and sit on the terrace.'

She accordingly led the way across the room, through the French doors and on to the wide sunny terrace which stretched the whole length of one side of the house, with a short flight of stone steps leading down into the garden. Bernard fetched four garden chairs with Geoffrey's help and arranged them in the sunniest and most sheltered spot. Margaret took one end and Bernard the other, so that Helen found herself sitting between him on her right and Geoffrey on her left.

At first the conversation was general, but as Helen could not conceal her feelings any longer, she took advantage of a pause to say,

'Mr Lyndon, I can't keep quiet another minute. I must tell you how much I enjoy your books – I think you're marvellous.'

'How did you know I wrote?' asked Geoffrey, not looking very pleased.

'We told her,' explained Margaret. 'At least, we gave her some titles and let her guess, which wasn't very difficult, as she knows them all by heart – she's been quoting you for the past two days. I hope you don't mind.'

'She'd probably have found out anyway,' put in Bernard, 'she's so clever.'

Geoffrey laughed good-humouredly.

'Oh well, in that case, I suppose I can't say any more,' he said, 'but' – turning to Helen – 'don't let it get any further, will you, Miss Wentworth. You see, I hate to be known.'

'No, indeed I won't,' she replied. 'But please call me Helen, Mr Lyndon. *I* hate it when young people go about calling each other "Miss This" and "Miss That".'

'Yes, so please call me Geoffrey,' said he, heartily. 'Usually it's much better, but there are some people one cannot call by their Christian names after only ten minutes' acquaintance. I know it was about three months before I dared to call Margaret anything but "Miss Robertson".'

Everyone laughed at this, but it only proved once again to Helen that her friend commanded respect as well as affection.

Gradually they began to converse in twos, as people will do on such occasions. Geoffrey, being next to Margaret, naturally talked with her, and Helen was left with Bernard.

Helen never felt at ease with Bernard as she did with Charles. There was something about him which seemed to put her under a restraint, partly because he was one of those difficult people whom one never quite knows how to take, and she always had to be very careful what she said to him. She liked him – indeed she was very fond of him, as she was of Margaret – but she could not fully understand him.

There was one thing about Bernard which she did like, however, and that was that one did not *have* to talk to him. He was perfectly content to be in the same room with her and never say a word, although he was not reading or playing the piano. For friends, conversation is not a necessary adjunct of sociability. She was rather glad of this now, for it meant that she could study Geoffrey, who had pulled his chair nearer to Margaret's and was deep in discussion with her over the far arm, without having her thoughts interrupted by incessant chatter.

Once the shock was over, Helen discovered plenty in Geoffrey to examine and like. His face had attracted her at once, for it was kind and pleasant, and though quite well-featured, was not too good-looking to lack irregularity and interest. He was not at all what she imagined an author would be like. In fact Bernard looked the more literary of the two, at least as far as clothes were concerned, for he was only comfortable in a pair of hardly-creased grey slacks, an old blazer and sandals, whereas Geoffrey, contrary to her expectations, was as neat and tidy as he possibly could be, even to the existence of all the tags on the shoelaces of his perfectly polished shoes. One of the first things Helen noticed, after looking at his face and trying to read what lay behind it, was his hands, whose long, tapering fingers denoted the scholar and writer, not the practical man. A particularly striking contrast between him and Bernard was that, while the latter could not keep still for two minutes together, Geoffrey, having settled himself in a comfortable position, hardly moved at all, except to blow his nose once, and to aid, with his hand, a description which even he found difficult to express in words.

After lunch, which they ate indoors, Margaret proposed a walk, and having donned outdoor clothes, they started out.

The countryside was, as Helen put it, 'really glorious'. The leaves were already turning red and yellow and in the woods the gradations of colour, matched with that of the rich earth and the soft blue of the sky, convinced Margaret, at least, that Lincolnshire was one of the most beautiful counties in England.

At one point, where they were fairly high up and could look down on the surrounding country, Geoffrey suddenly cried out,

‘Oh Lord, if only I could paint that! What wouldn’t I give to be able to make it live for others as it does for us!’

‘Yes!’ responded Helen. ‘Do look at that tree down there – isn’t it just – just wonderful!’

The tree she was referring to was a tall poplar whose silver featheriness seemed to mingle imperceptibly with the blue-grey mist of the sky behind it, contrasting with the glow of a hawthorn tree growing in the hedge below.

‘There are times,’ said Bernard after a pause, ‘when words cannot express one’s feelings. They can’t express mine now.’

‘Nor mine,’ added Margaret. ‘The only way to get it out seems to be by singing.’

‘You are right,’ said Geoffrey, ‘that is the only way. It doesn’t matter what one sings – anything – but one must sing!’

‘Let us hope the weather keeps up all the time you are here, Helen,’ said Margaret.

On the way home, Margaret purposely walked with her brother, so that Helen could talk to Geoffrey.

She found him a most interesting person to be with, for he seemed to know something about everything, and could convey his meaning and draw pictures as clearly in conversation as he could with his pen, which pleased her, for she had thought he might perhaps be the type who, though they can be very fluent and happy in their choice of words on paper, are quite lost when it actually comes to speaking them.

The more they conversed, the more she liked him, for his manner was as pleasing as his face. He was not particularly witty, but he had a way of telling a story which made her laugh merely because of the way he told it. He had a deep insight into human nature, and as Helen was not at all difficult to understand, he soon knew enough about her to like her in his turn.

When, after tea, Geoffrey had to depart, she was quite sorry, for as she said to Margaret later, he was like a walking encyclopaedia – one only had to ask him a question and he seemed to know everything there was to know about it. He bade them adieu and Margaret went to let him out.

‘Well,’ she said when she returned and they settled down once more, ‘what do you think of the great Mr Jeffries now you’ve met him, Helen?’

‘I think he’s marvellous,’ replied Helen. ‘What a lot he knows! There wasn’t one question I asked him he couldn’t answer. You’d *never* think he was only twenty-six!’

'Try him on maths,' suggested Bernard. 'You'll find a weak spot there.'

'Unfortunately,' laughed Helen, 'my maths were never my strong point, so I probably shouldn't be able to tell whether he were right or wrong anyway!'

Chapter XIV

'I had an idea last night,' said Margaret at breakfast next morning, which they were eating in the dining room at the front of the house.

'Oh, what was it?' asked Bernard, helping himself to some more marmalade.

'Well,' began Margaret, 'your next concert is being held at Ilton in about a fortnight's time, isn't it? So, don't you think it would be a good idea if we made a party with Geoffrey and arranged to meet the Brisleys there – it would be a good way of seeing them and we could thus combine two things.'

'Yes,' said Bernard, 'that would certainly be one way of doing it.'

'And I thought you could write to Penny, Helen, and see if she could come too – it's a Saturday afternoon.'

'I'm sure Penny would love to come,' said Helen. 'Thanks awfully; she was only saying the other day that she'd never heard Bernard play properly.'

'Good; well, you write to her and I'll write to Helen Brisley, and we can ask Geoffrey tomorrow when he comes. Do you agree, *mon frère?*'

'Yes, rather – jolly good idea ,' agreed Bernard enthusiastically. 'Then we can book a table at The Windmill and have a meal afterwards.'

'That's settled then. There's another thing,' went on Margaret, turning to Helen 'We don't intend to make plans for every single day so that you find you have no time to yourself. I'm sure you'll want to write letters or read or be alone sometimes, and we always make it a rule that each of us makes his own arrangements, such as going into the village to do some shopping, or going for walks and so on. If there is any expedition decided upon we all join in as a matter of course, but otherwise, your time is your own. Will that suit you?'

'Yes, very well, thank you. It's a very good arrangement.'

'The only condition is,' continued Margaret, 'that if any of us goes out, he lets the others know so that they know where he is.'

'Very wise. Is there anything on this morning?'

'I don't think so. Why? Do you want to go out?'

'No, I've got several letters I ought to write, and if there's nothing on, I could write them this morning.'

'Oh well, that's all right. Bernard, how about you?'

'Practising,' said Bernard briefly.

Helen came downstairs to the drawing room later during the morning in search of a suitable place to write her letter, and found it empty. Bernard was not practising, in spite of what he had said, for he had remembered something important he had promised to do for Geoffrey, and had ridden over to his house on his bicycle to see about it; Margaret had taken the car into Strowsby to do her shopping. Helen pulled up a small table and set to work.

First of all there was Penelope to write to, to tell her of their plans and ask her to find out whether it would be possible for her to join their party. Then there was a brief note home, just to let her parents know that she had arrived safely. A long, newsy letter to Charles took up more time, and finally she gave her attention to the question of Philip. For some time she sat idle, wondering what she should say and how she should begin. She decided to tell him the news first and leave the 'delicate task' until afterwards. She accordingly began by telling him about her journey and what they had arranged so far to do; then she set about the task of explaining his family to him as well as she could without seeming to 'preach', for she knew that there was nothing Philip hated more than the thought that she was 'moralizing'.

'You remember what you said to me the other day (she wrote) about not getting on well with the rest of the family? I was most distressed to hear you say that because I'm sure with a little effort on everyone's part it could be set right. I think you should perhaps try to get to know them better, and of course, they you. It is difficult, I know, when you live at home, or even when you see as much of it as you do, to appreciate your family. It is only when you are away from home longer than usual that you begin to realize what each person is worth. I daresay you think this is an unnecessary thing to say, as we have all been away from home at boarding school, and now you are at Cambridge, but in this case, I think you should try a little harder to understand each other. Of one thing I am certain, Phil, and that is, that however unkindly it may seem that Mother and

Father behave towards you, they do not intend to be indifferent and overbearing, and I know they would hate to think that that was how their behaviour appeared to you.

You said that Father hardly ever speaks to you. I hope – indeed I'm sure – that this was an exaggeration, wasn't it? If he does speak to you less than he does to the rest of us, I think it is because he never quite knows what to say. Your tastes are not similar and he probably does not know how to converse with you in such a way as to interest you. Father is very shy, you know, Phil; he doesn't make friends easily, and no doubt your university manners rather awe him. You have to plumb deeply before you can really get to know Father. Give him the right atmosphere, and he will blossom forth in a wonderful way, but put him in a room or in company, even of his own children, which is the least bit strange, and he will recoil within himself, and it is extremely difficult to get anything out of him. I think you will find that if you try to be interested in his books and his stamps, even if you are not really – if you *appear genuinely* to be interested – he will open out and tell you a great many things you would never be able to find out for yourself. Luckily, I have always understood him and consequently have never experienced this strangeness, but I can quite see that to anyone who was not wholly sympathetic towards him, this difficulty would arise. It can be overcome, though, but it is you who must make the greatest effort, because you are not by nature shy as Father is and therefore it would be easier for you than for him.

The reason you don't get on well with Mother is because you are too much alike. You both have a will of your own, and neither of you is willing to give way to the other. Also, you both have tempers and though Mother has learnt by age and love for her family to control it to a large extent, you have not, and where there is the least tendency for heatedness, only a small spark is capable of lighting a big blaze. You both like your own way, and when those ways conflict, you find contention. Am I not right? So long as you can both have what you want, all well and good, but the moment your desires cross – well, you know better than I do how you feel. You must be very gentle with Mother, Phil, because in her heart of hearts, though I know she would never admit it, she is afraid of you. She always has been afraid of you, even when trying to make you obey her, and that is why you have been allowed to do so much as you like. Try to remember this, and be a wee bit more considerate – she has a right to every attention you can give her. You are the eldest son, and she wants to be proud of you.

I think I have said enough about Alban for it to be unnecessary for me to do more than urge you not to quarrel with him. I'm sure you will try, and when I see you again, I hope to see you good friends.

Penny and Gerry are too young even to think about trying to understand you, and I think it is up to you to see that they have no reason to quarrel when they are older. Gerry, I know, is inclined to fear you, but he takes after Father in that he is terribly shy and sensitive. So do try to be patient with him.

Well, you will be bored by now, so I had better stop telling you about the rest of your family, and get on with something more interesting which I have just remembered.

Helen read through what she had written several times, wondering whether she had told him all she wanted him to know, and put it in such a way that he would not be offended – it was very easily done, as she knew only too well. She even thought of tearing it up and not sending it at all, but she decided something must go. She accordingly folded up the letter, slipped it into an envelope and stamped and addressed it. She propped it up against one of the ornaments on the mantelpiece so that she would not forget to post it, and then took her writing materials upstairs. By this time Margaret and Bernard had both returned and it was lunchtime.

The arrangements for the concert were all completed and everyone concerned was able to come. Penelope was thrilled, as Helen knew she would be, and looked forward to the event with eager anticipation. They had agreed to meet outside the hall where the concert was being held, to save time and misunderstandings.

Bernard himself left during the morning, going into Ilton by bus, so that his sister could bring Helen and Geoffrey in the car and not have to start unnecessarily early. The drive took just under three quarters of an hour and was soon over, and the car parked safely in the car park The three of them then walked up the hill to the hall, and found Penelope waiting for them, looking very neat in the black jacket and grey skirt and hat which was the 'Sunday best' uniform of her school. She greeted them cheerfully and explained that she had been there a quarter of an hour, she

Benjamin Brisley 'Bristles' (1945)

was so afraid they would go in without her. This caused a general laugh, and then she was introduced to Geoffrey.

'I wonder where Helen and Ben are,' said Margaret, when the first excitement of meeting was over. 'I hope they won't be late, though it would be just like Ben if they were.'

'Is he not very good at being on time?' asked Geoffrey.

'He's hopeless!' Margaret said. 'Helen, do you remember that awful time when – oh, here they are. Good.'

The remaining members of the party having arrived and everyone been introduced, Margaret searched in her handbag for the tickets, and they followed her through the immense main door into the foyer. People were crowding in all the time, and it was quite an effort to keep together, but by dint of clinging on to each other's arms they managed it and were shown upstairs into the great hall. Penelope was not the only one who felt a thrill of excitement as they went in, for there was a buzz of talking from the people already in their seats, and the hall was beautifully decorated, with a stage at one end of it, from behind whose heavy plush curtains there came the sound of tuning up. Their seats were in the middle of the circle and easily found. Penelope volunteered to get the programmes, which Ben, much to Margaret's disgust, insisted on paying for. These procured and coats removed, they settled down to study them. Penelope turned to Margaret, who was sitting next to her, and pointing to the name of the soloist on the cover, said,

'Doesn't that make you feel proud, Margaret?'

'What, dear?'

'That – "Bernard Robertson". Gosh, I'd be proud if it were *my* brother.'

'I am proud – very proud. Who wouldn't be?'

'I'm so glad I could come. It was jolly decent of you to ask me.'

'I'm glad you could, too. I thought you would probably enjoy it.'

'Rather!'

Helen leant over to Geoffrey and whispered audibly, with a twinkle in her eye,

'Penny's got what we used to call at school a "pash" on Bernard, you know!'

'Rot!' exclaimed Penelope

'Dear me, and so young, too,' replied Geoffrey, ignoring the denial. 'Do you dream about him, Penny?'

'No, of course not. Helen's inventing it.'

'Ah, Penelope, my child,' said Ben seriously, 'never be led astray by one of us men. You will be told by every man who has the chance to tell you that you have eyes like stars, neck like a swan, hair black as the raven's wing –'

'Oh, I say, that would hardly be true of Penny!' interrupted his sister. 'Don't you mind what they say, Penny. I've got a 'pash' on Bernard too, so we're quits.'

'Have you?' cried Penelope in surprise. 'Fancy admitting it! I thought when you were in love with a person the last thing you did was to say so.' She wondered why her remark caused Margaret to blush so hard that she had to become intent on her programme in order to hide her face. She had not seen the glance which Geoffrey had given her over her head.

A few minutes were spent in gazing round at the other people in the audience. This was an intriguing occupation, as there were so many types to be seen, from long-haired musical-looking men to members of her own staff. There was plenty to take in, and as the concert did not begin promptly (what concert ever did?) she had plenty of time to do it.

At last the heavy curtains were drawn slowly aside, revealing a large orchestra arranged in tiers on an equally large stage. The conductor and the leader of the orchestra were still to appear. There was a magnificent grand piano a little to the left of centre, on whose glistening proportions Penelope gazed enraptured. Only two pieces to get through and then Bernard would be playing it. It was true, to a certain extent, what Helen had said, though she would never admit it.

As the curtains parted, a hush fell over the assembly and when the leader came on to the stage and took his place with a bow, everyone clapped politely.

'Why do people always clap the leader?' Penelope asked Geoffrey in a hoarse whisper.

'Well, he's rather important,' replied Geoffrey. 'He keeps the orchestra together.'

'I thought the conductor did that,' pursued Penelope, but there was no time for further argument, because the conductor now walked on to the stage and bowed over his baton to the terrific applause which greeted him.

He turned to face his orchestra, turned up the corners of his score, and tapped on his stand with his baton. The orchestra prepared itself for the first beat while the audience coughed and rustled programmes for the last time, and soon the hall was filled with Mozart's beautiful Symphony in E flat. When it came to the famous Minuet and Trio, Penelope nudged Margaret and whispered 'They play this in the orchestra at school – nothing like this, of course.' Margaret nodded, and gave herself up to enjoyment.

The applause was tremendous when the symphony was over, and the conductor turned with a gratified smile to bow to his audience. He was not one of the most popular conductors of the day, but he had one of the finest orchestras to follow him that afternoon. He had engaged Bernard, knowing that he himself would not be the attraction, so that the brilliant young pianist should have all the glory. He was conscious of having a first class orchestra and soloist behind him that evening, and it was no wonder that his smile was a gratified one.

There was a hasty change of music, then once more the two short taps and the baton held in the air. This time it was Dvorak's music which filled the hall, contrasting well with the delicate finesse of Mozart. Penelope much enjoyed watching the antics of one of the double-bass players, whose facial expression was never the same from one minute to the next. During his rest bars he drew out a large white handkerchief and mopped his brow, pushing his hair back from his forehead, over which it had dropped. There was much entertainment to be had in watching the orchestra, and it must be admitted that Penelope, at least, was more interested in doing this than in concentrating on the music.

The piece finished with a string of forte chords, and the applause broke out again. Even while she was clapping whole-heartedly, Margaret's heart began to beat wildly; she had been to many of her brother's recitals, but still experienced a thrill of anticipation whenever he was going to play. The conductor disappeared into the wings and Penelope, whose heart was beating almost as fast as Margaret's, nudged her for the second time, and grinned broadly. The others all exchanged glances and nodded as if to say, 'Now for it.'

The conductor reappeared, followed by Bernard, who was looking very neat and trim in his evening dress, and towering above him. He was greeted by deafening applause, and bowed rather self-consciously in response. Penelope clapped so hard that the seat shook beneath her, and her sentiments were shared by everyone in the party. While Bernard seated himself at the piano, the orchestra and conductor were arranging their music and score. Bernard had no music.

Although Margaret and Helen had heard the solo bars of the Beethoven Concerto No. 4 enough times in the past fortnight to make them thoroughly tired of it, neither of them was. Indeed, they appreciated it more for being familiar with it, especially when there was the orchestral background. Bernard excelled himself and Margaret told herself that he had never played so well before.

The applause was simply deafening when the last note was played, and Bernard had to come back and bow three or four times. Even that was not enough, and the clapping continued long after he had gone out for the last time, and the curtains had swung to for the interval.

'Oh, Margaret, he *is* marvellous!' cried Helen, unable to express all she felt. The others were equally eager with their praises, and Margaret was obviously very pleased.

'Gosh! To be able to play like that!' exclaimed Penelope.

'It seems impossible that there should be such terrific practising necessary to do it,' said Geoffrey. 'It all looks so easy, when Bernard does it.'

'That is the art of playing,' put in Helen. 'What wouldn't I give to be able to play as he does!'

'I suppose he had his donkey-work stage once,' said Ben. 'It was that that got me. I never could be bothered to practise properly. I wish now that I had.'

'One always does wish things like that when it's too late,' added his sister.

'You get a very good view up here,' remarked Geoffrey, changing the subject.

'Yes. *Did* you see that chap on the double-bass?' asked Penelope eagerly.

'Which one? There were two.'

'The one who pulled all the awful faces.'

'Oh, him. Yes, he was funny, wasn't he?'

'Playing a double-bass is no easy job, though,' said Margaret, 'especially when there are a lot of quavers. It's such a wide stretch for the fingers.'

Sounds of tuning up gradually made themselves heard behind the curtain, the orchestra preparing for the second half of the programme. All inharmonious sounds were over before the curtains were drawn again, as this orchestra was never allowed to tune its instruments in front of its audience. The last notes were silenced and once more the curtains swung apart. The leader walked on and received his polite clapping, soon to be followed by the conductor, whose greeting was much louder. Throats were cleared and programmes folded and the second half of the programme began. A suite of dance tunes based on Russian folk songs by a composer Penelope had never heard of, let alone try to pronounce the name of, some chamber music by Vaughan Williams and a series of short pieces by French composers came first, Bernard's second piece being last on the programme. The conductor had arranged it like this purposely, so that Bernard could have an encore and choose his own. This time his piece was by Chopin, and there was not one person in the audience who was not stirred to the depths by the passionate intensity or quiet gentleness of the music. Had Bernard's technical skill not been perfect, his interpretive sense would have won him praise, but the most experienced ear could detect no wrong notes, and in spite of the fact that he played without music, there were no faults in his performance. Margaret and Helen, who were the most musical of the party, listened as if they were in another world, and even Penelope, who understood least about music, was carried completely out of herself. Bernard himself was obviously far away. He seemed to know without looking how wide he must stretch his fingers, and no apparent worry as to whether or not he would hit the right note marred his performance.

The Chopin was played even better than the Beethoven, if that were possible, and the enthusiastic audience clapped as if it would never stop. Bernard came on to the stage and bowed three or four times, then, as the audience continued to clap and call out 'Encore!' he returned to the piano and made to sit down. The clapping ceased, and when there was silence he said, rather self-consciously, 'I am going to play the first movement of the "Moonlight" Sonata.'

It was Helen's favourite piece, and she could not help wondering if the glance he threw in their direction – he knew roughly where they would be sitting – meant that he had chosen it on purpose. The minor harmonies appealed to her, for they seemed to express better than words the strange, unfathomable longings that sometimes filled her heart.

Margaret wondered how it was that her brother managed to play the chords so softly, the accompanying quavers forming a harmony whose component parts were scarcely distinguishable from each other. Memories of learning the piece herself, or hearing other amateurs learning it, were of unimportant notes given too much stress, and notes in the tune not enough. Bernard showed how it should be played, ending so softly that the slightest sound would have drowned the last three chords.

Once again the clapping broke out and Bernard took his last bow. The National Anthem was played and the curtains swung to for the last time. People began to collect their wraps and make for the exit. The usual crush followed.

Margaret looked so happy and was obviously so thrilled at her brother's success and the praises of her friends that several people near them guessed she must be some relation, and leant over to add their praises. Neither she nor Helen nor Geoffrey spoke. They could not; they were far too deeply moved to be able to say anything. They were halfway towards the door before Margaret came down to earth and said,

'We'll go straight to The Windmill. I left it that Bernard would meet us there as soon as he could.'

At last they were out in the street.

'Coo! Fresh air!' exclaimed Penelope, as they emerged. '*Wasn't* it marvellous?'

'Yes,' said Geoffrey briefly. 'Absolutely wonderful.'

They made their way to The Windmill café and went in. They selected a table in the room upstairs, and Margaret ordered tea.

'I don't expect Bernard will be very long,' she said. 'He usually gets away as quickly as he can before people have time to stop him and keep him talking, so don't wait.'

Bernard duly arrived after several minutes.

'Sorry to keep you waiting,' he said, when he had greeted them all, 'but I made it as soon as I could.'

Then the praises began to flow forth, until Bernard looked so embarrassed that his sister took pity on him and said,

'My dear, it was marvellous. And now, ladies and gentlemen, too much praise isn't good for anybody, however well deserved, so shall we get on with our tea?'

This caused a general laugh and Bernard gave his sister a grateful glance.

When this was over, Bernard volunteered to take Penelope back to school, and Ben murmured remarks about having a train to catch. So the party split up, the Brisleys departing with profuse thanks, and the others making for the car park. Margaret suggested they should all go in the car as there was plenty of room, to save time afterwards, and everyone agreed.

Penelope having been safely deposited back to her house at Ilton College, the car was turned round and was soon speeding on its way to Strowsby. Bernard insisted on dropping Geoffrey off at his own front door, in spite of that gentleman's repeated protestations, and finally drove in to his own gate. Margaret and Helen got out, and leaving Bernard to put the car away, went into the house and upstairs to their rooms.

Later that evening when they were sitting by the drawing room after supper, all three became thoughtful. Bernard stared into the fire with his hands thrust deep into his trousers pockets; Margaret was doing some embroidery and Helen knitting a jumper.

'Are you glad it's over, Bernard?' asked Margaret after a pause.

'Pardon?' Bernard woke up with a start. 'Oh! Yes, I am, rather.' There was a short pause, then he added, 'It's always a bit of an effort.'

'I'm sure it is,' said Helen. 'It leaves you feeling flat after it, though, doesn't it?'

'Mm, yes, but it's a relief.' There was another long pause, then Bernard, who had been watching the progress of the knitting in a dazed, half-conscious way, suddenly said,

'That's an awfully pretty pattern you're knitting, Helen.' He got up and went over to the sofa where she was sitting, to examine it better. 'How do you do it? It looks terribly complicated.'

'It's not really, once you get into it,' responded Helen. 'It's going to be a Fair Isle jumper when it's finished – I hope!'

'Well, it's marvellous; and what pretty colours. Is it for you?'

'Yes.'

'It will suit you; won't it, Margaret?' he added, turning to his sister.

'Yes, I've been admiring it all the time she has been making it,' said Margaret, looking up from her work. 'You must get it finished to wear before you go, Helen.'

Helen laughed.

'Well, I don't know about that,' she said.

Bernard walked over to his sister.

'What are you doing, *ma chère?*,' he asked, sitting on the arm of her chair.

'I'm making an antimacasser,' said Margaret with a twinkle, glancing at Helen.

'A *what?*' asked Bernard.

'An antimacasser,' repeated Margaret.

'What on earth's that?'

Margaret and Helen both laughed.

'A chair back cover, *mon frère*,' returned the former. 'Surely you've heard it called that before now?'

'Never in my life. Why not call it a chair back cover and be done with it?'

Margaret merely laughed again, and they relapsed into silence. Bernard remained on the arm of Margaret's chair, leaning back with one arm stretched out along the back behind her. Margaret resumed her sewing and Helen went on with her knitting, unconscious of what a pretty picture she made or the effect she was having on him.

Chapter XV

One afternoon about three weeks after her arrival, Helen was listening to Bernard playing the piano and wishing for the hundredth time that she could play like him, when he stopped and said abruptly,

'Let's go out, Helen. I'm tired of being indoors.'

'All right. What about Margaret?'

'Oh, she went out with Geoffrey some time ago. He called.'

'Then we needn't worry. Where shall we go?' They were going towards the door.

'Shall we go to Our Wood?'

'Yes, that will be lovely. Tell me, why do you call it your wood?' She paused. 'Before you tell me, just let me go up and get my coat.'

This accomplished they crossed the hall and Bernard opened the front door.

'Well,' he said, as they went out and he shut it behind him, 'it's not our wood really, of course. We call it that because nobody but us ever goes there and we've no idea whom it belongs to. We are very fond of it, and we could take you to any spot in it we liked.'

'I see,' replied Helen, 'Is that the one you can see from Margaret's bedroom?'

'Yes, that's it.'

They came out on to the road and turned left. Almost immediately Bernard turned again, to the right this time, down a green lane which Helen had noticed when she first came. Its hedges, still green, were high and one could only see through them in a few places. It certainly was not the best time of year to see it, for the plants all looked overgrown and seedy, but Helen knew that in spring, Cuckoo Lane, as it was called, was a perfect paradise of beauty.

They had not gone very far before they heard voices on the other side of the hedge.

'Sh!' said Bernard. 'Don't move. I think it's Margaret and Geoffrey.' They paused to listen. Bernard was right.

'...and what would he do if you were to get married?' they heard Geoffrey ask.

'I don't know,' Margaret replied. 'I've often wondered. We've always been together, you see, and I don't know how he would get on...' She laughed. 'But there's no likelihood of my getting married just yet! The man who marries me must be better than Bernard, and I don't...'

They had passed too far for them to hear any more. Helen smiled and turned to speak to Bernard. His face, however, stopped her, and she never said what she intended. For Bernard was staring at her in a way which he only used when moved to the depths – an eager, passionate gaze with his head on one side and his hands clutching, in this case, an ash switch that he had broken from its tree. There was no mistaking that gaze, and Helen was for a moment hypnotized by it. Then she pulled herself together and began to walk on, fearing what was coming.

Bernard caught up with her.

'Helen!' he cried. 'Dearest Helen!'

She stopped and looked at him imploringly.

'Please, Bernard,' she begged, '*don't!*'

Obediently, and much to her surprise, he walked on for some seconds in silence. She followed him hesitatingly, preparing herself for the worst, and yet feeling strangely incompetent to deal with the situation.

'I can't stand this!' he exclaimed, turning suddenly and gazing at her even more ardently than before. 'Helen, you *must* listen to me!'

'No, –' she began, but he ignored the interruption.

'I can keep silent no longer,' he went on. 'I adore you, Helen. I cannot make speeches – my feelings are too deep; but I know that I cannot live without you. Say you love me, quickly, and end this agony!'

Helen realized that the only way of preventing total hypnotism was to keep walking, so that she did not have to look at him. She had never dreamed that his feelings for her were any stronger than those of a friend, and she was at a loss for words. She remembered Margaret's warning, 'I'm so afraid that if anything happens which upsets him more than usual, he will do something which he would be sorry for afterwards.' She realized in a rush that the thing was now about to happen. How could she tell him in such a way as not to hurt his feelings? Any refusal must be cruel, but she could do nothing but refuse.

'Bernard,' she began doubtfully, 'I – I –' Then she stopped, unable to proceed.

'Well?' he cried, ardently. Something *must* be done. His tone was too hopeful.

'Oh, Bernard – I can't!'

They had reached the gate into the wood by this time and Helen, thankful for some support, leant on it with her back to him. He stood behind her, unable to believe what he heard.

'What does this mean?' he demanded. 'I thought you loved me, Helen.'

'I do,' she replied almost with a sob, 'but –'

'Well, then what is wrong? Oh Helen, my own dearest Helen, say you will marry me!'

'Oh, you don't understand!' she cried, with another half sob, turning to face him. 'I do not love you like that. I couldn't say I didn't love you because I do and always have done, but not in the way you want. I love you as I love Margaret, but no more.'

'Isn't that enough to go on? It would increase.'

'No, Bernard, it would not. We could never be happy. We are not suited to each other. You may understand me, but I do not understand you. I do not know how to manage you. I am not sufficiently like you to make you happy, even though you may not think that matters now. You need somebody like Margaret, who has known you all your life and who *can* understand you; somebody who can sympathize with you, whom you can confide in, who would never displease you or hurt you. I am not that person – oh, you must believe me!'

'I *don't* believe it. I know you are the only person in the world who can make me happy. You could learn to love me, and as for understanding me, what does that matter so long as we are happy? Without you my life is a blank; it is worthless; it is all night. If you refuse me, I shall kill myself!'

This threat was so awful that Helen very nearly gave in. She could not bear to see Bernard in this state of mind. After all, she *was* very fond of him and it might grow, as he had said. Why should she deny him the happiness which was his due? The objections she had raised were not, on the whole, insurmountable.

She was on the point of giving in when she was stopped by a sound which she thought was somebody calling her name. She never knew what it was – whether there really was a sound or whether it came from inside her; but whatever it was it saved her from a decision which she knew would prove very foolish. She saw that if she consented to marry Bernard, she was taking a step in her life which could only be taken when both parties felt alike. She would ruin her own happiness in making his, and she was by this time not entirely devoid of dreams herself, comparing Bernard with somebody else, the scales weighing in favour of the latter.

'I have told you I cannot marry you, Bernard,' she said, as gently as she could, 'and I meant it. I am sorry to give you pain, but you will forget me, and find somebody else. Please don't ask me again.'

She turned back to face the wood.

'As if I could *ever* find *anybody* else to mean as much to me as you do! You don't know what you're doing. If you had any affection whatever for me, you would not treat me like this. Well, I said I should kill myself, and I don't care what happens to me now!'

With that he strode off down the lane. Helen turned hurriedly to stop him, but she never did. She watched him till he disappeared round a bend. She had a terrible feeling of apprehension but she could not think of any better way of expressing herself. If she had not been firm, she would have given him an impression contrary to the one she wished to give. But what would he do? – and how would she face Margaret if he did as he threatened to do? It was a problem whose solution she did not relish.

She turned once more and allowed her gaze to wander through the wood. The gate on whose moss-covered bar she was leaning opened into a long avenue of trees, the end of which she could not see as there was a slope downhill some hundred yards from her. It was beautiful, but she was not in the mood to appreciate it. She was busy with her thoughts until she spied two people emerge from the undergrowth on the left, near enough to see their actions but too far away to hear what they said.

She recognized them as Margaret and Geoffrey. Deciding to see how long it would be before they saw her, she did not call out, but remained where she was, silent.

Margaret, who was leading, was carrying some twigs of autumn leaves. As soon as she came into the avenue, she ceased to admire them and looked about her, particularly at the roof over her head. She threw out her arms as if embracing everything but she did not turn round. Helen strained her ears in vain to hear what she said.

She had advanced a few steps ahead of Geoffrey, who was now standing quite still. He said something which made Margaret stop and look at him, then become deeply interested in her twigs. Whatever *were* they talking about? It was like watching a film when the sound track has gone wrong. Helen was completely mystified. Geoffrey had a lot to say and it was obviously very important, for Margaret listened without interrupting him. He finished with a shake of his head and began to walk on. Margaret held out her hand and spoke one word, which, judging by her action, Helen was sure was 'Wait!' It seemed to fit, for Geoffrey did wait and turned back. Margaret said something else, not much longer than before, and then action followed rapidly. Helen was quite excited as to what all this was about. Geoffrey's step towards Margaret and her nod. A second's pause – and then they were in each other's arms.

Had Helen been nearer, she would have heard what passed between them. They had climbed over the fence into the wood and had slowly found their way to the glade where she saw them. Margaret had picked some autumn leaves with which to decorate the hall and up to this moment had been admiring them as well as minding where she trod. When they came out into the avenue she looked around her and up at the tall beech trees above her head, soaring high and making a cathedral roof, which was already turning gold, through which filtered the afternoon sunlight.

'Oh Geoffrey, isn't it beautiful?' she exclaimed. 'A wood is lovely at any time of year. I don't know which I prefer, spring or autumn; and when I look up at an avenue in a wood like this it always makes me think of a cathedral.' She took a few steps forward and then threw out her arms in an all-embracing manner. 'When I'm in here I feel as if I could love the whole world, don't you?'

Geoffrey did not move, but said,

'I should do, I suppose, but I'm afraid I'm more selfish than you, Margaret, because at this moment I feel I can love only you.'

Margaret stood still and turned to look at him. Geoffrey then poured out his feelings, hesitantly at first, but gradually gaining confidence while Margaret listened in silence. He concluded by saying,

'But what right have I to hope you can love me? Heavens! I'm totally unworthy of your friendship, let alone anything more. I can't ever hope you can love me the way I love you!'

He shook his head and began to walk on in front of her. Margaret held out her free hand and said, as Helen had thought, 'Wait!'

Geoffrey stopped and turned to face her.

'Geoffrey, I do love you,' Margaret assured him.

'You do? Really?'

Margaret nodded. The rest was self-explanatory.

Helen turned hastily away with a guilty feeling. This, coming on top of what she had just gone through with Bernard, was unbearable. Margaret must never know; she wished she had not seen them. There was such a contrast between the two scenes that she could hardly refrain from tears.

She suddenly felt very lonely. Margaret would no longer tell her all her secrets; she had Geoffrey now and would not need her. As for Bernard, she did not expect he would ever be quite the same, even supposing he did get over this passion, which did not at present seem likely. There was an inexpressible longing in her heart which was not directed to Bernard. She saw that now more clearly than ever, and for the first time she realized fully what it was she wanted.

She was so engrossed that she did not hear the twigs crack in the wood behind her, nor the muffled 'Good Lord!' which followed the crackings. The newcomer made a step towards her and called,

'Helen!'

She started from her thoughts and turned to face the voice. Was it merely by accident, or was there some unseen Power which had brought to this spot the very person she had all this time been longing for?

'Charlie, oh Charlie!' was all she could say, and had the gate not been there she would have flung herself upon him. He had soon climbed on to the top bar and was sitting beside her.

'Well, this *is* a surprise! I knew you were staying with Bernard and Margaret, but I didn't think I should find you here,' said Charles, in a tone of obvious pleasure.

'I certainly never expected to see *you* here,' responded Helen, now quite composed. 'Last time I heard from you, you were in London. What's brought you to this part of the world?'

'I'm staying with an uncle about two miles away across the other side of the wood' – he waved his arm vaguely behind him – 'so I thought I'd just come over and look in on the Robertsons, as I haven't seen them since I've been home.' Charles did not add that the real reason for his visit was a chance of seeing Helen. 'But where are the others?' he added. 'Are you alone? Well, I can see you are, but you know what I mean.'

'Yes. Well, actually, I came out with Bernard, but he – had to go. Margaret went out before that with Geoffrey.'

'Geoffrey? Who's Geoffrey?'

'Geoffrey Lyndon. Don't you know him?'

'No, I don't think so.'

'Oh. Well, he's one of their friends. You didn't see anybody in the wood, did you?' she added anxiously, hoping he had not witnessed what she had.

'No. Why?'

'I just wondered. Margaret says people never do go into it. I'm so glad you've come!' she continued, after a moment's silence. 'I was beginning to get all mopy.'

'What!' cried Charles, laughing. 'Helen Wentworth moping? I can't believe it.'

'It *is* unusual, I suppose, but – well, I've had quite a lot to think about this afternoon.'

'You must have had.' Charles, observant as he was, had not failed to notice certain symptoms of unrest in his friend, and it did not escape him to wonder, when she said she had been out with Bernard, and the rather unsatisfactory reason she had given for his not being there, if he had not had something to do with it. He was puzzled, and it must be admitted, a trifle jealous. He could not ask her a direct question, but he determined to obtain at least a hint of how the land lay, and so made her face an excuse to ask,

'Helen, has anything happened? – you're looking very pale.'

Helen immediately altered the situation by blushing to the roots of her hair.

'Well, I –' she began confusedly, trying in vain to appear calm. 'No, nothing of importance.'

'Are you…*sure?*' He looked at her scrutinizingly.

'Yes…No – oh, please don't ask me any more questions!'

Charles obediently said no more. He frowned and bit his lip. This only served as further evidence to his suspicions; yet she had said she was glad he had come, and her cry on first seeing him had been such as she could hardly have expressed if she had not wanted him very much. Then, he had dared to hope, and was he now to see his hopes dashed to the ground by the intrusion of another into her affections? Being Charles, however, he managed to cover up his feelings, and turned the conversation to a subject less painful to both of them.

But try as she might, Helen could not entirely exclude Bernard from her thoughts. She had an awful apprehension preying on her of where he had gone and what he intended to do. Knowing his passionate nature, she knew he might quite easily do something on the spur of the moment which, as Margaret said, he would be sorry for afterwards; and would love for his sister and his home in such a moment hold him back? These thoughts went coursing round and round in her brain and she found it extremely difficult to concentrate on what Charles was saying to her. She was not one of those people for whom, when a thing is out of sight, it is also out of mind.

'Stop worrying,' said Reason. 'You did your best when you weren't prepared. He must bear the consequences.'

'But he is so sensitive,' responded Conscience. 'You were too abrupt.

You don't know what you have done. You may have killed him. Poor Bernard! What will he do?'

This went on for so long that Helen could have screamed. She felt the only thing to do was get away from this place before she went mad. It was nearly half past four. She gave an inward sigh of relief when she saw that it was tea-time and she could give her mind to something else.

'Shall we go back now?' she said. 'We have tea at half past four. You must stay.'

'Thanks,' replied Charles, jumping down from the gate, 'I will.'

They accordingly wended their way homewards, Helen feeling that she could never go down Cuckoo Lane again.

Chapter XVI

Helen opened the door with the key Margaret had lent her for convenience and they went in to find nobody there. Helen showed Charles into the drawing room and went in search of Cook. She was alone, as it was the other maid's half day. On enquiring whether anyone had been in she was informed that Mr Bernard had dashed in about an hour ago and had gone off in a great hurry on his bicycle, and that Miss Margaret had been out all afternoon.

Helen returned to the drawing room.

'Everybody's out,' she said. 'We shall just have to wait, that's all. Do sit down.'

It was nearly five o'clock before Margaret appeared with Geoffrey. She apologized for being late, but they had been for a long walk and forgotten all about the time. Helen knew why. Then Margaret saw Charles and greeted him cordially.

'I'm sorry Bernard isn't here,' she said, when she had introduced him to Geoffrey, 'but I don't know where he is. I expect he will be here shortly, though. Do stay and have some tea.'

Charles accepted once more and tea was ordered.

The meal was a gay one and Helen almost forgot Bernard. Margaret and Geoffrey looked very happy, and Margaret, Helen thought, more beautiful than ever. But the time went on and even Margaret seemed anxious, for never, during the past three weeks, had he been late for his tea.

'It's twenty past five,' she said, consulting her watch. 'He's never been as late as this before. I wonder what can have happened to him. Have *you* any idea where he is, Helen?'

Helen felt the colour rush to her face, and she rested her hand on her knee so that Margaret should not see that it was trembling.

'Well,' she said, 'actually, he went out with me earlier, but he remembered something – and went off. He didn't say when he would be back.' It was not strictly accurate, but anything – *anything* – to take the spotlight off herself.

'Funny,' mused Margaret unsuspectingly. 'Well, I suppose he'll turn up. There's no point in leaving the tea things here. Will you all help to clear away, and then we can settle down sooner?'

Everyone lent a willing hand and in five minutes not a crumb was to be seen on the carpet.

Bernard did not come home until darkness had fallen. When they at last heard the front door close, Helen, at least, was intensely relieved. He had not killed himself. But he did not come in. Instead, he went straight upstairs and into his bedroom. Margaret rose, puzzled.

'Excuse me,' she said. 'I think something must have happened.' So saying, she left the room.

Helen never knew whether or not Bernard told his sister what had passed, but it was fully half an hour before she came down again. Meantime, the conversation in the draw-ing room dwindled to a discussion between Charles and Geoffrey on the relative merits of Norway and Switzerland as the ideal country for a winter holiday, in which Helen was content to sit and listen. Margaret reappeared when they were in the middle of talking technically about skis, and they had to stop.

'I'm sorry to have been so long,' she said, 'but he seems to have had an accident' (here Helen could not suppress a start) 'which has upset him rather. He's all right now, though. He'll be down in a minute – and please don't say anything.'

Helen was inwardly grateful that only the standard lamp was lit and that it stood behind her, so that her face was in shadow. In the few seconds left to her, she endeavoured to put on an unconcerned exterior.

The door opened and Bernard came in. His face bore lines of suffering and his eyes had lost their usual fire. The lids lay heavily over them and there was no pleasure in them when he came forward to greet Charles. He smiled, but it was only with his lips.

Geoffrey was shocked to see his friend so changed and could hardly refrain from asking him what was the matter. Charles glanced from Bernard to Helen, who was looking at her feet. Bernard shook hands with him listlessly and said, with an attempt at cheerfulness which was a complete failure,

'Hullo, Charlie, old chap. How are you?'

Charles had sense enough not to reply, 'Very well, thank you. How are you?' for it was obvious that Bernard was far from well. So instead, he said,

'Oh I'm fine, thanks. How's the piano?'

The preliminaries were got over somehow and they sat down, Helen feeling devoutly thankful that Bernard had taken absolutely no notice of her. They sat round the fire and talked about many subjects as though there were nothing unusual; but underneath there was not one of them who was not thinking about something else. Bernard talked in an absent-minded way to Charles, who was by this time convinced that the afternoon had not been uneventful as far as his friend and Helen were concerned, and he would have dearly liked to know what had occurred, and its outcome.

An hour passed in this unsatisfactory way, then Bernard rose abruptly and muttering something about having forgotten to put his bike away, left the room. The atmosphere at once cleared but it was still uncomfortable. Helen made a headache an excuse to go outside for some fresh air. She slipped into her coat, which she had not taken upstairs since the afternoon's walk, and let herself out of the front door.

It was not too cold, and the stars were shining. She walked, hardly knowing where she was going, to the gate. She had almost reached it before she saw a dusky figure leaning on it. It was Bernard. Her first impulse was to turn back. She would have done so, had he not called her without turning round.

'Helen, don't go!'

The best thing to do was to make a bold front of it. She advanced and stood beside him.

'How did you know it was I?' she asked.

'I could tell by your footstep,' he replied.

Helen leant on the gate and gazed above her.

'Look at those stars!' she said, hoping to keep his mind off herself. 'Aren't they beautiful?'

'Yes,' he replied, without paying any attention to them. A pause, then, 'Oh, Helen, can't you?'

'No, Bernard, I told you –'

'Yes,' interrupting her – 'I know you told me that this afternoon, but people so often don't mean what they say.'

'Do you mean me when you say "people"?'

'Perhaps I do. I hoped you might not. You sounded too definite at first and when I went away I was miserable; but I thought it over and I knew that some women kept people waiting in doubt for years before they gave you the final answer.'

'Did you think *I* was one of those women?' asked Helen, rather indignant at being classed with what she considered a shameless tribe and an insult to her sex.

'I did not know. Forgive me if I did you wrong but – oh, I could not believe I was to have no hope. Helen, say you did not mean it!'

This was far harder to resist than all his threats, but she was prepared for him now. There was no hope, but she could afford to be kind.

'Dear Bernard,' she said, 'I wish for your sake that I could!'

'Oh God!' he murmured below his breath, and Helen could see his knuckles gleam white where he gripped the top of the gate. 'Then… this…is my answer?'

'Yes, Bernard.'

'It will never be any different?'

'No, Bernard.'

He stood and gazed at her a moment longer and then turned and walked back to the house.

At that moment the front door opened and Charles' voice was heard to say,

'No, don't you bother. I'll find her – she won't be far away.'

Helen looked over her shoulder. She could see an elongated patch of light thrown out over the drive from the hall, and in it the shadow of Charles, who was standing in the doorway. He emerged as another shadow appeared and Margaret's voice was heard to say,

'Very well, only tell her not to stay out too long. I don't want her to catch a cold.'

'Righto. Well, cheerio, and thanks so much.'

'That's all right. We're always glad to see you. Goodbye.'

'Cheerio, Mainwaring,' said Geoffrey's voice. 'We'll meet again soon, I hope.'

'I hope so, Lyndon. Cheerio.'

Everybody shook hands and Charles started to walk down to the gate. Bernard, who had stopped when the door opened, now went on again, and met Charles halfway up the drive.

'Going?' he asked, as though he had not heard.

''Fraid I'll have to,' Charles said. 'Anyway, I'll see you again sometime.'

'I'm sorry it wasn't longer, but – well, I wasn't to know you were coming,' Bernard excused himself as well as he could.

'No, of course not. My fault for not giving you warning. Personally, I like surprise visits.'

'So do I…Well, I mustn't keep you. Goodbye, Charlie.'

'Goodbye, Bernard.' They shook hands. 'Oh, by the way, have you seen Helen?'

'She's down by the gate.'

'Oh. Thanks. Goodbye.'

'Goodbye.'

There being really nothing more to say, they parted in opposite directions. Charles came up to Helen and leant on the gate beside her.

'Star-gazing?' he asked.

'Yes. I could stay here all night looking at them, couldn't you?'

'Yes…I've got something to tell you,' he said. 'I didn't tell you before because I wanted to leave bad news till the very last possible minute.'

'Bad news?' Helen looked at him in alarm.

'Not that sort of bad news,' he went on reassuringly. 'You see, I heard from the Civil Service a few days ago – you remember I told you that firm I applied to wouldn't have me as I hadn't enough experience (I didn't expect they would, actually, and I'm not really sorry), and I've got to go for a six-month course, at the end of which an exam is to decide which of the candidates is to get the job.'

'Another course! But that doesn't sound very bad news to me, except that you'll have to do more work.'

'No, *that's* all right; but the thing is it's in Scotland.'

'Scotland! Why should they want to send you right away up there?'

'Don't ask me! You know what these big-wigs are. If they take it into their heads to send you to the Desert of Arabia, you go and that's all there is to it.'

'Scotland! Well, even that's not as bad as it sounds because you'll be able to come home for Christmas and Easter, won't you?'

'No,' replied Charles sadly, 'that's just it. We're only having a week's holiday at Christmas and as it's bound to be buried in snow, the journey would take up more time than it's worth bothering about; besides, there's always the risk of being stuck.'

'Then do you mean,' said Helen, the real truth of the matter beginning to dawn on her, 'do you mean that I shan't see you for six whole months?'

'It will more likely be seven, because we have to wait till the exam results are out before we know where to go next.'

'Seven months! But I can *never* live all that time without seeing you, Charlie!'

'I'm afraid it's a case of having to,' laughed Charles, 'and it will be equally impossible for me; but we must just grin and bear it.'

'Oh dear! But it's terrible, Charlie! You must write to me every week and tell me what you're doing and all about yourself.'

'Indeed I will try, Helen, but I can see from the syllabus that there's not going to be much time to do anything but work. You should see the stuff we've got to get through! So if my letters are short, you must forgive me.'

'Yes, of course' – it was a never-ending source of joy to Charles that Helen was blessed with a mind capable of understanding everybody's difficulties – 'so long as you write *something* every week.'

'Of course I'll write something; but you must write me good, long, newsy letters to cheer me up, or I shall become very dull.'

'Yes, I'll tell you everything. Will you have time to come and see us before you go?'

'I'm afraid not. I'm due there in five days' time.'

'Oh dear! So this is the last time I shall see you until you come back?'

'Yes.'

'Well, the very best of luck, Charlie boy – and take care of yourself, won't you?'

'Yes.' Charles grasped her hand in both his. 'Write to me *often*, Helen. I shall miss you.' He would very much have liked to take her in his arms and kiss her just then, but he did not. Instead, he squeezed her hand until it was quite painful, and said,

'I mustn't keep you out any longer, or you'll be catching a cold and then Margaret will never forgive me, for she told me to send you in. Goodbye, dear.'

'Goodbye, Charlie.' Helen ignored the first part of his remark, for her heart was too full to worry about such things as colds. She felt that this was goodbye indeed.

The next minute he had opened the gate and was gone – she did not know where, or care. All she could think of was that he was going to Scotland and she would not see him again for seven months – perhaps never, for anything could happen to him before then.

She walked back to the house with a very heavy heart.

Chapter XVII

She found Margaret and Geoffrey alone when she went into the drawing room. Bernard had gone upstairs, explaining that he did not want any supper. She therefore determined to put on a brave face and try to forget her troubles for a while. She succeeded fairly well until supper was cleared away and they returned to the drawing room. They sat by the fire and did not light the lamp, for as Margaret said, it was more cosy that way. Suddenly Helen said,

'Margaret, may I play?'

'Why yes, dear, certainly, if you wish.'

Helen rose and went into the adjoining room. It was dark, for the moon, which had risen during supper, was shining on the other side of the house. Helen felt her way across the room to the piano – Bernard's own grand piano – and switched on the standard lamp which stood beside it. She pulled out the stool and sat down.

Now Margaret knew that Helen never asked to play on Bernard's piano unless she were deeply moved by something, for she regarded it as his sacred property, which she had no right to touch. Very occasionally before, she had made the request while staying with them, and Margaret had always been able to tell what sort of mood she was in by the music she played. She therefore listened now for a clue to her friend's extraordinary and very unusual mood of the evening. When the first solemn bars of the "Moonlight" Sonata reached her ears she was satisfied that she had not been far wrong in her surmisings.

It was hardly surprising that Helen should choose the "Moonlight" Sonata, for she was very fond of it. The minor harmonies appealed to her. But tonight they appealed to her even more strongly, for all her thoughts were running in a minor key. She played as she had never played before. Experience had taught her grief and she let her heart and not her brain dictate to her. Margaret listened enraptured and even Bernard, whose bedroom was overhead, moved to his window in order to be able to hear her better. The Pathétique Sonata followed, then several unknown pieces whose weird, unearthly harmonies Helen found particularly appealing just then.

Suddenly she stopped playing and got up. She did not push the piano stool into place, for she might go back again. As she reached the arch between the two rooms she could see that the drawing room was empty, but the French doors on to the terrace being open, she guessed that its occupants must have gone outside Further looking proved she was correct, for leaning on the stone balustrade, gazing intently at something high on the wall to the right of the door, was Margaret, with the moonlight streaming full on to her face. She was framed in the doorway like a picture and Helen thought to herself that she looked even more beautiful, if possible, in the cool, silver light. She listened to the conversation and as she watched, forgot her own feelings for a while.

'There's a lovely one here,' came Geoffrey's voice. 'I'll see if I can reach it.'

'Do be careful,' said Margaret anxiously. A few seconds later, something fell at her feet. She bent down and picked it up. It was a rose.

'It's wonderful,' she said, smelling it. 'I'd no idea we had such fine ones in the garden, especially as late as this in the year.'

'It is a beauty, isn't it?' replied Geoffrey. Then he too came into the picture. He took the rose from her and arranged it carefully through one of the buttonholes of her dress. The smile which she gave him when he stood back to admire the effect was more heavenly than ever, and it was no wonder that he drew her close to himself and kissed her.

Once more Helen turned away with unpleasant feelings. *Why* was she always having to experience other people's happiness? This was unbearable. Before, Charles had not seemed so far away, but now, it would be seven whole months until she would see him again and she wanted him more than anything else on earth. She sat down again on the piano stool and covered her face with her hands. She did not cry, but her breath came and went so uneasily that it sounded like a sob.

She had not been sitting there very long before she felt an arm steal round her and somebody perch on the edge of the stool beside her. She moved a little to one side to make room and lifted her head. It was drawn gently back until it was resting on the somebody's shoulder. Helen knew who it was, and remained like this until she felt better. Then she said softly,

'Margaret, dearest, you are a great comfort.'

Margaret's reply was to rest her head on top of Helen's and take her hand. Margaret was blessed with a gift of sympathy which did not need words to express itself and Helen felt that, even if she did not know the reason for her strange behaviour, at least she would sympathize. In another few minutes she had regained her composure and looked up.

'There, I feel better now,' she said. 'I'm sorry to make such a fool of myself, Margaret.'

'No, no,' interrupted Margaret gently, 'you're not. I understand.'

'I'm rather tired,' said Helen. 'I think I'll go to bed.'

'Yes, I should, then.' They got up. 'Can't you tell me what is the matter, Helen?'

Helen shook her head sadly.

'I can't,' she replied. 'It's the first time in my life that I have refused to confide in you, but this time, I'm afraid I can't.'

'All right. Goodnight dear.'

'Goodnight, Margaret; and thank you so much.'

The quiet of her room was very pleasant after such an unhappy day, and she was able to reflect on what had happened with a calmer mind. She had found by experience what immediate relief was felt when one took one's troubles to God, and it was natural for her to call on Him for strength and guidance in hours of trial. Her distressed spirit was soothed by these few moments with the Father, and the peace which followed was very sweet. She was able to fall asleep with a quiet mind, to dream strange, pleasant dreams about Charles, of whom she had been thinking all day.

The last week of her visit was an uncomfortable one for Helen. Bernard ignored her except when it was absolutely impossible to do otherwise, and Margaret, though she did not mean to neglect her friend, was preoccupied with Geoffrey. It was natural, and Helen did not complain, or even show, by look or word, that she was not enjoying herself as she might. Margaret, realizing that first evening that Helen was not in the mood to be told how matters stood between her and Geoffrey, kept her engagement a secret and bided her time to break the news, little dreaming that Helen already knew.

She found an opportunity one evening towards the end of Helen's visit, and told her of all their arrangements.

'We shall be married in the spring,' she said. 'There is nothing to wait for, really, as I know Father and Mother would like Geoffrey – who could help it? – and he has no parents; but we both agreed it would be nicer in the spring, as a symbol of new life beginning. You may think it foolish, but we are foolish at times.'

But Helen did not think it at all foolish; she liked the idea. Margaret went on to say that Bernard would give her away and she would very much like Helen and Penelope to be two of her bridesmaids, the other two being a relation of Geoffrey's and Helen Brisley. Helen was very pleased and, knowing that 'Penny would be thrilled', agreed for both of them.

The last day came, and though sorry to leave Margaret, Helen was not loath to part from the places which brought back too many painful memories. She was taken by car as far as Grantham and all three of them came to see her off. She conversed with them through the corridor window, and it was not until the whistle was blown and the guard had waved his green flag that Bernard looked at her properly and spoke.

'Goodbye, Helen,' he said, and there was a note of awful finality in his voice. 'I shall always remember this visit.'

Helen did not know what she answered – she could not say much, as the train started to steam out of the station. The last picture she had impressed on her mind was that of the contrast between Bernard's fixed gaze and motionless attitude and the ease and grace with which Margaret leant on Geoffrey's arm while both smiled and waved until they could no longer be seen.

Chapter XVIII

The journey home was uneventful and Helen had plenty of time to think. In some ways she was sorry to be going home, and in others she was unfeignedly thankful. The past week had been very uncomfortable; although she was happy on Margaret's account, her ordeal with Bernard was not so easily forgotten, and it was to cause her much uneasiness for several weeks to come. She could not help thinking about Charles; seven months was a terribly long time to wait before she could see him again. His first long letter from Scotland, which she had received that morning and had kept to read in the train as she had not had a moment to spare until then, did a lot to cheer her. Charles knew how to write good, newsy letters, very well expressed and full of his usual humour. He described the place as 'dreadfully out of the way'. The village, he said, called itself Braeloch, but as yet he had only seen one other house besides the one in which he and his fellow-students were billeted, and two houses was not his idea of a village. There were about a dozen, including himself, taking the course. As yet he had not found out a great deal about them, but had 'rather palled up' with an aristocratic-looking young man called Bentley, who had the most exaggerated Oxford accent in existence but who was, all the same, 'a very decent sort of chap.' Then came a lot of talk about his work, which he managed to make interesting and which was so well written that a far less intelligent person than Helen would have found it understandable. After this came questions and information of a more personal nature and a plea for 'really long epistles' to keep up his spirits. 'I shall get frightfully mournful, dejected and low-spirited if you don't tell me about *everything*,' he concluded.

Helen smiled and put the letter back in its envelope. She felt like writing there and then had it been possible. She would do so as soon as she could after she got home and she did not think she would find much difficulty in sending him a 'really long epistle'.

*

It was already beginning to be dark by the time the bus swung round the corner by the first house in Edmuston. Helen wondered who would be there to meet her – her mother had said one of them would be; she quite expected it to be her father and she was therefore very surprised, when she descended from the bus, to find it was Alban who helped her to lift down her luggage.

'Why, Alban, I didn't expect to see *you* here!' she exclaimed. 'What's happened? Why aren't you at Dartmouth?'

'Oh, just a spot of leave,' said her brother unconvincingly.

'Funny time to have it, isn't it?'

'Well, actually, it's sick leave. I had flu.'

'Flu? My dear Alban, why didn't you tell me?'

'Why should I?' he replied with a smile. 'Nothing to worry about. I'm all right now.'

By this time they were walking towards the house, and before Helen had time to say any more, Alban said seriously,

'Helen, I want to tell you something before you get home.'

'Well, what is it?'

'I can't tell you here. It's private.'

'Well, wait till we get to the gate, then; nobody is likely to overhear you there.'

They walked on in silence until the gate was reached, then Helen said,

'Well, here we are. Now, what have you got to tell me?'

Alban put down the case he was carrying and said,

'It's about Phil.'

'Oh? What's the matter with him?'

'That's just what we don't know.'

'Why? What's wrong? Is he ill, or something?'

'I don't know, and anyway, it's far worse than that.'

Alban's accusation about gambling returned vividly to her thoughts and the fear that he might have lost money made her grip her brother's arm and ask, in no small degree of alarm,

'Alban, what has happened? Has he? – were you? –'

As if by some telepathy Alban seemed to understand what she was trying to say, and his hasty assurance that that was not it relieved the tension somewhat. But Helen was still afraid.

'Don't keep me in suspense,' she begged. 'If he's done something bad, tell me at once – don't keep me waiting.'

'He hasn't *done* anything exactly –'

'Then what is it?'

Philip
(1945)

Alban
(1945)

'He has disappeared.'

Instantly hordes of ominous possibilities came crowding into Helen's mind.

'Disa – ppeared?' she got out at last.

'Yes. And that's not all. He's been sent down.'

'*What?*'

'It's true, Helen. I had to tell you before you went in so you shouldn't ask awkward questions. You see, only Father and Mother and I know. Penny and Gerald haven't been told. It happened about three weeks ago. Father had a letter from the Principal explaining that he couldn't keep Phil any longer, as he had been getting into debt and not been working properly and lots of other things. He was awfully decent about it. He said he'd told the dons and whatnots there that unfortunately Phil had had to leave them and that he did not wish Father's reputation to be lowered by having it known. He said there were two others besides Phil who had been sent down and that Phil wasn't the worst of the three.'

'I'm sure he wasn't,' put in Helen.

'You always believed in him, didn't you? Well, now you see he's let you down.'

'Oh Alban, don't. It's not fair to hit a man when he's down.'

'I know; but it's a disgrace, Helen, not only to himself, but to us; to Father and Mother particularly. That's why we don't want the youngsters to know. And on top of that, instead of coming home and owning up like a man, he goes off somewhere and nobody has been able to trace him.'

'Did the Principal say that?'

'Yes. He said Phil and these other two were missing the very evening he'd told them they'd been sent down, Nobody knew where they were, nobody had seen them go, and yet although they searched the town and tried every way they could think of to find them they had completely disappeared.'

'Oh Alban, that's *awful*. Where can they be?'

'I've no idea. But I must say, I wasn't surprised it happened.'

They talked a while longer, Helen asking questions and Alban doing his best to answer them. Then they picked up the cases again and walked to the house. Alban rang the bell, and immediately Mrs Wentworth opened the door to let them in.

'Helen, dear,' she said, as she embraced her daughter. 'We are so glad you are back. It has been very lonely.'

Helen returned the embrace willingly, for she felt there was a deeper meaning in her mother's words than there had been on the previous occasion. Mr Wentworth was standing in the hall when she arrived and now advanced to embrace her likewise. Helen's sympathies went out to him at once as she felt his arms tighten around her. She knew what a terrible blow this must be to him, and that it would take him a long time to get over it. Her own griefs were forgotten in this great one which concerned them all, and in that brief moment she felt united with her father more strongly than ever before, although there had always been the closest affection between them.

Chapter XIX

Next day Alban's leave was up and he returned to Dartmouth. On the Monday Helen was to start her work again with the children and right glad was she of something definite to do to take her mind off her troubles.

One afternoon, on her way back from the village school, which she used for some of her lessons, she was overtaken by the Rector, the Reverend Moore. He relieved her of her books and seemed glad of her company to walk home with. He had worked in the Parish of Edmuston for many years and had made himself universally beloved. His gentle manner and kindly expression brought sunshine to every home he entered and he never passed by any member of his congregation without a smile and a few cheering words. Everybody loved him because he loved everybody, and set the example of what a good and noble life should be. He seemed to have an air of peace about him which was shed around him wherever he went.

His wife was another such gentle and serene person, who went about doing good and giving help to all who needed it. Unfortunately, she was not very strong and could not take an active part in many of the various occupations of her life; but she was always in the background, to give a word of advice or to do any little service that might be asked of her, an inspiration to all who came in contact with her.

The Moores had no children. Mrs Moore had had a bad time with the first baby, who had died, and the second, Colin, on whom they had lavished all the love and care which parents can give, had been killed by falling from a horse when he was only nine years old. Nobody had known how great had been their grief over this tragedy, for they had borne it well, upheld by that faith which alone knows that death cannot part those who truly love each other. When the first bitterness was over they devoted themselves to the children of the parish, telling each other that, as they had been denied the blessing of caring for children of their own, they would try all the harder to give what they could to others. Consequently, not only the fathers and mothers loved them, but the children also learned to do so, and proved to be, though they did not know it, an unending source of comfort to them. Helen had known them ever since she could remember, and though this had happened some years before she was born, she had heard all about it from her father and mother, and had always felt sorry for them.

'I have some news for you, Helen,' Mr Moore said as they walked along. 'Sad news – for us at least. We have got to leave you.'

This was sad news indeed.

'Oh, Mr Moore, you haven't, have you?'

'I'm afraid so. My wife isn't well, and must go to a warmer place. Besides, I think I have been here quite long enough. We must give the youngsters a chance, you know.'

'Oh, but Mr Moore, we don't want any "youngsters"! We shall never be able to carry on without you to lead us.'

Mr Moore smiled.

'Oh, you will,' he said, 'but it is not for me really; it is for my wife.'

'I'm sorry. Where will you find to go warmer than this?'

'To begin with we are going to spend the winter in the south of France and shall probably come back in the spring when my wife is strong enough. We have found a little house not far from here, a little nearer the coast, which suits us excellently, so we shall not be very far away.'

'I'm glad to hear that. When are you going?'

'At the end of the month.'

'We shall miss you very much, Mr Moore.'

'Thank you. We have tried to do our best.'

'And are you not rewarded? There are no two people in England more beloved and respected than you and Mrs Moore. There is not one person in the village who doesn't bless you and who will not know what to do without you. Do you not feel that?'

'Perhaps,' he said slowly, then repeated, 'We have done our best.' There was a pause, then he went on, 'But you have not asked who is to be my successor, Helen. You will not entirely lose contact with us, because my nephew, Robert Ward, will be taking over from me in November.'

'Your nephew?'

'Yes. He's a nice boy. He's coming to stay a few nights next week. You must come in to tea one day and meet him.'

'Thank you. I'd like to very much.'

'I will ask my wife what day would be suitable and let you know on Sunday. Will that be all right?'

'Perfectly. Thank you.'

They had reached the Rectory by this time, and having bade Mr Moore adieu, Helen made her way home.

So he was leaving. That did not seem possible after all these years. She wondered what Robert Ward would be like. Of one thing she was certain, that however good he might be, he could never mean as much to the village as Mr Moore had done.

After service on Sunday morning, Mr Moore had told her that his nephew was arriving the next afternoon and asked if Tuesday would suit her. Helen had replied that it would, and accordingly, about four o'clock on Tuesday afternoon she rang the front door bell of the Rectory and was admitted by Mr Moore himself.

'Come in,' he said cordially, 'Come in.'

'Thank you.' Helen obeyed. She had no coat to remove and so Mr Moore led her straight into the small drawing room at the back of the house. He opened the door for her and followed her in. The only occupant of the room was a young man of about twenty-seven or twenty-eight, who was standing by the fireplace with his back to the fire. He looked up with interest as Helen entered, for he had heard a lot about her from his uncle.

'This is my nephew, Reverend Ward,' said Mr Moore. 'Robert, this is Miss Wentworth.'

The Reverend Robert Ward looked at her with a pair of mild, serious blue eyes and held out his hand.

'How do you do?' he said.

'How do you do?' murmured Helen, shaking hands with him. His eyes were *very* mild, she thought, and he looked far too serious for a man of his age.

They sat down. Conversation did not flow freely at first, for he was rather shy. However, Mr Moore helped, and soon they found plenty to talk about.

'I hear you teach the children, Miss Wentworth,' said Reverend Ward after the usual preliminaries had been gone through.

'Well, I don't exactly *teach* them – not like an ordinary school teacher, you know. It's more extras that I go in for, like music and sewing and art.'

'Helen teaches them all the beauties of life,' put in Mr Moore. He was very fond of Helen and admired her for what she tried to do. He had been glad when she had decided, after she left university, to take up work

The Rev. Robert Ward 27 (1945)

amongst the children of the village, because he was interested in them himself. He never lost an opportunity to speak a word in her praise.

'Do you? That is good. I am fond of the arts myself. I think we shall have something in common.'

'Yes,' went on Mr Moore. 'You see that footstool, Robert? That is the handiwork of two of the children. One of the boys made the stool and one of the girls embroidered the top.'

'It's beautiful. How old were they?'

'One was fourteen and the other twelve,' replied Helen.

'Well, I think it's excellent work for children. Have you got anything else?'

'Not here. But aren't you getting up a concert for the end of term, Helen?'

'Yes. We try to do something every Christmas,' she explained. 'This time it will take the form of a variety show. There will be handicrafts displayed in the afternoon and a concert – singing, plays, recitations and various other things – in the evening. You must come.'

'Thanks. I shall be glad to. My only regret is that Uncle Alec won't be there too.'

'No, I know. We shan't be at all the same without him.'

'Excuse me,' said Mr Moore. 'I don't think my wife knows you're here. I'll go and fetch her.'

When he had left the room, the Reverend Ward said,

'Miss Wentworth, you will have to be very patient with me.'

'Why?' asked Helen in surprise.

'Because I shall make hopeless mistakes. It is not easy for anyone to follow in the footsteps of a man who has become so much part of his people's life as my uncle has.'

'No, I can appreciate that.'

'I may be lucky enough to be received favourably because I happen to be his nephew, but I don't know that it won't be a handicap.'

'You mean you think people will be continually comparing you to him?'

'Yes. It will be a very difficult task and I cannot help viewing it with a certain amount of uneasiness.'

'I know it will be difficult,' said Helen, 'but you may not find it as daunting as you think.'

'Indeed I hope not. But think how careful I shall have to be. Everything I do will be criticized and I can hear people saying, 'His uncle *never* would have done a thing like that!' At every turn I shall have to say to myself,

"Now am I carrying on Uncle Alec's tradition?".' He paused, then said, 'I don't know why I'm telling you all this when I've only known you a quarter of an hour.'

'I understand how you feel,' said Helen, and indeed, that was the reason, though she was unconscious of it. She was sympathetic and the sort of person one *could* confide in after only fifteen minutes' acquaintance.

'I don't want you to think I'm complaining,' continued Mr Ward, 'because I'm not. I should be a very ungrateful wretch if I were, when I'm lucky enough to be coming here. I suppose it's a desire for pre-understanding, if you know what I mean, so that I can be sure that at least *one* person in my congregation can appreciate my difficulties.'

'Indeed, I don't think you need worry about people not appreciating them. There are always, of course, some people who don't and who gossip and create rumours, but you may be sure that nobody who knew Mr Moore could fail to recognize the impossibility of being exactly like him.'

'Well, I sincerely hope it will be as you say. I don't know how I shall manage to keep up all his traditions and go on with all his jobs when I haven't a wife like Aunt Frances to help me with them.'

Helen had just time to say, 'Oh, you'll manage somehow,' when Mr Moore returned with his wife and they had to stop.

'I do apologize, Helen, dear,' Mrs Moore said warmly as she shook her guest's hand, 'but I'd no idea you were here, and of course, it never entered my husband's head to come and tell me!'

There was a general laugh, then Mrs Moore rang the bell for tea.

It was getting on for six o'clock when Helen eventually left. There seemed to be so much to talk about once Reverend Ward had got over his shyness, and it was always a delight to her to be with the Moores. One felt better as soon as they came into the same room, and to sit for two hours with them meant the absorption of their ennobling influence, which Helen always said acted like a tonic. She was not aware that one reason why she received so much from them was because she gave so much in return, and was always ready to receive.

She walked home in an uplifted frame of mind, satisfied that although Reverend Ward would not be at all an adequate substitute for their beloved Mr Moore, he was none the less a very nice person, even if he were inclined to be over-serious.

Chapter XX

Next weekend was Penelope's half-term and she came home with an ardent plea to be allowed to do gym and games again.

'My leg's perfectly all right now,' she said to her mother. 'Please, please, *please* ask Doctor Kennedy if I can play games again. I shall be hopelessly out of practice if I don't play soon!'

'But you've only been back at school just over a month,' began Mrs Wentworth. 'I think it's a bit soon yet –'

'Oh Mother, it's not!' cried Penelope desperately. 'I've been running about the school all the term and I fell downstairs about a week ago and it wasn't any the worse. *Please* ask him.'

'Well, we'll see,' said Mrs Wentworth.

On the Sunday afternoon Helen and Penelope went for a long walk over the down with Rex. Although Penelope's accident held for both of them unpleasant memories, they did not say much about it, and Helen had enough consideration for her sister's feelings not to 'rub it in', as the latter would have expressed it. Instead, she told her about Margaret's engagement and asked how she would like to be a bridesmaid.

'A bridesmaid? Ooh, how lovely!' was Penelope's first remark. 'When is it to be? What are we to wear? What's his name? What's he like?'

Helen laughed.

'Do give me time to answer one question at a time!' she exclaimed. 'Now, what was the first? Oh yes. When is it to be? It is to be in the spring. Margaret is designing the dresses herself and is going to send me our sketches as soon as she's done them, so that I can make the dresses.'

'Are you making them? Oh, good. They'll be decent, then.'

'Thank you. The next question, I believe, was "What is his name?" Geoffrey Lyndon. You met him at the concert last month.'

'Geoffrey? Is she marrying him? Oh, good.'

'Why "good"?'

'I *liked* him. I should think he'd be just the right person for Margaret to marry.'

'Yes,' replied Helen.

'Margaret's awfully nice, isn't she?' said Penelope after a pause.

'Yes,' replied Helen, 'awfully.'

'I've never been a bridesmaid before,' mused Penelope. 'What is one supposed to do? I suppose you just walk up the aisle carrying the bride's train and then just stand and wait while they are being married.'

'Yes,' said Helen, with an amused smile, 'I suppose that's about all.'

'Doesn't the bridegroom have to kiss you, or something? I know he did when two of the girls from school were bridesmaids, because they told us all about it afterwards. Do you think Geoffrey will kiss us?'

'I've no idea,' responded Helen. 'He may do.'

'I hope he isn't bristly, then,' said Penelope.

'Penny!'

'Well, I hate being scratched. I always used to hate it when Uncle Raymond said goodnight to me, because he was always so prickly. It was all right in the morning when he'd shaved, but by bedtime it had had time to grow.'

'Well, I don't think you'll find Geoffrey as bristly as that,' laughed Helen, 'because they will be married long before bedtime, and anyway, I expect he will have shaved only just beforehand.'

'That's good.'

There was a pause for a minute or two while each was deep in her own thoughts. Penelope was the first to break it.

'Margaret's very beautiful, isn't she?'

'Yes,' replied Helen, 'she is the most beautiful woman I have ever seen.'

'Mm.' Penelope returned to her thoughts.

'I say,' she went on after a while, 'would you call Geoffrey good-looking?'

'If you mean handsome, no,' said Helen, 'but he has a good, pleasant face, and he has a refined air about him which many merely *handsome* men have not. He looks, and is, a gentleman, in fact.'

'Good enough for Margaret?'

'Oh yes.'

'He *must* be decent, then.'

'He is. With them it's not a case of one being good enough for the other; they are so much one that the marriage ceremony seems unnecessary; it is only an external rite to make the connection lawful.'

They had come to the very top of the down by this time and sat down to admire the view on a smooth boulder jutting out from the turf.

Penelope was unusually thoughtful that afternoon and Helen could not help remarking on the fact.

'I was just thinking,' said Penelope, 'how funny it is that you don't stay friends for ever – funny peculiar, I mean, not funny ha-ha.'

'Who?'

'Anybody. You sort of grow up different, somehow.'

'Yes, that's natural. Have you anyone in mind?

'Yes, I was thinking of Valerie. Two years ago she was my best friend, but now she's quite different.'

'She's a good bit older than you, isn't she?'

'Yes, three years, but that never used to make any difference.'

'No, because when you were small, your ideas ran roughly along the same lines; but as children grow up, they naturally develop along different lines and it very rarely happens that the friends you have when you are small remain your friends when you grow up.'

'No, I suppose not; but I wish it didn't happen.'

'But you wouldn't want to keep up with Valerie if she has nothing in common with you now, would you?'

'No, but the thing is, I can't believe yet that she hasn't. Oh me! Thank heavens she's not the only friend I've got. How's Charlie?' she added, abruptly changing the subject.

'Fine, as far as I know. He's terribly busy, studying till I don't know what time at night, but having a good time, from what I can gather.'

'Why did he have to go right away up there?'

'Heaven only knows! I should have thought Scotland was the last place to send people for courses in the winter.'

'Yes, so should I. I suppose they think it's a nice hardy place, with no opportunities for slacking.'

'But good heavens! They must have *some* time off! You can't expect people to work well if they're never allowed any free time.'

'I wish you'd tell that to our English Mistress. She thinks we never have to do anything else but English, it seems to me. Honestly, the amount of prep we get from her is about as much as we get from all the other staff put together.'

'Is that Miss Ross?'

'Yes.'

'I remember her. Yes, she had a reputation for piling on the homework. I know we always used to think her awfully weak when we were juniors, because she could never keep us in order. It wasn't until we got to the sixth form that we really appreciated her. She's a wonderful teacher, Penny, and I admired her intensely. I still do.'

'Oh, I'm not saying I don't like her – I do; but that doesn't alter the fact that she expects us to do a dickens of a lot of work. I say, *do* you think I shall be able to do gym and games again soon?' she demanded, changing the subject again.

'I've no idea. If you plead your case strongly enough, Doctor Kennedy might let you.'

'Oh, I *do* hope he does! It's awful seeing them all go trooping out to the games field in the afternoon and me having to stuff indoors doing mouldy prep!'

'Oh, well, tell Doctor Kennedy you're all right, and I daresay he'll let you.'

'I don't expect he will. He'll tell me not to do acrobatics on it and say I'll break the other one, or something equally daft.'

'You wouldn't think it daft if you did break it again, would you?'

'No, but I shan't. It *must* be healed by now.'

'Well, suppose we get back to tea,' suggested Helen, looking at her watch, 'or Gerry will have eaten all the crumpets.'

'Crumpets! Yippee! Come on then.' Penelope jumped up and whistled for Rex, who had gone rat-hunting. Helen rose in a more dignified manner, and they set off down the hill towards home and crumpets.

On the way through the village they met Reverend Ward, who was 'down for the weekend' as he explained when he had shaken hands with Helen and been introduced to Penelope.

'Are you preaching tomorrow, then?' asked Helen.

'Yes. My uncle is very busy, so I said I would take the service for him. It's a good way of getting to know your congregation.'

'Yes. Well, we mustn't stop, and I'm sure you have plenty to do.'

'Yes. Goodbye, Miss Wentworth. Goodbye, Penelope. I shall see you tomorrow morning.'

'Yes. Goodbye, Mr Ward,' said Helen.

'Goodbye,' echoed Penelope. 'So he's to be the new Rector,' she added, when they were out of hearing distance. 'He seems a bit placid, doesn't he?'

'Very. Indeed, he's about the mildest person I've met, I think; but he may give very good sermons. People are not always what you think, you know.'

'No. Well, we shall have to see what he's like tomorrow. Now for England, home and crumpets!'

Chapter XXI

The weekend passed all too quickly and Penelope had to return. She had tried her hardest to persuade Doctor Kennedy to let her go back to a normal life, but he was adamant and refused, telling her that next term was plenty soon enough. The poor child was much upset on hearing the verdict and shed bitter tears after the doctor had gone.

Gerald, in the meantime, was becoming very excited about going to his new school, and worried his mother almost out of her wits telling her all the things he wanted to take when she was packing his cases for him. He felt so pleased with himself in his uniform – everything brand new – that it was difficult for the rest of the family to keep from laughing. Helen sewed the name-tapes on all his clothes, marked his shoes and sewed initials in the corners of his handkerchiefs.

Normally, the children travelled alone to and from school, but this time Mr Wentworth accompanied them on the train to see that Gerald was safely delivered to his new guardians and make sure that everything was all right. His school was the brother of the one to which Penelope went in Ilton, and the colleges were two of the best and most famous in the country. Ilton College for Girls had started life as a monastery, and so had a small church, and a graveyard full of interesting tombstones surrounded by cloisters, besides the original buildings, which had been enlarged and added to until now it catered for nearly four hundred girls. Modern equipment had been installed and the school owned its own private swimming bath and theatre. The grounds covered about a hundred acres, through which flowed a tributary of the Ile. There was also a lake where boating was the joy of all water-loving youngsters, in summer especially. A wood at one end of the grounds, commonly known as 'The Jungle', boasted many different species of wild flower and oh! never-ending source of delight – wild strawberries. The gardens were extensive and beautifully kept, all on slopes and different levels. Each girl was responsible for her own particular bit, and took a pride in keeping it neat and full of bloom. Wide lawns stretched away on all sides and on summer evenings the sound of tennis in progress could be heard from the courts. There were twenty of these, ten hard and ten grass, excluding two private ones for the staff. There were also pitches and courts for rounders, cricket, hockey, lacrosse, netball, squash and fives.

The five houses – Normandy, Tudor, Stuart, Hanover and Windsor, each presided over by a Housemistress and House Captain – stood behind the school, each with its lawn, garden and big shady trees, under whose protecting foliage the girls liked to do their homework in summer.

On the other side of the road stood Ilton College for Boys, a pupil of which Gerald was about to become. Its origin was similar to that of its sister school and the two together represented the very rare occurrence of two monasteries in such close proximity to one another. The two were closely connected and the boys and girls saw a good deal of each other. The respective Heads were both married, and in consequence seemed to have a much deeper understanding of their charges, and both had the children's interests very much at heart. Providing they adhered to certain necessary rules and regulations, they were allowed more freedom than children in most schools. The Heads believed in making the school houses as much like home as possible, and nearly all the children, the older ones particularly, appreciated it and were grateful. As many activities as possible were run in a co-operative manner, for the Heads believed that by encouraging right relations between the boys and girls, allowing the children to see their brothers and sisters often, they would minimize the amount of stupidity and 'flirtation' which was rampant in towns where the school rules were much more confining. Consequently, parties of friends were permitted to go off for picnics, cycle rides or expeditions to the theatre in Ilton – the colleges were about a mile from the centre of the town – providing there was with them a responsible boy or girl old enough to take full charge.

Mr Wentworth delivered his two children to their respective schools, assuring himself that Gerald was in good hands; and having spent the night in a hotel in Ilton, returned home. Helen met him at Mereford Station with the car, and was very anxious to hear how her brother responded to his first 'big' school. Gerald seemed remarkably shy, Mr Wentworth said, considering he had had four years at a prep school and before that in a kindergarten in Mereford.

'I expect he will settle down eventually,' he went on. 'The first few weeks are the most trying, particularly as he has had the disadvantage of not having started with the rest at the beginning of term. We may see big changes when he comes home at Christmas – boys are ruthless beings, you know. I have suffered some uncomfortable hours at their expense myself.'

'He'll catch up on the academic side,' said Helen. 'It's the games and sports he'll come down on – and Ilton has always been proud of its athletics. By the way, did you ask about his going on with his music lessons?'

'Yes, they have several excellent teachers, and he has done very well so far, so he shouldn't find that difficult to pick up.'

'Good.'

'It's a pity we didn't have one of you learn the violin, you know, Helen. I wish we had made Penelope go on with it, but she wouldn't practise and obviously wasn't musical. You could have had a great deal of fun together now you all play reasonably well.'

'Penny would never do well in the musical world, I'm afraid. She isn't cut out for it. She can sing nicely, but that's about all.' She laughed. 'She wants to bring honour to the family on the games field, and I don't doubt she will be the school Games Captain at some not very far distant date. She is very good already, judging by the reports she has and all the matches she plays in.'

'Yes, she certainly is our champion. Well, here we are. Thank you for meeting me, my dear. I wasn't looking forward to that bus ride.'

Helen smiled.

'That's all right,' she said. 'I thought you'd probably prefer the car.'

Tea was served round the lounge fire, and Gerald's news had to be gone over again in every detail to satisfy his mother, who could not help worrying over his luggage – whether he had 'got everything'.

'You and Helen made enough lists and did enough sewing to stock him up for ten years,' said Mr Wentworth with a laugh, 'and anyway, he'll write if he wants anything.'

There was a pause while they all sat thinking.

'Well,' said Helen at length, 'this is the first time we have been back to normal since you went away in August.'

'Yes, it's nice to be quiet once more,' replied her mother. 'When do you start work again?'

'Tomorrow, I think. There's no point in hanging fire. It will seem quite strange to be back there. Still, there is a lot to be done getting ready for the concert at the end of term, so I shan't be idle.'

'By the way, my dear, I forgot to tell you,' said Mr Wentworth. 'While you were away we had several officials down from the Ministry of Education.'

'Oh?'

'They made all sorts of enquiries and suggestions and I shouldn't be surprised to find there will be big changes soon. They were talking about a new Education Bill which is soon to be brought before the House, and from what they said, it seems to be going to make great improvements.'

Helen was immediately interested. She had very pronounced feelings on the subject, particularly for children like those in her own village, who had no opportunities to develop what talents lay dormant within them.

'What did they say?' she asked eagerly.

'They were talking about all children having the chance of the same good education, including, as far as possible, secondary education. More teachers were to be trained –'

'I hope they'll get the teachers,' put in Helen.

'Yes. In such schools as yours, where up till now, no "extras" have been taught except when somebody has the energy to do them, as you have, my dear, they mean to introduce art, music, cookery, laundry, carpentry, etc., as part of the daily curriculum.'

'Good. That *is* a good idea. I always wished somebody would think of that.'

'Yes, but Helen, think of all the staff they are going to need; and then they are proposing to build a great many new schools, all of which need to be equipped and staffed, and as they want to make all education free, where is the money coming from?'

'What, free even in the public schools like Ilton?'

'That I'm not sure about. The fees I pay to keep Penny and now Gerry are ridiculously low already, in spite of all the extensive uniform they both need. I don't think they were considering public schools. Their main concern seemed to be that of improving the elementary schools and leaving for the present the schools which had already proved their worth.'

'I see. Well, I *am* glad something is being done at last. These schools do need improving, heaven knows. I mean, one teacher to forty or fifty children is quite ridiculous – there can be no individual help at all, and it's only with individual help that you can make any real progress. You can never find out a particular child's particular difficulties unless you have time to get to know him – shall I say personally?'

'Exactly. The larger the class the more difficult it is to manage and teach it, especially with rough village lads like ours. Individually, they are very pleasant and helpful, but together – well, you know better than I do how trying they can be.'

'Trying! That's putting it mildly!' exclaimed Helen. She well remembered several exhausting tussles she had had with the village boys when they had been in a 'plaguing' mood. 'I wonder what they *will* do,' she went on after a pause. 'I must say, I hope the House will have the sense to see the good in the proposals, and not try to be destructive.'

'Surely they wouldn't,' said Mr Wentworth, while his wife, who had remained silent up till now, asked,

'What do you mean?'

'Well, you know there are some people who will never let you have more than they have without creating no end of a fuss. They say, "Why should So-and-So have that when we haven't?" and so do their best to take whatever it is from him instead of saying, "So-and-So has got that; there is no reason, therefore, why we should not have it *as well*". Now what I mean in the case of education is this: I heard a fellow lecture once – I don't know who he was or what political party he belonged to but all he wanted was to take away all individual lessons in schools, such as music and elocution and so on, because certain schools could not have them, and it wasn't fair that some children should have the opportunity of learning and others not. I got up afterwards and asked him if there were any reason why the "certain schools" should not have these extras included in their timetables. I can't remember what he said, but I know it wasn't very convincing.'

'Yes. It seems quite wrong to want to tear down instead of building up,' agreed Helen. 'Surely the right way to progress is to recognize a good thing when you see it and try to copy it.'

'You would have thought so, certainly,' put in Mrs Wentworth.

'Did the Ministry of Education representatives think it would pass the House?' asked Helen.

'They seemed very sanguine about it,' replied her father. 'Both of them were full of it. I wished you had been there to hear them. I think you would have been interested.'

'Indeed I should. Oh, I do hope it gets through! I must follow it up in the newspaper. There's sure to be an account of these enquiries. I shall be able to start work in a very happy frame of mind now.'

Mr Wentworth smiled.

'Good. Well, hurry up and drink your tea. It will get cold.'

Chapter XXII

Helen started her work next morning, as she had predicted, in a happy state of mind. She was devoted to her tasks, and if they were sometimes taxing, they were also extremely interesting. Children are surprising creatures and the most unlikely often produce the most amazing results. Helen believed that every child was capable of doing something well, and did her best to find out what it was. Some, she knew, had proved themselves to be particularly good at their ordinary lessons, and when this was the case, she took care that they should have every opportunity to read suitable books on the subject they were most interested in. Some were good artists; these she encouraged by taking them out sketching or arranging trips to exhibitions in Mereford at her own expense. For the musical ones she arranged lessons with private teachers at very reduced fees, took them to concerts, organized trios and quartettes and had a very flourishing choir. Those keen on cooking and needlework were encouraged to do what they could at home, and make things for the exhibitions and sales of work which were held every term. The carpenters made things for their homes. The gardeners not only kept their own home gardens neat and trim and colourful, but were also given jobs to do in the Wentworths' garden and those of other people living in the district. It was Helen who worked to procure an extra piece of land for the school so that the children could learn how to cultivate flowers and grow vegetables. There was not one who had not some task he was good at. It took longer to find out what it was with some of the children than with others, but Helen never felt satisfied until she had discovered what the dullest one could do. Above all, she pursued her task with such a charming manner, never angry and always quick to understand, that there was not a single child among the hundred odd attending the school who did not love her and work hard to procure her praise.

Consequently, she was welcomed in a very gratifying fashion when she appeared in the classroom doorway next morning, after an absence of three months. One of the children had seen her coming and hastened to spread the good news amongst his class-mates and organize a rapid 'plan of procedure'.

As Helen entered the room the children all rose simultaneously from their seats, to which they had all rushed when they heard she was coming. They knew she liked them to be there and, young as they were, realized that they could hardly give her a better welcome than by being all she liked them to be. Then, at a signal from the self-appointed leader, who audibly counted 'one, two, three' under his breath, they all called out cheerfully, 'Good morning, Miss Wentworth' and remained standing there in silence, grinning from ear to ear while she walked to the desk, returned their greeting and settled herself.

It was satisfying, when they had all begun their various tasks to be asked by first one and then another, 'Please Miss Wentworth, 'ave you 'ad a good 'oliday?' or 'Did you 'ave a nice time, Miss Wentworth?' Helen insisted on their calling her 'Miss Wentworth' and not just 'Miss', which she loathed, and usually they remembered. One or two forgot under the strain and she had not the heart to correct them, especially when one of the shyest of her youngsters, who adored her from afar in secret, plucked up enough courage to say, with a blush, 'We're glad you're back, Miss', thinking that by hiding behind the impersonal 'We', Helen would not discover her passion.

In spite of her apparent happiness, Helen never ceased to worry about Philip. Mr Wentworth had done all he could to find him, but there was still no trace of him. Nobody answering to the description was discovered, and they were forced to believe that he must have left the country; none of them would admit the worst fear they all felt, that it might mean he was drowned or buried. It was a very worrying time for them all. To Mr Wentworth it was a deep disgrace; indeed, it was so deep that he hardly spoke a word about it. He was far more upset over the actual event than he was about Philip's present whereabouts, though he was naturally anxious about that as well. Mrs Wentworth scarcely let a day go by without some reference to the subject, but though she worried herself almost ill at times, it was always what might happen to him that concerned her and not what he might be doing. Alban made one or two sarcastic remarks in his letters, whose truth Helen could hardly doubt, much as she would have wished to. It was not difficult for Alban to express his feelings in the most vivid terms and he made full use of his ability. Helen often wondered what could be his source of information, and when she finally asked him, it came out that one of his friends at Dartmouth had a cousin at Cambridge who told him all the news (and scandal) and he had passed it on to Alban.

It was not easy for Helen, with all this at the back of her mind, to carry on with her work as though nothing had happened. It was lucky that she had plenty to do which prevented her from brooding over it. Then, quite suddenly, something happened which made them all forget their own cares in the face of a far greater one.

Mrs Moore, who at the best of times, was never very strong, was knocked down in the High Street by a passing motorist and fatally injured. Mr Moore was away in London at a conference and had to be wired immediately. Even so, it was next day before he was able to return home. Doctor Kennedy came at once, and owing to the lack of a trained nurse, ordered one of the many anxious villagers who hovered near the Rectory door, to go and fetch Helen, whom he knew he could trust. She hurried to the house and did all she could before the ambulance arrived to take Mrs Moore to the hospital in Mereford. She was so badly hurt that Doctor Kennedy could hold out no hope for her; he could only pray, as he said to Helen, that the end would not be too painful.

Mrs Moore made a valiant struggle, but her body was so frail that the little effort she was able to make did not avail her very much. For a week her life hung in the balance, then, after one final struggle, she died.

Mr Moore's feelings were too deep for tears. Helen watched his calm face as he came out of the ward and marvelled that he could bear such a terrible blow with such steadfast courage. She longed to comfort him, and he, feeling her unspoken sympathy, put his arm round her and they walked out together. The first thing he said was, 'She has seen Colin.'

When they arrived back at the Rectory gate, Helen made to go, thinking he might prefer to be alone; but he held her back, saying,

'No, Helen, don't go. I need you.'

There was such a pathetic look in those kind eyes that she found it impossible to keep down her feelings any longer. Her eyes filled and her lips quivered. Mr Moore put his arm round her once more, and said quietly,

'Don't cry, Helen. She is happy now.'

'Oh, Mr Moore, you are so brave!' she cried between her sobs. 'I don't know how you can take it all so calmly!'

'I have known grief, Helen,' came the reply. 'I have known death. In my life I have had to make many sacrifices. When I was young I used to cry out against them, wondering why God, in all His infinite mercy and loving kindness, could permit them; but as I grew older, I came to realize that it was *not* God's will that such things should come to pass; that He, a loving, merciful Father, did *not* ordain that any particular person should be killed or hurt by any particular accident; but there are laws in nature, Helen, and if a man breaks one of them, wittingly or no, he must not expect God to lift up His finger and suspend those laws so that he shall not have to suffer the consequences. This I believe, as firmly as I believe in the Almighty, and this it is that helps me to bear the greatest sacrifice of all.'

'I believe that, too,' said Helen, 'but I have not the courage to bear things without tears as you have. I try to live up to my beliefs, but it is so difficult not to give way to your feelings when it is someone you love very much who is taken from you.'

'Yes,' he replied simply. 'It is – very difficult.'

Mrs Moore's funeral took place four days after she died, and was conducted by a friend who had known them both for many years. The little church was packed, for there was not one of the villagers who had not loved Mrs Moore. The service was simple and straightforward, for Mr Moore would not have anything but sincerity in the ceremony. Most of the women shed tears and there was a hardly-stifled sob on more than one occasion; one or two of the men had to blow their noses hard, or wipe a sleeve hurriedly over their eyes to clear their vision. Helen, with a great effort, managed to control her feelings, but she found it impossible to sing the hymns Mr Moore had chosen. She glanced at him while the first – 'He who would valiant be' – was being sung. His nephew was standing beside him, and though they both started singing together, it was not long before Robert Ward had to shake his head, and swallowing hard, bow it over his hymn book. Mr Moore continued to sing, his head held high and his eyes shining. He seemed to be sustained by some unseen Power, and Helen found herself wondering even more at the calm, steadfast courage of the man. She was not surprised when, instead of the lugubrious *Funeral March*, it was Purcell's *Trumpet Voluntary* that rang out from the organ. She guessed why he had chosen it and thought how well it fitted in with his whole attitude to his loss.

The death of his wife caused all Mr Moore's arrangements to be altered. Instead of going to the new situation at the end of the month, he decided to stay until Christmas had passed, and let his nephew take over in the New Year. There was a great deal to be seen to and he was glad of the extra time in which to do it. Robert Ward helped him considerably with his church duties, and several times, when the poor man was too busy to prepare a sermon, took the service in his place. Helen had offered her help that very first day, and was only too willing to do whatever he asked her. His unswerving faith in the goodness of the Almighty, his great courage and, indeed, his very presence, helped and inspired her, and she had several long talks with him on the subject of religion and life – for with him they were inseparably connected – from which she reaped much benefit. They helped her to see her own troubles in their right proportion and gave her greater confidence in her methods of dealing with them. At first, she had been very wary of talking about such things, fearing it might give him pain; but finding it did not apparently hurt him to mention his past griefs, she gradually overcame her shyness and conversed freely with him, little dreaming that it helped him, as well as herself, to have someone sympathetic and interested to talk to, someone whose presence cheered his lonely moods – for he was very lonely at times, and longed for something on which to pour out his love. He was very fond of Helen, and was always glad when she came. This she was quick to realize, and her heart went out to him. Consequently, she paid him visits as often as she could, and he always seemed to be cheered by them.

When the Reverend Ward was not busy with his work, he made a third in their party and joined in with their discussions, and as the days passed, Mr Moore noticed that the amount of work he seemed to find it necessary to do became less and less, until one day he himself opened the door to their guest, conducted her to the drawing room, and did not leave it at all the whole afternoon except once to answer the telephone.

Helen herself was quite unaware of this, and treated him with the same respectful ease that she did Mr Moore. She had no disturbing thoughts about him, for all her dreams were connected with Charles, and she had far too many things to think about to have time for the Reverend Ward, or the contemplation of possible attentions from that quarter. She looked upon him as a very mild young man, but with a strength of character behind his mildness; he spoke little, not because he was shy, but because he thought a great deal. When he did speak, his words were well-considered and forceful. He was the type who say little and do much, and only his uncle knew to any extent how far this was true.

Chapter XXIII

One afternoon, shortly after Helen returned from a visit to the Rectory, the front door bell rang and when she went to see who it was, she was handed a telegram. It was addressed to her and she opened it with a beating heart. She always hated receiving a telegram, for she felt it must bring bad news. The telegraph boy stood with a bored expression on his face, only waiting for her to say 'No answer' to dash away to his bike and go whistling down the High Street with his hands in his pockets and his hat on the back of his head.

Meet me tonight church porch 9.30 Phil, read the telegram. Helen suddenly felt sick with relief. 'No answer,' she said hurriedly, 'thank you.'

The boy disappeared and she closed the door. Her heart was beating so wildly that the telegram trembled in her hand. She sat down on one of the hall chairs to recover her strength. It was such a relief to know that he was at last safe and tangible, and would tell her himself where he had been and what he had been doing. She decided to calm down a little before telling her mother and father, so went upstairs to her study; she locked the telegram away in her desk and sat down to think it over. The terrible waiting for news had been so wearisome; day after day dragging on and still no word had come to them. Was he at last going to come home, or would it be some other man she would see tonight, come to tell her what Phil could not do himself – that he was very ill, had had an accident, or worse still, that he was dead? It was so like a dream that she had to go to her desk and unlock it again to find the telegram, in order to assure herself that she had not imagined it all.

Pulling herself together, she ceased worrying about the past, and began to wonder about the future. What would he do when he did return? He could not go back to Cambridge, and he was not qualified for any kind of job. With his unruly temperament he might get himself into serious trouble – for all she knew he might already have done so –without something to keep his mind and hands occupied. It was not a pleasing prospect, but one which they would all have to face.

Philip (1945)

She rose, and trying to assume a composure which she did not feel, went back to the lounge. Her expression gave her away, however, and Mr Wentworth, looking up as she entered the room, saw it.

'Helen, my dear, is anything wrong?' he asked, laying down his book.

Helen seated herself on the buffet in front of the fireplace.

'No,' she replied, 'don't be alarmed. It was only a telegram.'

'Only a telegram?' exclaimed Mrs Wentworth.

'What was it, Helen?' asked Mr Wentworth. There was an anxious note in his voice, as if he half feared another blow, and Helen paused before she answered, simply,

'It was from Phil.'

'Philip!' they both cried together.

'Thank God he is safe!' cried Mrs Wentworth.

'Where is he – is he all right?' demanded her husband. 'What did he say?'

'As far as I can tell he's all right – he didn't say. He wants me to meet him tonight. I will bring him home.'

Mrs Wentworth suddenly surprised them by bursting into tears. Helen jumped up and perching herself beside her on the arm of the chair, put her arms round her and whispered,

'It's all right, Mother. He's safe now.'

Mrs Wentworth laid her head on her daughter's breast, and in her fit of selfish grief, cried out,

'Oh, Philip, Philip! What have I done that you should treat me like this?'

Helen sighed inwardly. Her mother did not seem to care what had happened to Philip during the past six or seven weeks; only how his behaviour affected herself. She made no outward sign, and merely gave her mother a comforting hug and said,

'You haven't done anything, Mother dear – it's just that Phil is different from the rest of us; but he's in England and you will see him tonight. He will come home and ask you to forgive him if he has done anything which needs your forgiveness. It's only one more case among many thousands of the story of the Prodigal Son. Don't let him hear you say that.'

While her mother was being soothed. Helen glanced several times at her father. He had said nothing during this scene; she saw then, what she already felt, how far deeper was his sorrow than that of his wife. It made her want to cry – a thing which she hardly ever did. She took advantage of her mother's going out of the room to go across to him and kneel down at his feet. She took the hand that lay motionless in his lap in both her own, whereupon Mr Wentworth laid his other hand on top of hers, and lifted his eyes. He looked sadly old just then. They said nothing, for neither could think of what to say, but each felt the other understood. Finally Mr Wentworth said,

'I don't know what to expect tonight. He is bound to be different.'

'Yes, he will be different. I am sure he will have learnt a lot from this.'

About a quarter past nine Helen put on her coat and scarf and, taking a pair of thick gloves, for it was a very cold night, set out for the church. It was black out of doors; no moon and not a single star helped to lessen the darkness. Luckily, she knew the way perfectly and did not stumble over any unexpected stones. As she approached the churchyard, the qualms which kept repeating themselves in the pit of her stomach increased in rapidity until she felt almost sick. There was no sound to be heard and the click of the church gate sounded alarmingly loud. She walked up the path to the porch, inside which a dim light was burning. If she had not been too busy thinking about Philip, she would have been a little frightened to be alone amongst the gravestones; there were so many stories circulating in the village, that even the most insensitive could not go there after dark without some feelings of apprehension.

She entered the porch, which was always kept open, so that travellers could pause there for a rest and shelter if necessary, and sat down.

Everything was still. Not even an owl hooted.

Suddenly the half-hour chimed out, sounding so near that it made her jump. As the last bell was rung, a dark figure appeared as from nowhere and stood in the middle of the archway. Helen rose to her feet with a little cry that was the sharp intake of breath,

'Phil!' she cried.

The figure said nothing but took two steps forward. In the dim light it was difficult to recognize it. Helen, gaining courage because those two steps were made in a familiar manner, approached and, taking hold of his arms, drew him under the lamp to examine him more closely and find out if it really were he.

When the light, such as it was, fell on to his face, she started back a step, unable to believe that this was her brother. His hair, which had never been very short, was long now from neglect and his unshaven chin and upper lip made him look at least ten years older. The black brows were knitted into an even deeper frown, and the eyes, when at last they dared to look at her, were ashamed yet rebellious and full of fear. His hands were thrust far down into his pockets, and his clothes looked as though they had not been cleaned or mended for months.

'Phil!' she cried again. 'Oh, Phil!'

Still he said nothing. He could not think of anything to say, for amongst other feelings he knew he had let her down, and was ashamed of it. He wanted to say so, but it was not in his nature to do so. Instead, he blurted out at last,

'Well, I've come home. What are you going to do with me?'

'Oh, Phil!' she cried yet again, 'are you quite safe and well? Where have you been? We've been so worried!'

'I'm OK. I've been to France.'

'France?'

'Yes.'

'What have you been doing? Oh, I'm so glad to see you, I could weep!'

'Are you really?' he demanded. 'How can you be? I've been so rotten.'

'Oh yes! You don't know how anxious we've been these last few weeks.'

'Couldn't show my face after that,' mumbled Philip. 'The pater would never have forgiven me.'

'Oh Phil!' Helen was gently reproachful.

Philip had dreaded this meeting even more than Helen realized. He still had enough good feelings to be heartily ashamed of the way he had treated his sister, and knew so little of character that he had expected her to be furiously angry. It had taken days of struggle to pluck up enough courage to come to this meeting and he very nearly did not turn up even at the last minute. The only thing which had made him come at all was that it was dark and nobody but Helen would see him.

Now the first few words had passed and she was not angry – indeed, she had almost hugged him and had said that she was so glad to see him she could weep. Suddenly he saw his mistake and felt even more unworthy of his welcome. Had she scolded him, or been coldly distant, he would have recoiled within himself and never told her anything; but she was just the same, and he felt an immediate desire to pour out his troubles in her ear. He only waited for her to ask again, because, much as he wished to, he could not begin of his own accord.

'What have you been doing?' she asked, drawing him to the seat and pushing him into it.

Philip paused before he answered, then he plunged into his narrative, slowly at first, and with many gaps, but gradually gaining confidence with his sister's friendly encouragement.

'I suppose you heard all about my being sent down?' he said.

'Yes, I was told that.'

'Well, Moresby and Dilke were sent down too. We all said we couldn't go home – decided it was best to quit the country. We managed to get to France in a fishing vessel – we'd enough cash between us to bribe the old chap to keep his mouth shut if there was a stink.'

'In a fishing vessel! How uncomfortable!'

'Only safe method.'

'When was this?'

'Same night as we got kicked out.'

There was a pause.

'What happened in France?'

'We started off gaily enough, going immediately to Paris, of course. We went out to get some supper, and Moresby won some cash playing cards afterwards, and that kept us going for a bit. It didn't last long, though, and so we all three played. At first our luck held and we made quite a bit, but Moresby and Dilke spent most of theirs on getting tight, and didn't like it when I wouldn't do the same thing every night. I was bad enough but I wasn't as bad as they were.'

'I'm glad you wouldn't give in.'

'I didn't consciously.' Philip did not tell of several occasions when he had been held on the floor and robbed because he refused to let his companions take what he had won.

There was another pause, then, coming to the interesting part of his tale, he got it all out without another break.

'This went on for some time, but then our luck turned and we lost all we had and got into debt. Something had to be done in order to live, and without telling me, I found one day they had come to some sort of agreement with a horrible crowd of swine, and thus got enough cash to buy themselves more drink. I know I'm a bad lot, but even *I* didn't like that, and told them so. There was an awful row and it ended in my being knocked on the head and what few francs I had taken. I refused to go with them on their nightly prowls, then one night they doped me and took me along. I was quite conscious enough to be aware of what was going on and I shall never forget those beastly women.' Helen's arm tightened round his own. 'I stood it as long as I could, but I soon began to wish I'd never gone on the damn chase. So one day, I set off north, and by means of lifts in carts and wagons, made my way to the coast. I got back three days ago.'

'How did you get back?'

'Never mind how. I just did.' He did not like to admit that he had taken the first motor boat he could lay his hands on with sufficient petrol on board to get him across the Channel. Nor did he admit that the same motor boat was at that moment sitting under a rock at Cuckmere Haven.

Helen said nothing, and Philip, not understanding her silence, said,

'Well, now you know. What are you going to say to me?'

'Oh Phil!' she cried. 'Thank God it was nothing worse!'

'Oh, I'm not pretending I wasn't just as bad as the rest of them. I won more cash and I didn't care how I got it. Tell me I'm a swine; I know.'

The bitter shame and the old rebelliousness were returning, and hoping to avert them, Helen asked almost tearfully,

'But you're not! Oh, why didn't you come home?'

'How could I? I would never dare.'

'Oh yes! How much misery you would have saved yourself! But don't let's think about that. You're home now and Father and Mother are waiting for you.' She got up. 'Come.'

The fear which he showed at first and which had disappeared as he told his story, came back in a rush and he clung to the seat as if paralysed.

'Come home!' he cried. 'I could *never* come home!'

Helen looked at his cowering figure. He was trembling all over.

'But of course. Why ever shouldn't you?'

'I could never come home,' repeated Philip. 'Not after all this.'

'Oh, rubbish, what are you thinking of?'

'No, Helen! How could I ever face Father? No! Let me go!' – for she had taken hold of his arm, and tried to make him get up. 'I'll go anywhere, but I won't go home.'

She gazed at him in amazement. She understood that he was ashamed of himself, that it had been difficult to tell even herself what had happened to him, but she had never for one moment had a single doubt that he would come home with her. She found that he had not changed, and that his mood was just as he used to be when he was small, and having done something wrong was afraid of the consequences; only in this case the fear was magnified a hundredfold. She sat down beside him, and putting an arm through his, said gently,

'Listen, Phil. When I came back from my holiday, Alban met me at the bus stop and told me what had happened, so that I should not ask any awkward questions when I got home. You see, he knew that Father and Mother were terribly upset at your disappearance, and as soon as I got back I saw it too. Mother has been so worried and anxious and Father has looked so old and lonely. When your telegram came, I took it in, and read it over several times before telling them. If only you could have been there, you would not doubt that they have missed you terribly. Before I left tonight, Father said to me, "Tell him to come home, Helen; that he does not need to have any fears of his reception. We were never angry with him; only anxious and lonely." Can you now refuse to come back with me?'

Philip still hung back, unconvinced.

'Will he really forgive me?'

'He forgave you as soon as it happened. You *must* come.'

'I wish I could – but I can't.'

'But *why*? Oh, Phil, surely you don't *still* doubt me? You *must* come. They're waiting.'

'Are you *sure* they won't be angry?'

'Of course not. Do come.'

'Well, if you're certain…' he began. Then he stopped. 'My hair – my face – oh, I can't come like this!' He was going to back away but Helen caught him.

'Nobody minds what state you're in!' she cried, desperately now. She was beginning to be afraid herself, now, that he would slip from her grasp even yet. 'Who cares about your hair or your face? It's *you* they want – you, yourself!'

Philip looked at her. She was almost in tears with desperation and her sincerity was such that he was at last convinced that she must be right. He gave in.

'All right,' he said, 'I'll come.'

When they reached the house, Helen preceded him into the lounge and bidding him wait for a few minutes, went in to tell her parents he had arrived and give them a hasty warning.

'You will have a shock,' she said, 'but don't let him see it; and be kind to him. I've had an awful struggle to make him come at all. He is in a really fear-ful state.'

Then she came out again, and holding the door open for him, waited till he had gone through it, then closed it behind him and hurried to her room. She never knew what passed between them in the lounge, and they stayed there so long that she went to bed. Before climbing into it, she dropped on to her knees by its side and cried in her heart,

'Oh God, help him to keep straight! Help him, help him!'

Chapter XXIV

Philip did not come down to breakfast next morning and Helen had to leave the house without seeing him. When she came back for lunch she found him wandering listlessly round the garden, now and then giving a kick to Rex's ball, while its owner hovered near, expectant, or went off to nose for it amongst the bushes. He did not see her as she walked up the path, as he was busy with his own none-too-pleasant thoughts, so she crossed over the lawn and came towards him.

'Hullo, Phil,' she said cheerfully, 'did you have a good night?'

'Not very,' responded Philip. 'I didn't sleep.' He certainly did look tired, and now it was daylight, ill as well. But his chin was shaved and except for his hair, he was more or less the same as he used to be; but there was still an air of rebellious shame about him which would accept no pity, or even sympathy, from anybody.

Helen linked arms with him and they began to pace round the lawn.

'What are you going to do this afternoon?' she asked.

'Don't know.'

'Well, I'm off this afternoon and I'm going into Mereford to do some shopping. Would you care to come with me?'

'Are you going in the car?'

'Yes.'

'May as well – I've nothing to do.'

'Good. I've got all my Christmas shopping to do, and I haven't even got Penny a birthday present yet and it's her birthday next week.'

'Is it? 'Spose I'd better get her something too, then. What sort of things does she want?'

'Oh, she wants lots of things, I assure you! But let's go in now. It's nearly lunch-time, and after that I'll cut your hair, if you like.'

'Will you?' Philip looked at her eagerly. His long, dishevelled locks served as a constant reminder of the one thing he wished to forget, and until they were quite short, he could not be comfortable. 'Then I can wash it – it's filthy dirty.'

After lunch Philip and Helen departed to the bathroom armed with comb, scissors and clippers. Philip took off his jacket, threw a towel round his shoulders and sat on the stool. Helen set to work.

'How do you want it?' she asked.

'Cut it all off, please, really short. I'm fed up with it flapping around my eyes all the time.'

Helen worked in silence for a minute or two, then broke into a stream of small talk, hoping to keep his thoughts from the channel in which they were bound to flow.

'I wonder what sort of a birthday Penny will have,' she began. 'She was full of plans in her last letter. Did you see it?'

'No.'

'Oh well, she said she was going to try to get to the theatre in the evening, with some friends, and of course, take Gerry with them. She was going into Ilton the day she wrote to book the seats – they were going to see *The Gondoliers*, I think she said. The D'Oyly Carte is there for a fortnight. Lucky girl!'

Philip did not seem to be impressed with his sister's good fortune, so Helen tried a new line.

'What do you want for Christmas, Phil? I've got absolutely no ideas at all. Men are so difficult.'

'Oh, I dunno.' Philip shrugged his shoulders. 'Don't worry about me.'

'Don't be silly. Of course I shall worry about you.'

'I'll tell you what I do want; but it's not a thing you could give me, however much you might want to.'

'Why, what is it?'

'A visit to the Continent.'

'Oh Phil!'

'No, no, not like *that*. I mean a real, properly organized trip. At least, organized as far as cash goes, not places to sleep. I'd prefer to find those as I went along.'

'Well, I don't see what is to prevent your going. Ben Brisley covered the whole of France and Germany on just over ten shillings, so I've no doubt you can do the same.'

'Who's Ben Brisley?'

'He's a friend of Bernard Robertson's.'

'Oh.'

'But why do you want to go?'

'Oh, don't you understand? I'm fed up of living in this poky little village, having the same old sort of life year in and year out, and now I've been sent down from Cambridge I haven't even got that to take me out of it for half the time. I'm tired of it – tired of England – tired of all its limitations! I want space and opportunity – to live my own life and not be bothered by stupid old-fashioned conventions!'

'But would Europe give you this?'

'Yes! And I can tell you this – if I don't get out of here, and pretty quickly, too, I shall do something far worse than running away.'

The spirit was roused, and it seemed best to let it burn itself out; so Helen did not try to cross his feelings, hoping that, by letting him talk, there would consequently follow a lessening of the desire to escape.

'If you think I've come to stop, you're wrong,' he went on. 'I couldn't stay here where everybody knows what a mess I've made of things.'

'But nobody does know, Phil, except Father and Mother and Alban and me – and Alban doesn't know what you told me last night.'

'They may not know now,' responded Philip, 'but they'd find out. Things have a way of getting round, and when they saw I didn't go back to Cambridge, they'd begin to ask questions, and start rumours, and cast pitying glances on me when they met me in the street; and if there's anything I won't stand, it's pity – especially when you know everybody gossips about you the minute you're gone.'

'Well, don't go till after Christmas,' said Helen. 'Nobody will wonder things just yet and there's plenty of time to get away after the New Year.'

'No, but I shan't stay any longer than I can help.'

'I understand that; but Phil, promise me something.'

'What?'

'Try and forget all this while you are here. At present nobody knows and if you don't say anything nobody *will* know. So don't spoil your Christmas by being morbid – there are plenty of plans afoot which you can help with – and we shall be glad of an extra pair of hands. Will you promise to try and forget?'

'That's easier said then done.'

'I know it is – but you can do it if you make up your mind to it.'

'All right – but on one condition.'

'What is that?'

'That you won't try and stop me when I *do* want to go.'

'No, I won't stop you.'

'Good. Then I'll try to seem satisfied until the New Year, but after that I won't promise anything.'

'I'm content. Now will you get up and see how that looks? I've chopped an awful lot off – I hope it's not too much.'

Philip got up and went to the mirror to look at himself. His reflection was more pleasing than it had been for some time past, and after a few minutes' silent scrutiny he said,

'Yes, that's OK, thanks. Nice to have it short for a change.'

'It's not too short, is it?' asked Helen anxiously. 'I know you always used to like it a respectable length.'

'No, it's fine. Help me to forget.' He turned from the mirror with a wry smile. 'Thanks a lot; now I'll wash it. I'll be ready to leave in half an hour.'

'Will you be wise to go out with it wet? It's cold today, you know.'

'I know. I'll be OK. Now hop off and leave me to it.'

'Very well. I've got one or two things I can do till you're ready, so give me a call. I'll be in my study.'

'OK.'

Helen retired and 'left him to it'. She made out a list of friends and relations to whom she must send presents or cards or both; she found Penelope's birthday-and-Christmas list, and chose from its lengthy columns two things which were within her means to buy – rather a difficult task as her sister seemed to consider impossible presents like television sets and a fully equipped gymnasium essential to her happiness. What Philip would do she did not quite know.

She found a small note-pad and divided several sheets into quarters to use as labels for her presents, but as she had not yet bought anything she could not write on them. She liked to make her labels appropriate to the present and – according to the person – in some degree funny. Then she scribbled a hasty note to Margaret, and filled up the rest of the time by darning her stockings.

At the end of half an hour there was a tap on her door; it was opened two inches and Philip's voice said,

'I'll be ready in five minutes.'

'All right, thanks. I'll go and get the car out.'

The door closed again. Helen tidied up her belongings and, taking the two precious lists, went through into her bedroom and put on her outdoor clothes. Then she hurried downstairs with a large shopping bag and had the car outside the front door just as Philip appeared in it.

'Nicely timed,' he said.

'Yes, wasn't it?' laughed Helen. 'I'll just nip in and tell Mother we're going, and see if she wants anything.'

Mrs Wentworth did not want anything, however, and they were delayed no longer.

'Would you like me to drive?' asked Philip, when his sister joined him again.

'Oh, no, thanks, I'll do it.'

'Sure?'

'Yes, quite sure, thanks.'

They got in and were soon out of the village on the way to Mereford.

'What's the programme?' asked Philip, when the last house had been passed.

'Mainly to try and find what I want for people,' replied Helen. 'It might be easiest to park the car, and start at one end of Mereford and go on till we get to the other. There might be a chance of getting things that way.'

'Why, do you know what you want for everybody?'

'No, not everybody by a long way, but I have one or two ideas.'

'Well, who have we got to provide for?'

'To begin with, there's the family; then we always send something to Uncle Raymond and Aunt Edith and family –'

'There won't be much left by the time we've finished with them! Why on earth did they have such an enormous family?'

'They're both very fond of children, and if you can afford it, I think it's a jolly good thing to have a large family. I'm all in favour, personally. But we're digressing. We always deal with them *en masse* – don't you remember? Then there's Granny Carter, and sundry other relations, and of course, I've got a lot of friends to provide for. Oh, there's going to be some fun.'

'I'm glad you think so. I think it's going to be ghastly. I've no idea what anybody wants.'

'Well, Father wants a new tie, so there's one idea for you.'

'Oh? Well, what sort of a tie?'

'Just an ordinary black knitted one – you know the kind he likes. Mother wants a torch – a really good big one; so you can start with that.'

'Yes, that's all right, but what about all the rest? I haven't the faintest idea what people like. I was always bad at choosing presents.'

'Well, you come round with me, and if I see anything that I think anyone would like and I've already got him something, or have something else in mind, you can get it.'

'OK. Suits me.'

Mereford was crowded that afternoon and Helen had some difficulty in getting to the car park; but she managed it at last and they set out to comb the town.

Christmas cards were not unduly difficult to find, but even they took up more time than Helen had anticipated, and it seemed at one point as if they would have to come a second time. However, Philip proved to be more helpful when they really began the search, and by the time half-a-dozen presents had been bought, his mood was forgotten and he was really enjoying himself. Helen rejoiced within herself that the afternoon's excursion was so successful, and hoped that his brightness would continue. By half past four nearly all the people on her list had been provided for, and Philip took her into a delightfully old oak-timbered café to have tea. When this was over they completed their shopping and drove home, the back of the car piled high with boxes and tins of all imaginable shapes and sizes. Several journeys were necessary to empty the car of its luggage, and when it was finally driven into the garage, Helen found a small parcel hiding away in a corner which had been overlooked. She could not help smiling when she saw what it was. A chocolate pipe covered with silver paper which Philip had found in Woolworth's and which he had declared would do nicely for his mother, who could not bear smoke of any description.

All the purchases had, at Helen's request, been put on to the table in her study, and Philip was busy sorting them out when she came in.

'Hullo, I'm just finding which are mine,' he said.

'Good. You left this in the car,' Helen replied, handing him the pipe.

'Oh, thanks. I was just thinking I hadn't seen it around. I say, when are you going to tie all these things up?'

'As soon as possible – but we must do Penny's birthday presents first, or she won't get them in time.'

'Oh, righto. Which are they?'

'Well, that looks like mine, but I don't know which yours is. What sort of shape is it?'

They began to turn over the rest of the parcels and Philip put his collection down again in order to be able to help. After some searching, the right packet was found and Philip departed to his room. Helen sat down and wrote to her sister, tied up the parcel and letter, and when all this was completed it was time to go down for supper.

Chapter XXV

Preparations for the school concert continued daily, Helen working hard to train the children up to the standard she wanted. On the whole they were very good and remembered what she told them, but most of them had no idea of recitation or time, and even after repeated corrections, when she thought that at last they understood, they came to rehearsals next day and made exactly the same mistakes without seeming to realize they were wrong. The several small plays she was trying to produce were more successful, for here the children felt there was some point in their efforts and for the most part threw themselves into the spirit of the various pieces with consequently better results. She had more trouble with the Nativity Pageant, as there were no words, and all movements had to be slow and graceful, keeping in time with the music provided behind the scenes by Helen on the piano, and a couple of bamboo pipes which two of the boys had made. It was so difficult to get the children to move anyhow but jerkily, and they were usually right the way across the space allowed – for no stage had been erected yet – before the third beat had been played. During rehearsals, the piano was placed in a position to enable Helen to see all that went on, and as long as she was there to direct, things went smoothly; but the minute she played without making any sign for the actors to follow, one of them was sure to forget something and spoil the piece. Helen was patient, but when they were still making the same mistakes only about a fortnight before the day appointed for the performance, she began to wonder whether she had been wise in attempting such an undertaking. However, she was always hopeful, and cheered herself with the thought that bad rehearsals often meant a good performance.

The making of costumes for the different items provided a good deal of amusement, and it was surprising what the children could produce when they got down to it. Nothing more was bought than was absolutely necessary, and as the Wentworths had a fairly extensive property box, nearly all the work was reduced to altering garments to fit. A tuck here and a stitch there were all that was necessary, and the children looked forward eagerly to the day when they would tread the boards in all their finery; and the fact that it was borrowed did not seem to lessen the fascination.

Philip, oddly enough, took a keen interest in the proceedings and made a good many of the 'stage props' with his own hands. Before, he had regarded the children more or less as barbarians who could never absorb any sort of learning or turn out anything worth notice, and his sister's attempt to teach them some of the beauties of life as being rather a waste of time. After one or two visits to the school when preparations were in full swing, he changed his opinions, and had to admit that there was talent as well as ability amongst them.

'You've done some mighty fine work there, Helen,' he said, as they walked home one evening after a couple of hours' extra toil. 'I thought they were all quite brainless.'

'Oh no!' cried Helen, quick to defend the children she loved. 'Far from it! Why, some of those youngsters have real talent and I only wish it could be developed. It seems so unfair that they shouldn't be given the opportunity of a better education; but Father says that they had a couple of Ministry of Education officials down while I was away who were very full of a new Bill which will help to raise the standard of education in schools like this.'

'Good idea. It needs it. But I must say, I think you've done a good job.'

'Don't give me all the credit. I'm only an extra – I'm not really a teacher and they only let me do this work after much pressure. I don't *teach* them – not actual lessons, such as reading, writing and arithmetic – I try and give them some ideas of what I call the Higher Arts of Life.'

'Wish there were more like you.' Philip meant more than just teachers in the Higher Arts of Life in that remark, but Helen, whose mind was still with her children and their education, did not appreciate it.

'Sometimes I wonder if it's not silly to go on with this concert,' she said. 'They're hardly any better now than they were a month ago, and it's only ten days to The Day. It seems that either they have the gift or they haven't, and that no amount of coaching will make those who haven't understand what they have to do. If they have a spark of intelligence on which one can work, it's not too difficult, but if they haven't – well, it's practically impossible.'

'Can't you choose the best children and leave the others?'

'To a certain extent, yes, and for things that matter, like the Nativity Pageant, you have to have the better ones if you want to get any sort of result; but they are so disappointed if you leave them out that you can't, especially when they are so anxious to help and be "in it". The difficulty is finding something the duller ones can take part in without ruining the whole thing.'

'Certainly not easy, I should say.'

'No, not at all; but they're all singing in the carols, so if they can't do anything else, they can do that.'

'I shall be interested to hear this concert when it comes off. When's it going to be?'

'On the twenty-third. We wanted it to be as near Christmas as possible, and there is a carol-singing expedition arranged for Christmas Eve, so we thought that would be best.'

'Where is it going to be held? You'll *never* get all the village in the school hall *and* a stage.'

'No, Mr Moore is lending us the church hall, which has the advantage of a platform at one end and fittings for curtains, and can hold a fair amount of people as well. We may have to do it twice, but I don't think we shall.'

'Well, all I can say is, I hope for your sake they pull their socks up a bit on the night.'

'So do I!' said Helen, with heartfelt agreement.

Chapter XXVI

Hanover House
Ilton CollegeGirls
Ilton

My dearest Family, December 19th

Thanks awfully, all of you, for all the lovely presents – they're marvellous, and just what I wanted. How on earth did you know? I suppose Helen told you because she had a list. Anyway, thanks tons, everybody.

I had a simply marvellous birthday. It was Saturday, so there was no school. There were tons of things on my plate at breakfast, but I wasn't allowed to open them till afterwards so as not to hold things up. I suppose it's sensible really but I was simply aching to open them.

We toddled upstairs to my dorm and I undid them on my bed, while the others sat round and looked at them when I'd finished with them. There were tons of things and umpteen birthday cards; the old dorm looks quite festive. I won't tell you all the things I had because it all takes time, and I haven't much, and anyway, you'll see them when I come home.

It began snowing on Thursday evening and all day Friday, so Winkle (the Gym Mistress) said she would take anybody who liked tobogganing and some of the prefects said they'd help her, so we all set off armed with toboggans to Bunker's Back, which is absolutely top hole for it. I'd have asked if Gerry could come, as several of the girls had their brothers, but I didn't think he'd want to, knowing him (silly ass!) so I didn't. Funnily enough, when we got there the boys had had the same idea and were already in full possession. And would you believe it, Gerry was there!!! And I think he was having a jolly good time, too. See what Ilton has done for him! We did have some fun, especially riding on our stomachs, four on top of each other and rolling off at the bottom so as not to go into the hedge. One of the boys got winded, but I don't think there were any bad accidents. It was his own fault, because the idiot didn't fall off properly and landed on his chest.

After lunch we had a *merveilleux* time. Ten of us, including Gerry, and two of the girls' brothers, went into Ilton to see *The Gondoliers* by the D'Oyly Carte Company. I'd got the tickets some time ago, and if you are lucky you can get into the best seats for a shilling, providing you go in uniform. I must have hit the right day (or else the ticket chap was captivated by my sweet smile!) Anyway, we got into the front row of the circle for a shilling each. Not bad going, what? It was a grand show and very funny. Most of us knew it, *arkshully*, but it's the type of thing you never get sick of, at least, I don't. I love the song about Lord Chancellors being as cheap as sprats, don't you? As a matter of fact, the Maths Mistress my form has looks exactly like a tabby cat; her hair's a funny sort of mottled colour, and she always makes purring noises when she's correcting an exercise. We call her 'Pussy'. She doesn't wear a shovel hat, though.

Well, after that we found a café and had a simply scrumptious tea, with some luscious chocolate éclairs. I do love them. You ought to try and make some, Helen. I'm sure it's quite easy.

We got back about half past six, and there were more letters and cards for me, come by the afternoon post. Amongst other things, Uncle Raymond and Aunt Edith sent me a cricket bat. Uncle R says it's 'rather out of season, but will do for next summer'. I don't care what season it is, it's a lovely bat, and I'll be able to beat all England with it!

I cut your cake after supper when we were all assembled in the dorm, and oh boy, is it good! It wasn't damaged at all getting here, which says a lot for your packing.

Now I've got streams of letters to write. I wish my birthday wasn't quite so near Christmas. I shall have them all to write all over again after it!

Now I must tell you about the plays and things we've been having. Exams finished about a fortnight ago, and we've been getting used to our results before plunging into the usual end-of-term activities, which began last Thursday with the finals of the House hockey matches. Oh, I was so jealous! And I felt such a fool having to stand on the touch line and watch them fog around with the ball! Scream,

scream! Hanover won, so it didn't really matter, but I'd like to have had a share in the victory. I mean to play next term, and Doctor Kennedy's not going to stop me, either!

On Friday morning after break there were two plays done by the seconds and lower thirds and Form Upper VA. They were good, but nothing to go wild about. Then in the evening there was the Seniors' Party, given by the sixth form for the lower fifths upwards. That was good fun, and they had the whole thing organized to the minute. We've got a jolly good set of prefects this year, much better than last, and they made it go with a hum. Of course there was competition for dances with certain members of staff. I won an elimination walze with Miss Dicock and we got a bar of chocolate each. Then there was a treasure hunt all over the building, with clues which were quotations suitable for the place, like 'Where should this music be? I' the air or the earth?' being applied to the Music Room, and other things like that; very clever really, though it was rather difficult because so many people wanted to try for it. There were tons of other competitions, and I think nearly everybody got a prize of some description. It went on till about ten o'clock. The Middle School had theirs on Monday, and the Juniors are in full swing at the moment. I'm writing in the study attached to our dorm.

Saturday you know about, and Sunday was pretty quiet. We had an end-of-term Service in the Chapel, which I quite enjoyed. The afternoon was very quiet and spent mostly in tying up parcels and sticking Christmas cards into envelopes. I got a lovely one for Charlie, of an Oxford graduate complete with gown and mortar-board trying to skate on Port Meadow (wherever that is, I suppose he'll know), only he's come a cropper and is in a very undignified position. Underneath it says 'Don't be got down by degrees – a second is all you need to come down' and then over the page something that follows on. Well, I don't quite know what it all means, but I thought it was appropriate, and anyway, he would appreciate it.

We've been very busy decorating our form-room, and the sixth form did the hall and the Chapel in time for the party on Friday, though the Chapel wasn't needed till Sunday.

Monday was a terrific day. We had Prayers as usual, then one or two lessons. We didn't do much work, actually. We gassed and played games most of the time, then we had to go over to the theatre.

We didn't know what was going to happen, but somebody said the staff were going to do a play, and of course, the rumour spread rapidly (rumours like that always do). But it wasn't the staff so we were a little disappointed. It was the sixth and lower sixth. They did two plays, both very good, and the second one was screamingly funny. It was a thing called *The Man in the Bowler Hat* by A.A. Milne, and was really awfully clever. The school howled with laughter, so much so that it was quite embarrassing for the poor actors, who couldn't go on till they were silent. Oh dear, my sides still ache!

There was nothing more in the morning, then in the afternoon we trooped over to the theatre again and this time it *was* the staff. They did a sort of skit on school life like an *In Town Tonight*, having all sorts of queer people up to the 'microphone'. It *was* funny. To see the staff descend from their pedestals and put on the most idiotic costumes was funny in itself, but when they began to talk – well! – you can't imagine the picture unless you have experienced it yourself. A fresh shriek of mirth greeted every new character who came on to the stage.

Today there was nothing much doing in the morning, and this afternoon we had our usual Carol Concert. It was in the Chapel, as usual, and went off very well. The choir did its stuff, with yours truly trying to hit the right note at the right time, and the school sang with its usual gusto, though I must say, Miss Williams trains them pretty well. I suppose the fact that she's Welsh helps. Anyway, I like the carols we sing; they're different from the well-known ones, and I've not come across them anywhere else, except at home, and that was only after you started at Ilton, Helen.

The evening has been spent packing, and I must admit, at one point I wondered how on earth I was going to get all my stuff in. I seem to have accumulated a dickens of a lot, what with birthday presents and what not.

We break up tomorrow, and I suppose there will be the usual Assembly, the usual reading out of marks, the usual clapping of the 75%s and overs, the usual 'Term Report' from Miss Radcliffe, with its usual attempts at humour which are never funny.

Then there's one more night to be got through and we'll be coming home. Yippee! We should get to Mereford at the usual (oh dear, I seem to be rather fond of that word) time, i.e. about four o'clock, and if somebody feels like meeting us…

Well, this is some letter, but I thought I'd better write it all down, as it's easier to remember than saying it, so I hope you haven't been too bored.

Tons and tons of love

from

Penny

Chapter XXVII

Penelope and Gerald followed this letter up in person on the afternoon of the same day as it arrived. Helen had taken the hint in Penelope's letter and driven over to Mereford to meet them, and she hardly had time to draw up in front of the house before Penelope had jumped out and was pulling out the luggage. Gerald followed suit, and leant over his sister's shoulder to play a joyful chant on the horn – 'just to warn them,' he explained.

Penelope seized a case in each hand, rushed up the steps to the front door and pressed long and hard on the bell. This was practically unnecessary, however, as both Mr and Mrs Wentworth had seen them come up the drive and heard Gerald's announcement of their arrival. The door was opened even while Penelope was ringing.

Then there was much joy and excited talk; anxious enquiries as to the children's welfare, voluminous thanks for birthday presents again, and general family rejoicing. Above the uproar, Gerald was heard loudly demanding his tea. They had had nothing since breakfast, and he, at least, was 'starving'.

When the noise had quietened down a little, Philip appeared from the lounge, where he had secluded himself, to escape from the first reunion – the kind of 'silly nonsense' he despised. The greetings were less affectionate, but Penelope was genuinely grateful for his 'lovely present'.

'It was marvellous,' she said. 'How did you guess what I wanted?' Then without waiting for an answer, 'What's that scar on your chin?'

The rest of the family looked up in alarm, for up till now nobody had noticed it. Philip turned scarlet and mumbled something about a razor.

Helen rose to the occasion and saved it.

'He did it weeks ago. It's nothing much. Come and help me to put the car away, Phil.'

Gladly, Philip obeyed, and Penelope had soon forgotten about it in the bustle of hauling luggage upstairs.

They were soon all seated round the tea-table, the two youngest members of the family doing full justice to their appetites and the ample spread provided for them.

'When's Alban coming home?' asked Penelope, covering a thick slice of bread and butter with a liberal helping of apricot jam; being her favourite, it had been specially opened for the occasion.

'Tomorrow afternoon,' replied Mrs Wentworth.

'Good. Can I go and meet him?'

'Certainly, if Helen will take you.'

'Will you?' Penelope addressed her sister across the table.

'I might consider it,' said Helen, with a twinkle.

'Well, Gerald,' said Mr Wentworth, turning to his youngest, who had been silent since the beginning of the meal. 'How do you like Ilton, now you've got there at last?'

'I love it,' responded Gerald briefly.

'You did extremely well in the exams. Your results pleased us very much – only half a term's work, too.'

'Oh, Gerry would pass exams on only half a *day's* work,' put in Penelope. 'Brains, and all that. Wish I knew how he did it!'

'Well, you got 71 per cent as a final, so what are you grumbling about?' asked Gerald.

'Mere fluke, I assure you! And anyway, that's the result of past terms' learning. I couldn't possibly go to a new school, and after only half a term, take exams and get 87 per cent. Some people have all the brains,' she added with a sigh.

'I think you've both done wonders,' said Helen, 'and anyway, Penny has the consolation of being brilliant at games and gym, so you're about equal, really.'

'You've not seen my report yet,' said Penelope ominously.

'Look, don't let's spoil tea with the comparative brains or brawn of our two scholars. It sounds too much like work,' said Philip.

'Good idea,' agreed Gerald.

The conversation turned to topics of more general interest and when everyone had had his fill, Penelope and Gerald departed to their rooms to unpack. The former's belongings were soon scattered all over her bedroom, for as she explained, she could not tidy up properly unless there was a really good mess to tidy up. Gerald, on the other hand, put his things away as he came to them and his bedroom was always the last word in neatness. The first thing he did, when everything was stowed away, was to go to his bookcase and scan his precious books with the affection and pride which only a true book-lover can know, taking one out here, and pushing one into place there, and finally selecting one of his favourites, and retiring with it to lie on his bed, once more to devour its much-thumbed pages, though he knew it almost by heart already. He was outwardly less shy, but inwardly the same, for not even the athletics of Ilton could destroy Gerald's love of books.

The next afternoon Alban arrived; he came earlier than was expected, and was already halfway through the twitt'n while Helen and Penelope were thinking it was time they got ready to go and meet him. He walked up the drive grinning to himself over the surprise he was going to give everyone, just as Charles had done several months before. The front door was not locked, so he walked straight in, and having relieved himself of his luggage, lifted up his voice in a mild shout:

'Ahoy there, you landlubbers! The fleet's in port again!'

Penelope was the first to reach the hall, and flung herself upon him almost before he had had enough time to recover his breath. The others followed more sedately, but were no less joyous in their welcome, and Alban was escorted into the dining room to the accompaniment of *Rule Britannia* from Penelope and a very life-like imitation of a drum from Gerald.

Helen had told him that Philip had returned but she had not given any details of his behaviour during his absence. She had begged Alban to pretend nothing had happened and not spoil Christmas with any suggestion of tension, and Alban, who had had plenty of time to think things over since they last met, was perfectly willing to obey. The result was they both got on a great deal better together than they had ever believed was possible. Alban forgot his contempt and Philip his desire to escape, and Christmas promised to be a very happy one after all.

Chapter XXVIII

At breakfast the following morning there was quite a considerable mail. Christmas cards came pouring in, and notes from uncles and aunts who could not think what to give them, and solved the problem by sending them the wherewithal and letting them choose themselves. All parcels and any letters that were obviously presents were intercepted by Mrs Wentworth and hidden away on top of the wardrobe in her bedroom to await the actual day. She did not believe in spoiling the fun of the day itself by letting the children receive and open their presents in ones and twos. Having grown up with the idea, they were quite used to it, and never raised any objections.

A great deal of fun was to be had in guessing whom the card was from by the writing on the envelope. Most of them were easy to identify, but one or two caused a certain amount of doubt at first.

Mr Wentworth passed round for inspection the cards addressed to him and his wife or to the whole family, and when everybody had looked at everybody else's, Mrs Wentworth seized the opportunity to tell her news.

'I've had a letter from your Aunt Edith,' she said, 'and she wants us all to go there to stay for a few days over the New Year for the twins' twenty-first birthday.'

'Oh lovely! When is it?' asked Penelope,

'Teddy and Eleanor?' asked Helen,

'When are we to go?' asked Gerald, all speaking together.

'Hush! Don't all talk at once!' cried Mrs Wentworth. 'I'll read you what she says.'

'Yes, my dear, please do,' said her husband.

'I'd no idea they were anything like twenty-one,' said Alban. 'I thought –'

'Never mind what you thought; let's hear the letter,' interrupted Penelope.

'You shouldn't chip in,' reproved Alban loftily. 'It's very rude. You should let me finish my sentence even if you do want to hear the letter.'

'Oh, dry up!' exclaimed Philip. 'Go on, Mother – what does she say?'

Mrs Wentworth looked round the table as if expecting another outburst, but nothing came, so she began.

'She says "As you know, Teddy and Len are twenty-one on the thirty-first of this month; we are arranging a dance for them and we want as many of their relations as possible to come for it. As it's hardly worth your while to come all that way for only one night, will you stay a little longer – say, arrive about tea-time on the thirtieth and stay for two or three days? We haven't seen any of you for such a long time that we shall need all the time we can get." '

'Oh, we must go,' said Penelope, 'especially after such a broad hint.'

'I don't see any reason why we shouldn't,' mused Mr Wentworth.

'No reason at all!' agreed Penelope. 'Let's put it to the vote. One, two, three, four, five, six and yourself, seven. Motion carried unanimously. Good. We go.'

Mr Wentworth laughed.

'You see, my dear, the question is taken out of our hands. Our children say we are to go, so I presume we had better do as we are told!'

'What on earth shall I wear?' said Helen, mentally running through the possibilities of her wardrobe.

'Your Elizabethan, of course,' responded Penelope. 'I suppose I shall have to wear my old pink thing. I don't like it, but I haven't got anything else.'

'Oh, you're all right – you look quite respectable in the "old pink thing". I'm the one with nothing to wear,' said Alban. 'I left all my stuff down at Dartmouth, and I don't believe I've got a suit to my name up here. Still, there's nothing like going in a bathing costume.'

'They *would* be thrilled,' said Philip scathingly. 'Can't you get into any of my old suits?'

'*Yours?* Dear me no. What, with my sylph-like figure? Why, they would hang on me like washing on a line.'

'If you really have got nothing, you'll have to try, Alban,' said his mother. 'I don't think there would need to be much alteration. After all, you're nearly eighteen, and Philip had his last suit two years ago.'

'But he was fatter than I am,' objected Alban, 'and I don't like not having a suit of my own.'

'Ah, now we're getting down to the root of the trouble,' laughed Helen. 'No suit, no party.'

Mrs Wentworth looked down the table at her husband. There was an indulgent twinkle in his eye, and she guessed what would be the result of the argument. Mr Wentworth did not like his children's enjoyment to be spoilt by lack of clothes, and she saw that, unless she put in a word quickly, Alban would have a complete new evening suit.

'But you've got a suit somewhere, dear,' she said. 'Where is it?'

'I said, I left it at Dartmouth. Anyway, I never wear it, because it's too small.'

'What do you wear for dances, then?' enquired Gerald.

'I think we are wandering from the point.' Alban ignored his brother and turned to Mr Wentworth. 'Yes, Father, you were saying?'

'I wasn't saying anything,' replied Mr Wentworth.

'Oh, I beg your pardon. I thought I heard you murmur something about a new evening suit,' the naughty lad explained. He was bound to get his wish by fair means or foul. He turned his head and winked at Penelope. She rose to the occasion but not in the way Alban expected.

'If he has a new suit, I want a new dress,' she said decidedly. 'My pink thing is out of date and falling to pieces.'

'Now, Penny, you keep out of this,' said Helen. 'Let's deal with one of you at a time.'

'I think it would be best if you went upstairs and tried Philip's old suit on,' Mrs Wentworth told him. 'We shall never settle anything by talking.'

Alban sighed. His new suit, in which a few seconds before he had seen himself walzing round his uncle's ballroom with everybody's eyes upon him, now receded to the distant horizon and he felt that unless he made a drastic effort, it would fade away altogether.

'All right,' he agreed reluctantly, 'but I'm sure it will be miles too big.'

However, it proved to fit him near enough to be usable, and Helen volunteered to take in the back of the jacket and let the sleeves down, which was all that needed altering. Alban was disappointed, but had to admit that it 'didn't look too bad' when finished.

'Who would have thought,' he said, 'that Phil had ever been small enough to get into that!'

Chapter XXIX

The village school had broken up, but preparations still went on, with more fervour than ever now that the day was so near. Helen begged to be allowed the use of the church hall for final rehearsals, so that the children could get accustomed to its acoustics and to a proper stage. Philip and Alban and several of the older boys set to work on the Saturday afternoon to fix up the stage; it did not take long, as there were brackets and hooks in all the right places. The hall had been used so many times before that experience had taught where such things were necessary.

Of course, one of the children went down with flu at the last minute, but Alban nobly stepped in and filled the gap; luckily the part the child had to take in one of the plays was one which he knew, and he agreed to perform some conjuring tricks at the time when the rightful actor should have been showing off his double-jointed back.

They rehearsed hard all Monday afternoon, and although things did not go as well as could have been wished, they were better than they had been a week or two before.

While Helen, Philip and Alban were busy with this, Penelope and Gerald undertook to cut the evergreens for decorating the house. They found a pair of clippers, the garden steps and a large 'tin' bath in which to wash the sprays when they had cut them. Penelope did the actual clipping, and Gerald ran to and fro depositing them as she handed them to him. When the pile had grown to a considerable size, they paused in their labours.

'Do you think that'll be enough?' asked Gerald.

'No, I don't think it will. Let's cut some more,' replied Penelope, rubbing the back of her neck. It was stiff with so much craning to look for branches over her head.

'Mother said we weren't to get too much,' said Gerald, doubtfully.

'*That* won't be too much! And anyway, if there is any over it'll do to decorate the church hall. Helen said she didn't know where the stuff was coming from. Come on.'

They searched further and soon the pile was half its size again.

'That'll do,' Penelope decided. 'Now we must wash it. Help me fill this.'

They each took a handle of the tin bath and carried it to the scullery sink. Penelope turned on the hot tap.

'It'll take ages to fill,' she said, perching herself on the corner of the table.

'Did you remember the dust sheet?' asked Gerald, who knew the procedure by heart from previous years.

'Oh, no! I'll get one.' Penelope disappeared into the kitchen and soon returned with a large dust sheet. She threw it on to the table and went to see how the filling of the bath was progressing. It was still only half full.

'Oh, hurry up, water!' she cried impatiently. 'Just look at that tap! And it *won't* go on any further.' Indeed, the tap was running remarkably slowly. 'Remind me to tell Mother,' she added. 'It ought to be seen to.'

However, the bath was full at last, and after some difficulty they succeeded in carrying it round to the garage. Gerald unlocked the door and spread out the dust sheet.

'Now,' said Penelope, 'I'll squish the twigs round in the water and you can shake them outside and put them on the dust sheet.'

This operation was carried out successfully, with a good deal of pausing to warm up frozen fingers, for the air was decidedly chilly.

'I wish,' said Penelope, 'squishing' a spray of holly energetically in the water, 'that we could have a really proper Christmas for once. It never snows nowadays.'

'No,' agreed Gerald, 'or if it does, it thaws on Christmas Eve, or something silly.' He looked up at the sky. 'Do you think that's a snowy sky?' he asked.

'Don't expect so,' replied Penelope despondently. 'We shall probably have a beautiful sunny day with mosquitoes buzzing because it's so warm.'

'Well, I don't know much about the weather,' said Gerald, 'but that looks very heavy to me.'

'Let's hope it is. Anyway, here's the last of this. Is there room enough to get the car out?'

'Oh, yes. I've put it down the side.'

'Good. Help me to tip up the bath and then we've finished.'

They emptied the water away down the drain in the middle of the drive and, collecting the clippers, went back into the house to wash.

'I've still got some presents to buy,' said Penelope, standing over the basin. She had filled it with hot water and plunged her hands in above the wrist – a sure and rapid way to restore warmth and circulation.

'So have I,' responded Gerald, sitting on the edge of the bath drying his hands.

'Let's go down to the village and see what there is.'

'Righto.'

With a promise to be back for tea, they set off to see what they could find in the village. It was a custom in the family for their father and mother to have stockings on Christmas Day as well as themselves, and whereas their own were more or less serious, their parents' were largely funny, and the village shops provided just what was necessary. They went from shop to shop, mainly buying what they fancied for this purpose but also one or two 'proper' presents which they had been unable to obtain so far, until their funds gave out and they had to return. They hid their purchases and came down to tea.

Helen had said she hoped they would be finished by five o'clock, but that if they had not appeared by ten past, the rest were not to wait for them. As the children were becoming impatient for their meal, Mrs Wentworth decided not to wait any longer. However, they had not progressed very far before they heard the three come in at the front door. After a hasty 'wash and brush up tuppence,' as Penelope put it, in the cloakroom, they trooped into the dining room very ready for something to eat.

'Poof! Food!' exclaimed Alban, flopping down into his chair. 'Strange as it may sound on this beautifully sunny summer's day, I'm simply stewing!'

'Well, you've been working hard all the afternoon,' said Mr Wentworth.

Helen took her seat next to her mother, saying as she did so,

'A cup of tea is all I want just now, please.'

'How did it go?' asked Mrs Wentworth, pouring out the tea.

'Oh, not so badly, I suppose, considering. Oh dear, Willie Bell *is* such trial! – thank you very much – if he doesn't behave tomorrow I don't know what I shall do!'

'Oh, cheer up, he wasn't so bad,' replied Alban cheerfully, having recovered his spirits now that food was a real possibility and not merely an anticipation.

'The kid on the tin whistle's jolly good,' put in Philip. 'Where did he learn?'

'At home, I think. He was terribly shy about it at first. In fact I never knew until a few months ago, when I happened to call at his house for something and heard him practising. When I asked who it was and was told Johnny, I was amazed, because I'd no idea he could do anything of the sort. He was too shy even to play to me to begin with, but he's getting over it, and should do very well tomorrow.'

'I'm dying to see this show,' said Penelope. 'We've heard such a lot about it.'

'I only hope it comes up to your expectations,' answered Helen.

'Oh, don't worry, they'll be OK,' said Philip. 'There's no need to get het up about it.'

'That's all very well, but you're not producing it. I shan't be really calm until it's all over.'

'Bags of flap,' murmured Penelope.

'I'm sure everything will go without a hitch,' said Mr Wentworth.

'Father dear, you are very cheering. I sincerely hope you are right. Now, if everybody has finished, I believe there are one or two things that need attending to in my study, if *les enfants* would like to come.'

'*Les enfants*' took the hint, and soon they were all having a gay time comparing and camouflaging their purchases for the two stockings. When both were full, and the appropriate pieces of holly pinned to the tops, Helen took them and concealed them amongst the clothes hanging in her wardrobe.

'To bed, small fry,' said Alban in a superior tone. 'We, the hard-working labourers, are tired and wish to retire and have some well-earned rest.'

'Then why don't you go?' asked Gerald innocently. It was surprising how much less shy he was. Alban could not help commenting on the fact, and chased his small brother into his bedroom, into which the latter just managed to lock himself before he could be invaded.

'And don't be long in the bathroom,' he added.

Chapter XXX

The following morning they all set to work to decorate the house. Helen and Philip put up the evergreens, and Alban and Gerald the paper streamers which had come out every year since they had first been bought – when Helen was only a few months old – and which were very dear to all their hearts, tattered though they were. Penelope disappeared to her room with the little artificial Christmas tree and box of decorations and did not reappear for more than an hour. By then the house was nearly finished and certainly did look very festive.

In the afternoon the 'hard-working labourers' repaired once more to the church hall, taking with them what was left of the evergreens, to carry on there. Helen had had several offers of holly and laurel from the children, and had accepted all gratefully, knowing what a lot would be needed if the hall were to look anything but bitty. They dashed in for some tea about four o'clock and then dashed back again to begin preparations. The children were all to have arrived by five, giving them an hour and a half in which to get dressed and organized. Four of the boys had offered to act as programme-sellers and to usher the audience into its seats. The children had all given the number of parents and friends who would be coming from their respective homes, so that Helen should know how many to provide seats for, and with the help of half-a-dozen of the best artists, had made more than enough programmes for everybody. There were no tickets but a charge for admission was to be paid at the door. The two boys detailed to collect it felt very proud of themselves when they were settled behind a table just outside the door joining the hall to the ante-room, and were far too sharp to let anyone get in without paying.

Helen had warned her family to be there early if they wanted good seats, and consequently they were the first to arrive and could select their own position. A place was to be saved for Philip, in case he wanted to come and sit in the audience, but he had thought in all probability he would remain behind the scenes to help with the prompting and manœuvring of the curtains.

Soon the stream of fathers and mothers and friends began, keeping the ushers busy supplying programmes and directing them to their seats. A buzz of eager conversation filled the hall, as each family compared with its neighbours the upheavals and unearthings, the stitchings and the hammerings, the painting and the learning of parts which had been going on during the past few weeks. They all had some incident of which to tell, capping one impossible story with another until they were cut short by the lights going out promptly at half past six. Every eye turned expectantly towards the curtains, whose base was illuminated by the footlights which Alban had spent so long in fixing up. There was a pause of sufficient length to enable the audience to admire the effect, then the curtains were lifted apart by two invisible hands, just wide enough for a person to slip through. Two lights were switched on from the sides of the proscenium, and Helen appeared between the curtains, which closed behind her. She was greeted with loud applause and having made a short explanatory speech, retired through the gap again made for her amidst even louder cheers.

There was a moment's hesitation while places were found behind the curtains and subdued whispers hastily quietened by quite audible 'ssh!' noises. Then the curtains swung apart to reveal four rows of children, all in their Sunday best, ranged in a semi-circle round the stage, with Helen facing them in the centre. A chord was played on the piano in the wings, and with breath pent up and lips forming the first syllable of their song, the children waited for the raised baton to fall. The next minute it had done so and they had burst into the first bars of the opening chorus, a spritely rendering of *Twankidillo*, which Helen had considered a suitable opening to their concert. A dozen of the more musical ones were allowed to sing the descant, but otherwise they all joined in the main tune and tried their best to hit the right notes; but harmonious or discordant, it was happy, and served to put the audience in a good mood at the start, which was what Helen most desired.

The first item on the programme was announced, as was each subsequent item, by a girl of about twelve years of age, who slipped through the curtains and called out that there would now be a recitation by Johnny Deane, of a poem entitled *Christmas Eve.*

After the curtains parted, Johnny Deane, a small, dark-eyed boy of ten, whose hair shone as smooth as glass with brilliantine, walked doubtfully on to the stage, repeated the name of his poem, and began. He was not quite sure of himself at first and the rows of faces before him heightened his anxiety. But he was a good actor, and soon the simple, tragic story gained possession of his thoughts, and he forgot everything but the words of the old ballad. It was such a story of Christmas as may often be found amongst peasants and it had appealed to Johnny. This very fact had enabled him to understand its beauty and gave expression to his voice and face which none but his mother knew or even guessed that he possessed. The poem was long, but he needed no prompter, and several eyes were misty before he had proceeded very far. Helen was pleased and thought to herself that if all the children did as well as Johnny, the concert would be a great success.

Next came a selection of scenes from *A Christmas Carol* which Helen had dramatized and adapted for their limited means of production. A crosser, more selfish and grumpy Scrooge never graced the boards of any stage, and it was difficult to recognize Alban beneath the grey wig and beard and the husky, croaking voice. Helen could not help feeling that the rightful Scrooge would hardly have done so well, although she was sorry that he had to miss the concert. Good though he was in the part, however, he was no better than Tiny Tim, whose crutches and bent back brought tears of sympathy to the eyes of the audience.

This was followed by two piano solos given by one of the older children whom Helen taught to play. Philip, listening in the wings, remembered what she had said about there being talent amongst them, and felt that this child was gifted in a way quite disproportionate to his background. Why should there not be an opportunity for such to go on and learn from experienced teachers? Helen's services were given freely, he knew, because she enjoyed the work; but even she could not teach much more to this child, and what would happen then? Would all the progress which might be made have to be stopped because there was not enough money to make more advanced study possible? It was a ghastly shame, and he wished something could be done about it.

He had no time for further meditation, as the announcer came forward again to inform the audience that they would now be entertained with some conjuring tricks by Mr Alban Wentworth. The lights in the hall went up.

Alban was prepared to enjoy himself and had brought his best tricks along with him that evening to puzzle and intrigue his audience. He did not even mind the fact that as many of the children as possibly could had crowded into the wings to watch him.

The aim of all conjurers is to create an impression, and Alban certainly succeeded with his. Although his equipment consisted of nothing more than a small table covered with a black velvet cloth, a few bottles, boxes and packs of cards, his audience, to most of whom anything of this nature verged on the realm of the supernatural, were keyed up with excitement from the moment the curtain rose.

An endless stream of talk served to distract attention from his actual movements, and though everyone thought he was watching most intently everything the conjuror did, the most important and vital sleights of hand went by unnoticed, and time after time the audience was deceived. Tricks with coins and bank notes and handkerchiefs, all of which he borrowed from the audience, to be burnt, made vanish and reappear in totally different places; tricks with cards, lengths of ribbon, jam jars and cigarette boxes – nothing seemed beyond his powers of illusion.

Finally, he picked up a pack of cards, and shuffling them energetically, said,

'Now, for my last trick I want some active co-operation. Any offers? It's quite simple. All you have to do is select one of these cards and show it to the rest of the audience without my seeing it – no funny stuff, or making you go purple or disappear or anything. Who will come and take one?'

Penelope, always willing to oblige her brother in his games, and thinking there might be some glory attached to this, put up her hand and said,

'I will.'

Alban greeted her offer calmly, without betraying a single suggestion of treachery.

'Good,' he said. 'Thank you very much. Now come and take one of these cards' – he spread the pack out like a fan – 'any one will do, it doesn't matter which you take' – Penelope drew out a card – 'don't let me see it. Now go and show it to everybody – make sure they all know what it is' – Penelope, feeling very important, passed the card in and out of the rows while Alban prattled on about nothing in particular, until she returned with it to the front of the hall.

'Ah, has everybody seen it? Good.' He could see Penelope visibly swelling with pride as she held up the card with its back towards him, and could not resist a wicked twinkle which was quite lost on her. 'Are you all quite sure you know what it is?' he asked, as if everything depended on their knowledge. Murmurs of assent rose from the audience.

'Good. Then there's no need for me to tell you.'

Amid groans and laughs he bowed Penelope, scarlet with mortification, back to her seat, then, as thunderous applause broke out, he bowed and smiled his thanks till the curtains swung together and hid him from sight.

There was a ten-minute interval before the next half of the programme commenced, and when the curtain rose again, the stage was practically in darkness. This was for some carols, sung in two, three and four parts by the appropriate number of children. They were standing in a row diagonally back from the front of stage left, and two very dim lights were turned on to them, so that they could be seen but not identified. As the third or fourth was not required, he stepped back out of the light, to return when wanted. This effect had been created purposely, because Helen wanted all attention to be held by the carols, which she had chosen specially for the beauty of their words and music, and not by who was singing them.

The notes were played on the two bamboo pipes, and with Helen conducting in the wings, where she could be seen by the singers but not by the audience, they sang their first carol. It was a four-part harmony, in which it had been necessary to enlist the help of two boys who had left school, because none of the voices of the present scholars had broken.

The carols, with no accompaniment but the two pipes when wanted, were nearly all very old, dating from the sixteenth and seventeenth centuries. Helen had learnt them at school and loved them. As Penelope had said, they were unusual, and one did not often hear them. They were a pleasant change from the well-known ones which everybody sang, and Helen wanted the village children to know and love these also.

There is something very charming about the old tunes, written without key signatures and consequently having quaint and unexpected harmonies and often ending on the mediant. No modern tunes can quite equal them, be they never so beautiful. The children sang their half-dozen well, making every word distinguishable and every note clear. Helen had enjoyed teaching this quartette, because they seemed to enjoy learning, and had a pleasing appreciation of what they were being taught. The tunes and words were not, on the whole, difficult to learn; even the old English spelling was soon overcome and the words understood. It was in their very simplicity that their attraction lay, and more than one person went away with them still ringing in his ears.

Another play followed the carols. This time, it was a modern piece, written by Helen, about three children who had lived in a very fine house and had suddenly been reduced to very poor circumstances. They begin by grumbling over the 'flop' Christmas is going to be that year, with no parties or gaiety and no presents to speak of. They wish something would happen to bring them more fun and consequently more happiness. Hoping like this on Christmas Eve, they look out of the window to see if it is snowing, and find that it is, quite fast, and has been doing all the evening. Carol-singers come round, but their cheer is felt to be misplaced. They go away and one of the children, still by the window, watching them disappear into the darkness, sees one of them lag behind and then collapse in the snow. Forgetting their mood of a minute before, they hurry out to rescue him and bring him into the house. He is terribly cold, and they transport him to the sofa by the fire and cover him with what rugs they can lay their hands on, not quite knowing what to do to bring him round. They try various methods unsuccessfully, but at last the warmth revives him and he demands something to drink. He is given something hot, gaining sufficient strength to tell them that he was not really well enough to go out on such a night – but owing to lack of funds at home he had had to. He bore up as long as he could, but the others walked so fast in order to keep warm that he could not keep up with them, and when they had found him he had thought he was going to die. They give him food and tell him to lie there and stay with them for the night, which he is only too willing to do. They see that he is comfortable, then make up the fire and sit down near him, trying to keep awake in case he should want anything. He falls asleep and though they try their hardest not to let themselves drop off, they are too tired, and one by one their eyelids droop and they sleep too. The fire dies down until there is only a red glow in the hearth. Then suddenly the sofa is illuminated in a soft light, the boy rises from it and the light, which seems to be issuing from him, reveals that where there was a ragged coat and worn-out shoes, he is now wearing a long white robe, tied with a girdle round the waist. Stretching out his arms he blesses the children and disappears. Just at that moment the window, which has not been properly fastened, opens suddenly and closes with a loud bang. The children wake up with a start, put on the light, and of course, find that their boy has gone. They do not know what to make of it at first, until one of them tells a dream he has had, in which the boy rose 'all dressed in shining white' and blessed them, saying that they would find their Christmas happy, as they had so made another's. The children look at each other in wonder and amazement, and finally they all say what they are thinking – 'It was the Christ-Child'. The bells peel out and they realize it is Christmas Day.

A series of short monologues, given by one of the more humorous of the girls, followed this, and kept the audience in fits of laughter, for the speaker managed to be two different people at once, and by altering the pitch and accent of her voice with each impersonation, gave the impression that she really was two people. Expressive gestures with head and arms enhanced the effect and she obviously enjoyed herself as much as the audience did watching her.

The owner of the 'tin whistle' whom Philip had praised so much then made his appearance and played a solo. His instrument was really a bamboo pipe and had sweet and pleasing tones. Next he was joined by the other piper and they played several short duets, then broke into a hornpipe. Alban hopped on to the stage in full uniform and danced to their lively accompaniment, much to Penelope's joy, for she loved to watch him dance the sailor's traditional dance.

Next came a brief Nativity Play, performed silently by the actors with a musical and vocal accompaniment behind the scenes. This was the piece about which Helen felt most anxious; last warnings were given to move slowly and gracefully, to count as they had been taught while making any gesture or step backwards or forwards. The awe of the occasion kept the children on the alert, and they remembered everything they had been told; they managed their long robes and did not trip over them; they measured every movement and altogether went through their actions with creditable precision. It was a great relief, and the applause which broke out at the lowering of the curtain proved that it was appreciated.

Then there was a hurried rearrangement on the stage. The piano was rolled on to it and the entire company, half in costume and half not, assembled round it. When all was ready, the announcer slipped through the curtains to say that their finale would be carols, and everybody was to join in.

Everybody did join in, lustily, and even if the words were a little hazy, the tunes were familiar, and singing them to 'la' was just as enjoyable and quite satisfactory.

The audience was overwhelmingly appreciative when at last the concert was over; there was not one person who would not have liked more. They clapped and clapped and cheered; somebody more daring than the rest called out 'Producer!' and his call was taken up by his neighbours, and soon the entire company was yelling, 'Producer! Producer!' at the top of their voices. Helen slipped through the curtains once more, glowing with happiness at the success of her pupils, and received the redoubled applause with bows and smiles of gratified pleasure.

All the children had remained in their places for the National Anthem, and when Helen disappeared, she hurried across the stage to the piano and struck a chord. The curtains were parted and the audience rose to give full vent to their feelings.

As the last notes died away and the curtains swung to for the last time, people began collecting their coats and crowded to the door. Eager discussion broke out, one proud parent vying with another over the comparative merits of their children, and recalling amusing incidents which had occurred during the evening. But most of all it was a triumph for Helen. Her work, begun nearly eighteen months ago with so much opposition from the Education Authorities, and regarded with suspicion by these same parents, was now amply rewarded, and though not many people voiced their opinions, all of them would have acknowledged that it was her energy and ideas, her patience and skill, her untiring efforts, that had made this concert possible.

Chapter XXXI

As many of the children as were able to be, were dismissed at once, and the rest were helped with derobing and packing. Helen and Alban worked hard to clear the hall of all extras, staying long after everyone had left, to sweep and straighten and tidy up. They did not pause until everything was as usual except for the stage and the decorations, which were to stay over Christmas in case the hall should be required for anything else.

They had just finished, and were resting for a few minutes, drinking some cocoa that Helen had brought with her in a thermos, when the door at the end of the hall opened and the Reverend Robert Ward came in. He walked down the side aisle, explaining that he had come from his uncle to see if there was anything he could do. Helen thanked him and said they had just finished.

'I'm afraid I'm too late,' he said apologetically. 'I'm sorry, I should have come sooner.'

'That's all right,' replied Helen. 'There wasn't very much. We're rather dirty, but that's all!' She wiped her free hand on her overall. 'This is my brother Alban, by the way,' she added. 'Come and have a cup of cocoa.'

Mr Ward greeted Alban and said, 'No thanks. I've just had supper. Are you sure there is nothing I can do?'

'Quite sure, thanks. We shall be going home in a few minutes.'

'Very well, in that case I won't stay.' But the Reverend Ward did not move. 'May I congratulate you,' he went on, 'for this evening's concert? It was a fine piece of work.'

'Thank you, Mr Ward.' Helen accepted his praise on behalf of her children and did not think of taking any glory herself. But not so the Reverend Ward. He pursued his point.

'Yes,' he continued, 'everybody is full of it. Personally I haven't enjoyed anything so much for a long time. You must have worked very hard to procure such an excellent result.'

Helen laughed.

'Some of the work was a little exasperating at times,' she admitted, 'but I enjoy it so much I don't call it work.'

Alban had remained silent while this conversation was in progress, smiling alternately at his sister and at the Reverend Ward. Although he had heard a great deal about the new Rector, this was the first time he had met him. Mr Ward lingered a while longer, then said, as if loath to depart,

'Well, if you're sure there's nothing I can do…?'

'Quite sure, thank you. We have finished, really, haven't we, Alban?'

'Pardon? Oh – yes!' responded Alban. A thought had just struck him and he was busy following it up when Helen spoke.

'Thank you very much for coming, all the same,' said Helen. 'It was very kind of you.'

'Not at all,' replied the Reverend Ward hurriedly. 'I wish I could have been of service to you. Well, thank you again for a most enjoyable evening. Goodnight.'

'Goodnight, Mr Ward.'

'Goodnight,' echoed Alban.

They remained where they were until the door had closed behind him, then Helen got up, saying,

'We'd better be getting home, I think. Come along.'

But Alban did not move.

'Do you know,' he said slowly, as if turning over a new idea in his mind, 'I think the Reverend Robert Ward is in love with you.'

'*What?*' exclaimed Helen in astonishment. 'With *me?* My dear Alban, wherever did you get such an idea?'

'Well, it's rather obvious, isn't it? You've only to see the way he looks at you.'

'I haven't noticed it.'

'*Haven't* you? You surprise me.'

Alban scrutinized his sister's face, but she showed no sign of what he perhaps expected to see, so he tried a new line.

'I suppose,' he said, 'that having lived with him from the beginning, as you might say – I don't mean literally! – you wouldn't notice it, but I must say, I think you must be rather blind if you haven't.'

'Considering that I never gave a moment's thought to the possibility, I don't see that I can be so blind. Such an idea never entered my head. I don't go about looking for them.'

'Neither do I; but I still fail to see how it can have escaped you. However, as you didn't seem to know, I imagine you don't mind.'

'Mind what?'

'I mean, don't mind whether he is in love with you or not.'

'He doesn't cause me any sleepless nights, if that's what you mean; but it's rather worrying, if it's true, as you say, to think that all this time he may have been mistaking my attitude for one which I never intended.'

'Well, of course, I don't know the gentleman, but I certainly should watch your step if you feel that way about it.'

'Thank you,' Helen smiled amusedly. 'I will take your advice.'

'Oh, I'm sorry! But you're always so kind and friendly to everybody – a lot of fellows would take it the wrong way.'

'He wouldn't.'

'No, I shouldn't imagine he would, although as I said before, I don't know him. He looks far too sensible to pursue anything he could see wasn't any good.'

'Even sensible people are sometimes persistent at such times,' said Helen, more to herself than to Alban.

'All the more reason for you not to give him any encouragement,' continued Alban, ignorant of the cause of her last remark.

There was a pause while she thought over his statement. It was very disturbing, and she wondered whether by any chance her manner could possibly have been misunderstood, even by the Reverend Ward, who, of all people, she knew was the least pretentious. Surely he could not be mistaken as to her feelings? Alban must be wrong. After all, he had never seen the man before, and how could he form a correct opinion on one brief meeting? But she was bound to admit the truth of what he had said, that whereas she, who had been in contact with him all the time, might not have been aware of any increase in his addresses, anybody else, coming suddenly amongst them like this, might see matters in quite a different light. Even so, he must have heard her speak about Charles, and must have realized that nobody else could possibly fill his place in her affections.

'Oh dear,' she said eventually. 'Why is life so complicated? Are you *sure*, Alban – how can you be, when you've only seen him for five minutes?'

'I'm quite sure. You keep your eyes open, and you'll see what I mean.' He got up. 'Of course he may not *say* anything – if he sees it's hopeless he probably never will say anything. It's rather improbable, but there you are.'

Helen was still standing with the cup in her hand, and it was Alban this time who urged their departure. They collected as many of the things as they could carry between them, and having switched off all the lights, they left the hall, locking the door behind them.

'Would you mind popping round to the Rectory with the key?' asked Helen of her brother, as they emerged into the darkness. 'He ought to have it tonight.' Besides the real reason, this provided a good excuse to get rid of him for a few minutes, and give her time to think alone. 'And Alban, I charge you not to mention a word of this to anybody,' she added.

Alban acquiesced and they parted in opposite directions.

Helen had plenty of time, during the walk home, to meditate and look at the question from all sides. When she came to consider it, she was forced to admit that the Reverend Ward had been much more attentive lately. He never gave himself away by word or look, but on more than one occasion he had accompanied her home when he had met her in the street after dark, and he had quite often chanced to pass by the school gate just as she was returning home after an evening's rehearsal. Was it not so much chance as she had imagined? When she called at the Rectory, *he* always opened the door; *he* it was, during tea, who saw that she was supplied; *he* helped her into her coat when she left and invariably asked if he could see her home. How glad she was that she had as invariably refused. And yet, none of these things was such that he could not perform it for anybody. She tried in vain to think of some little action, some hint, that would give a clue to his feelings, but there was nothing. He was so unassuming in his attentions, if such they were, that she found it extremely difficult to believe Alban's assertion; but in case it were true, she would be on her guard, and not let herself say or do anything that could give him the least bit of encouragement. With this conclusion, she dismissed the subject from her mind.

Gerald had gone to bed when she got home, but Penelope was still up, although in her pyjamas and dressing-gown, and fell upon her the moment she opened the door. Seizing her by the arm, she dragged her to the lounge, hardly allowing her time to deposit her burdens in the hall before pouring out her praises in such a way that Helen could not get a word in edgeways.

'Well!' was her father's greeting, and his wife added, 'There you are!' both senseless remarks when one comes to analyse them, but common to most families.

'Now dear, you must be hungry,' said Mrs Wentworth. 'Come and have something to eat. Where is Alban?'

'He's just taking the key back to the Rectory; he'll be along in a minute.'

'I'll go and put the kettle on,' said Penelope, dodging under her mother's arm as she was going through the door. Mrs Wentworth called her back again.

'No, no, Barbara will do that. You run along to bed.'

'Oh, Mother!' cried Penelope, in a please-don't-make-me-go-yet tone of voice, 'I wanted to stay and hear Helen.'

'Let her stay, Mother, just once,' begged Helen. 'I don't know what she expects to hear, but it *is* Christmas.'

'*Please!*' added Penelope in her most coaxing voice.

Mrs Wentworth gave in.

'Very well, you may stay up for half an hour, but not a minute longer.'

'*Thank* you!' cried Penelope.

They had crossed the hall to the dining room and now sat down round the table. It was laid with two places, and by the time Barbara had brought their supper in, Alban had returned and joined them.

Then began the praise, the reminiscences and stories of mishaps at the last moment which are the inevitable sequel of any show, and enjoyed by great and small alike. In a village as small as Edmuston, where few events of importance occurred to colour the monochrome of daily life, it would be a subject for discussion for many weeks, whether it was over a pint of bitter in the local, over the garden wall on wash day, or over the counter in the shops. Every household in the village was talking about it that evening, not the least of them being the Wentworths.

Penelope retired obediently, if reluctantly, when her half hour was ended, and one by one the rest of the family followed suit. Helen climbed into bed with a feeling of relief now that the concert was over and of great pleasure at its success. The only thing which spoilt her peace of mind was the anxiety occasioned by Alban's disturbing, if unfounded, suggestion.

John Mainwaring
(1945)

Charles
(1945)

Chapter XXXII

The morning of Christmas Eve was spent in making final preparations for the morrow, tying up odd presents which had been overlooked and adjusting decorations which had somehow got out of place. Alban went off to collect the rest of their belongings from the church hall, then he and Helen sorted them out and put them away.

Towards mid-day the front door bell rang, and Helen, who was passing through the hall at the time, went to see who it was. A fair-haired youth of about eighteen years was standing on the doorstep. He was so like Charles that she was quite startled.

'Hullo, Helen,' said the youth cheerfully. Even the voice was similar, but the likeness soon ceased to be surprising when she realized that it was John Mainwaring.

'Why, John!' she exclaimed. 'This is a surprise! Come in.'

John entered the house.

'Take off your coat,' said Helen, and while John proceeded to do so, went on, 'Well, this *is* nice. What brought you over here?'

'I was in Mereford, so I thought I'd come over and see you.'

'I'm so glad. Come and sit down and let's hear all the news.'

She ushered him into the lounge and called the rest of the family. It was most refreshing to see him, and he was so like his brother that she could hardly keep her eyes off him. Although Alban was his particular friend, he was none the less popular with the others. Philip was the only one who was indifferent, for the very reason of his being like Charles; for no amount of 'moralizing' would ever alter his feelings towards his sister's best friend. They all came in, even Philip, to welcome their guest and press him to stay for lunch. He accepted with the proper degree of reluctance to encroach on their hospitality; but he was human, and had planned his visit in the hope that he would be asked. Also, as he had no idea where he should eat if they did not ask him, he was very glad to accept.

They all plied him with questions, and learnt that he was now Head

Boy at Rugby, and going to be a doctor. Ursula, who came between him and Charles, was in her last year at Oxford, where she was reading History; she was going to teach.

Helen was burning to ask after Charles, but she felt that, just for the moment, she had not sufficient control over herself; John's sudden appearance had thrown her slightly off her balance. Penelope saved her any embarrassment by enquiring eagerly at the first opportunity,

'Have you heard from Charlie lately?'

'Yes, we had a long letter from him yesterday,' replied John. 'By the way, that reminds me,' he added, diving into his inner breast pocket and producing a fat-looking envelope. He took out two snapshots and handed them to Helen. 'He sent these. I thought you might like to have them.'

Helen tried to look composed as she took them, but she could not help smiling as she looked at them; they were so very good and he seemed to be so happy. Both were taken in deep snow.

'You can keep them if you like,' repeated John.

'May I really? Don't you want them?'

'No, it's all right, we've got some more.'

'Thank you very much. I'd love to have them.'

They were passed round for general inspection and returned to their new owner, who put them in her pocket.

John stayed until three o'clock or so, then departed, intending to get home before it was dark. He carried many messages and a good deal of happiness with him, for like Charles, he was naturally contented, and loved home and homely families.

'John is a nice boy,' was Mrs Wentworth's comment when he had gone.

'Yes,' agreed her husband, 'he is. So is Charlie. They are a charming family.' Even so, Charles was the one he liked best.

The carol-singing expedition was due to commence at six o'clock and Helen had asked to be allowed to have her choir round to the house for 'a good tea' first. Mrs Wentworth was rather alarmed at the idea when she heard of it, thinking she was about to be swamped by all the children in the village, but when she learnt that there would only be sixteen of them including Helen, she was quite willing to co-operate. An enormous spread was laid out on the dining-room table, which nearly collapsed beneath the weight, and by half past four all the choristers were assembled in the lounge and longing to attack the meal. They had often been

John Mainwaring
(1945)

Alban
(1945)

to the house in ones and twos for odd meals after music lessons, but never before so many together, and the occasion overawed them. They became painfully shy and said 'Yes, Sir,' and 'No, Ma'am' when they were spoken to, otherwise remaining self-consciously silent, either staring at the floor or casting furtive glances round the room. Even Helen failed to make them feel perfectly at ease. It was Alban who finally broke the ice, by bouncing in through the door and announcing,

'Tea-boat, m' hearties! All laid out in the Mess. Tread the deck gently or you'll go through to the hold. Now, who's for the dining room and hot teacakes?'

Nobody could resist so tempting an offer and they all laughed, immediately relieving the tension.

Places were found for everybody in the room, and with Mrs Wentworth presiding over the teapot and Alban over the teacakes keeping warm under a cover by the fire, the meal commenced in very gay style. Food is a wonderful uplifter of spirits, and even the hardest man has been known to soften almost to the point of becoming amiable under the spell of good English roast beef. This was hardly a feast of roast beef, but as the company assembled to partake of it was neither hard nor unfriendly, a lighter meal was all that was necessary. The effect was the same, and many confidences were exchanged over thick slices of bread and jam, cakes and sugar-biscuits that would never have been divulged in normal circumstances.

When no more could be eaten and even Johnny Deane, whose appetite was reputed to be the largest in the village, declared he could not manage another thing, and the children were getting tired of sitting still, Helen sent them off to play in the loft with Alban, Penelope and Gerald, while she and her mother helped Barbara to clear away and wash up the tea things; she said she would call them in half an hour and they must be ready for a final rehearsal before setting out on the evening's excursion. As the last shouting youngster disappeared up the stairs, the four elders with one accord looked at each other and uttered exclamations of exhaustion.

'Poof!' cried Philip, 'What a crowd!'

'My poor head is going round and round!' complained his mother. 'Those children!'

'I sometimes wonder, my dear, how you ever manage to keep your sanity,' said Mr Wentworth.

'Oh, they're not always like this!' laughed Helen. Being used to them, she was the first to recover.

'I should hope not!' ejaculated Mrs Wentworth.

The clearing up did not take long with four pairs of hands, and with Barbara washing and Helen drying, the job was soon done.

Mr Wentworth retired to his study for some well-earned peace; Mrs Wentworth and Philip occupied themselves with the weekly darning and books, and Helen went into the lounge to prepare for the final rehearsal. She gave the children the full promised half hour then pulled the bell in the hall which rang on the top landing, and thus recalled them to more sober things. They had had a good romp and were quite ready to sing. No mishaps occurred during the practice, and they had their coats on ready to leave promptly at six o'clock. They were bade good luck in the hall, and then Penelope opened the front door. Thick white flakes were falling outside.

'Boy! It's snowing!' she cried joyfully.

The children crowded round the door as if they found it hard to believe. When they saw that it was genuine and not just Penelope's imagination, they let out a shout of jubilation and surged forth into the night.

'Goodbye! Goodbye!' they called; then remembering their manners, forgotten in the excitement of the moment. 'Thank you very much for the tea!'

'Goodbye,' responded Mr Wentworth. 'We're glad you could come.'

'Where are you going first?' asked Mrs Wentworth, as Helen made to follow her tribe.

'Doctor Kennedy,' answered Helen with a smile.

Penelope groaned.

'I'm glad I'm not coming then,' she said.

'No – well, goodbye.'

'Goodbye, and good luck!'

'Thanks. We'll be round here sometime during the evening, so don't go to bed. Goodbye.'

Armed with torches and bicycle lamps with which to light their path, and their hands clutching their little carol books, thrust deep into their pockets for warmth, they set out, chatting and humming snatches of their tunes, every now and then pausing to rejoice over the snow, which all had feared would disappoint them and mean yet another mild Christmas.

Doctor Kennedy lived in a large square house on the main street and his door was soon reached. A convenient lamp post just opposite provided all the light they needed and, dividing into their four parts, they grouped themselves round it. Johnny Deane had brought his pipe to give the note, and everybody hummed his harmony to get it fixed into his head. Helen counted – one – two – three – and they broke into *O Come All Ye Faithful*, one of the simplest, and yet most pleasing harmoniously, of all the more popular carols.

The doctor was not expecting this visitation, and being occupied at the time, was not a little annoyed at the disturbance. He strode over to his window with the intention of telling the singers to be off, for although he was not really unkind, he was extremely busy; but as he neared the window, his conscience got the better of him and he turned to go and open his door. He listened for a few seconds and decided that these were no ordinary carol singers, of the 'Hark-the-Herald-Angels-go-jingle-jangle-jingle' variety, and he turned to the window once more to see who they were. He pulled the curtain aside, threw up the sash and leant out. The cold air and snowflakes hit him in the face, but he did not mind them, and when the singers, hearing a movement, looked up, he recognized them, withdrew hastily and came downstairs. By this time they had finished *O Come All Ye Faithful* and were halfway through a second carol. This they sang to its close while the doctor and his housekeeper stood in the doorway.

'Good evening, Doctor Kennedy,' called Helen brightly.

'Good evening,' responded the doctor. 'What's all this about – disturbing me at this hour of the night?' He twinkled fiercely round the company.

'We thought you might like it.'

'Oh, you did, did you?' twinkling even more.

'Don't you?' demanded one of the children bolder than the rest – they were all intimidated by the doctor.

'Eh?' he uttered in surprise. But the child's boldness deserted him, and he did not repeat his question. Helen took it up for him.

'As you are so unappreciative, we won't trouble you any longer.'

'Rubbish! Very good concert. What are you collecting for, eh?'

'Oh, we're not collecting for anything.'

'What, dividing the profits amongst yourselves, are you?'

'No!' cried the children indignantly.

'Well, if you're not collecting and not keeping the money for yourselves, what are you going to do with it?'

'We are not collecting any money at all,' Helen explained. 'We're doing it for the love of it and hope to give some people a little pleasure.' She could not help giving extra stress to the 'some people'.

'I see,' he said. 'Well, can we offer you a cup of tea, or anything?'

'No, thanks. We've just had a meal.'

Helen and the carol singers (1945).

'Not allowed to do anything, eh? Well, where else have you been?'

'Nowhere. You are the first.'

'Oh! Well, good luck to your further efforts.'

'Thank you.'

'Thank *you*. Goodnight.'

'Goodnight!' cried the children. 'Merry Christmas!'

They passed on to the next port of call. They planned to include the homes of all the singers and as many of the others as they had time for, finishing up at the Rectory, where Mr Moore had invited them all to come and have some cocoa and buns as near half past nine as possible.

There was a delicious feeling of Christmas in the air, not only because of carol-singing but because, as the evening progressed and the snow went on falling, the ground and every corner that could trap it was being covered deeper and deeper in the white mantle, traditionally necessary to complete the scene. Nobody would deny that Christmas feels more like Christmas if there is snow on the ground.

Every household they called at welcomed them and wanted to give them something; it was quite a new experience to have anything done for the pure love of the thing, and they liked it.

'That's Miss Wentworth,' they said to each other. 'God bless her!'

Chapter XXXIII

They arrived at the Lodge about half past eight and sang their best in the hall with all the lights turned out and only the firelight flickering in the lounge, where the family was sitting listening. Helen had arranged this with Alban and it proved to be an excellent idea, for the children were not distracted by their surroundings or embarrassed at having 'Miss Wentworth's' parents, brothers and sister in sight. The same parents, brothers and sister came out of the lounge to applaud them when they had completed their performance, and sent them off once more upon their way, all with half-a-dozen toffees in their pockets.

They went to three or four other houses and by the time conversation, congratulations on the previous evening and seasonal greetings had been exchanged, it was getting on for half past nine and they had to direct their steps to the Rectory.

Gathering round the old porch, they sang *Silent Night.* Helen knew it was Mr Moore's favourite, and she chose it first for that reason. The Rector and his nephew came to the door and stood in the porch until they had finished, then Mr Moore welcomed them and asked them to come in; but Helen declared they had not yet earned their reward and should sing at least one more carol before going in. Mr Moore did not agree, but Helen was firm, and the children were eager to sing another as it was nearly the end of their expedition, so he had to give in. *Lullay Myn Lyking* gave an opportunity for little Dicky Wilde to show what he could do. His voice was sweet and clear, though his pronunciation was not all it might be. That did not matter, for the spirit of the words was there, whether they were sung in the accents of the Sussex Downs or the 'purest' English of the BBC.

At the close of the last refrain both Mr Moore and the Reverend Ward gave them a round of applause and bade them come in. They filed into the hall with much brushing of clothes and stamping of snow-covered boots and shoes on the step, and crowded into the bright Rectory dining room. Mr Moore, in his usual pleasant way, succeeded in finding a seat for them all, and he and his nephew supplied them with cups of steaming cocoa, sweet and frothy, and delicious cakes that almost melted in the mouth. They soon drew the children out into conversation, for now that Reverend Ward was no longer a stranger in their midst, they had accepted him as a friend and decided they liked him. He had the same serene, quiet manner as his uncle, with an added mildness that gave no clue to the unplumbed depths of his character. This very mildness was his handicap, for on first impression he appeared too ineffectual to accomplish the strenuous tasks of a village parson; but this impression was only fleeting, and beneath his peaceful exterior there burned a fire of ardent faith which gave eloquence to his words and force to his sermons.

The old man and the young moved about among their guests, filling a cup here and replenishing a plate there, chatting with the youngsters and thoroughly enjoying themselves. Both were very fond of children, Mr Moore especially. At one point he found himself next to Helen, and paused for a few minutes' conversation.

'Well, my dear, you have given us a delightful entertainment, and I wish we could do something to show how much we appreciate it.'

'You are very kind; but we are greatly indebted to you, Mr Moore. I don't know what we'd have done last night if you hadn't let us use the church hall.'

'I'm only too pleased that you should have had it. You have only to ask, if you want it, you know.'

'Thank you very much. I will.'

'Do you find it easy to train the children?'

'Oh yes – they are very good on the whole. We derive a lot of fun from it.'

'I'm sure you do. Have you heard anything from Charlie lately?' he asked, abruptly changing the subject.

'Yes, we had his brother John in for lunch today.'

'Did you?'

'Yes, he dropped in quite unexpectedly, and it *was* nice to see him. He's awfully like Charlie, you know. In fact, for a minute, I really thought it was he.'

The Reverend Ward, who was talking to one of the children behind where Helen was sitting, heard what she said and could no longer give his whole attention to his partner. He had to listen, and while he tried to appear interested in the family troubles of his small friend, he was in reality not hearing a word, merely saying 'Yes' and 'No' automatically. Helen's voice and the obvious pleasure with which she mentioned this

'Charlie' rang in his ears and obliterated all other sounds. In one flash of insight, quickened as it was by his own experience of the most sacred of human emotions, he realized that the happy dream he had been nursing and developing almost since his first meeting with her was tumbling about his ears and forcing him to wake and face the facts. For a second a pang of jealousy caused a shadow to cross his face – a natural feeling when one learns that those whom one had considered one's exclusive property, whether they are or not, have equal or higher claims of affection elsewhere. But the Reverend Ward was so used to thinking of himself last that the jealous feeling was only momentary. God, Who knew all things, would give him strength to bear this. As she could never be his, he would see that she, of all people, should never know how he felt about her. He would cover his heart and throw himself with renewed ardour into the service of God. Few men have the courage to do this unflinchingly; least of all those who have not a deep faith in the goodness of the Almighty, Who alone has the power to comfort and revive.

When he stirred from this reverie Helen was showing his uncle some photographs. He made an excuse to find another chocolate cake for his companion, passing behind Mr Moore so that he could catch a glimpse of Helen's face. It was glowing with happiness – yes, there was no doubt. Well, he would leave it for God and time to heal.

The children had eaten all they could and were becoming silent with weariness. Helen was quick to sense the atmosphere and made to go. Mr Moore, understanding, did not detain them. They wrapped themselves up and thanked their hosts most heartily for their kindness, and followed each other into the hall. The Reverend Ward preceded them to open the door, and he and Mr Moore shook hands with them all and wished them a 'Merry Christmas'. Their rosy faces, framed with a variety of scarves, caps and hoods made a pleasant contrast with the gleaming white snow, which was still falling steadily, and were a greeting in themselves. Helen waited until they had all stepped out on to the path, then gripping the Rector's hand, said,

'Thank you so much, Mr Moore.'

He held on to her hand as he answered,

'My dear, we are only too pleased to do anything we can for you who do so much for us.'

'Oh, Mr Moore, I don't do much.'

'But you do – doesn't she, Robert?'

'Yes, indeed! We are much indebted to you.' The Reverend Ward smiled his grave smile, and there was a wistful look in his eyes which Helen saw and, owing to Alban's timely warning, understood.

'You are very kind. Thank you.'

She turned to shake hands with the Reverend Ward.

'The success of my work and your appreciation is ample reward; if there were anything more I could do for you, I would be only too glad to do it. Goodnight.'

'Goodnight,' he replied dazedly. The grasp of her hand and the unmistakable look of sympathy she had given him as she said those words – could she possibly know?

'Goodnight, Mr Moore, and thank you.'

'Goodnight, my dear.'

'Merry Christmas!' cried all the children in chorus. 'Merry Christmas!'

They moved away, picking a careful path through the snow, which was now several inches thick and still falling. It was going to be a 'proper' Christmas after all.

The porch, which was built out square from the door, with the entrance not at the front, but facing sideways down the path towards the gate, had an electric light fixed in the roof and was always illuminated after dark until the inmates of the Rectory went to bed. This light cast a glow for some yards round the porch, and it was only when the carol-singers were a step away from the gate that they could no longer be seen. Mr Moore and the Reverend Ward stood and watched them disappear and called a final goodnight before going back into the house.

'Well,' said Mr Moore, as they heard the gate close behind the last, 'that was a most enjoyable little interlude.'

'Yes,' said the Reverend Ward inattentively. She *must* have known.

'Helen has trained those children amazingly well.'

'Yes.' How *could* she have known?

'You'd better come in, Robert. I don't want any colds tomorrow.'

'No.' Had he, after all, given himself away? He made no effort to move from his position leaning against the wall of the porch, and allowed his thoughts to wander back to the realm of the might-have-been. Mr Moore looked at his motionless figure and its dreamy attitude. He had a suspicion.

'Robert!'

'Yes, Uncle?'

'Are you coming in?'

'No, I think I'll stay and watch the snow for a bit it's so beautiful.'

Mr Moore's suspicion was increased to a certainty and a full summing up of the situation.

'I would rather you came inside, Robert,' was all he said. It had its effect. The Reverend Ward would never do anything his uncle did not want him to do. He turned and walked slowly into the house, halting by the table in the hall to pick up a book and flick its pages before his unseeing eyes. Mr Moore shut the door and came and stood beside him. He put a fatherly hand on his shoulder, and said,

'I know, my boy, I know.'

The Reverend Ward put down the book, but he did not speak.

'Is there no hope?' asked Mr Moore gently.

'No.'

'How do you know?'

' "Charlie".'

Mr Moore understood.

'Come and sit down by the fire,' he said. 'It's warmer in there.'

The Reverend Ward felt his unspoken sympathy and they walked together into the drawing room. Remembering his decision of not giving in, he put his thoughts in order and raised his head. Nobody, not even his uncle, should see that he was weak enough to be overcome, even for a few minutes. He was ashamed that he had been discovered, for until now he had thought that nobody shared his secret; and yet *she* knew – in some strange, unaccountable way, *she* knew. Well, as that was a part of him that would never know expression, he would never refer to it.

Mr Moore noticed his enlivened manner, as he stood against the mantelpiece and talked about what they would do on the morrow; and knowing his nephew, realized that he did not wish to have any more said on the subject, and respected his silence.

The children were happy with their outing and all declared they must come again next year. They went the round of their various homes, saying goodnight to one here and one there, all wishing each other a 'Merry Christmas!' before they went into their houses, until they had all been safely restored to their families.

Helen stumped home happily through the snow, listening to the church bells, which would be ringing until half past ten. They chimed a Christmas message of peace in the stillness of the night, a blessing the full significance of which she found she appreciated more than gifts and parties, pleasant and seasonable though they were. She thought of the tiny Baby born again each year in the hearts of his disciples, symbolizing the gift of eternal opportunity of renewed life and endeavour; that not only one isolated spot, but the whole wide world celebrated this night the Christ Mass, that all thoughts were turned towards it; the angels' song of love, everlasting yet ever young, and above all, the essential simplicity of the Christmas message. That the festival of the Christ Child's birth should be made an excuse for excessive eating and drinking was wholly repugnant to her and she felt how very misdirected were the thoughts of those who believed that it was necessary – how sadly astray were their lives!

She thought only happy thoughts of Christmas as she trudged homewards, but thoughts which nevertheless brought a lump to her throat; Christmas Eve always did. One of the beautiful carols they had sung that evening expressed her feelings better than words and she began to sing it softly to herself:

As up the wood I took my way the oaks were brown and bare,
And all about the snow lay white and bitter blew the air.

As up the wood I took my way the night began to fall,
When out a star shone fair and bright and I heard a sweet voice call.

'Come on, come on, thou weary man,' the sweet voice cried to me,
'For in yon shed where the cattle are I have good sight for thee.'

Then suddenly turned the snow to rose and the bare oaks grew to green,
The bitter wind was a gentle air and I felt not fear nor teen.

For Golden Gabriel took my hand and brought me to the shed
Where mid the cattle sat Queen Mary and rocked Lord Jesu's bed.

Then hie good shepherds and masters mine, we'll cease to moil and grieve,
For this brave Babe is the Lord of all and this is Christmas Eve!

By the time she had reached the end of the carol her feet had brought her nearly to her own gate and she covered the rest of the way in silence.

The children had all gone to bed when she got in, even Philip, who was not usually an early bird. Mr and Mrs Wentworth were sitting reading over the fire in the lounge. She pulled up a buffet and joined them, stretching her hands out to the fire to warm them.

'Well, how did it go?' asked Mrs Wentworth

'Very well. They sang really beautifully.'

'I'm so glad,' said Mr Wentworth.

'I don't know whether it's the atmosphere out-of-doors, or the fact that it was snowing, or its being Christmas Eve, or what, but they sang a lot better tonight than they have ever sung at rehearsals.'

'Good! I was sure you would be successful,' said Mr Wentworth, beaming with pleasure, and his wife added, 'How did the people like it? We've had several others round while you were out.'

'Have you? Oh, I think they quite enjoyed it. They seemed to, anyway.'

'I'm sure they did.'

'We shall miss Mr Moore very much when he goes,' Helen murmured, thinking over the recent visit, and how he won the hearts of the children.

'Yes, we shall.' Mr Wentworth felt sad at the thought of his coming departure, for he would lose a dear friend in Mr Moore; they had had so many happy hours together talking religion, philosophy and books, or sitting silent by each other's fireside, reading or dreaming in the content of a relationship which needed no words to express itself.

'We shall indeed!' agreed Mrs Wentworth. 'I'm sure this young man Ward won't be a patch on Mr Moore.'

'Give him a chance, my dear – he is somewhat younger!' exclaimed Mr Wentworth.

'He hasn't had anything like his experience,' added Helen, 'but I think he will prove to be far better than anyone imagines at present.'

'He is so mild! He hasn't any go about him,' objected Mrs Wentworth.

'That is only a blind. Underneath he is one of the most ardent men I have ever met, and I'm sure, if need arose, you would find he had just as much go as little Johnny Deane. He doesn't show it, that's all.'

'Well, I hope he turns out better than he seems,' said Mrs Wentworth, sticking to her point.

They stared at the fire for a few minutes, then Helen got up.

'I think we'd better go to bed, or we shall still be up when Santa Claus comes, and that would never do!' she said.

'No, indeed!' agreed Mr Wentworth. He picked up his book and put the guard in front of the fire, securing it in place by leaning the tongs against it with their legs stretched out in the hearth. Mrs Wentworth rose slowly from her chair and plumped up the cushions. Leaving Helen to see that all doors and windows were locked or shut properly, they proceeded upstairs to their room.

Half an hour later, when Santa Claus had filled the children's stockings – for they still hung them up; they could not bear to give up one of the most thrilling of Christmas institutions – Helen crept out of bed, found the two they had filled for their father and mother, and tiptoed across the landing to hang them on their door handle.

Everything was very quiet, and she had a final peep out of the window to look at the weather. It was still snowing hard, and she was glad to be inside. She wondered how Charles would be spending Christmas. She did hope they would have a good time – it was such a hopeless place to be in for it; but she would hear in a day or two, when he had had time to write.

She climbed back into bed, and it was nice, after the chill air out of it, to find it warm within. She snuggled down amongst the bedclothes and was soon asleep.

Chapter XXXIV

Penelope and Gerald were awake long before anybody else on Christmas morning, and both lay wondering what the time was and wishing their mother would get up. They were not allowed to look at their stockings by themselves or before the appointed hour, and they were far too honest to do so, although Penelope did creep out of bed just to make sure that Santa Claus had not forgotten her. Satisfied on that point, she got back into bed and wished even harder that someone would make a move.

After what seemed like hours she heard her mother's bedroom door open, and knew it must be about seven o'clock. She scrambled out of bed once more and waylaid her on the landing.

'What's the time?' she asked.

'A quarter to seven. Not nearly time to get up yet. Get back into bed this minute.'

'How long will you be?'

'About a quarter of an hour. Get back to bed; I'll call you when I'm ready.'

'Righto.'

Penelope returned to bed.

At last Mrs Wentworth's tea was made and brought upstairs for herself and her husband. She called her children, finding Penelope and Gerald all ready in their slippers and dressing-gowns and only waiting for the word 'go' to unhook their stockings from the handles of their chests of drawers and tear into their parents' bedroom.

They all appeared more or less at once, shouting 'Merry Christmas!' to each other, and climbed into the big double bed, which Mr Wentworth, in his dressing-gown, propped up against pillows, was still occupying. He moved over as far as he could without endangering his existence at the edge of the bed, and Gerald and Philip squeezed in next to him. Helen, Penelope and Alban sat under the eiderdown with their backs resting against the high foot of the bed, and Mrs Wentworth hovered round, filling her husband's cup and laughing over the treasures produced from her family's stockings in the intervals of looking at her own.

Shrieks of laughter and exclamations of delight greeted each new treasure as it was pulled out. Mr Wentworth looked 'quite the thing' with a tiny hat made from a walnut shell with a cardboard brim and trimmed with ribbon, tied on his head. Everyone munched happily and Mrs Wentworth enjoyed her chocolate pipe, for all her loathing of tobacco. Santa Claus seemed to know exactly what would be most acceptable for each of them, from the different tricks and gadgets sticking out at the top of their stockings to the first tangerine of the season stuffed into the toe.

The children were loth to move when the last thing had been extracted, and lingered in the warm bed even after Mrs Wentworth had said they must go and get ready for breakfast.

Helen and Philip moved first and challenged the rest of the family to a race, to see who could be ready first. They accepted and scrambled out of the bed and into their slippers.

'Bet you I win!' cried Penelope, disappearing through the door with her box of oddments.

'Bet you don't!' countered Alban, as he followed her. 'You've got to wash behind the ears, you know!'

Then there was a rush for towels and soap, and while they were getting washed and dressed their father and mother were able to clear up and get ready in peace.

Alban won the race. He was used to rapid changes and had worked out a system of procedure on which he could not improve. Penelope and Gerald were close upon his tracks and tore down the stairs in hot pursuit. Philip appeared a few minutes later and Helen last of all. Penelope laughed scornfully as her sister appeared, declaring she would never be any good if the house caught fire. Helen replied that her hair had refused to go up and had caused her a lot of exasperation and delay.

They stood round the table admiring the Christmas tree, then Penelope ran to the window and looked out over the garden. It had snowed all night, and the bumps and uneven pieces of ground were smoothed out under their white blanket. The sky was heavy and grey, and looked as if it would produce more snow any minute.

'*Isn't* it lovely?' she cried, her eyes glistening as she gazed. 'Look at the bird-table – there's about a foot of snow on top of it!'

The others joined her.

'What do birds do when it's like this?' asked Gerald, watching a solitary one hopping about outside.

'Stay in bed if they've any sense,' responded Philip. 'Erh! I hate snow.'

'Oh, you are silly!' said Penelope. 'I love it.'

'Wait till you're my age…' began Philip.

'Hrr-ahem!' interrupted Helen with a twinkle.

'I'm rather inclined to agree that a warm bed is preferable,' said Alban, 'or a fire.'

Mr and Mrs Wentworth came in just then, and they all sat down.

'Is there a post today?' asked Penelope.

'I don't know – I shouldn't think so,' replied Mrs Wentworth, while Helen added, 'Oh, surely not.'

'I wish there were!'

'Why? You've had millions of cards. What more do you want?' enquired Alban.

'Millions of cards more.'

'Well, you won't get them,' said Philip decidedly, 'because there isn't a post today.'

'I might get them tomorrow.'

'Oh, eat your breakfast!' cried Alban.

'Who's preaching this morning?' Mr Wentworth asked, to change the subject.

'Mr Moore,' replied Helen.

'Hm, thank you,' murmured Mr Wentworth. Secretly he was glad, but he would not have said so, not wishing to cast aspersions, intentional or otherwise, on the Reverend Ward's abilities. He liked the young man well enough, but he could never feel the same towards him as he did towards the older one. Mr Moore's exodus would be a sad loss for Edmuston.

The little church was packed almost to overflowing, for not only was it Christmas, but it was also the last time Mr Moore would be preaching there in his official capacity. All the usual carols were sung; indeed, the amount of singing on Christmas morning was always greater than any other part of the service, for Mr Moore knew that the majority of his congregation preferred to sing themselves rather than listen to long passages of Scripture, however appropriate. His address was short and seasonable, and he somehow managed, each year, to find a new theme on which to speak – a difficult task when he had preached for nearly fifty years.

After the service he came down from the pulpit and shook hands with everyone in the porch, wishing them all the season's greetings and receiving them in return. The snow glistened in the sunlight, for the sky had cleared by now, and the bright coats and hats of the people picking their way down the path, or standing chatting in little groups, showed up in cheerful contrast to the dazzling white. The atmosphere was sharp and frosty and the haze over the down in the distance was that peculiar shade of grey-blue that is only seen on a cold sunny day after snow. Everybody's breath condensed as it came in contact with the air, and Penelope, after watching it for several minutes, intrigued, remarked that the company looked like so many kettles boiling.

'Merry Christmas!' rang sharp and clear from one group to another and the people began to disperse to hurry home to their turkeys and plum puddings. The closing bars of *Jesu Joy of Man's Desiring* sounded sweetly from within the church as Mr Moore bade the last person to leave a 'Happy Christmas', and Helen, turning to have a parting look at the beautiful doorway, every gargoyle and carving capped with a heap of snow, wished that she had her camera with her and that she could take a coloured film of the picture.

The Wentworths covered the way home to lunch as fast as deep snow would permit. Gerald and Penelope threw one or two snowballs at each other, but their mother had too much respect for their best clothes to allow it to continue very long. A few minutes after this Penelope, showing off a jump in the snow to prove that her leg was now mended enough for her to play hockey next term, landed in the middle of an unexpected snow drift and sank up to well above her knees. Gerald shrieked with laughter and Alban said,

'Serves you right!'

'Meow! It's gone all down inside my boots,' moaned Penelope. 'And you needn't laugh,' she added, turning to Gerald. 'It's not funny.'

'Oh, but it is!' replied her brother.

'Wait till you sit in it – I'd like to see you laugh then.'

But Gerald did not sit in it and they reached the house without further mishap.

No time was ever lost over lunch because 'Cookie' and Barbara left immediately everything was cleared away and naturally liked to be off as soon as possible. There was still time to enjoy the turkey, with all its extras, and the mince pies which followed – for Mrs Wentworth did not believe in having too many rich things at once, and left the plum pudding until Boxing Day – and they did full justice to Cookie's excellent work.

'When can we open our presents?' asked Penelope during the meal.

'How do you know there are any?' responded her mother.

‘Of course there are!’

‘She looked,’ accused Gerald.

‘Yes, I did,’ Penelope admitted shamelessly. ‘I got on to the bed to see how the pile was growing on top of the wardrobe.’

‘Then I don’t think you should be allowed to have any,’ said Mr Wentworth, with a glance at his wife.

‘No indeed!’ cried Mrs Wentworth. ‘You certainly shan’t have any after that!’

‘Not till Mother and I have had our forty winks, anyway,’ added Mr Wentworth.

‘Well, that’s what I wanted to know,’ persisted Penelope. ‘How long are you going to be snoozing?’

‘At least two hours. And why are you so anxious? You’ve got all Father Christmas’s things to look at. Surely they’ll last you till three o’clock?’

‘Of course they will,’ declared Helen, ‘and if they don’t, we’ll go for a walk on the down and have a snow fight.’

‘Good idea,’ agreed Alban. ‘Pipe down, Penny and eat your lunch.’

Penelope pulled a face at her brother but did as she was bid.

Chapter XXXV

When Mr and Mrs Wentworth had retired to the lounge for their forty winks, Penelope attacked Helen on the subject of going out.

'I say, Helen, were you serious just now when you said we could go for a walk on the down?'

'Well – er – I –' began Helen. If the truth be known, she had merely said that to satisfy her sister's insatiable curiosity and had not really meant what she said; but Penelope obviously liked the prospect, and she saw that it would keep them all from becoming bored and getting into mischief; so she went on hastily, 'Er, yes I was.'

'Well, let's go?'

'Certainly, if you're quite sure you want to.'

'I do. What about the others? Boys! Coming for a walk?'

'Lord, no,' grunted Philip. 'Who on earth wants to go for a walk on a day like this?'

'Do you good,' said Alban. 'Very bad, all this stuffing indoors. Fresh air, that's what you want. And you –' turning to Gerald.

Gerald pulled a face, but submitted.

'Oh, come on, Phil!' cried Penelope pleadingly.

'Yes, do come,' added Helen. 'We haven't all been out together for ages.'

'We went this morning.' Philip really did not relish the prospect.

'Oh, but that was different. Do come. I want somebody to talk to.'

'All right.' Philip gave in reluctantly. 'But don't take me very far.'

'Just on the down – that's not very far.'

Ten minutes later they were all ready in the hall, muffled up in overcoats, scarves, hoods and gloves and boots, and felt equipped to defy the coldest of days. They stumped through the twitt'n, avoiding the drifts, and came out into the main street. It was a very different scene from that of a few months before. Everything that could trap the snow had done so, making the simplest shapes assume the most grotesque and incongruous proportions. Hardly any traffic had passed down the street, and where it had, the imprint of the tyres had left ribbons of compressed macaroni patterns and narrow channels which it was fun to walk in and try not to overbalance. A large white tom cat had found this and was carefully treading its velvet-padded way homewards, a streak of dirty grey against its white background. Helen remarked that puss had not been washed in Persil, and they passed on. They met nobody and even the birds had flown away.

Penelope and Gerald followed the car tracks, with the others behind them. It was easier to climb the hill thus than trudge up through the untrodden snow. It was a case of single-line traffic in each track, for only one car has passed that way. When the gate on to the down was reached they encountered deeper snow where the wind had blown it into weird shapes. Somehow, they managed to push the gate open – and there were no attempts to vault over it this time – and having floundered through eighteen inches of snow, emerged on to the pathway over the down. Here, although it was covered, and indistinguishable from the turf on each side, the snow was not deep, and here and there the land was blown nearly bare; but every bush and pebble had its windward side covered and piled with snow. Penelope shrieked with delight when she saw it, declaring she had been learning all about winds in Geography and that this was a perfect example of what 'Old Whatnot' had been talking about.

Helen warned everybody to keep together, as snow was treacherous even when you knew the area as well as the back of your own hand. For this reason Rex had not been let off the lead, although he would have dearly loved to have been.

When at last the top of the down was reached everyone was feeling delightfully warm and had cheeks glowing with the cold air and hard work. It was strange being up there on Christmas afternoon, with not a soul in sight, nor even a car on the road below. All around was an endless and undisturbed sea of white – not even the road could be distinguished. Just slopes merging gently into each other as they stretched away into the distance, where the grey-blue mist enveloped them and you could not tell where snow ended and sky began. Only the village was visible as a separate thing; the smoke from the chimneys curled with the wind, and the walls of the houses where there was no snow showed up strangely dark against their background. Even the sun looked very wintry, although he was doing his best to be cheerful.

Helen gazed at the scene in wonder, thinking that in summer it was hardly more beautiful. Philip shivered and thought he had never seen anything so dreary in his life. Alban took off his gloves and blew on his fingers, wondering whether he would be murdered if he asked for a second piece of Christmas cake at tea. Penelope looked round for prospective tobogganing sites and anticipated fun ahead. Gerald, who had come out to walk and not to stand and stare, soon got bored and threw a snowball at Alban to relieve his feelings. Alban, wakened suddenly from his dreams of food, retaliated, and soon all of them were engaged in a lively snowball fight. They hurled snow at each other for five or ten minutes and then, exhausted with the effort of trying to aim straight and avoid being hit at the same time, ceased by mutual agreement and went on with their walk.

The snow lay thicker on the far slope of the down and progress was difficult. All signs of the track disappeared and knowledge of the right direction was their only guide. Even Penelope did not venture far ahead of the rest and Helen had no necessity to issue orders for her to keep with them.

As they descended the slope, the wind, which, although not strong, blew chill on the top of the down, grew less until they could hardly feel it at all. They went on slowly, picking their way carefully, for nobody had been along previously to show where drifts had collected, until the snow was almost over the tops of Gerald's boots. Here Helen called a halt, and said she thought they had better turn back.

'Oh, Helen,' cried Penelope mournfully, 'do let's go on – it's only a little way to the bottom.'

'No, it's getting too deep to be safe. Gerry's nearly out of his depth already. Besides, we want to be back by a quarter past three and it's half past two already.'

'Yes, let's get home,' said Philip, who was not enjoying the walk at all. 'It's beastly cold up here.'

'But it's just as quick that way,' persisted Penelope, unwilling to give up her fun without a struggle. 'We can carry Gerry.'

'Ooh-hoo! Can we!' exclaimed Alban. 'You speak for yourself – *I'm* not going to!'

'No, come on; we must go back this way,' said Helen firmly. 'The known is better than the unknown, and I'm sure it's far quicker really.'

'As you will, but let's move!'

They accordingly retraced their steps and found that following their footprints made the journey comparatively easy, so it did not take nearly so long to get home. Snowy boots were kicked against the doorstep and stamped on the mat, then taken into the kitchen to dry in front of the range. Cold hands were warmed in hot water and everyone reappeared looking neat and respectable once more. Helen went into the lounge to see if their father and mother were ready for the onslaught, and finding that they were, bade the others, who were waiting patiently in the hall, collect their boxes and go in.

Chapter XXXVI

Suddenly everyone became painfully polite, and stepped out of each other's way and helped each other into comfortable chairs, apologizing profusely when toes were trodden on or elbows jogged.

The table on which the presents were piled was put on one side of the fireplace and the family grouped itself in a semi-circle round the hearth. Mrs Wentworth occupied the sofa, with the string basket beside her and a washing basket at her feet, so that she could tidy up string and paper as it was strewn about the floor and not have it all to do at the end. A large pad on which she wrote down each present, whose it was and whom it was from completed her outfit. This habit had gone on from year to year and was a good one, because it enabled the children to see exactly whom to thank for what. Mr Wentworth sat next to the table, and the children between him and his wife, with their boxes on the floor in front of them, and Rex occupied what space was left.

'Now, Father,' said Penelope, when everyone was settled, 'you begin.'

'No, the baby should begin,' said Mr Wentworth. 'Don't you think so, my dear?'

'Yes,' replied Mrs Wentworth. 'You begin, Gerald.'

'Shall I?' Gerald looked round the assembled company.

'Yes,' said everyone.

So Gerald got up and walked over to the table and picked up a parcel. He could not see whom it was for until he turned it over, because all the parcels had their names facing downwards on to the table. Gerald turned it upright and read the inscription:

> To Mr Wentworth,
>
> In remembrance of a friendship which will never grow old
> and many happy hours spent in his company,
> With all good wishes for Christmas and the New Year,
>
> from
>
> Alexander Moore

He handed the parcel to his father, who took it with pleasure. It was like Mr Moore to do this. He removed the wrappings and disclosed a complete set of the works of Francis Bacon, beautifully bound in soft cherry-red leather and illustrated with woodcuts and engravings by contemporary artists.

Mr Wentworth's pleasure found no expression in words. He turned over the leaves of the top one, only his smile and eyes devouring every detail of the binding, print and paper telling how thrilled he was with the gift.

They took it in turns to pick, delight increasing with each new treasure, from Gerald's Shakespeare's *Histories* – his parents' present – which would hold an honoured place beside the *Comedies* and *Tragedies* already on his bookshelf, to Helen's beautiful jumper whose exquisite workmanship and intricate patterns were not only executed, but designed by Margaret herself. All of them had many things which they really wanted, for when exasperated aunts and uncles wrote to their mother asking what their nephews and nieces wanted for Christmas, she was able to quote several of the most suitable items and thus help both the relations and her children.

Last of all on the table was a large flat box which had so far not been picked. Alban, whose turn it was, lifted it off the table, turned it over and read,

To Penny,

Wishing her a Happy Christmas
and an even happier Twins'
Twenty-First-Birthday-Party,

With love from

Helen

Penelope took the box and grinned with a puzzled expression at her sister, who maintained a perfectly straight face, although her eyes twinkled. She read the label through twice and then said,

'May I cut the string?'

'No!' said Gerald. 'That's cheating.'

'Well, she's done it up so jolly tight.'

'Pull it off the corners,' suggested Philip. Penelope tried to do this, but Helen's packing would not allow it, and she had to untie every knot. Anticipation increased with delay, and when at last the paper was off, her excitement was such that she could hardly get the lid off the box for trembling fingers.

Inside the box were several layers of crinkly white tissue paper. Penelope lifted it off with more haste than care, for she had already guessed what her present was. She transferred the box to the floor, and as the last layer of paper was removed, gave a joyful shriek and made a dive, seizing the shoulders of a pale blue party frock, consisting of a taffeta base covered with layer upon layer of filmy net and trimmed with narrow black ribbon. As she held it up to her the skirt fell in clouds round her legs and on to the floor.

'Oh Helen, it's *marvellous*!' she cried in ecstasy. 'Did you make it?'

'Yes,' said Helen.

'It's lovely! Thanks *awfully*. Oh boy!' She threw the dress over one arm and crossed to kiss her sister while the rest of the family was exclaiming over it and admiring Helen's handiwork.

'Hold it up properly and let's have a look at it,' said Mrs Wentworth. Penelope did so.

'It's very pretty, Helen,' said Mr Wentworth. 'Did you make it from a pattern or out of your head?'

'Out of my head.'

'Gosh!' exclaimed Gerald.

'Now you won't have anything to complain about, Penny,' said Alban. 'You ought to consider yourself jolly lucky to get a new dress. All I get for the party is an outworn suit of Phil's.'

'*Don't* start that again, *please!*' begged Helen, gathering up the tissue paper which Penelope had scattered far and wide when she pulled the dress out of the box.

'Well,' said Mrs Wentworth when the excitement had subsided, 'how about some tea?'

'Good idea!' cried Philip and Alban together.

'I'll lay it,' volunteered Penelope. 'Here, Helen, you fold this up – you know how it goes. I shall spoil it – please,' she added.

'We'll all help,' said Mrs Wentworth. She gave a task to each and soon the lounge was as tidy as ever, and the table in the dining room laid with everything but the cake. This was never allowed to be seen before teatime on Christmas Day, and Mrs Wentworth shoo'd everyone out of the kitchen and dining room while she brought it through, complete with several other dainties seasonable to the occasion. When the scene was set, she sounded the gong and the family made a general rush, eager for their tea although they had been eating more or less solidly all day. But Alban found, when he came to it, that he could not manage a second piece of Christmas cake after all, for Mrs Wentworth's mixture was so rich and her icing so thick that it was as much as he could do to get through one.

Helen and Penelope cleared away the remains and then joined the others in the lounge, to look at presents again and lose themselves in new books.

The 'best' present which Helen had received – even better than Margaret's jumper –was a photograph from Charles. The book token he enclosed with it was acceptable too, of course, but the photograph was far superior. It had been taken in Edinburgh – she remembered he had said in one of his letters that he had been there – and was excellent. She looked at it again, and the more she looked the more it grew upon her. There was something so personal about a gift like this, which none of the other things she had received could possibly be. Dear old Charlie! How she wished he were with them to share in the fun!

So the day drew to a close and one by one the young people retired to bed, reluctant to let it go for another year, yet tired and well pleased with what they had done and the presents they had received. They soon fell asleep, Gerald with his Shakespeare's *Histories* on his bedside table ready to read in the morning – fear of the consequences being the only thing that kept him from doing so now. None of them was allowed to read in bed, at least until they were eighteen or more, and so far, he had not dared to break this rule.

Philip got into bed with mixed feelings. True, he had enjoyed his Christmas on the whole, but the longing to escape from the cramping atmosphere of this small village was increasing daily and he was becoming more and more discontented. He could hardly go before the twins' party (bother the twins!) as he supposed he would be expected to attend and it would be difficult to give a water-tight reason for his absence if he did not; but once that was over, there would be no excuse for tarrying and tarry he would not. He would be sorry to leave Helen – but – well, she would write.

Chapter XXXVII

Boxing Day and the following few days were rather an anticlimax, as they always are after the excitement leading up to Christmas, but sledging parties organized in the village by Penelope and Alban helped to pass the time more quickly. Parts of the down were admirably suited to tobogganing and a night or two's frost gave the snow just that degree of crispness required to make the toboggans glide smoothly over its surface and add a touch of danger to this best-loved of all children's winter sports. Penelope was utterly fearless and loved the swift descent and the feel of the snow blowing up in clouds into her face as she shot down the hill, with the rolling off at the bottom to avoid being carried into the hedge. The tumbles were almost as enjoyable as the ride and no amount of mishaps could deter her from it. Not so Gerald. He went with them, under pressure, the first day and one accident was enough for him. He left the field vowing never to return, and refused to allow them to drag him out again. When sport on the down was mooted, he retired to the lounge with Shakespeare and did not reappear until he was called for meals. When the others returned with high colours and even higher spirits and he was laughed at by his younger sister for being so silly, he merely smiled and responded mildly, 'Oh well, each to his taste.'

The week thus slipped away and at the end of it they were all on their way to Oxford, where lived their Uncle and Aunt Herrick and their family of five boys and five girls, of whom the eldest were to celebrate their twenty-first birthday on December 31st.

Travelling was crowded, but Mr Wentworth had taken the precaution of booking seats all the way, so they were at least able to sit down and have a carriage to themselves. They set off early in the morning, paused for lunch in London and then went on to Oxford. They arrived about half past three, and found Gordon Herrick, the next in age to the twins, waiting outside the Way Out to meet them, with a taxi to carry them and their luggage to his home. Hullos and Happy New Years having been mutually exchanged, and Gordon informed that he had grown out of all recognition, they stowed themselves and their cases into the taxi and drove off through the city and out along the Banbury Road. The light was already fading, so they could not see very much of the colleges and houses they passed on the way. After some minutes' driving past suburban houses of a spacious late Victorian and Edwardian style, they turned in between high stone portals on the right and wound round a curling drive until they pulled up at length outside the Herricks' impressive mansion and began to sort themselves out. Gordon rang the bell, and half a minute later Uncle Raymond and Aunt Edith had opened the door and came down the steps to welcome their guests. Gordon settled with the taxi-driver while nobody was looking, and it was not until he moved off that Mr Wentworth thought of anything so prosaic as fares. They argued for two or three minutes but Gordon won and they followed the others into the house.

Mrs Wentworth had remarked on the journey that her sister believed in doing things in style and that the party would probably be in keeping with the rest of her *ménage;* but if Aunt Edith did like to be lavish, she also liked plenty of youngsters round her, and all those who came in contact with her were her loyal adorers for evermore. Uncle Raymond, too, liked formality, but was as kind as any uncle could be, and loved to give pleasure to his children and his nephews and nieces. This party was therefore as much their own as the twins', and both were looking forward to the family gathering the next evening.

'We are so glad you could come,' purred Aunt Edith, as she took them up the wide, thick-carpeted staircase and showed them to their rooms. 'I only hope the journey hasn't tired you too much.'

'Not in the least,' responded Mrs Wentworth.

'Good. I'm afraid we have had to put several of you children together. We have one or two other relations staying tomorrow night, so we couldn't let you all have a room each.'

'Of course not; that's perfectly all right.'

'Well, this is your room, Augusta. Do make yourselves at home – and James, the door on the opposite side is a dressing room.'

'Thank you,' murmured Mr Wentworth, following his wife and sister-in-law into the bedroom. High, richly furnished and comfortable to the last degree, this was the pattern of all the rooms, although some of them were smaller than others.

Aunt Edith emerged, telling them to come down to the drawing room when they were ready, and leading the way, went on,

'Now, Helen dear, I have put you and Penny together; I hope you don't mind' – Helen interrupted with 'No, not at all' – 'Here we are.' She opened another door. 'And you three boys are all in here – Gerry we've had to put in the dressing room, but you're all together really. Now you won't scrap, will you?'

The boys laughed. Secretly, all three of them would have preferred to have been alone, but Aunt Edith had such a cheery way with her that she seemed to instill the right spirit into you the moment she spoke to you. Perhaps she knew how they felt; she was a very understanding sort of person. Assuring her that they would do their best not to come to blows, they began to take off their coats and scarves.

'Come down when you're ready,' repeated Aunt Edith, 'and meet the children – how long is it since we last saw you? Six or seven years at least – then we'll have tea. I expect you're hungry, aren't you?'

'We are rather,' admitted Alban.

'I'm sure you are. Well, it will be ready when you are. You know your way down to the drawing room, don't you?'

'Yes, thank you,' they replied in chorus.

'Good. Well, I'll leave you to it.'

When the door shut behind her Alban said,

'I *like* Aunt Edith, you know. She's a sport.'

'Yes. What a marvellous house!' Gerald exclaimed. 'Let's go and have a look at my bedroom.' He opened the door and went through to a small but equally comfortable, if somewhat improvised, bedroom and was pleased to see a row of books on a shelf above his bed. Aunt Edith knew his tastes.

Alban pulled one end of his scarf and released it from his neck and then sat on the end of his bed and looked round.

'Tiddley isn't the word,' he said.

'Too tiddley for my liking,' responded Philip, who was used to Alban's phraseology. 'Fancy making us sleep together – why couldn't she have put *me* in the separate room?'

'Oh, don't start dripping, for heaven's sake,' begged Alban. 'Look on the bright side of life. This is going to be Fun with a capital F.'

'For you, perhaps,' grunted Philip. The journey had not left him in the best of tempers.

'I say,' cut in Gerald, appearing in the doorway with Chaucer's *Canterbury Tales* in his hand, 'Aunt Edith has put some books in my room.'

'Has she?' murmured Alban uninterestedly. 'Nice of her.'

'It's grand. I'll be able to read them all.'

'Well, come and get ready for tea,' said Philip.

'Good idea,' agreed Alban, rising to wash his hands. 'My inner man has been calling for the last half hour.'

When everyone was ready they all descended *en masse* and went into the drawing room. Uncle Raymond stood with his back to the fire; Aunt Edith occupied an armchair on one side, and swarms of children were grouped around, sitting on the sofa, in chairs, perched on arms and even on the floor. All rose to their feet and stood looking pleasantly self-conscious, waiting for their mother to reintroduce them to their cousins. All of them had grown so much since they had last seen each other that it was difficult to recollect who each one was.

Having first introduced the Wentworths to her family, Aunt Edith proceeded to name her children.

Edward and Eleanor, never called anything but Teddy and Len, were alike in looks but not in expression. Teddy's mouth, though slightly weak, was kind, and his eyes, if somewhat wistful, lit up when he was addressed. He had a quick, mercurial way of speaking, remaining silent until he was spoken to and then replying in odd little bursts. He was shy, and jumped if you spoke to him when he was not expecting it. Eleanor, on the other hand, had a slightly sulky curve to her mouth and was inclined to look down her nose; in fact, as they soon discovered, she was always being teased about her 'snooty' airs. Helen decided that she preferred Teddy, and was immediately sorry for him. Eleanor was obviously the more important of the two, in her own eyes at least, and liked life to revolve around herself. The sulky curve turned into a definite pout if she thought Teddy was getting too much attention.

'Gordon you have met.'

'Yes.' Everybody bowed and smiled. Gordon was nearly twenty and one of the only two dark-haired members of the family.

'Basil.' The hair of this grave-looking youth of eighteen-and-a-half was a peculiar silvery-yellow colour, and Helen caused much laughter and protestations by exclaiming, 'Yes, I always thought Basil's hair was like the colour of the underskin of a sardine.'

'Anne.' Anne was seventeen and her real name was Angela, but she was never called by it. Anne bowed with a quiet smile. She, too, was grave, and reputed to be very clever.

'Rupert.' Mischievous, green-eyed Rupert attracted Penelope at once, with his mop of golden curls and ready, flashing smile She felt that here was a kindred spirit, and remembered how she had thoroughly enjoyed joining in his pranks when she was small. He was a year older than she, but at fifteen and sixteen the difference was not great.

'Monica.' Monica was fourteen, her hair was red, and she giggled.

'Liz.' Elizabeth bowed, and her brown hair immediately flopped over her shoulders. She tossed it back again as she straightened herself and grinned. Elizabeth was twelve.

'Charmain.' A fair-haired, long-plaited young lady of eleven smiled in a very attractive, open way.

'And the youngest, Brefni.' The other dark-haired member of the family was nine, and smiled in a quick, boyish fashion when his turn came. He had only been two or three years old when they had last met and he did not remember his cousins at all; and they only remembered him as the toddler he then was.

'Well, now, don't stand on ceremony,' said Aunt Edith. 'Everybody knows everybody else, so find somewhere to sit and have a good pow-wow. I'm sure you must have lots to say. There are so many things I want to ask, I don't know where to begin.'

But the tinkling of the tea-bell just at that moment delayed Aunt Edith's questions and her thirst for news had to go unquenched until they were all sitting round the huge circular table in the dining room. As far as possible the two families were alternated, but Aunt Edith placed her sister next to her and they were soon talking away 'nineteen to the dozen', as Rupert put it, discussing their families, what they were all doing or hoping to do, dipping into the past and remembering their own childhood; in fact, hardly pausing to eat at all. Mr Wentworth and Uncle Raymond were soon deep in Oxford history and politics. They had both been at Christ Church together, where the one studied classics and the other medicine, and it was at his friend's wedding that Uncle Raymond had met his wife. He was now an eminent brain surgeon. Mr Wentworth, when his career had to come to an end because of his health, had devoted himself to writing, and had several books on ancient Greece and Rome to his name.

The children chatted and laughed, discussed Christmas and the presents they had been given, and picked up old threads in no time. Gerald and Elizabeth found their memories of each other's families rather vague and Charmain's and Brefni's were non-existent, while Helen and the twins remembered many details of previous visits and the fun they had all had together.

'Did Mum remember to tell you to bring your skates?' asked Rupert. 'Jam, please, Liz.'

'Yes, she did. Where do we skate?' replied Penelope

'On Port Meadow, or if you like to go further afield, we could go to Blenheim and skate on the lake,' said Gordon.

The Herrick family. (1943)

'Of course, if it freezes about twenty degrees of frost every night, the river might freeze and then we could skate on that,' added Rupert, 'but it's not very likely.'

'Pity you didn't come in the summer,' said Eleanor, 'then we could have rowed on it.'

'Oh, but skating's marvellous fun!' cried Elizabeth.

'It's so dangerous.'

'Don't be so daft. You used to love it.'

'Well, I don't now.'

'Oh, leave her alone!' said Rupert. 'She needn't come if she doesn't want to. It won't be much loss.'

'Let brotherly love continue,' murmured Helen. 'Really, Rupert!'

'Well, I don't know what's the matter with her lately. She's been too high and mighty for words. Won't do this and won't do that. Swelled head, I suppose, at attaining years of discretion. That's it, isn't it, Len?'

Eleanor looked down her nose at her brother across the table.

'I don't consider that such wild sports are any longer suited to my age; and don't call me "Len".'

Rupert burst out laughing, and even Helen could not suppress a smile. Eleanor obviously had a very good opinion of herself.

'Not suited! Yoo-hoo! Hark at that!' shrieked Rupert. Monica giggled and Anne exclaimed 'Oh Len!' in a tone of mingled amusement and disgust.

'Don't call me "Len"!' cried Eleanor.

'Why not? You've been called "Len" all your life, haven't you?'

'Yes, but I don't like it any more. My name is Eleanor and I want to be called by it. I told you so this morning.'

'I'll call you "Elly-anna" if you're not careful,' responded Rupert, which caused another round of laughter. 'Eleanor indeed! Who do you think you are – Lady van Wollop or something?'

'Really, Len, I think you're being rather foolish,' admonished Basil.

'What's wrong with "Len" anyway?' asked Alban. 'It sounds the obvious thing to call you, to me.'

'Of course it is. She's just being stupid,' declared Rupert. 'I suppose you want us to call Teddy "Edward" too?' (Teddy jumped at the mention of his name and said, 'What? Oh.')

'You'll just have to want, that's all. *I'm* not going to suddenly stop calling you "Len" just because you're twenty-one. Anyway, you aren't yet.'

'I'm sure Helen wouldn't care two hoots what she was called,' said Gordon, smiling at his cousin, 'would you?'

'Not in the least.'

'Wouldn't you really?' asked Eleanor.

'Of course not – though I suppose I'm hardly the one to ask, never having been called anything but "Helen" all my life.'

'Do you think I'm silly?'

'Frankly, yes.'

'Good for you!' cried Rupert, waving his hand at her. The others voiced their approval and Eleanor, somewhat reluctantly, agreed to let them continue to call her 'Len'.

'And will you come skating?' asked Charmain.

Eleanor hesitated. She glanced at Helen as if to say 'Help me to decide.' Helen rose to the occasion.

'Yes, do come,' she begged. 'It will be such fun if we all go.'

'But supposing somebody saw me.'

'What's it matter if they do?' enquired Penelope, while Elizabeth ejaculated, 'Oh, don't be so daft!'

'Are *you* going?' demanded Eleanor of Helen, ignoring them.

'Yes indeed! I'm looking forward to it immensely.'

'Then I will.'

'Good! Good! Helen, you ought to come and live with us,' laughed Rupert, 'she'd soon see sense then.'

'I don't think she's entirely lacking now.'

'Just a little silly at times,' said Basil quickly.

'Well,' said Aunt Edith, coming back to the present, 'has everyone had enough? Gerry, another piece of cake?'

'No, thank you, Aunt Edith.'

'Helen, another cup of tea? Penny, finish those éclairs? Phil? Pass the coffee kisses to Alban, Brefni.'

'No, thank you; no thank you, really I've had enough.'

'Sure?'

'Yes, quite sure, thank you.'

There was a pause while Mr Wentworth and Uncle Raymond ended a discussion. Aunt Edith beamed round the table and tried to persuade somebody to eat some more of something, but she was unsuccessful.

'Well, shall we adjourn?' she said at length. 'Now, children do anything you like, but don't get into mischief.'

Chapter XXXVIII

Gradually they dispersed to various occupations about the house, the older members of both families returning to the drawing room to talk, the younger looking at Herrick Christmas presents or playing games in the 'nursery', as the children's playroom was still called.

Helen, Philip, the twins, Gordon, Basil and Anne settled themselves on the opposite side of the fireplace to their parents; Rupert and Penelope lay on the floor doing their best to beat each other at 'Peggity', Rupert and Clarke, the great St Bernard, propping each other up back to back.

The Herricks' drawing room, if large, was friendly, and could be made very cosy when the standard lamp was the only lighting besides the fire. The shade of the lamp was intriguing, for it was a hand-coloured map of Oxford, oiled and thronged to a detachable frame. Coming in at the door, the group formed a delightfully homely picture. Aunt Edith, in her love of style, did not sacrifice taste, and most of her furniture was antique and solid. The room was panelled in oak and everything matched, from the tapestry seats and backs of three Jacobean chairs to the long heavy richness of the curtains drawn across the windows. It looked particularly attractive just now with sprigs of holly and silver shreds over all the pictures and round the walls. The hearth was wide and the crackling logs piled high in the centre filled the air with their aromatic fragrance. The firelight danced on the two fair heads bent so absorbedly over their game, glinting on Rupert's curly mop and turning it to a glowing copper. For once the jack-in-a-box was still, and his countenance was wrapped in concentration. Helen looked at him often during the evening, thinking that for all his faults, and they were many, he was a good-hearted lad and she could not help liking him.

The group on the left of the fireplace were soon deep in each other's affairs and found out what plans and careers each had in mind for the future. Teddy was at New College studying for a science degree – the Herricks had a strong bent in that direction – and Gordon was following in his father's footsteps at Christ Church. Basil was still at school, but would be leaving at the end of the summer term, when he hoped to join Gordon. Eleanor was the exception that proved the rule, for she was at the Slade School of Art, where, as Gordon put it, she was 'wasting her time drawing people's bodies instead of finding out how they worked'. Eleanor retorted that she knew as much about anatomy as he did, the only difference being that she studied it with relation to exterior forms and left people's 'disgusting insides' alone. This started a lively argument on science versus art in which Helen supported Eleanor and both of them defended their case nobly against the onslaught of the scientists. Philip took little part in the argument, not particularly caring one way or the other.

The Herrick household dined at half past seven, the youngest members taking their supper in the nursery and going straight to bed. Gerald was included in the supper list but Penelope, to her great joy, was considered old enough to stay up for dinner. The bell rang at seven as a warning that it was time to get ready, and again, twenty minutes later, to say that the meal was about to be served and everyone was expected to come down.

Gerald did not much care for the idea of having his supper with his three youngest cousins. Elizabeth's wild habits scared him and he was never quite sure where he was with her. Charmain and Brefni looked up to him, not only because he was older, but because they had been told that Gerald was 'brainy'. This was something of a salve to his soul, so used as he was to being the youngest himself. They had spent the evening exploring the attics, Gerald from politeness more than desire, and he was feeling somewhat exhausted. Elizabeth had led them into the dirtiest, pokiest corners, and he was wearing his second-best suit of clothes. When he asked if she and Charmain ought to crawl in the dust in such tidy skirts, she replied casually that it didn't matter a bit, they'd done it in far better than these old things. However, by bedtime some of her energy had worn off and she merely proposed they should all race through the washing processes and see who would be in the nursery first. Gerald could have a bath if he liked; there was plenty of hot water.

Gerald did like. Contrary to most boys of his age, he hated feeling dirty, and having travelled for most of the day with but a scanty wash between that and travels in dusty attics, he was feeling in need of a bath. There were several bathrooms in the house, but he only knew of one, that nearest to his own bedroom. Contrary also to the usual way of boys, to be thorough with Gerald did not mean taking two hours over it and even then forgetting the back of his neck. Gerald was thorough and quick as well, and he was in the nursery several minutes before the others

Gerald in his pyjamas (1945).

appeared. Elizabeth was quite surprised to see him, and having bounced in and warmed her hands unnecessarily in front of the fire, she bounced out again to run downstairs and bring up their supper. It was ready on the kitchen table as usual, but with enough for four. The three Herricks were all pleased to have company. It made a change from their normal routine, and while Charmain and Brefni said very little, Elizabeth put herself out to make it enjoyable for her cousin. She chatted gaily, crouching in her pyjamas and dressing-gown on the rug in front of the fire, trying not to talk with her mouth full. The other three sat down with her, having first switched off the light at Brefni's suggestion, and they transferred the trays on to the floor between them. They munched away at the food provided, which, if it was not so elaborate as the main meal going on below, was full and satisfying. Altogether, Gerald found supper with his young cousins not so bad as he was expecting and then went off to bed to enjoy reading the *Canterbury Tales* for a short time before settling down in his extremely comfortable bed to go to sleep.

Downstairs in the dining room the privileged 'grown-ups' were seated round the circular table enjoying some of the Herrick household's excellent cooking. The cut glass and highly polished silver sparkled and flashed, reflected in detail in the surface of the table, which was also highly polished. Lace mats, of all shapes and sizes, over cork ones, protected it from hot dishes and drops of water. Penelope's eyes grew wider and wider until Rupert asked her what she was staring at.

'Oh!' Penelope blushed at being discovered. It was very rude to stare. 'I'm sorry, I – I didn't know I was.'

'You were – eyes like saucers – weren't they, Mon?'

'Yes,' giggled Monica.

'Well,' said Penelope, feeling terribly embarrassed and blushing still more, 'I was just thinking I'd never seen anything like this before in my life!'

Everyone laughed and Uncle Raymond said,

'And do you like it, Penny?'

'Yes,' replied Penelope untruthfully. She hated formality but could not very well say so.

'How about some music,' suggested Aunt Edith, when they returned to the drawing room. Everyone agreed enthusiastically, for the Herricks were musical as well as scientific, and all of them except Uncle Raymond played some instrument. There was a rack full of music beside the grand piano, and a cupboard in the wall was also full. Violins, violas and cellos were brought out, Helen, Basil and Aunt Edith taking it in turns to play accompaniments. Duets, trios and quartettes were alternated with songs from Gordon and Rupert, and the evening passed before they realized how late it was. Monica and Penelope were rushed off to bed, and were closely followed by Rupert, Anne and Alban.

Aunt Edith slipped her arm through Helen's as they walked up the stairs half an hour later, leading the way as the rest of the company retired to bed. In the brief time since they arrived she had become very attached to her elder niece. She remembered her as a long-legged schoolgirl like Penelope and the change was remarkable. Helen, in her turn, felt the attachment between herself and her aunt had become even stronger after the gap since they had last met, and their reunion proved it a hundred-fold.

'Oh, Aunt Edith, that *was* fun! There's nothing to beat home music, is there?'

'No indeed! It makes all the difference.'

'You get something from playing with others that you never would learn playing by yourself – and it's so good for you, too. I *did* enjoy it.'

'I'm so glad. We must have some more.'

'May we? We have so little opportunity at home.'

'I wish you could come more often. What a pity we don't live nearer to each other.'

'Yes.' They reached the top of the stairs. 'This visit is going to be grand, Aunt Edith. I feel the fun is just beginning.'

Aunt Edith gave out a little motherly laugh.

'Good. Well, I'm sure we shall enjoy it as much as you. Goodnight, dear.'

'Goodnight, Aunt Edith.' Helen kissed her affectionately. Goodnights and 'sweet dreams' were exchanged all round and they dispersed to their various rooms.

Chapter XXXIX

Next morning everyone except the twins was ready for breakfast at nine o'clock, and eagerly discussing what the plan for the day should be. Rupert was all for skating, as there had been a hard frost during the night, and Penelope supported his suggestion, but Anne said they would all be too stiff to dance if they hadn't been before and that it would be better to leave it until the next day. After some argument, it was decided that this was the better proposition, and a tour of colleges was mooted instead. That it was not the best time of year to see them was mutually accepted, but as Anne pointed out, they looked better covered with snow than they did with just dead plants and bare twigs in their gardens.

'What *are* Teddy and Len doing?' asked Aunt Edith. 'We can't wait much longer.'

'Making themselves pretty, I expect,' said Rupert. 'I wish they'd hurry – *moi, je suis très* hungry.'

'Liz, run up and find out how long they'll be, there's a good child.' Elizabeth assented and raced out of the room. 'Really, I can't think why they are taking so long.'

Elizabeth reappeared a minute later, saying that they were 'just coming'.

'Well, let's sit down,' said Aunt Edith.

The twins appeared, looking slightly flurried, apologizing for being late. Their excuses were drowned in an uproar of Happy Birthdays, Congratulations and Many Happy Returns of the Days. Having kissed their parents and uncle and aunt, and smiled happily at the company – for they refused to kiss everybody – they took their places at the opposite side of the table to their mother. Everyone became overwhelmingly attentive; Rupert forgot to tease and even Elizabeth passed the sugar without being asked. Aunt Edith explained that there were so many presents, they had better leave them till after breakfast, or they would never get anything eaten. The twins laughed and said they would hold a viewing in the drawing room, anyone wishing to be present to be there at nine-forty-five sharp.

Porridge, golden eggs and pieces of toast and marmalade disappeared with alarming rapidity, and nobody was late for the viewing. There were, as Aunt Edith said, so many presents that they could never all have been opened during breakfast. Grandparents, uncles, aunts, cousins, friends, neighbours, acquaintances – practically everyone they knew had sent them a gift, and soon the drawing room looked like a multiple store. It took at least a couple of hours to look at them all, by which time it was hardly worth while to begin a tour of colleges and the expedition was postponed until the afternoon. Many willing hands were lent to help to carry the twins' new possessions up to their rooms, where they lingered to look at them again, and exclaim over some piece of generosity, wholly unexpected, and all the more pleasant in consequence.

Eleanor decided to refrain from joining the outing after lunch. She did not wish to make herself tired for the evening, and anyway, she had seen all the colleges at least a dozen times before, and their party would be quite large enough as it was. Philip also remained behind – the idea of looking over colleges was too painful, even if they were not the ones he knew.

They caught a bus into the city, discussing on the way which college they should go to first, and finally decided on Christ Church. They got off the bus and pushed their way through the crowds. Helen remarked that she had never seen such a crush: long queues for buses blocking half the pavement, making one-way progress on the inside of the path the only possible method. Those going in the opposite direction to the mainstream stepped off the pavement and walked in the road, avoiding cars and buses and the endless flow of bicycles for which Oxford is famous, with uncanny skill. If you were in a hurry, which fortunately was not the case on this occasion, you were nearly driven crazy by the slowness of the people dawdling along in front of you, stopping to look in shop windows about a foot from the glass, chatting on the kerbstone, or lounging in doorways. Even the cold did not seem to have any quickening effect on the inhabitants of Oxford.

'What a *terrible* place!' exclaimed Penelope, after they had stood on the curb at the main crossroads for five minutes without being able to reach even the island halfway across the High Street approach.

'Oh, this is nothing,' responded Rupert airily. 'You ought to be here in term-time; it's far worse than this.'

'I've no wish to, thank you. This is quite bad enough for me.'

They reached the other side at last and proceeded down to Christ Church. Basil knew all its history, from its early beginnings as the

Monastery of St Freidswide, to its present-day structure with its unfinished cloisters and its Wren Tom Tower. They went into the cathedral, whose tall white arches and delicate tracery made them catch their breath in wonder at their beauty, the hall with its rows of portraits of dignitaries ancient and modern connected with the college, Peckwater Quad and the Library with its weathered stonework, and finally the kitchens, which could only be seen during vacations. Helen and Penelope were thrilled with them; for although modern ovens had been installed in place of the old spits, the actual kitchens were the same as when they were built and, as Gerald said, probably did not smell much better.

As they emerged once more into the busy street, Alban said that to come out and find traffic seemed to be quite wrong after the atmosphere of the past inside the college. The others agreed, and Anne, in passing, pointed out the 'Sheep's Shop' further down the road, where Alice went and found all the dolls and toys went up through the ceiling as she looked at them, and the sheep behind the counter was knitting with fourteen or so pairs of needles. There was no time to go and examine it, although Penelope would have loved to have seen whether the toys still did the same peculiar things.

They turned into 'The High' and walked along until they reached a music shop, then crossed the road – for once, it was fairly easy – and passed down a narrow street, which Gordon said would come out by two of the best bookshops in Oxford, then they would go and look at Trinity and Balliol. Gerald's eyes lit up at the mention of bookshops. He had been given several book tokens for Christmas and wanted to spend them. They paused on their way to peep through the gateways of Exeter and Jesus Colleges, the last causing Rupert to break forth into a strong Welsh accent as he told the story of the man calling to see his friend Mr Jones…

Gerald was not allowed to have more than the merest glimpse into the bookshop windows. They wanted to 'get round' their programme before it became too dark to see properly. Anne promised to bring him 'next year' for a whole morning to look at bookshops if he wished and, thus satisfied, he followed them down the road to Trinity. The gardens were very beautiful in the snow, the long strips of lawn unimpaired by footprints, every leaf and twig weighted down under its white burden. All periods of architecture were displayed in the component parts of the college, yet the whole effect was pleasing, for the snow united the separate buildings and made them one.

A quick look round Balliol had to suffice, because Anne was anxious that they should see St John's gardens before the light faded. St John's was the last on the list as it was the nearest to their home. The gardens were well worth the visit, but even so, Alban said he preferred Trinity.

The light was beginning to turn blue and Basil thought they should return, as tea was to be early, to give everyone plenty of time in which to prepare for the dance.

'I expect Granny will have arrived by the time we get back,' he said, 'so we mustn't be too late.'

'Who else is staying the night?' asked Monica.

'Heaven knows!' responded Basil.

'Don't expect Mum does either,' added Rupert.

Monica giggled.

'Why didn't Len come with us?' enquired Elizabeth.

'She had to have her beauty sleep,' said Gordon. 'I hope the bus isn't crowded, or we shall have to get on in relays.'

'What does she want a beauty sleep for?' persisted Elizabeth.

'Don't ask me! What does any girl want a beauty sleep for? Ask Helen.'

'Helen, why –'

'Oh, shut up, Liz!' exclaimed Rupert. 'You wait till you're her age, then you'll know.'

'I shan't have one.'

'No?'

'No, I shouldn't do anything so daft.'

'Huh! We shall see,' murmured Gordon.

'What are you wearing tonight, Penny?' asked Elizabeth, abruptly changing the subject, and while Penelope was enlarging on the glories of her new dress, Gordon lent over to Helen and said,

'If the truth be known about Len, we think – mind you, we make no definite assertion, but we *think* – that she wishes to make an impression on a certain gentleman, who shall be nameless, who is coming to the dance tonight.'

'Oh, I *see!*' replied Helen slowly.

Monica had spotted a bus in the distance and as it came nearer it proved to be the right one and they all managed to get on it.

When they reached the house, they found that not only had their maternal grand-mother arrived, but also several other relations who had come a long way and were staying the night. Penelope wondered where they were all going to sleep, but she did not know how many rooms there were in the house, nor how many of the family members would be put into one.

Tea was a lively meal, with so many relations from both sides to talk to, and Granny, mother of Mrs Wentworth and Aunt Edith, kept them laughing all through the meal. A little, white-haired lady, but with a dignity that made tall men feel awkward and pretty girls aware that they lacked something, she could be strict and unbending, but her eyes could twinkle and her tight little mouth had a mischievous twitch when she was not serious. She loved all children but believed that they should be kept in their places and only allowed loose on very rare occasions; but on the rare occasions when she did allow them to be let loose there was no end to the pranks she enjoyed. Her daughters divided her traits between them, Mrs Wentworth inclining to the strictness and Aunt Edith to the pranks.

She waltzed round the room (1945).

Chapter XL

Eleanor did not appear for tea, Aunt Edith explaining that she did not wish to be seen now until the party and that she was taking her tea in her bedroom. Rupert passed a remark to the effect that it was 'all a lot of blah', but they were too busy talking to take much notice of Eleanor.

'Well,' said Aunt Edith as they rose from the table, 'have as many baths as you like, but don't catch cold. We begin at eight o'clock and I hope everybody will be prompt. If anybody wants anything, come and ask me.'

There was a general dive for bedrooms and for the next two hours preparations were in full swing. Aunt Edith supervised the final arrangements downstairs while the thickest of the fight was going on above, leaving her dressing until the coast was clear.

Basil, but recently promoted to a full evening dress suit, had some difficulty in getting into it, and Teddy had to come to the rescue with the tie, which Basil just could not tie into a bow. Gordon oiled down his hair until it shone again, and insisted on oiling Rupert's as well, much to that young gentleman's disgust. In fact, he was so annoyed that he went to the basin when his brother was out of the room, and washed it out. It still looked sleek and shiny and Gordon did not discover it until it was too late. Rupert entered the ballroom with an even brighter and curlier mop than before.

Helen spent an hour ironing out the creases in her own and Penelope's dresses, but they had travelled well and did not need much doing to them. Aunt Edith had placed a small clothes-horse round their fire, and they hung their things on it to warm while they washed. Penelope began to get excited and could hardly keep still while Helen did up all the hooks and eyes at the back of her dress. She waltzed round the room holding out her skirt with one hand and waving the other in the air, ending in a sweeping curtsy, smiling and laughing so happily that Helen, as she watched the lithe, graceful young figure, could not help thinking that Charles was indeed right when he had compared her to Venus.

'Oh, Helen!' Penelope exclaimed, 'this *is* a marvellous frock! However did you guess it was what I wanted more than anything else in the world?'

'Oh, intuition,' laughed Helen. 'Look, *chérie,* can you come and do me up? I can't get at the fastenings.'

'Of course.' Penelope performed the necessary operation, saying as she did so, 'You know, Helen, you look awfully good in this.'

'And you look awfully good in that, so we're quits! We'll take the ballroom by storm.'

'Where *is* the ballroom?'

'I'm not sure, but I think they'll probably use the long room that opens on to the garden.'

The front door bell rang continually from about a quarter to eight and at five minutes to, when they were both ready, Helen and Penelope descended. Helen had been right: the long room that stretched the entire width of the house, had been cleared of furniture, chairs placed round the walls and a special dais erected at one end for the 'orchestra', a company of half-a-dozen musicians hired for the occasion. Heavy curtains stretching almost from the ceiling to the floor kept out the cold, and the light from the chandeliers and lamps cast a bright glow over the gathering assembly.

The rest of the Wentworth family were waiting in the hall. Helen and Penelope joined them and they stood and admired each other for a few minutes before going in. Everyone agreed that Penelope looked very pretty in her new dress and that Helen's 'Elizabethan' was as effective as ever. It was made of stiff crimson brocade, embroidered all over with patterns in gold thread and would stand up of its own accord. Alban made a deprecating remark about his borrowed finery, to which his mother responded that nobody would have known it was not his own.

Rupert appeared from the ballroom and bade them hurry in and see the exhibition before it was smothered in the crowds. They laughed, knowing Rupert's opinion of his eldest sister was not very high. They followed him into the ballroom and found it moderately full already in spite of the fact that parties seldom warm up until at least half an hour after they are due to start. Uncle Raymond and Aunt Edith stood with the twins just inside the door, ready to receive and welcome their guests, Teddy with a nervous little bow and rapid smile, Eleanor with charm and self-confidence. She certainly did look well in a white dress with black, full-length gloves and black patterns round the waist. A blood-red rose at her bosom and another in her hair gave the final touch to her colour scheme; but she was conscious that she attracted attention, and this, in Alban's eyes, spoilt the whole effect.

They shook hands and wished the twins a 'Happy Birthday' once

Helen in her 'Elizabethan' (1945).

more. Penelope's dress was duly admired, and Helen told that she looked like a page from the past. Helen, knowing by Eleanor's expression that a return compliment was necessary, gave the expected praise and Eleanor was happy.

Passing on from their hosts, they were immediately seized by Basil, who presented them all with programmes and told them that Gordon and Rupert would introduce them to anybody they did not know (they also introduced them to several guests whom they thought they ought to know). While introductions were still in progress the orchestra struck up and the MC called out to the company to take their partners for the first dance.

Those who had not so far secured partners hastily found them. Teddy led his twin into the dance, and Gordon took Helen. Soon the floor was thronged with couples whirling round in time to the music, and everyone who had a Herrick for a partner discovered that all of them were excellent dancers.

'Who is the tall, aloof-looking man dancing with the girl in the pink frock?' asked Helen, struck by the gentleman's look of utter boredom.

'Where?' Gordon looked about him. 'Oh, there, do you mean?'

'Yes.'

'Oh, he's the chap I told you about for whom our dearly beloved had a beauty sleep.'

'The one who was to be impressed?'

'That's right.'

'Oh?' Helen sounded interested.

'The gent in question goes under the confoundedly stupid name of St John St Verax.'

'Good heavens! What a name!'

'Isn't it? Actually, he's quite decent really, except when Liz calls him "*Saint* John *Saint* Verax", when he gets rather annoyed. I'll introduce you to him at the next opportunity. He will probably ask you for a dance, which will cause Len untold pangs of jealousy.'

'Oh, Gordon, don't be unkind!'

'It would do her good. She can't have her own way all the time, you know.'

'Yes, but is it fair to steal him from her if she particularly wants to dance with him?'

'Bless your heart! She's got all the other dances vacant! She mustn't be selfish.'

Helen raised no more objections, although she rather dreaded the consequences of the plot, for Eleanor could make herself very unpleasant when she was in a bad mood. However, as Gordon said, there were all the other dances, and she had to admit that she would rather enjoy watching Eleanor's expression when she saw what was happening. She did need bringing down a peg or two, and if this would help, she would welcome the chance of doing it.

Gordon was as good as his word, and the unwitting St John fell. He booked Helen for the next dance, and Gordon walked away chuckling to himself over the success of his mission. He purposely sat out the next dance in order to watch his sister's reactions, and he was not disappointed. Eleanor's face registered first surprise, as if she found what she saw difficult to believe, and then sulkiness. Her nose was raised several degrees into the air and she would not look at either of them when they passed. Gordon was satisfied and rose to go in search of Rupert, who, he knew, would relish this game against his sister. Gordon had outgrown the stage through which Rupert was passing, but he still enjoyed teasing Eleanor, who, more than any of them, 'asked for it'.

There were several young people invited for the express purpose of keeping the younger members of the family out of mischief, and Rupert was well supplied with three school-fellows, who provided partners for Penelope and Monica and the latter's friends. It was obvious that the company was divided into two camps, the 'grown-ups', with whom Anne chose to include herself, and the 'children', which included everyone from Rupert downwards. Alban vacillated from one to the other, equally at home in both. He suggested that they should separate themselves and dance in the hall, where they could still hear the music and yet 'not be bothered by the grown-ups'. This was a very satisfactory arrangement, and Aunt Edith, when passing through the hall, where she was nearly sent flying by an enthusiastic schoolboy walzing round with Monica, did not forbid it, but realized that the more sedate dancers inside would be glad to be rid of the wilder youngsters.

Inside the ballroom, uncles and aunts and cousins, brothers and sisters and friends circled round the floor unhampered by children who did not know how to dance properly, and their existence was forgotten.

Helen found her programme filled up almost before she was aware of it and she danced with nobody twice. She gave herself up entirely to the enjoyment of dancing, a thing she had not indulged in for a very long time. Many of her partners were college friends of Teddy and Gordon, and she found them extremely interesting and amusing to talk to; and they, finding her alert and receptive, chatted freely and told her their best

Penelope
(1945)

Helen
(1945)

college stories, sure of their being appreciated. Teddy and Gordon were pleased that their friends were accepted by their cousin and both vowed that they would press their mother to invite her sister's family to stay again as soon as it was possible.

Philip, who had been dreading this dance ever since the receipt of Aunt Edith's letter before Christmas, found it even as he expected. He hated meeting strange people, and even though Gordon saw to it that he was introduced to plenty, he shrank from asking them to dance on so short an acquaintance. He danced with Helen and Anne and his aunt, but he did not ask Eleanor. Her manner froze him and he did not like the patronizing air she used towards him. So if Eleanor expected him to ask her, which he told himself was not very likely, she would be disappointed.

Eleanor herself, although she seemed light-hearted enough, was really acting for effect. Beneath her apparent happiness, an increasing feeling of jealousy was growing. Instead of herself being the centre of attraction, the gaiety revolved around Helen. Not that she lacked partners – far from it, she did not sit out a single dance except for choice; but during the intervals it was the group round Helen that attracted adherents rather than her own; and the irritating thing about it was that she could not accuse her of flirting. Helen treated everyone alike, with the same easy respect that she treated Teddy: polite without being tedious, friendly without being familiar. She also knew that one of the reasons why people liked Helen was that she was a good listener and did not spend the whole time talking about herself. The fact that she was jealous made Eleanor become spiteful. She began finding fault with her cousin to herself, and it was surprising how much she could find to pull to pieces once she began.

Helen, unconscious of the black thoughts coursing round in Eleanor's mind, was enjoying herself tremendously. She did not often have the opportunity of talking to people of her own age who had some definite purpose in life and who could talk familiarly about subjects of which the average person knew nothing, with whom comprehensive knowledge of music, literature, pictures, history and politics was part of daily existence, not acquired only after years of study.

Teddy was torn between loyalty to his twin, whose self-centred conversation he found excessively boring, and spending his time in Helen's circle, which was a very lively one. Be it said to Teddy's credit that he only deserted Eleanor on one occasion, when a heated discussion on women students at the university was in progress. Other discussions were conducted without him, and he did his best to be attentive to Eleanor and her friends. Eleanor did not appreciate the struggle her twin was having to stay with her. She took his presence for granted; when he was not there she thought him neglectful and rude, but when he was, her manner towards him was condescending. Poor Eleanor! In her desire to captivate she only repelled, and the one man in the room whom she really did want to impress was pained by what he saw and found Helen's company far more attractive. However, like Teddy, he remembered his manners, and when the time came for refreshments, he it was who took Eleanor through to the dining room. Eleanor recovered herself and proved to be as charming as ever. Having secured the now attentive St John for a second dance, she forgave Helen and magnanimously handed over all the rest of the company to her. As long as St John St Verax was willing to admire her, she did not care tuppence for anybody else.

The youngsters sat on the stairs and in the hall, Rupert and his school friends making daring raids into the dining room and waylaying unfortunate maids carrying trays of dainties from the kitchen, and bringing back the spoils to divide amongst the company, amid triumphant cheers and shouts of approval from their band. Nobody stopped them or even disturbed them, and they made as much noise as they liked. At one point Helen came into the hall with Gordon to get some fresh air, and Rupert, recognizing two friends at court, called out to them to come and join them. Helen looked first at them and then at Gordon; the latter, much to Rupert's disgust, suddenly remembered his years and his dignity and walked back into the dining room. Helen took one glance over her shoulder, and made for the stairs. She was greeted enthusiastically, and the youngsters made room for her in their midst. It was an exciting interlude, especially when the lads discovered that she had hardly had anything to eat, and once more braved the throng for her benefit. Rupert poured scorn on Gordon's head for not looking after her properly and no doubt stuffing himself, until Helen corrected him, saying that it was not Gordon who was supposed to be looking after her, but a friend of Teddy's, who was absorbingly interesting to talk to, but hopelessly forgetful when it came to filling anything but his brain.

'He went to get me a sandwich,' she said, 'and I never saw him again. I expect he became deep in a discussion on the vitamin content of the chickens' dinner.'

There was a general laugh, and Helen was regaled with plunder of all varieties, so much so that she had to beg them not to be so attentive, as she could not eat more than one thing at a time.

'Stay and dance with us, Helen,' begged Rupert.

'I'd love to, but my programme is full,' replied Helen.

'Can't you cut one of them?' suggested Elizabeth.

'Oh, no!' replied Helen.

'Of course she can't – don't be stupid,' said Rupert. 'Wish you could, though,' he added.

The meal was hilarious, and Helen enjoyed the break. It was good to be a child again sometimes. Couples returning to the ballroom recalled her, however, and scattering liberal thanks, she bade them a hasty adieu; her first after-refreshments partner would be wondering where she was. She mingled with the guests wending their way slowly across the hall, and her band of now faithful adorers saw her joined by her partner and pass on with an air of complete innocence except for a glance which she threw in their direction – Rupert even swore that she winked.

The second half of the evening was even more enjoyable than the first, for Eleanor, having reinstated herself in St John's good opinion, put herself out to be as charming as she could. The tense atmosphere around her cleared and even some of Helen's group migrated to Eleanor's.

At midnight everyone crossed arms round the room and sang the New Year in with *Auld Lang Syne;* the orchestra paused for a few minutes' break, then began again and played for another couple of hours, by which time nearly everyone was willing to stop. Most of the children had retired to bed or been fetched after the singing, and those that had to remain because of their parents had a hard job to keep awake.

Final adieux were exchanged between hosts and guests and between guests and guests, until all but those sleeping under the Herricks' hospitable roof had departed. Aunt Edith closed the ballroom door, saying it could wait till the morrow when they would feel more like clearing up. They must all go straight to bed – and need not get up till they felt like it in the morning.

Helen mounted the stairs with Eleanor, saying as they began the ascent,

'Well, that was grand, Len!'

'Did you enjoy it?'

'Oh yes! I've not enjoyed anything so much for a long time. Thank you very much.'

'Don't thank me! Mum did all the arranging. I'm glad you enjoyed it, though. I did too. I thought I wasn't going to at first.'

'Oh, Len! Why?'

'Oh, I don't know! Everyone was so boring and did nothing but talk learnedly about Shakespeare and politics and the National Gallery and lots of other things.'

'That's just what I liked about it – there were so many people who *knew* things – besides, I should have thought you would have liked talking about the National Gallery.'

'It's all right for you – you don't have it week after week. Teddy's sweet and so are some of his friends, but I get so *sick* of listening to their everlasting talk.'

They had reached the landing by this time and here parted company.

'But I did enjoy it,' Eleanor added. 'Well, goodnight.'

'Goodnight.'

Chapter XLI

Nobody was disturbed after such a late night – or as Gordon later put it, early morning – and it was lunchtime before everyone had appeared. Those who were merely staying the night had already left and the Wentworths were the only ones left in residence. Over lunch, all were enthusiastic in their praise of the dance and their expressions of enjoyment.

'What about the skating?' asked Rupert, changing the subject. His question immediately altered the course of the conversation.

'Let's go this afternoon,' urged Penelope.

'Yes. Who's for skating?' asked Gordon. 'I vote we go to Blenheim,' he added, amidst a general shout of 'Me!'

'Don't you think Blenheim is a little dangerous, dear?' queried his mother anxiously. 'If Gerry and Liz and the two youngest want to go, hadn't you better go to Port Meadow?'

'Oh, no! It'll be far too crowded – everybody goes to Port Meadow.'

'But is it safe? I don't want the children –'

'Oh, they'll be all right,' put in Rupert.

'Please, Aunt Edith,' said Gerald hestitatingly, 'I'll not go if it means they –'

'Not go!' echoed Aunt Edith, 'but of course you'll go!'

'No, really, Aunt Edith, please – I'd rather not.'

'Why ever not?' asked Elizabeth.

'Well, I – I can't skate and – and I'd rather read!'

Everyone laughed, and Aunt Edith said,

'Very well, dear, you needn't go if you don't want to; but what about the others?'

'Oh, we'll be all right,' said Elizabeth confidently.

'Will you?' Her mother sounded doubtful.

'They'll be OK,' confirmed Rupert. 'Besides, there'll be tons of us there to see if they go through.'

'How will you get there?' asked Uncle Raymond.

'By car,' said Gordon. 'Teddy and I can drive.'

'What condition are the roads in?' Uncle Raymond was thinking of his tyres.

'Oh, not too bad. If we go slow-and-careful-like we'll be quite all right. Shan't we, Teddy?'

'Oh yes. Yes, quite.'

'Very well. But mind you *are* careful. I don't want the cars ruined.'

'Don't worry. They'll come to no harm.'

'Right. But you must stop as soon as it begins to get dark. I don't want any accidents.'

There was something in Uncle Raymond's tone which would allow for no argument, and even Rupert did not press the point. Having gained permission to go, the plan developed rapidly. Gordon and Anne rang up friends who lived in Oxford, asking them to join them on the lake – they could not offer transport – and the climax was reached when Basil suggested booking tea for their own party at the Marlborough Arms in Woodstock, in whose vicinity Blenheim Palace stood.

Accordingly, armed with skating boots, hockey sticks, walking sticks and a piece of wood with which to play ice hockey, they set off for Woodstock.

Outside the city the snow lay thicker, and they began to wonder whether it would be possible to skate on the lake at all. The sky was an even grey and merged into the near horizon all round them. It took half an hour to cover the eight miles to Woodstock, for Teddy and Gordon kept their promises to drive slowly. Not many cars were on the road, and the only signs of life were in the villages passed en route.

Passing the main entrance to the Palace on their left, they drove on into Woodstock so that their cousins could see and admire its stately Queen Anne houses, broad streets and old-world atmosphere. Helen was thrilled and thought how Margaret would love to sketch here. It was quite unspoiled by anything modern and her imagination began to work, seeing men and women in frock coats and flowered waistcoats, sweeping skirts and flowing wigs coming out of the doors and walking down the streets. They pulled up for a minute or two outside the Marlborough Arms for Gordon to go in and order tea. This accomplished, they drove on, through the back gates of the Palace and into the park. It looked beautiful in the snow, but Blenheim Palace itself almost brought tears to Penelope's eyes, it was so ugly.

Luckily, time was too precious for much commiseration over the Palace. They parked the cars and, collecting their skates and sticks, descended to the lake. One or two people were already there but there was plenty of room for more. Hastily changing into their boots and leaving their shoes in a pile by some bushes, they scrambled on to the ice and made one or two preliminary turns to get accustomed to the feel. The Herricks, who had been several times before that season, were quite at home, but the Wentworths were at a disadvantage, not having been on skates for a year or more, and had a succession of tumbles, which caused much laughter and rude remarks. It did not take long to 'get into it' again, however, and they were soon as proficient as their cousins.

While awaiting the arrival of the six friends who had promised to come, they practised turns and glided off round the lake to explore. The ice was hard and smooth, for enterprising people had previously brought brooms and swept the snow off the surface. In one or two places where the water had frozen in ripples, it had been caught and refused to be dislodged; but these areas could be avoided, and added to the fun – swift and sudden turns to be accomplished with sitting down.

By the time the rest of their party had arrived they were all feeling confident on their skates. Rupert and Alban seized hockey sticks and the putt and began a match between themselves which drew in everyone until the game became fast and furious. Here they paused to welcome their friends, pick sides and mark out an imaginary pitch and goals. They agreed upon some impromptu rules and took their places.

Their main theme was similar to ordinary hockey but there were no restrictions as to where they could go; consequently the play became somewhat involved and not a little dangerous. There were some good skaters amongst them and the game was so swift that even Penelope found it difficult to keep pace with it. Back and forth spun the putt, the attacking side in hot pursuit, whizzing over the ice at break-neck speed, until one of the defenders checked it and sent it shooting back in the opposite direction.

At the end of half an hour the score was two all and they paused for a break before beginning the second half of the game. Nearly everyone had discarded at least one jumper and scarf and more were to follow – skating is the best-known sport for getting thoroughly warm.

The game progressed evenly, another goal being scored on each side. Gordon, who was acting as umpire, cheered on his side with encouraging remarks and Basil, not to be outdone, yelled to his. As the second half drew near to its end the play became even more furious, both sides trying to secure the winning goal. Collisions became more frequent and their impact more stunning, but nobody was hurt.

Gordon was just about to blow the final whistle when the opposing side, spurred to greater efforts by the fleeting time in which goals could be accomplished, rushed forward with the putt, displayed some excellent team-work and brilliant play. Penelope caught it and whizzed with it over the ice; when attacked, she sent it out to wing, who avoided further attack and returned it to her a few yards from the goal. An unforeseen descent from behind laid her by the heels, but she first managed to hit the putt so hard and straight that the goalie could not stop it and it sailed through the goal and away across the lake. The whistle blew as Penelope picked herself up, her opponent apologizing for the accident and everyone exclaiming, 'Well played!' and 'Good shot!'

There was a short period of relaxation, everybody puffing and panting, talking and laughing at the same time. Helen produced a bag of toffees and passed it round, and they all sucked happily. Already the daylight was fading and Teddy, true to his promise, bade them collect their belongings and make tracks for the cars. Rupert, naturally, objected, and urged one more spin round the lake, but Teddy insisted and Gordon backed him up. Rupert was forced to submit and remove his skates.

They straggled back to the cars in ones and twos, saying goodbye to their friends, and drove back to the Marlborough Arms for tea. This was eaten in the cosy old-world lounge, round the wide stone hearth in which a log fire crackled merrily, sending sparks shooting up the chimney.

It was dark by the time they had finished and the drive home was accomplished at a slower pace than before. Rupert urged more speed, but Teddy and Gordon would take no risks – the responsibility of so many lives in their hands was too great.

Back at home, when the party had left, Aunt Edith suggested to Gerald that he should accompany her into town to look round the bookshops. Gerald jumped at the idea and Mr Wentworth, hearing of it, decided to go too. In fact he insisted that Aunt Edith should not trouble, as she must be very busy. Aunt Edith, after a short protest, submitted, for she *had* a lot to do.

The two booklovers accordingly set out alone and spent a blissful afternoon browsing in Blackwell's bookshop, lost to the world outside and forgetful of time. It was not until the lights were switched on that Mr Wentworth realized he had been straining his eyes and that he and Gerald ought to be returning. He looked round for his son, but he was nowhere to be seen. Mr Wentworth did not worry, knowing that he could not have wandered far, so he paid for the books he had chosen and searched out Gerald afterwards. He was eventually found in a corner in the second-hand department, devouring hungrily the pages, worn and yellow, of an old edition of Milton's shorter poems, which he desired to buy. Unfortunately, his book tokens covered only half the cost, but 'Christmas money' came in handy, and he walked out of the shop clasping his treasure firmly to his side.

'Oh, Father!' he exclaimed as they walked down Broad Street towards the bus stop, 'this *is* a lovely place! Couldn't all these old buildings tell some stories if they could speak!'

'Yes; and the more you see it the more you love it, Gerald. If you stop and listen there are many voices which will whisper in your ears and tell you secrets that you little dream of. I hope one day you will be privileged to come here, as I did, to study.'

'Oh, may I? There is nothing I should like more.'

'Then work hard, my boy, and it will be possible. The future is in your hands.'

'Indeed I will! And may I go to Christ Church and read Classics, as you did?'

'I cannot promise which college you will go to. You will have to work doubly hard if you want to go to Christ Church.'

'Oh, I will, I will!'

It was a source of great pleasure to Mr Wentworth that Gerald should have developed so early such a strong affection for the beautiful city he loved so much himself, and he could have wished for nothing more than that his son should follow in his footsteps. He was clever and learned quickly, and more important, he had an aptitude for study. In ten years' time he would have completed his course, and then anything might happen – who could tell? Mr Wentworth fell to dreaming of the possible careers that Gerald could follow, and planned for him a life brilliant with success – such a life as he had once dreamed of for himself and which only ill-health had prevented his following. Gerald, he hoped, would be more fortunate.

He became aware that Gerald was speaking.

'I wish we could have stayed longer,' he was saying. 'It would take about three weeks to go round properly.'

Thinking he was referring to Oxford, Mr Wentworth agreed.

Aunt Edith had an appetizing tea waiting for them and they ate it round the fire in the drawing room with the lights turned out, and only the standard lamp lit. Mr Wentworth and Gerald showed their purchases, the latter praising the city and all it contained until Aunt Edith suggested he should stop talking and eat his tea.

The remainder of the time was taken up with shopping, more sight-seeing and music and an evening at the theatre. By the end of the visit, which passed all too quickly, the cousins were firm friends, all except Philip, who, as usual, made no effort to be friendly. Rupert expressed his opinion privately to Gordon that he thought his cousin 'a disagreeable bounder, not worth bothering about', and he wondered why the dickens Mon was so fond of him – for Monica, oddly enough, had developed an abject kind of adoration for Philip; blushed when he spoke to her and giggled at everything he said. Philip at first despised her for being a 'silly schoolgirl', then pretended to be indifferent, and finally, as the others retracted, became, in his condescending way, quite friendly. This suited Monica: she thrived on distant recognition. One of her heroes was Lord Byron, and Philip reminded her strongly of him. She liked to imagine him in a loose neck-cloth and tight-fitting trousers, pacing up and down his room reciting 'She walks in beauty like the night' to some unseen fair one (she was honest enough not to imagine herself in the part) and it was a little disappointing that when her idol did open his mouth, nothing the least resembling poetry ever came out of it.

Having discovered her passion, Rupert teased her mercilessly, but Monica, whose temper corresponded to her fiery locks, was quite capable of standing up for herself, and got her own back by calling him 'Rupe', an abbreviation he could not bear and which his family used when they wanted to tease or annoy him.

There was a general wail on the last day at the thought that tomorrow the Wentworths must go home. The children begged them to stay longer, but Mrs Wentworth replied that they had already stayed two days longer than they had intended and they could not spare any more time. Further visits were pressed for in the near future, but Mr Wentworth said that it was their turn to go and stay with them; he did not quite know where they would all sleep, but no doubt it could be managed somehow, even if it meant making improvised beds in the summer house. Rupert replied that he was quite willing to sleep in the coal house if need be, so long as they gave him black sheets to lie on.

With some difficulty they all squeezed into the larger of Uncle

Raymond's two cars and Teddy drove them to the station, the others making their adieux at the house and gate.

'Have you got the tickets, Uncle James?' Teddy asked when they arrived.

'Yes, I think so,' replied Mr Wentworth. 'At least, your aunt has. Augusta my dear, have you got the tickets?'

Mrs Wentworth had, and all was well. They secured their seats and settled themselves in the carriage, bidding Teddy a last goodbye through the window, and waving in turns until they could see him no more.

'I *like* Teddy,' said Helen, as her father's newspaper came out and her mother began to search for her knitting.

'Yes, he's a nice lad,' agreed Mr Wentworth.

'He's so kind and considerate,' went on Helen. 'Do you know, he came up specially to carry Penny's and my cases down for us, and nobody asked him.'

'He's always very nice to me,' said Mrs Wentworth. 'I must say, I do like young people to show a little respect for their elders, even if they don't feel it.'

The whole family was brought to the bench for discussion and this served to pass the time to London. By the time Mereford was reached it was quite dark and the taxi-driver who took them home was cautious in the extreme, not knowing the way very well.

The house looked dark and cheerless as Mr Wentworth unlocked the door and pushed it open.

The Wentworths (1946)

Chapter XLII

'Put the kettle on, Helen,' said Mrs Wentworth, almost before she had had time to turn round, 'and let's have some tea.'

'A cup of tea, the Walrus said, is what we chiefly need!' cried Penelope, and added as an afterthought,

'Biscuits, butter and cheese besides, are very good indeed.'

She sounded hopeful, but Helen disillusioned her by saying, as she departed to the kitchen,

'There's no food of that description in the house.'

Mrs Wentworth put on a business-like air and soon had the family disposing of the luggage, which had been strewn all over the hall:

'Penelope, take those into the kitchen and empty them – Philip, Alban, carry the cases upstairs – Gerald, put all the newspapers and books where they should go – James, switch on the fire in our bedroom if you're going up; the place feels like an ice-house.'

The children completed their tasks and came back for more, and Mrs Wentworth, still in her coat and hat, issued further orders. Penelope switched on electric fires, while Philip, Alban and Gerald helped their father to unpack. Helen laid a hasty meal in the kitchen, as being the least trouble, and opened tins – their only food supply until the orders were collected from the village. Mrs Wentworth went upstairs to take off her outer garments and have a wash, and Helen had just finished laying the table when the kettle boiled and everything stopped for tea.

Alban and Penelope did full justice to what Helen had been able to provide, but Gerald was too sleepy to care much for food.

'Golly, I'm tired!' he exclaimed after yawning for about the tenth time since he sat down.

'I'm sure you are,' said his mother. 'We seem to have been travelling for hours.'

'Well, we have, quite a few.' Alban attacked another tinned pear with zest, chasing it round and round his plate with his spoon until his patience ran out, when he told them all to 'look the other way' and got rid of it in an easier, if less 'dining room' manner.

'Well, I hope everyone enjoyed it,' Mrs Wentworth said later. 'Edith certainly has a beautiful house.'

'Rather!' responded Penelope enthusiastically. 'But I shouldn't like to live there always.'

'Why not?' asked Mrs Wentworth.

'Well, it's sort of – stiff, somehow…'

'Formal, do you mean?' asked Helen.

'Partly, yes; and it's so grand – and – oh, I dunno. I can't explain it. I prefer home, anyway.'

'Too confoundedly poshocracy for my liking,' grunted Philip. 'I like things plain and simple.'

'Well, that's Edith,' responded Mrs Wentworth. 'She always did like to do things in style. She used to say that if she ever had the money she wanted to have at least six children and live in a big house and run it like a palace.'

'Well, she's got her wish,' said Alban, 'with a quartette of extra brats thrown in.'

'Precisely which ones are you referring to when you call them "brats"?' enquired Helen.

'Liz for one!' chimed in Gerald before Alban could open his mouth.

'And I should say Rupert and Monica,' suggested Mr Wentworth. 'I don't know which is the more "brattish"!'

'As I was about to say…' said Alban, 'only was not permitted to do so…incidentally, as we are on the subject of bratterie – when are you going to bed, Gerry?'

While Gerald was replying to this insult, Penelope murmured,

'New French verb: *Je me bratte, tu te brattes, il se bratte;* perfect tense, *ils se sont brattés!*'

There was a pause of more idle sitting, then Penelope suddenly jumped to her feet and exclaimed,

'Do you know what? I quite forgot to see if there were any letters! That comes of having a letter box you can't see into!'

She dashed out of the room and was heard to call out joyfully when she reached the front door.

'Bags of them!' she said, returning with a handful of letters. 'Let's see…J.P. Wentworth, Esquire, postmark, Mereford; Mrs J.P. Wentworth, postmark, Aberdeen; J.P. Wentworth, Esquire, postmark, London; Mr J.P. Wentworth, postmark, um-um-um-Bris – Bristol; Miss

Hot-and-Cold-Water – I mean, Miss H.C.Wentworth, postmark, Edinburgh –'

'Oh good, that's Charlie,' interrupted Helen, seizing the fat-looking envelope which Penelope handed to her. 'I was hoping that would be waiting for me.'

'– Mrs Augusta Wentworth,' continued Penelope, as though there had been no interruption, 'postmark, Mereford; Philip Wentworth, Esquire, with a foreign stamp – don't snatch!' she exclaimed, looking disapprovingly at her brother, 'Mr James Wentworth, postmark, London; Miss H.C. Wentworth, postmark, Strowsby, Lincs –'

'Oh, that's Margaret,' said Helen happily.

'– and J.P. Wentworth, Esquire, postmark – um – somewhere in Kent.'

'Why, that's Mr Moore,' said Mr Wentworth, scanning the last envelope. 'I wonder how he is.'

'Nothing for me?' enquired Alban in an injured tone.

'No.'

'I never get any letters,' moaned Alban.

'Well, you never write any,' said Penelope.

'There *is* that, of course –'

'Oh, Charlie's sent some snaps!' cried Helen delightedly, unfolding the lengthy epistle he had written and causing half-a-dozen photographs to fall into her lap.

'Let's have a look,' begged Penelope, leaning over the table.

Helen looked at them herself and passed them on, then deciding she could not enjoy Charles' letter until she had time to take it in, put it back in the envelope.

'H'm, nice lot of bills, and other such interesting documents,' said Mrs Wentworth. 'Only one –'

'Damn!' cried Philip, giving the table an angry thump with his fist.

'Philip!' exclaimed Mr Wentworth.

'Oh, I'm sorry,' growled Philip. 'No, I'm not. Damn, damn, damn, and damn again!'

'Philip, Philip!' cried Mrs Wentworth in dismay, while the others looked alarmed, 'Whatever is the matter?'

'Oh my God, I can't stand this!' Philip jumped up, stormed out of the room and slammed the door behind him, leaving his family staring blankly at each other, wondering what his wrath was about.

Mrs Wentworth recovered herself first and ordered her two youngest to bed. Recognizing the note of authority in her voice, they went without a murmur. Even Alban was subdued, and left the room at his mother's bidding to go and finish unpacking, without even so much as a query.

'What was all that about, do you think?' asked Mrs Wentworth. There was a nervous quiver in her voice.

'I don't know,' replied Helen quietly. She mustn't get excited.

'Helen, Helen!' cried Mr Wentworth dazedly. 'What is it? What has happened?'

'I don't know, Father, something in the letter, I think.'

'It must have been pretty serious to make him exclaim like that,' said Mrs Wentworth.

'I hoped I should never live to hear him swear,' Mr Wentworth added.

'I'm afraid he's a long way from us,' sighed Mrs Wentworth.

'Helen dear, find out what the trouble is. He won't tell either of us, I'm sure.'

Her father's words struck coldly against Helen's heart, for they made her realize more strongly than ever that there was no bond between parents and son. She had been so hopeful during the past month. Philip had tried to be more sympathetic; he had not quarrelled once with Alban, and had been such a help with the school concert; she really had begun to think he was forgetting his past and turning over a new leaf.

And now this letter had come, causing all the good to be undone, and Philip to break out in a way which he must have known would hurt his parents, particularly his father, who detested swearing, whatever the provocation. She could not suppress a sigh at the thought that everything must be gone through again, and this time it would be more difficult.

'Yes,' she said, 'I'll do my best.'

She rose sadly from her chair and began to clear away the cups and plates. Mrs Wentworth made to assist, but she would not allow it. They sat for a while longer, Mr and Mrs Wentworth not quite knowing what to do, for although they longed to be master of the situation, both felt utterly helpless. The atmosphere was tense and they were secretly relieved when Helen said there was no point in their sitting up and they'd better go to bed.

'I shan't sleep till I know what the matter is,' said Mrs Wentworth, half-reluctant to leave Helen to deal with Philip alone and yet glad to be relieved of the responsibility. 'Helen, dear, come and tell us before you go to bed.'

Helen said nothing. She was not at all sure that Philip would communicate anything, even to herself, in his present mood. Luckily, her mother did not wait for a reply before going on,

'Are you sure you can manage? It doesn't seem quite fair to go to bed…'

'Now, don't you worry,' replied Helen, speaking with a cheerfulness which she did not feel, 'it will be all right. Go to bed and have a good rest. I'm sure you're tired. I can tell you tomorrow.'

'Well, yes, I am,' admitted Mrs Wentworth. 'Goodnight, dear.'

'Goodnight.' Helen kissed her mother affectionately and she went out of the room.

Mr Wentworth lingered, wanting very much to express his emotions, but he found it impossible.

'Helen, I –' he began. 'I'm sorry,' he ended lamely.

Helen understood.

'Goodnight, Father,' she said.

'Goodnight, my dear.' He kissed her. 'God bless you.'

Chapter XLIII

When the clearing up was completed, Helen mounted the stairs slowly, trying to summon up enough courage to ask Philip to tell her what was wrong. Somehow, she dreaded doing it, probably because something told her that she would meet with no success. She knocked on Philip's door. There was no answer, so she knocked again.

'Go away!' shouted Philip from within.

'Phil it's I – Helen. Can't I come in?'

'No! Go away!'

'I only wanted to say –'

'I don't care what you wanted to say!' Philip's voice rose in a wrathful crescendo.

'Very well,' she said, after a moment's silence. 'Goodnight, Phil.'

The word 'hopeless' loomed up in large letters before her eyes. She walked slowly across the landing and into her room. It was very cold and she was miserable. She shut the door and switched on the electric fire in a very distressed state of mind, and was glad of Charles' and Margaret's letters to cheer her up. She sat down on the edge of her bed and began to read Margaret's. It was full of happiness and Geoffrey and joy over the fact that her father and mother were coming home and so would be there for her wedding. She enclosed designs of her and Penelope's bridesmaids' dresses and a rough sketch of her own to show how they fitted in. Helen read it through twice, studied the designs and felt better. Charles' lengthy epistle – also full of content, though assuring her he was working himself to the bone – which she also read through twice, served to revive her spirits to normal and she soon ceased to be downhearted.

Her suitcase still remained to be unpacked and she set to work to put her things away where they belonged. She was in the middle of doing this when there was a loud knock on her door, causing her to jump so much that she nearly dropped what she was carrying. Without waiting for a reply, the door opened slightly and Philip's voice said in a brusque manner,

'Helen! Come here – I want you.'

Helen went to the door and opened it properly. Philip was standing there, rebellious, fiery-eyed and dishevelled. Indeed, in the dim light, he was quite a frightening figure.

'What is it?' she asked.

'Come into my room.' He crossed the landing without looking round. Helen followed.

'Shut the door.' She did so. 'Read that.' He pointed to a letter lying on his bed. Helen walked over to the bed, sat down on it, and picked up the letter. Philip watched her, noticing her expression change as she read it.

'Well?' he demanded, when she had finished.

Helen gazed at the floor and ran her finger and thumb repeatedly along the fold.

'Well?' demanded Philip again, seeing she made no effort to reply. 'Why don't you say something?'

'What is there to say?'

'There's a confounded lot to say!' he began, stumping up and down the room. 'Do you wonder I swore? Wouldn't you swear?' He stopped in front of her and waved his finger angrily at the letter. 'Do you think I could read how that chap's enjoying himself over there and think of the mouldy existence I'm leading at the moment and not want to go too? I'm sick of it!' He began to stump again. 'If I stay here another day I shall kill somebody! I *must* go – I can't stand it any longer!'

'But Phil, you can't go without any preparation –'

'Can't I? That's what you think! I did it before, and I can do it again. I must – do you understand? – must! I loathe this place and everyone in it – they all hate me – they all wish I were dead! I can't stand it, I tell you! I want life – excitement – I'm not meant to stay in a deadly dull hole like this. I'm going to France – and you're not going to stop me!'

'But Phil, you were happy –'

'Oh, was I?' Philip was bitter. 'I'm glad *you* think so. Happy indeed! Oh yes, I may have appeared to you and everyone else to be happy. Happy, in a place like this!'

'But I thought you enjoyed it. You liked helping with the concert, didn't you?'

'The concert – oh yes, that served to make a change, but I'm not made for that kind of thing. I want freedom and variety! I can't stick in one place all my life!'

'But didn't you enjoy going to Oxford?'

'Oxford? No, I hated it. Do you think I liked going to a place that reeked so of learning? I only went because I had to – they'd have wanted to know where I was if I didn't. And as for the Herricks! Eleanor's a silly, simpering idiot and Teddy's as weak as water. Gordon thinks he's the cat's whiskers and Basil's a smug little prig. Huh! Thank heaven I'm not likely to see them in France!'

'You weren't so anxious to go yesterday.'

'I hadn't had the letter – but I'd have gone anyway, don't imagine it's made any difference to that! It's just made me hate it all so much I could scream!'

'Have you thought what it will mean to Mother and Father?'

'I don't care a damn what it will mean! What do they care about me? What does anyone care about me? Nothing! Particularly Alban – blast him!'

'Phil! Phil!'

'Oh, I know, I'm a worthless scoundrel – all the blackest sins – I know! Oh, you can talk. Anyone can talk, but what do they know about it? They don't know what I did at college, they don't know what I did in France; they don't know a thing! And they don't care! Oh, yes, you can say they do, but I know jolly well that they don't!'

'Phil! Don't say such things! They're not true.'

'They are, I tell you! What do you know of my life? Oh, I know you've tried to reform me, but I'm not the type to be reformed. You can talk anyone into doing things for a time – you're about as good a talker as that Charlie Mainwaring you're so fond of –'

'Leave Charlie out of this!' cried Helen, her cheeks burning with indignation. 'You can say what you like to me, but I won't have you insulting Charlie!'

'What's it to you what I say or think? I don't believe even *you* really care two hoots what happens to me!' The words stung and Helen felt hot tears rush to her eyes, but she bit her lip and said nothing. 'What's it to you?' he went on. 'What do you know of life? You haven't seen what I've seen – how can you know? What do you care if I never come back? Tell me that!'

'Perhaps I *don't* know much about what you've been doing during the past eighteen months – you're not very communicative at the best of times. I don't doubt for a minute that you've been through some pretty unpleasant experiences, especially in France; but you've no right to say all these things about me' – she began to talk very rapidly, trying to overcome the choke in her voice – 'they're neither fair nor true. You're my brother – and I happen to be very fond of you, and if anything happened to you – I should be – very unhappy. I thought that – even if you didn't – trust anyone else – you did at least – trust me – and I think you are – very unkind –' She could not go on.

Philip, so far as he was able, repented having been so rude to his sister, for she was, as he well knew, the only true friend he had and he would be foolish to turn her against him just when he needed her most.

'I'm sorry,' he said gruffly. 'I didn't mean to hurt your feelings; but – oh God! I'm so fed up and sick of it all! Oh, Helen, don't you understand? I *can't* stay here! I'm not made for this deadly dull existence – I want life! Freedom! Adventure! I shall go mad if I don't get it!'

'Of course I understand. Isn't this just what you've always said? I know you're not happy here, nor ever will be. As for your being a worthless scoundrel, that isn't true either. There's a lot in you that will only come out in the right atmosphere. Perhaps I *have* tried to make you see things the way other people do, but I see now that I was wrong. You're not the type – as you said –'

'That I'm not!'

'Now listen, Phil. I know nothing will keep you once you have made up your mind to go – but are you *sure* you want to go to France? Have you forgotten – ?'

'No, but Dilke won't be there this time – he was always the ring-leader. It will be all right without him. I must go – I don't care what happens – I *must* get away.'

His first passionate rebelliousness was beginning to abate, and in a calmer frame of mind Helen knew she could handle him better.

'How long will you go for?'

'Dunno.'

'How will you live? You've no money of your own.'

'I'll manage somehow. I managed before, so I daresay I can manage again.'

'I don't like it.'

'Oh Lord! For heaven's sake don't start worrying! I'm quite capable of earning a living.'

Helen was not so sure, but Philip obviously thought he could, so she did not press the matter further.

'Phil,' she said after a pause, 'I've listened to all you have said and though I'm perfectly certain a great deal of it is wrong, and though I do think you *could* like Edmuston if you tried hard enough, I think that just now you do need a change. I'll not object to your going; but I don't think you ought to stay away longer than three months.'

'Why?' demanded Philip.

'Well, you can't go on like this for ever –'

'I can! I tell you, I'm not meant for a quiet, monotonous life. I'm not a settler – I'm a wanderer. I want adventure and variety!'

'Well, I still think you should come home occasionally.'

'I won't promise anything.'

Philip had never, as far as Helen could remember, made one single straightforward promise in his life – and it did not look as if he ever would. He was always afraid to do so in case it let him in for something unpleasant. Either he flatly refused or attached one or more conditions to it.

'There's one thing that I do want you to promise, and that is to write *at least* once a fortnight.'

'There may not be time.'

'You must make time. It doesn't take long just to give an account of your doings. You needn't write a book, but some sort of record – regular record – is essential if you want me to keep in touch with you. I can't write freely to somebody who doesn't answer my letters.'

'Oh, I'll send you something. How often I can't say – it'll depend on what I'm doing.'

'If you expect me to write to you as often as I've been doing, you must do something. I don't agree with a one-sided correspondence.'

'I'll write when I can – I can't say more than that, can I?'

Helen rose to her feet.

'No, I suppose you can't…I really must go to bed. You can tell me anything more you want to say in the morning.'

'OK – but I intend to go tomorrow.'

'Oh, Phil, don't be silly! How can you? You'll want a passport, and all sorts of other things.'

'Hmph! We'll see,' mumbled Philip, and with this half-disguised threat, they parted.

Chapter XLIV

Philip announced his intentions at breakfast the following day without any preparatory words whatever. He was brief and to the point but he gave no explanation even when asked. His mother protested and his father begged him to reconsider; Alban made a sarcastic remark about his sudden love of France, and Penelope, not knowing what had gone before, said she wanted to go too. Philip would not be shaken; he was going and he was going alone. He wanted a change; more than that he would not say. His mother wanted to know what he would do when he got there; he did not know. His father wanted to know how he proposed to get there; he did not care, so long as he did. To all their questions he was unresponsive and when his mother began making objections, Helen answered for him, supporting him and capping each objection with a better reason for overruling it. Seeing that she could not obtain mastery that way, Mrs Wentworth concluded the argument by forbidding him to go, and would listen to no more talk. Philip was apparently squashed, but nobody saw the gleam of exultant defiance and the contemptuous curl of his lip as he bent his head over his plate. They had a poor idea of his will if they thought a mere prohibition would have any effect.

The atmosphere was tense that morning. Philip spoke to no one, and every time he appeared, everyone instinctively drew back. Nobody dared do more than glance at him, half-bewildered, half-fearful. He was like a schoolboy in disgrace; each one of them wanted to say something but not one of them dared.

He went out about eleven o'clock and did not come back for lunch. Helen returned from shopping in Mereford to find her parents in such a state of nerves that they could not keep still for two minutes together. Lunch was eaten in strained silence; pleases and thank yous were said as shortly as possible, and the sound of knives and forks on plates was painful in its loudness. Penelope, trying to make no noise, let her fork slip through her fingers and clatter on to her plate, making everybody jump.

After lunch, Helen beckoned to Alban and asked him to take Penelope and Gerald to the pictures. Alban, half understanding, agreed, and they spent the afternoon in Mereford. She herself had work to do to prepare for the new term starting in two days' time.

Philip returned in time for tea, bringing with him the tenseness which had abated somewhat during his absence. He went up to his room and locked himself in, only coming down for supper. Penelope and Gerald were in bed by this time, but Alban was up and ripe for another quarrel. He had suspicions, and watched his brother closely, waiting for an opportunity to begin. He did not understand why they all accepted his behaviour without complaint, and had no intention of doing so himself. He knew that Philip would ignore his mother's words, and wanted them to know too.

'What are you doing tomorrow, Phil?' he asked as if it did not matter, the first to break the silence, which was even more strained than at lunch.

'What's it to you?'

'Oh, nothing. I was just wondering, that's all.'

'Well, you can wonder.'

'What time do you intend to get up?'

'In time for breakfast.'

'Oh, you will be here, then?'

Philip did not answer, so Alban went on,

'Do you know, Father, it's a funny thing. I meant to tell you before this, but I forgot. One of the cadets had been doing something he adntorta last term and he got a dickens of a bottle for it besides some extra duties, and he was so fed up he decided to run. So one night he went to bed early and pretended to go to sleep, and then when all the crew was asleep he got up under pretence of going to spend a penny and tried to escape.'

'Did he?' asked Mr Wentworth.

'Of course not,' replied Alban, who had been glancing at Philip all through this invented narrative. 'People who try that kind of thing never do. By the way, Phil, I shall probably come in and collect my stuff out of your wardrobe on the way to bed, so don't lock the door.'

'Just what are you getting at?' growled Philip menacingly.

'Oh, nothing, nothing,' responded Alban airily.

'Then shut your beastly little trap.'

'Oh!' exclaimed Alban, in mock surprise. 'I *beg* your pardon?'

'Oh, for heaven's sake dry up, can't you?' Philip was infuriated.

'Alban, I think you're being rather trying,' said Mr Wentworth gently.

'Yes, Alban, be quiet.' added Mrs Wentworth firmly.

Alban was amazed. His family did not fathom his plan, and he could not bring himself to accuse Philip openly – somehow, it seemed like tale-telling, and Alban had an abhorrence of tale-tellers. But he did not intend to be silenced so easily. Really, they must be *blind* if they couldn't see what was going to happen. He tried again:

'But Mother –'

'That is *enough*, Alban.'

Alban sat back in his chair and stared open-mouthed. His mother was calmly pouring out another cup of tea with an expression of complete absorption in what she was doing, which he considered almost unforgivable in the present circumstances. He wanted to argue further, but he was so used to 'discipline' and 'not answering back' his senior officers – unfair advantage they had! – that he did not dare to venture another word in argument. He shut his mouth and sat up, and offered one final opinion:

'All right – but don't say I didn't warn you.'

'May I go?' demanded Philip, rising from his seat. 'If he opens his mouth again I shall strangle him! – No I don't want any more.'

He went, and as the door closed, none too quietly, Alban began again.

'Father, you *must* listen! He's desperate – don't you understand?'

'I've told you once to be *quiet*, Alban,' said Mrs Wentworth severely.

'I'm sorry, Mother, but I *can't* be quiet. Don't you realize he's defying you? Are you going to let him? – without even trying to stop him?'

'Now listen to me, Alban,' said Mr Wentworth seriously. 'Philip isn't like you, and he doesn't behave like you. He has made up his mind to go, and if he will not stay, it isn't for want of talking on our part – just remember that. But the methods you employ are more likely to urge him on than hold him back and anyway, I think we know a little more of the circumstances than you do; and if we are satisfied, that should be enough.'

'But I don't understand how you *can* be!' cried Alban. 'Good Lord! If he was in the Navy and behaved like this he'd get into the dickens of a rattle.'

'Then perhaps it's as well he's not. He's always had a distaste for discipline.'

'Do him good,' muttered Alban.

'No, I don't think it would. Service life can either make or mar a man, and while admitting that in nine cases out of ten it makes him, the tenth case is marred beyond repair. Philip is a case in point.'

'So you're just going to let him defy you?'

'I have told you, Alban, we are satisfied. Now stop arguing and finish your supper.'

Alban obeyed, but he was quite unable to see their point of view, and was incredulous that they were apparently not able to see his. When supper was over he attacked Helen, catching her on her way up to her study, and held further argument on the stairs.

'Helen, do *you* think it's right?'

'What?'

'Why, to let Phil go off like this?'

'Oh, Alban, still on that subject? I thought we'd done with it.'

'They may have, but I haven't. Surely, *you're* not blind?'

'No, my eyes are very wide open, thank you.'

'Then why don't you do something? Oh, gosh! Is there nobody in the house who'll stand up to him?'

'I'll stand up *for* him. You seem to be doing all the standing up *to* that is necessary.'

'Believe me, I don't *want* him to stay. Far from it. Nobody will be happier than I when he's gone, but I don't like the way he's doing it.'

'He hasn't done anything yet.'

'No, but he's going to.'

'Well?'

'Well, are you going to let him?'

'Father and Mother said they were satisfied, and I should have thought that was enough.'

'They don't know anything about it. And anyway, Father knows he couldn't stop him – oh yes, I'm not blind, though I may be only seventeen.'

'Shall we let the matter drop? We don't seem able to agree on it.'

Once more Alban stared. Such obstinate blindness from Helen, who he had thought would have been more observant, was astonishing. His hold of the banisters, which had tightened in his excitement, lost its grip, and he fell back a step. For a second he said nothing, trying to take it all in, then said, in a voice slow and subdued with incredulity,

'I believe you take his part.'

'Of course I do. Haven't I always?'

'Yes but – this time…Honestly, Helen, don't you think he's a cad?'

'No, I don't.'

'Well, you wouldn't admit it if you did, I suppose; but you can't *like* the way he's behaving.'

'I don't like the way *you're* behaving.'

Alban came up with a bump. A direct reproach from Helen was unusual, and something to be taken notice of.

'Why?' he demanded.

'Well, to begin with, you don't know anything about what's been happening to Phil during the past few months; you don't help to improve matters by nagging; and Father did say they were satisfied with Phil's behaviour – and I don't think it's right to go on arguing after that: "Judge not that ye be not judged".'

Helen began to mount the stairs.

'All right, I'll dry up, as I see it's no use; but don't blame me if anything happens to him.'

'I shan't blame anybody, least of all you.'

Helen could not resist that final cut. There were times when Alban's insistence on playing the game was a little wearing.

Chapter XLV

That night Helen dreamed that Philip came into her room and stood for several minutes by her bed to see if she were asleep, then fumbled around in the dark until he found her dressing table and left a note on it. On the way out he tripped over her bedroom slippers and kicked one across the room. A muttered oath escaped from his lips as the shoe hit the wall, and he made a hasty but noiseless exit.

When she got out of bed next morning she discovered that one of her slippers was missing. She found it sitting under her chest of drawers at the other side of the room. On her dressing table was an envelope addressed to her in Philip's handwriting.

She began to wonder if she *had* dreamt it.

At first she was almost afraid to open it, but pulling herself together, she did, and read in Philip's fiery scrawl,

> Dear Helen,
>
> Am going to France. Will write when
> I get there. Please tell Mother that
> I couldn't stay.
>
> Phil

She stood for a few minutes taking it in and wondering how she was going to break the news. Another scene with Alban would be more than she could bear, and yet she knew what he would say when he heard. She couldn't keep it to herself, because Philip's non-appearance at breakfast would make them suspicious. How could she avoid telling them at once?

Suddenly an idea presented itself, so daring that she did not know whether she would be able to carry it off successfully. If only the truth could be kept back until Alban had departed, all would be saved. He would leave for Mereford on the ten o'clock bus. Could she withstand his questioning until then? She slipped into her dressing-gown and peering round her door to make sure nobody was about, crossed the landing and opened Philip's door. Everything inside the room was in order and his bed untouched. She extracted the key from inside the door, retreated and locked it after her. She went back to her room, took a deep breath, counted ten and got on with her dressing. The plan unfolded itself by degrees, one idea opening up another until, subject to no awkward questions, she had the whole undertaking complete.

She was down to breakfast before the rest of the family and so had even more time to make the plan watertight. Mr Wentworth was the first to appear, but he was soon followed, and all but Philip sat down to breakfast.

'Where's Phil?' asked Alban, as Helen hoped and thought he would.

'He won't be down for breakfast,' she replied firmly. 'He wanted to sleep on.'

'Huh!' said Alban scathingly. 'What's the matter with him?'

'He's very tired. We sat up talking late last night and I promised he shouldn't be disturbed.'

'Have you tried his door?'

'Of course not.' Really, Alban was playing the cards into her lap with incredible innocence.

'I should try it, if I were you,' Alban warned darkly.

Helen ignored him and tried not to think of the key sitting in her dressing-table drawer. She was thankful, therefore, when her father began a new topic of conversation. The first phase had been successfully accomplished and nobody had suspected anything. She had to be on her guard, however, for soon Alban would realize that he wanted his mackintosh and great-coat out of Philip's room.

The rest of breakfast passed with no more reference to Philip and it was not until their rising from the table that Alban remembered his clothes.

'Oh, by the way,' he said, 'my great-coat and mac are in Phil's wardrobe. I must get them.'

Helen was ready for him.

'You go and finish your packing,' she said. 'I'll get them.'

'Oh, you needn't bother, I can do it,' responded Alban. Helen sensed the ulterior motive behind his seeming politeness and silenced him with,

'No, you'd wake him with your heavy shoes on. I'll get them.'

'Oh, all right. Why are you so anxious for me to keep out? Has Phil run and you don't want me to know, or something?'

'I told you, Phil left strict instructions that he wasn't to be disturbed, and you know you always make more noise when you're trying to be quiet than you do when you're not.'

The truth of this Alban could not deny, and he had to submit. He retired to his room rather out of temper and finished his packing with the door open so that he could see when Helen went into Philip's room. If she wouldn't let him go in, she couldn't stop him putting his head round the door. Unfortunately, his little plan was spoilt because Helen did not go straight to Philip's room from her own, but into her mother's, and thence to Philip's, so that Alban neither saw nor heard her unlock the door and close it behind her. Thinking she was being an excessively long time, he came out on to the landing just as she appeared with his coats draped over her arm. This final outwitting displeased him and he took them from her with hardly so much as a thank you. Helen did not reproach him, although she would like to have done so. It was too dangerous a game to play when she was not sure of her ground.

She had not relocked Philip's door, but now she began to wonder whether she had not better do so, because Barbara would soon be up to help with the bed-making, and if Philip's bed were seen to be tidy she might quite innocently ask awkward questions. When Barbara came up she explained that Philip did not wish to be disturbed and that she would make his bed when he got up.

Mrs Wentworth suddenly decided that she had shopping to do in Mereford, and she would go on the bus with Alban. Penelope thought she would like to go too, so the last half hour was a scramble to be ready in time, and nobody thought of Philip.

Alban's last remark to Helen was,

'This time you win, but – you'll see.'

'When you have time, just give a little thought to the word "toleration", will you Alban?' replied Helen, 'and also to what somebody said, though I can't remember who just now, that "to know all would be to understand all".'

Alban looked at her for a few seconds in silence, then climbed on to the bus. As it prepared to leave and adieux were said, he added,

'I'll think about it.'

Helen smiled and waved until they were out of sight. She walked home with one load off her mind. It would be easier to tell Alban by letter.

Mrs Wentworth and Penelope would be back for lunch and she wondered whether to leave the news until then, when they would all hear it, or tell her father at once. She decided on the latter, because if Mrs Wentworth asked where Philip was, as Helen knew she would when he did not come down to lunch, and had to be told without preparation, there would be a scene – and the one thing they particularly wanted to avoid was Philip's history being disclosed in front of Penelope and Gerald.

Mr Wentworth was in his study. Helen collected Philip's note and tapped on the door.

'Come in.' Mr Wentworth looked up and when he saw who it was, hastily put down his book and made room for her.

Helen handed her father the note without saying anything and he read it through twice before making any comment. When he did, it was quiet and free of all bitterness.

'So Alban was right after all.'

'Yes, he was right. I knew that.'

'Poor Philip! I'm afraid he has had very little understanding from anyone but you. We couldn't expect to keep him.'

'I could wish it had not happened, though.'

'Yes; and yet we mustn't complain. He was never happy here – but it is a pity it came like this. He has had so little time to think.'

'My main concern is what he'll do when he gets there – he has no money and he knows no trade – he's an easy prey to all the winds that blow.'

'Don't you think he had enough of that sort of thing last time to keep him away from it in future?'

'I don't know – he certainly had enough – but things like that are always attractive, and there is no guarantee he may not be fascinated again. He isn't very well equipped to withstand temptation, you know.'

'No...we must just pray he comes to no harm. Poor Philip.'

Mr Wentworth took the blow remarkably well, Helen thought, and she admired his courage more than ever. To a man of his refined and idealistic nature, family troubles must be extremely distasteful and irritating; and yet he never lost his temper or showed any signs of annoyance. Mr Wentworth's calm philosophy had always been a subject of wonder, at first during his college days and later amongst the staff of the school where he had been Classics Master. Having no pride or false sense of dignity himself, he had never been ruffled by petty insults which had upset other masters twenty times a day. Of course, he had been 'played up' mercilessly by the boys – masters of mild temperament always are – but they had loved him all the same, because he was so kind. Then he had become a Head Master, and Helen knew that when he had to give up his work because his health broke down, the school showed how it felt towards him by mountains of gifts and letters of appreciation. In those days, however, he had not had the family upheavals that he had been having lately. Indeed, there had been as much trouble during the past three months as there had been during the whole of his married life, and if he had been angry, Helen would have forgiven him. But he was not. Like Mr Moore, with an increase in his trials he seemed to have increased courage to bear them. Helen knew that it was because of his supreme faith in the goodness of God, and had often prayed that she might have it too.

'Does Mother know?' he asked after a pause. 'She will be very upset, I'm afraid.'

'No, she doesn't. I kept it from her – indeed from everyone – until Alban had gone. I'm afraid it was very cowardly, but I just couldn't have borne another argument such as we had last night.'

'No.' Mr Wentworth smiled sadly, knowing Helen's feelings on this matter. 'Poor Mother,' he went on. 'She won't like it at all. We must break it to her gently.'

'Yes.' Helen felt she had been doing rather a lot of gentle breaking lately, and never enjoyed breaking things gently with her mother. One never knew how she would take them, especially when they concerned Philip.

Mrs Wentworth and Penelope returned in time for lunch, full of their adventures and the success of their expedition. Alban's train had been punctual, so they had wasted no time at the station – if there was anything Mrs Wentworth particularly hated, it was waiting on platforms for trains which were late. She always thought of the important things she might be doing. She was far too absorbed in her purchases to listen to confidences, and Helen was forced to leave news-breaking until after lunch. She hoped Philip's absence would cause no disturbance. He had been out to lunch without warning so often lately that perhaps it would not be noticed.

Mrs Wentworth's reception of the news when Helen at last did find an opportunity to tell it, was, as usual, unexpected. A swift outburst of wrath was followed by complete calm and self-control. She asked questions, but they were not flustered. The almost unbearable qualms Helen had experienced with the first 'Mother, I've got something to tell you,' died down, and she heaved a great sigh of relief. The three of them sat down and discussed the situation together, and by tea-time were calmed down sufficiently to tell Penelope and Gerald that Philip had gone to France for a holiday.

Chapter XLVI

Although there was a constant worry about Philip at the back of her mind, Helen found life more or less normal once she returned to school. There was always a great deal to do, and when she was not working there were letters to write, the garden to look after, the darning to do and a thousand and one other little jobs in the house which needed attention. She also set about making the dresses she and Penelope were to wear for the wedding, and as she believed in doing a job properly if she was going to do it at all, she found her hands full. Penelope insisted on helping while she was still at home, but she was often more trouble than she was worth. Not knowing the first thing about dress-making, she had to ask Helen's advice on everything she did, distracting her attention from her own work, to the detriment of the product. In one morning, due to the constant 'What do I do now?' or 'I say, I can't get this right,' she joined two sets of seams wrongly, put the right sleeve into the left armhole (fortunately she had only tacked it) and very nearly cut the facings out of the skirt. In the end she decided it really wasn't worth it and if the dresses were not to be spoiled irretrievably she had better wait to continue until Penelope and Gerald had returned to school.

Mrs Wentworth continued to worry audibly about Philip and almost every day asked Helen if she had received any letter from him. Mr Wentworth suffered in silence but Helen knew it was none the less deep and sincere because it was unexpressed. She herself was worried, more particularly because she could not write to him or make contact in any way. He had not even said where he was planning to go, though she thought it was probably Paris, at least to begin with. She prayed fervently that he would come to no harm and that he would not be led astray a second time. She thought he had probably learnt his lesson as far as that went, but he had left in such a rebellious mood that she trembled, sometimes, when she thought of what he might do.

It was therefore with the most tremendous relief that a week or two after Penelope and Gerald had gone back to school for the spring term, she received a letter with a French stamp on it and recognized Philip's unmistakable scrawl on the envelope. She slit it open and took the letter to her chair by the fire in her study. It was only two pages, but as she read it, a great weight lifted from her mind and heart and by the time she had finished it she was feeling more hopeful of Philip's immediate future than she had done for a very long time.

Dear Helen (he wrote),

Here I am at last. I'm sorry not to have written sooner, but things have been happening rather fast since I left. Going over on the boat I met a very decent fellow called Anderson. We got talking more or less straight away and palled up. He said he was an explorer and was about to go to South America on an expedition and was looking for a strong young man to join his crew (six altogether, he wanted, including himself). He asked what my plans were, and when I told him I hadn't got any, he invited me to be Number 6!!! I must say, I was very surprised, but also that I liked the idea, and I have accepted. I told him I had no experience of this sort of thing, but I was fit and was prepared to do anything. He said they weren't going for a month and during that time I could live with him and his family and he would instruct me and see that I was equipped.

So here I am! What an adventure, eh? I know it will be difficult but I'm prepared for that, and it's a challenge, and I like that too. I'll let you know when we leave and I'll tell you where you can send letters when I know. In the meantime, wish me luck! Oh, I should say that Anderson is English although he lives in France. Mrs Anderson is very kind and the family, Stephen, Jane and Robert, are all very friendly. Stephen is about my age, Jane a year or two younger and Robert about seventeen. You will be pleased to know that for once in my life I'm enjoying myself.

Yours ever,

Phil.

Helen read the letter through twice and was thankful beyond measure that Philip seemed, miraculously, to have fallen on his feet. The tone of his letter was so different from his mood before he left, and she prayed silently that he had at last found an outlet for his energies; and that in struggling with nature, as without doubt he would have to, his rebelliousness would be tamed a little.

She went downstairs to the lounge and read Philip's letter to her parents. They were both pleased to hear the news and Mr Wentworth remarked,

'I think perhaps this is just what Philip needs. I should never have thought of such a thing for him myself, but I can see that the adventure – indeed, even the danger – of this expedition would appeal to him. He doesn't lack courage in that direction.'

Mrs Wentworth agreed, although she did express a certain amount of reservation about Philip's 'taking up with a complete stranger and agreeing to go halfway round the world with a man he knew nothing about'.

'But wait a minute,' said Mr Wentworth, ' the name Anderson does ring a bell. I think I've read something about him in connection with exploration. In fact, I rather think there was a paragraph about him in *The Times* this morning. Would you be kind enough to give it to me, please, Helen dear? – and I'll see if I can find it.'

Helen gave her father the paper and he began to look through its pages. After a few minutes he said,

'Ah yes! Here we are. I thought I'd seen something: "Mr Edward Anderson, the explorer, is about to embark on an expedition to South America to explore some previously uncharted areas of the Amazon hinterland. He has done valuable work already in connection with the Incas and has written a best-selling book on the discoveries he made. He plans to leave at the end of February and expects to be away three months. He will be taking five others with him." So that's it. It's strange, isn't it, that we should read about it in the newspaper before we hear from Philip where they are going.'

'I don't think he knew exactly when he wrote,' said Helen. 'I think it could be that Mr Anderson didn't tell him immediately – wanted to get to know him better before going into details, in case he didn't think he would be up to it.'

'Yes,' said Mrs Wentworth, 'but I wish he weren't going so far away. I hope he does write. I shall be on tenter-hooks all the time, waiting for news.'

'I'll answer this straight away,' said Helen, 'now I've got an address to write to. I'll tell him we're all pleased about it and wish him luck; and next time I go to Mereford I'll get Anderson's book out of the library and then we can get an idea of what sort of person Phil has got himself mixed up with. If it's a best-seller they're bound to have it and if not, they can get it for me.'

'Yes,' responded Mr Wentworth, 'that's a very good idea, Helen. You do that, and then we'll all read it; and I'll write a note to Philip too and send him a contribution towards his expenses – it can go in with yours.'

'That's very generous of you, James,' observed his wife. 'He doesn't deserve it, after the way he has behaved.'

'No, my dear, perhaps he doesn't,' replied Mr Wentworth, 'but I think it would be good to put that behind us and try and help him to turn over a new leaf – a bit of encouragement would probably be a great boost to him just now. There is also the fact that he will be twenty-one in a few weeks' time and it doesn't look as though he will be celebrating his birthday even in this country, let alone at home. So all things considered, I think it would be a good idea to make his present a money one, then he can buy what he needs over and above what Mr Anderson seems to be going to supply him with.'

Mrs Wentworth agreed that the first part of her husband's remarks was probably true and she saw the need to do something about Philip's coming majority in a way that would be most acceptable to him. Helen and her father then both rose to go to their respective studies to write their letters.

About halfway through February Philip wrote again, thanking them for their letters and their encouragement and acknowledging receipt of their monetary gifts (Helen had added to the contribution as her present) in a very grateful and appreciative way ('You see, my dear, he *has* got some good and right feelings underneath all that bluster,' his father commented). He informed them that the expedition would be setting out from Le Havre on February 28th.

> Send letters here (he wrote) and Mrs Anderson will forward them with any others. It's more likely I'll get them this way than if you try to catch up with me along the way.
>
> The Andersons are a really decent sort of family. I'm sure you'd like them. I've had some very interesting discussions with them and we agree on a good many things. I don't know when I shall be able to write again. Don't worry about me. I'm in good hands and I shall be all right.

'Yes,' said Helen aloud to herself as she read it, 'I do believe you will.'

Chapter XLVII

When Alban, Penelope and Gerald were told by letter what Philip was doing, their reactions were characteristic.

> Well (wrote Alban) I can only say I'm pleased. It sounds like a jolly good idea to me. I'm sure it'll do him good. Hope he doesn't get uppish with Mr Anderson, though. He'd not be able to get away *there.* He'll jolly well have to lump whatever he gets. Anyway, here's hoping the old reprobate finds his niche.

Penelope, whose vivid romantic imagination conjured up all sorts of wild notions, wrote,

> I *say!* How marvellous! I wish I was going too! All those lovely jungles, and pygmies (her geography was a little vague) and brightly-coloured birds squawking all over the place. I hope he doesn't fall overboard while they're sailing up the Amazon and get eaten by crocodiles, or something awful.

Gerald, who knew even less than Penelope about what was involved, wrote,

> I think Phil is very lucky to be going to South America. As a matter of fact, we are doing it in Geog. this term and when I told old Crocker (the Geog. Master) about it, he said I should get him to send me as much information as he could, because it would help me to build up a more accurate picture of the area than I could get from books. I've written the enclosed note to Phil, so please will you send it to him when you write?

Another letter was dispatched to Philip, timed to arrive just before his final departure, and then they settled themselves down to wait for news, which they all accepted would be a long time coming. Helen thought about Philip's imminent adventure constantly. She saw all sorts of dangers and difficulties ahead for him, not the least of which was how he would get on with the other members of the party. As Alban said, if he lost his temper in that enclosed little community, he could make life very trying for them all, including himself. She wondered if Philip realized just how strict the discipline would have to be, the need for obedience to Mr Anderson and the need for them all to pull together in harmony. 'Please, God,' she prayed every day, 'keep him safe and let this be the making of him.'

She wrote to him every week. Sometimes Mr and Mrs Wentworth enclosed a note, but more often than not Helen's was the only letter. Although relations seemed to be improved, they still found it difficult to know what to say to him. She also added her part of the weekly letters that went to Penelope and Gerald. There was plenty of correspondence between herself and Margaret about arrangements for the wedding and, of course, she wrote a long letter to Charles every week as well. So what with preparation for her school work, her usual activities in the house and some in the church and village, and all this correspondence, she was kept busy and had not too much time to worry over Philip.

Life seemed to settle down into a routine and kept on an even keel most of the time. There was always the odd upset with one of the children at school, but these were relatively minor and did not trouble her. As she often said to herself, they were 'all in the day's work'.

She was just congratulating herself that all was going swimmingly, it was only a few weeks to Margaret's wedding and then, after that, Charles would be returning from Scotland and she would be able to see him at last, when something happened that disturbed her peace of mind once again and threw her life into turmoil.

One evening at the beginning of March, Mr Wentworth asked her to return a book to the Rectory which Reverend Ward had lent him, with grateful thanks for the loan, and to tell him he had enjoyed it very much and looked forward to discussing its contents with him sometime. Helen took the book and was soon ringing the bell at the Rectory. Mr Ward opened the door and when he saw who it was, said,

'Good evening, Miss Wentworth. Do come in. It's cold tonight, isn't it?'

He ushered her into his sitting room and bade her take the seat by the fire. When she objected that he had surely been sitting there and she could just as easily sit somewhere else, he said No indeed, and insisted that she have the place by the fire. Helen therefore took the seat and explained her mission, passing on her father's message exactly as he had given it. Mr Ward said,

'Thank you. I'm glad he enjoyed it; I thought he would; and I'd be very pleased to discuss it with him sometime. Please tell him just to let me know when it would be convenient for me to come round and I shall look forward to it.'

He took the book from Helen and put it on the table. He sat down and then got up again and asked,

'May I get you a cup of tea? Mrs Smith can soon make you one.'

Helen declined the offer, but Mr Ward said,

'Well, as a matter of fact I could do with one myself. Please do take your coat off and join me. I'll go and see about it.'

Feeling it would be rude, under these circumstances, to continue to say No, Helen accepted the offer. She took her coat and scarf off and put them over the back of her chair. Shortly afterwards the tea was brought in and Mr Ward did the honours.

They chatted about various things to do with the church as they sipped their tea, and then Helen asked,

'Are you happy here, Mr Ward? Have you settled in all right? It's a bit of a change from the city church which I understand you came from, I imagine.'

'Yes, it is; but I *am* enjoying it, thank you. It's a challenge to have a church in a totally different setting, you know.'

They continued to talk and Helen noticed that Mr Ward seemed to become increasingly agitated. She wondered what the matter was. Was he, in spite of what he said, troubled about something in the church – or even some*body* in the church? In the end, her sympathetic nature was so sorry for him that she felt she had to find out what was wrong – perhaps she could help in some way. After all, she knew everyone in the village and had known most of them for as long as she could remember. She knew one or two of them weren't the easiest people to get on with and perhaps Mr Ward had upset one of them, not consciously, but because he had said something in one of his sermons which had been taken the wrong way; or perhaps he had done something which somebody had taken exception to. In the end, she felt impelled to ask, as gently as she could,

'Mr Ward, is anything the matter?'

The Rector looked startled, as if caught in something he would have preferred to keep to himself.

'No,' he began. 'No, thank you.'

There was an awkward pause, as if he were having an inward struggle with himself, then he got up, picked up the book and took it to the bookshelf, as if to put it away; but he did not do so. Then he turned and said,

'Why should I lie to you? There *is* something the matter. I *cannot* keep silent any longer.'

Helen's heart missed a beat. Alban's warning flashed into her mind and she feared the worst. Nor was she mistaken.

'Ever since I met you,' Mr Ward continued, nervously turning the book in his hands, 'I have admired you very much indeed. I like what you are doing with the children in the school. That Christmas concert was a masterpiece. You do so much for the church and the village and I know that everybody loves you and you are everybody's friend. I know many of the things you do which *you* would never talk about but which other people tell me of. My feelings for you have been growing stronger and deeper during the time I've been here, and now I *must* tell you that I love you, Miss Wentworth. My uncle discerned my feelings the night you came with the carol-singers. I told him then that I didn't think there was much hope because there was somebody else. I determined, if that were true, to overcome my feelings and put those sort of thoughts out of my mind.' Dropping the book on the table, he took a chair and placing it right in front of her went on, 'But it's no use – I can't. I tell myself that perhaps I was wrong. I haven't seen you with anyone, nor have you spoken to me of anyone in a way which would make me think your heart was engaged elsewhere.'

He gazed at her with all the passion that was normally well under control; so much so that Helen, glancing up, was amazed when she realized that this normally very mild young man had depths of feeling which she had never seen before. He went on,

'Miss Wentworth, you are the most beautiful and wonderful girl I have ever met and I love you with all the ardour of which I am capable. I like my work here, yes, but with you beside me, what a difference it would make! It would be heaven, and there is nothing we could not do together! Please, Miss Wentworth – Helen – will you marry me?'

Helen's feelings, as she listened to this declaration, were indescribable. Knowing that there was no hope for him and never could be, she felt almost overwhelmed with compassion for this suitor who meant so sincerely every word he said. She was silent, trying to find words with which to decline his offer without hurting him too much – for hurt him she would, there was no getting away from that. He seized on her silence and began again:

'You do not say anything. Perhaps I have been too sudden. Perhaps you hesitate to enter into a life of comparative poverty after what you have been used to. It is a life of sacrifice and I have no right to ask you to share it with me. But you would make a *wonderful* Rector's wife – you have all the right qualities, and what is more, you would have the tremendous advantage of having known everybody all your life and understanding all their needs and problems. I don't feel I can go on without you. But perhaps you need more time to think – get used to the idea. That I understand, and I'm quite prepared to wait for an answer – but please, not too long. I can't bear it.'

This time, Helen felt she simply had to say something and put an end to false hopes.

'Mr Ward,' she said, 'you do me the greatest honour and I appreciate that, believe me. Whoever marries you will be a very lucky young woman – and I mean that, most sincerely. As for poverty and sacrifice, that wouldn't matter at all if I could love you the way you want. But you are right – there *is* somebody else; and the fact that you haven't seen me with him is simply because he is up in Scotland for six months and won't be free to come here until the beginning of June.'

Mr Ward looked so distressed that Helen felt dreadful; but she knew it was no use letting him go on thinking there might be some hope when she knew there wasn't. It was true that Charles had not as yet *said* anything but she knew how *she* felt and it was quite impossible for her to marry Mr Ward.

He got up from the chair and pushed it back under the table. He, too, realized that there was no hope. He should have believed his earlier instincts and not gone on deceiving himself the way he had been doing all these months. In a very subdued tone of voice he said,

'I understand, Miss Wentworth. I should not have spoken. Forgive me.'

'Mr Ward, there is nothing to forgive. I just hope you don't think I have said or done anything which you might have taken as encouragement. If you do, then it is for you to forgive me, for I certainly didn't intend it.'

'No, no, you have been perfectly controlled and proper. I cannot accuse you of that; but it will be difficult to forget what has passed between us tonight when I see you every Sunday from the pulpit. I am not a saint and I shall need your help, Miss Wentworth. Please pray for me.'

'That I certainly will. I am desperately sorry to have caused you pain, Mr Ward. I would not want to hurt you for the world, but – well, there's not much more I can say.'

'No, I do not expect it; and you may be sure that I shall not again bring this matter up between us. I shall never forget you, but I am sure that, with prayer and the passage of time, I shall manage to continue somehow.'

'I know you will. Now I must go.' She turned to pick up her coat and scarf. Mr Ward helped her into her coat and saw her to the front door. In the porch he took her hand in both his as he bade her goodnight and Helen said,

'I'm sorry, Mr Ward. I shan't breathe a word of this to anyone – I know how gossip gets round Edmuston – you can trust me completely on that. You *will* find somebody in due course. Goodnight.'

Giving her hand a final appreciative squeeze, Mr Ward bade her goodnight and went back to his sitting room feeling as if the light had gone out of his life, and he had no idea how he would be able to go on.

Helen walked back to her home with her mind going round in circles. First Bernard and now Mr Ward, and she hadn't done anything, so far as she knew, to give either of them ideas of that sort. She realized that what Mr Ward had said about seeing her in church every Sunday would be his main problem; but it wouldn't be much easier for her, to have to sit and look at him for an hour every Sunday during service. She considered whether it wouldn't be kinder to stay away for a bit; but she decided that it wouldn't. In the first place, it would be noticed; secondly, in the end it would be no help and indeed, might even make matters worse, because, when she did reappear, it would start it all up again in his mind; and in any case, she didn't want to stop going to church. Then she thought of going to church in Mereford for a few months; but in the end she would have to come back and the same thing would happen. In any case, she was involved in the church life in more ways than one and she couldn't just leave without explanation and yet still be in the village. Whatever she did would start the tongues wagging – and Mr Ward must be protected at all costs. She considered the possibility of going to stay with Margaret for a week or two, but that idea was dismissed immediately, for two reasons. First, she could give no adequate reason for the request; she wasn't sick and nobody had died. Second, Margaret most certainly wouldn't want her so near her wedding; she would just be in the way.

No, there was nothing for it. Both of them must face up to the situation, and with the help of God's sustaining grace, live through it. She was sure that Mr Ward *would* find a suitable wife one day and she prayed that it would be soon.

Chapter XLVIII

Margaret's wedding was fixed for the last Saturday in March and as it was not quite the end of term, it was arranged that Penelope would just have the day off school to attend it and return to Ilton in the evening. Helen had finished both their bridesmaids' dresses by half-term and so had been able to try Penelope's on her when she came home for that long weekend. She was to transport all their things when she and her parents drove up a few days before the wedding. Margaret wanted her friend with her during her last days of single blessedness, she said, and as it would be silly – and very expensive – for them to travel separately, she insisted that Mr and Mrs Wentworth came at the same time. Helen Brisley and a cousin of Geoffrey's were to be the other two bridesmaids. Ben Brisley was to collect Penelope with his sister halfway through the morning, and Geoffrey's cousin, who was roughly the same age as Penelope, would be arriving with the rest of her family at about the same time. Mr and Mrs Wentworth would sleep in the house, as would various close relations, and friends in and around Strowsby were offering hospitality to selected others.

Margaret gave her friend a most warm and loving welcome on their arrival and looked, Helen thought, even more radiantly beautiful than ever, if that were possible. They arrived during the afternoon and Helen was pleased to be introduced – or rather reintroduced – to Sir Arthur and Lady Robertson, whom she had not seen for about ten years. Sir Arthur was tall and grave, a legal man with a brilliant mind and clear speaking voice. As she watched his courteous, old-fashioned grace and manners, with his long face and sensitive fingers, it was easy, Helen thought, to see which of his parents Bernard took after, in looks if in nothing else; and the quiet gentleness and refined good looks of Lady Robertson had certainly been passed on to her daughter. She, too, was tall, and both had kept their figures remarkable well.

Helen was very glad, in fact, that they were there, because it relieved her of having to have *tête-à-têtes* with Bernard while Margaret was busy –

which she was, naturally, most of the time. Bernard was also practising hard for a recital the night before the wedding and that took him away as well. He had greeted her surprisingly calmly, Helen thought, in view of what had happened on the last occasion when they met, but she knew that, had they been left together on their own for any length of time, it could have been embarrassing for both of them.

Geoffrey popped in and out, bringing parcels which had been left at his digs, and he and Margaret had a great deal of delight opening them and seeing who had sent them. They spent a lot of time discussing last-minute arrangements but Margaret found the time to go for one or two walks with Helen, and the two friends had plenty to say to each other; but at tea-time on the day before the wedding, Lady Robertson insisted that everyone have a pause and sit down. This was acceded to most willingly and all expressed the feeling that it was good to get off the feet for a short while and enjoy a cup of tea. The other Robertson relations had arrived by this time, so it was quite a little party that gathered round the drawing room fire for refreshment.

'Is everything in order, dearie?' asked Sir Arthur of his daughter.

'Yes, I think so. Everything that can be delivered today has come and only the things that can't be done till tomorrow are left – like the flowers.'

Helen turned to Geoffrey, who was sitting between herself and Margaret.

'Are you having a stag-party tonight, Geoffrey?' she asked.

'No, I'm not, actually,' Geoffrey replied. 'I've never liked that idea and in any case I don't have lots of friends locally, such as you'd have in an office and so on. My friends live all over the world, so it would be difficult anyway. No, I'm doing something far more interesting.'

'Oh, what's that?'

'I'm going to Leicester to hear Bernard's recital.'

'Oh! Lucky you. I wish we could all come but obviously it's impossible. You'll have to represent the rest of us.'

Geoffrey was, in fact, going to drive Bernard over to Leicester and the two of them made their adieux soon afterwards, amidst many wishes of 'Good luck!' 'Hope it goes well!' and 'Don't be *too* late back. We don't want you falling asleep in the service!' Margaret said goodbye to Geoffrey in the hall while Bernard was fetching his case containing his evening suit and they were soon away; then it was back to work to complete any little tasks which had still to be done.

'Now, my dear,' said Lady Robertson to her daughter about half past eight, 'it's an early night for you. I doubt if you'll sleep but you can at least rest and that's better than nothing. Helen, take her to bed, there's a dear, and see that she does as she's told.'

Once by themselves in Margaret's bedroom, which, because of extra guests in the house, they were sharing, Margaret sat down on the edge of her bed and cried,

'Oh, Helen, I'm so happy! All right, I'm beginning to get butterflies in my stomach, but I believe that's quite normal the night before one's wedding. Geoffrey is *the* most wonderful person I have ever met and I only hope I can live to be worthy of him.'

Helen sat down on the bed beside her and, putting an arm round her shoulders, said,

'*He's* the lucky one, dear! And I hope you will both be supremely, marvellously happy. I'm sure you will.'

Margaret hugged her.

'Bless you!' she cried. 'I know we shall too; and I hope it won't be long before you can say the same. Nothing would give me greater pleasure than to see you as happy as I am.'

Helen smiled, but refused to be drawn.

'Where are you going to live?' she asked.

'We've got a dear little house not far from here,' answered Margaret, mentioning the name of a nearby village. 'Geoffrey loves this part of the country – he says it inspires him – and I do too, so we are both satisfied; but I am expecting to be doing quite a lot of travelling with him, when he goes looking for new subjects to write on, so it seems I shall be having rather an exciting life, at any rate to begin with.'

'Am I allowed to know where you are going for your honeymoon?'

'I don't mind *you* knowing, as long as you promise not to tell a soul.'

'I promise.'

'At first we thought of Skye but we realized we would really hardly be out of winter up there, so we're going south instead, Cornwall, to be precise.'

They rose from the bed and prepared for the night. When they were finally settled, Helen said,

'Goodnight, Margaret dear, and God bless you.'

'And you too,' responded Margaret, putting out the light.

The following day dawned bright and sunny and was quite warm. The Brisleys and Penelope arrived about half past eleven, the last-named in a state of great excitement and hardly able to keep still. Bernard's recital had gone well, he said – and he was his own harshest critic always – but it has to be admitted that little attention was paid to it on this most important day. Only Helen Brisley spared more than a minute to discuss it with him.

An early and very quick lunch was followed by everybody departing upstairs to change. Bernard went off to Geoffrey's digs, for he was acting as best man, amidst reminders of 'Have you got the ring?' and showing that he had not forgotten it.

The church was beautifully decorated and was packed. Margaret was as much loved in Strowsby as Helen was in Edmuston, and Geoffrey, although he was not as well known, was liked by those who had anything to do with him. Margaret must surely have been the most breathtakingly beautiful bride anyone ever saw, and when she walked down the aisle on Geoffrey's arm after the service, followed by the four pretty bridesmaids in their delicate-coloured dresses, there were several in the congregation who actually did catch their breath at the sight of her. Bernard carried his responsibilities through with dignity even though he did have to walk down the aisle afterwards with Helen, as chief bridesmaid, beside him.

The reception was held in the Robertsons' house, which, though not the size of Aunt Edith's, was quite large enough for the purpose. Penelope much enjoyed her brief hour of importance and made the most of the respite from 'dreary old school'.

Helen went upstairs with Margaret when the time came to change, to help her friend out of her finery and into her 'going-away dress'. Just before they went down again, Margaret looked at the plain golden ring on her finger and said,

'Perhaps it's a funny thing to say, Helen, but I look at this ring and I think to myself, "Whatever happens to me, for the rest of my life, there's one thing that will always be safe and secure. I'm married to Geoffrey now, and nobody can ever take that away from me".'

Helen embraced her and with a few more words of thanks and affection on both sides, they descended to the hall, where Geoffrey was waiting. The entire company assembled to see them off. Lady Robertson was doing her best not to break down and even Sir Arthur was having a struggle.

When the newly-weds had finally driven off, guests began to disperse. Penelope said goodbye to her parents and Helen and got into the car with the Brisleys to be taken back to 'dreary old school', but as Helen said, it was only for a couple of weeks and then she'd be coming home for the

Easter holidays. With that cheering thought she waved goodbye and blew kisses to them until the turn on to the road hid her from sight.

When the last guest had gone, Lady Robertson turned her attention to supervising the clearing up and Helen went upstairs to change out of her bridesmaid's dress and carefully fold both it and Penelope's ready for packing. She would be driving her parents home in the morning.

She took a final look round the room and also out of the window. Cuckoo Lane and the fateful wood it led to were visible in the distance and she had a strange feeling of sadness as she realized that she would not be coming here in the future – well, not to stay, at any rate. Margaret's dress hanging on its hook from the picture rail brought other thoughts to her mind as well and she thought longingly of Charles. Why did time have to pass so slowly?

The Wentworths set out straight after breakfast next morning and were home in time for the evening meal. As she got into bed that night, Helen thought to herself,

'One more excitement over. What next, I wonder?'

Chapter XLIX

Easter came and went and a few days later, while Penelope and Gerald were on holiday and Alban home on leave, a fat letter arrived from Philip.

They had had an uneventful crossing, he wrote, and had sailed a good many miles up the Amazon before Mr Anderson had called a halt. He described in some detail, mainly for Gerald's benefit, the scenery, the wildlife, what adventures they had had and some encounters with the natives they had met. He wrote well and they almost felt they were with him.

He said he liked Mr Anderson more the more he got to know him. He was a good leader and knew his stuff. On the one or two occasions when the members of the party had had arguments or even nearly come to blows, he was strict but fair; and so far he himself had managed to avoid scrapping with anyone. He really sounded happy and was obviously enjoying the challenge. He mentioned certain discomforts – the cramped conditions and the insect-life which they had to contend with – but he made light of them and generally wrote an extremely good and interesting letter, and as Gerald said, it was legible for once. Gerald imposed on himself the task of writing out all the descriptive bits to show 'old Crocker' at school and so his remark about legibility was heart-felt.

Alban's comment was, 'You wait till I go to sea! Then he won't be the only one having exciting adventures!'

'Yours won't be like that, though, will they?' said Penelope. 'I mean, you'll be on board ship all the time, you won't be going exploring.'

'Who knows?' responded Alban airily. 'But I must say,' he went on, 'old Phil hasn't half changed his tune. D'you think our intrepid explorer is going to become famous, like Mr Anderson?'

'Gosh!' exclaimed Penelope. 'Wouldn't that be super? "Philip Wentworth Esq., SOS, RSVP, has just published his tenth book about the jungles of South America and will be signing copies in Foyle's on the thirteenth inst".'

There was a general laugh and Gerald added,

'Well, he might, you know, if this letter's anything to go by. I think it's very interesting – and well-written, too. I mean, descriptions like that can be jolly boring, but his aren't.'

They continued discussing the details of Philip's letter for a while longer, then Alban said,

'I'm for the down – who's coming?'

Helen and Penelope expressed their willingness to join him, but Gerald said,

'I can't. It'll take me *ages* to copy all this out and I've only got a few more days to do it in.'

'I think it would do you good to go for a walk, Gerald,' said his mother. 'You spend far too much time indoors with your books. James, make him go. He needs the exercise.'

'Yes, Gerald, I agree. You should. Too much work isn't good for anyone and you'll ruin your health if you don't have some balance. I'd come myself if I could, believe me.'

Gerald had a great love and respect for his father and always wanted to please him if he could, so he agreed, rather reluctantly, to put his labours aside for the rest of the morning and go for the walk. Of course, once on the down he enjoyed himself, and spent the time when he was not being chased by Alban, looking for flint arrowheads and other items of interest of that sort. Rex was thoroughly happy and dashed about between the four of them, barking ecstatically.

As they neared the top of the down, Penelope said,

'It doesn't seem eight months since I had my accident. Coo! I wouldn't want to do that again. It wasn't funny, having to lie on the sofa all that time. I wonder what Charlie's doing.'

She was walking with Helen, and the latter said,

'No, young lady, you'd better not! And Charlie's taking his exams right at this moment, I think.'

'Is he? Then I hope he does well. I bet he will. He's very clever, isn't he?'

'Yes,' replied Helen, amused at her sister's enthusiasm.

Penelope ran off to join Gerald in his search for arrowheads, and Helen and Alban walked on by themselves.

'Let's go to the tumulus,' suggested Alban, and on Helen agreeing, shouted to the others to join them there.

'You know, I simply can't get over Phil,' he went on. 'I've never seen anyone change as he seems to have done. It's amazing.'

'I think,' Helen replied, 'it was because, underneath, he himself didn't know what he wanted. He went to Cambridge more to please Father than for any other reason, I believe; but he wasn't really suited for that kind of life, and I think this contributed a lot to his misery.'

'Yes, I think that's probably true,' said Alban, 'but he was very bad-tempered even before that. I don't think Father was strict enough with him when he was a child and Mother – well, she spoiled him.'

Alban's understanding of the situation was pretty near the mark, Helen thought, and she realized that her middle brother was growing up into quite a perspicacious young man. This would be of immense value to him at some stage in the future, when he was commissioned and perhaps in charge of his own ship. He tended to be very critical but he was only young and she was sure he would mellow with time and experience.

'Phil has some excellent qualities,' she said. 'I've always known that. It's just that he's different from the rest of us and we've never understood his need for the kind of challenge this trip is giving him. When he returns, Alban, treat him with respect and try to see the best side of him.'

'Yes, I will, I promise you, now I can see there *is* a best side. I never found it before. Funny, how you can live with somebody all your life and know so little about them.'

'That's true, but don't forget, we have all either been to or are at boarding school and now you are at Dartmouth, and so we only see each other during the holidays. When you are away all term like that you love coming home and tend to behave better when you're there than you might if you were at school locally and took each other more for granted.'

'Yes, I hadn't thought of that.' Alban picked up a piece of chalky flint and examined it. 'You know, Monica Herrick thought he was the cat's whiskers and mooned on about him being the spitting image of Lord Byron. I thought, at the time, if she knew more about Byron's private life she perhaps wouldn't like to keep up the comparison! Thank heavens, though, that's one thing that Phil has never shown any signs of imitating.'

'No indeed!'

At this point Penelope, Gerald and Rex appeared, clambered up the rise to the tumulus and stood there panting, Rex with his tongue out.

'One of my ambitions,' said Penelope, when she had had time to get her breath back, 'is to spend a night up here in this tumulus. It would be super to lie in here and look at the stars.'

'You'd freeze,' said Alban briefly.

'No, I shouldn't. I'd be well wrapped up and I'd bring a sleeping bag to keep me warm.'

'Wouldn't you be frightened up here all by yourself?' asked Gerald.

'No fear, I'd love it!'

'What if it started to rain in the middle of the night?' asked Helen, smiling once more at Penelope's enthusiasm, which was very refreshing.

'I'd choose a night when it wasn't going to rain,' replied Penelope, 'like in the middle of a heat-wave.'

'I'd dress up in skins like a Neolithic man and come and haunt you,' grinned Alban.

'No, you wouldn't – and you wouldn't fool me, anyway,' replied Penelope stoutly. 'I'd know who you were immediately. I've got several ambitions,' she went on, 'and that's one of them.'

'What are the others?' asked Gerald.

'I'd like to drive a train, fly in an aeroplane and go down a coal-mine,' Penelope informed him without hesitation.

'I think that those are rather wishful thinking,' said Helen. 'You might go up in an aeroplane one of these days, but I'd be surprised if you managed to drive a train or go down a coal-mine.'

'I might,' responded Penelope, undeterred. 'You never know.'

Helen said she thought it was time they returned, as it would soon be lunch-time, so they retraced their steps and half an hour or so later they were back at the house, exhilarated with their exercise, and Gerald for once with rosy cheeks from his exertions. This was not lost on his father and mother, who both commented on it when they saw him.

A few days later the three youngest ones left for school and college, Gerald having packed his precious manuscript to show to the Geography master, and life returned to its usual term-time regularity.

Things had hardly settled down, however, when Mr Wentworth discovered a letter with a French stamp on amongst his mail one morning at breakfast. It puzzled him, for he did not recognize the handwriting. He opened the envelope and took out the letter. He turned to the back of it and read the signature at the end.

'Oh, it's from Mrs Anderson,' he said. 'Would you like to read it first, my dear, while I read my other letters? It's addressed to both of us.'

He passed the letter to Helen, who handed it to her mother. Mrs Wentworth took it and began to read.

Suddenly, she gave a little shriek and put her teacup down with a clatter.

'Oh no, oh *no!*' she cried out.

Mr Wentworth put down the letter he was reading and Helen looked at her mother in alarm.

'Augusta, my dear, what is it?' asked Mr Wentworth.

'It's Philip. He's had an accident and is very ill. Oh, I knew something like this would happen! We should never have let him go!'

'An accident! Gracious God, what has happened?' asked Mr Wentworth, while Helen hastily rose from her seat and went to put her arms round her mother's now sobbing figure. Mrs Wentworth gave her the latter, saying between her sobs,

'Helen – you read it – I can't.'

Helen took the letter and, with one arm still round her mother's shoulders, read it aloud:

Dear Mr and Mrs Wentworth,

I am afraid it is my very unpleasant duty to pass on to you some rather serious news. I have just received a cable from my husband and he asks me to tell you that your son Philip has met with a bad accident and is currently fighting for his life in a hospital in Georgetown. He says a letter of explanation follows and I will let you know the contents of this letter as soon as I receive it.

I am so terribly sorry to have to be the bearer of such news. I know it will be a great shock to you, but if it is any comfort to you, I must tell you that my husband has said several times that your son has been an invaluable help to him and is far and away the best and most reliable member of the team.

Believe me, you have my sincere sympathy, and I pray that Philip will pull through this crisis and soon be able to come home, where your love and care will quickly restore him to full vigour and health.

Yours sincerely,

Jean Anderson

Mrs Wentworth was in such a state of tears and shock that Mr Wentworth suggested she go and lie down on the sofa in the lounge. With Helen's help, she acted on this suggestion. Helen then went to the kitchen, and putting her head round the door, said.

'Barbara, please will you bring a hot water bottle to the lounge? I'm afraid Mother's not very well.'

Barbara moved to comply and Helen fetched a rug to put over her mother. She found her father trying to comfort his wife, holding and gently rubbing her nearer hand, but at present unable to stem the flow of tears.

'We should never have let him go!' wailed Mrs Wentworth again. 'He should never have gone! He should never have gone!'

Helen had too much to do trying to console her parents to be able to give way to grief herself, although she felt it keenly. She lent over the back of the sofa and took her mother's other hand.

'We couldn't stop him,' she said. 'He was determined to go, and nothing any of us could say would have made him change his mind.'

'Yes, yes, I know! But if only we knew what had happened! So far away! – and we cannot possibly go and see him – and he will die all by himself – and we shan't be there – and he will feel abandoned and –'

'My dear, don't talk like that!' expostulated Mr Wentworth. 'Don't think the worst right at the beginning! Let us hope, let us have faith that Philip will pull through and he will indeed come home as soon as they think he is fit enough to travel.'

Barbara tapped on the door at this point and came in with the hot water bottle. She asked no questions but Helen, realizing she would be wondering what had happened, said,

'Thank you, Barbara. Mother's all right but we've just had some rather distressing news.'

'Oh, I'm sorry, sir,' Barbara said, turning to Mr Wentworth. 'If there's anything else I can do? –'

'No, I don't think there is at the moment, thank you,' replied Mr Wentworth vaguely. He was finding it difficult to gather his thoughts. Helen added,

'I don't think we shall be going back into the dining room, Barbara, so if you would clear away the breakfast things, that would be the biggest help just now.'

'Yes, Miss Helen, I'll do that, straight away,' and she left the room to do so. Helen turned to her mother and said,

'Are you all right enough for me to leave you, Mother? Time's ticking on and if you don't need me to stay, I really should be getting ready for school; but if you want me to stay, I will; but I'll have to ring up.'

'No, of course you must go,' replied Mrs Wentworth. 'Your father will look after me and I daresay I shall be better soon.'

Giving her mother a final kiss, Helen reassured her with 'Everything will be all right; just pray for him, that's the best thing we can do at the moment.' She left the room to collect her things and go to school.

As she walked to her work, Helen turned over in her mind the immediate practicalities of the situation. She was fairly sure that, once her mother's initial violent reaction had passed, she would not want news of

Philip's accident to get out until they had something more explicit to communicate. The rest of the family must be told as soon as the news of what had happened had reached them, and although she was full of anxiety herself on Philip's account, she did her best, during the morning, to carry on with her work as though nothing had happened.

When she returned home for lunch, her mother had recovered herself, and the three were able to discuss the matter in a calmer frame of mind. Her father and mother both agreed that nothing should be said to anybody until they had heard again from Mrs Anderson. None of them voiced, however, what all of them feared, that that letter, when it came, would bring worse news rather than better. Once more, they settled themselves to wait, and prayed fervently that Philip's life would be spared and that he would make a complete recovery.

Chapter L

Another whole week passed before there was any further news, and this time it was from Mr Anderson himself, enclosed with a covering note from his wife. He told how, while out one morning exploring not too far from their overnight camp site, Philip had climbed a tree to obtain a better view of the lie of the land, and while he was negotiating a twist to get a better footing, the bough had broken and he had fallen some thirty feet to the ground. Fortunately, although there was a lot of rocky outcrop in the area, his fall had been slightly broken by a bush, otherwise it could have been a lot worse; but there *were* broken bones and he was unconscious when they got to him. They had *very* carefully carried him back to the boat, where one of the members of the team, who was a doctor, had examined him and pronounced the immediate need for hospital. He had attended to him as well as he could with what they had taken with them on the boat. He himself had called the hospital in Georgetown and arrangements were made for Philip to be taken there. He was in daily wireless contact with the hospital and understood that the broken bones had been mended but that Philip had contracted a fever of some kind – whether a bug he had picked up already or as a result of the accident, Mr Anderson did not know at present.

There followed a page of praises of Philip's contribution to the expedition and a promise to keep them informed.

Although the news was still obviously serious, it was a relief to know what had happened. Helen felt it would be all right now to tell Alban, Penelope and Gerald, and when her parents both asked her if she would do this, she agreed. At the end of the letter she urged her brothers and sister to write to Philip to cheer him up.

'You've no need to say much,' she wrote, 'or you could make him a card. He'll appreciate anything from us at home, I'm sure, so let me have something quickly and I'll send it with our next letter.'

All three responded immediately, with varying degrees of concern, enclosing their separate efforts for Philip himself. Alban, who was not particularly artistic, had found a shop card which he 'thought would make Phil laugh'; Penelope drew her own – quite well – and composed her own words; Gerald wrote a note and decorated it with little pen drawings as he went along. These were enclosed in the packet containing letters from all three at home and dispatched to France immediately.

Helen also wrote to her aunt and uncle in Oxford and to Charles and Margaret. General horror and sympathy were expressed all round, for although Philip had not made a good impression on his relations, they did not wish him ill-will in any way and were full of hope for a speedy recovery.

'We have bought a card,' wrote Aunt Edith, 'and all signed it, and as you say letters have to go via you to Mrs Anderson in France, I am enclosing it, stamped, for you to send on, please.'

Inside, the card was full of signatures with little messages, brief but sincere, and Helen was sure that Philip would appreciate the fact that all twelve of them had signed it.

Charles wrote at once, full of concern, addressing the letter to all three of them.

'Strangely enough,' he went on, 'I have a cousin of my mother's living in Georgetown, married to a banker out there. I am writing to them with this and have asked them to go and visit Phil. That way you'll get some first-hand information and much quicker than you possibly can via the roundabout route your arrangements are confined to at present. I've given them your address. I sent it by air, so I hope it won't be too long before you hear from them.'

This gesture brought considerable comfort to both Helen and her parents and they waited anxiously for more direct news.

When it came, by air, some time later, the news was good. Charles' relations had gone to the hospital more or less as soon as they had received his letter and had seen Philip. His fever had abated, they said, and he was better, though still confined to his bed and very weak; but the hospital authorities had pronounced him over the worst, and he would be coming home, they hoped, in about six weeks' time, depending on his speed of recovery. Philip himself was reasonably cheerful and thanked them for their letters and cards, which he had recently received. They would visit him regularly and send reports by air until he was fit enough to be able to write himself. They gave the address of the hospital, and this was much appreciated, because it meant that the family would now all be able to write to him direct and not have to go through Mrs Anderson any more. Mr Wentworth sat down and wrote to their unseen friend in France and thanked her for all she had done during the past weeks, and expressed the hope that they would all meet at some date in the not-too-far-distant future. He also wrote to Charles' relations in Georgetown and thanked them as well.

From then on letters flew across the Atlantic almost every day from one or other of Philip's family and relations, and Charles also wrote frequently. When the Reverend Ward got to hear of Philip's accident, he came round straight away to offer his condolences and see if there were anything he could do to help. After his visit Mrs Wentworth was forced to admit that the young man *was* a good pastor and that she had found his visit helpful and comforting. He, too, wrote to Philip from time to time.

Then, at last, the day came when there was his familiar handwriting on the envelope, and although only short, because he was not yet strong enough to write much, the letter inside was contented and reassuring. Mrs Wentworth, on reading it, broke down, releasing all the pent-up emotion of the past weeks. Helen also wept, and Mr Wentworth joined in quietly, not at all ashamed of his tears.

After this Philip was able to write every so often and eventually told them that he was now walking on crutches a little every day. They were pleased with his progress, he said, and he was hoping they'd let him come home about halfway through June.

There were also letters from Mr Anderson, and by the middle of May he was able to give some more definite news of a home-coming:

> My work in the Amazon hinterland is more or less completed (he wrote) and the rest of the party will return to France just as soon as we have tied up all the loose ends. I myself propose to move into Georgetown, so that I can visit Philip, and when he's well enough to travel I shall bring him to England by air. I feel extremely responsible for what happened and I shan't rest until I have delivered him all in one piece to you myself. As a matter of fact, I'm hoping it will fit in with a trip to London which the family is planning to make about the middle of June, and if it wouldn't overburden you, it would be very pleasant to meet the parents and at least some of the family of my excellent and much-valued young friend. I will let you know just as soon as I know when Philip will be allowed to travel, and you may be sure that I shall bring him by the fastest possible route.

*

What a kind man he must be!' exclaimed Mrs Wentworth. 'Philip has indeed been fortunate to have met such a person.'

'Yes, indeed,' agreed Mr Wentworth. 'We have been very blessed – and so has Philip. It will be a great joy to meet Mr Anderson and his family and I hope that idea comes off.'

'I think Phil will be pleased to see all of them again, too,' added Helen. 'He spoke so highly of them before the expedition set off.'

'Yes,' said Mr Wentworth, 'it is wonderful news. May God bring him safely home to us.'

'Amen,' said Mrs Wentworth.

Chapter LI

Helen wrote immediately to all those whom she had informed about Philip and all rejoiced at the news that he seemed to be pulling through his ordeal so well.

Charles expressed genuine relief and pleasure and after a page or two on this subject, then turned to his own concerns and immediate plans.

> The exam results won't be out till May 20th (he wrote) and we have to be here when they are released, because there's a job involved. We are all fairly apprehensive, I can tell you, because the exam was rather a beast and none of us is sure if we have passed. It's infuriating, because I'd hoped I could have seen you before this. Just to keep us from getting bored we have all been given an assignment to accomplish. Rotters! Anyway, you may be sure, dear old Helen, I shall be in Edmuston just as soon as I possibly can be. I'm hoping it won't be more than a week, so I won't write again, I'll just turn up. Expect me when you see me, as my mother says!

Just over a week later Charles rang the bell at the Wentworth home and waited until the door was opened by the maid.

'Good evening, Barbara,' he said. 'Is Miss Helen in?'

'Good evening, Mr Charlie,' she replied. 'Yes, I believe she's in her study. Will you come in?'

'Thank you.' Charles crossed the threshold and waited while Barbara shut the door.

'Shall I tell Miss Helen you're here, Sir?' she asked.

'No, I'll go up to her. I know the way – and Barbara,' putting his finger to his lips – 'mum's the word!'

'Very well, Sir; thank you.'

Charles mounted the stairs two at a time, smiling happily to himself, crossed the landing and knocked gently on Helen's study door.

There was no answer, so he tried again. There was still no answer.

Barbara had been quite definite that she was there, so he ventured to go in.

Helen was there, with her back towards him, in an easy chair by the fire. She did not move as he entered. She was too deeply engrossed in her book to hear or care for exterior sounds. Charles crept quietly up to her chair and stood behind it. He remained silent for some minutes, during which time Helen had raised her eyes from her book, staring in front of her in deep thought. A prolonged sigh made Charles feel it was time to let her know of his presence, so very softly he said,

'Helen.'

She turned, startled, then, seeing who it was, jumped up, crying,

'Oh, Charlie, Charlie!'

'Dear Helen! Have you missed me then?'

'Oh yes!' Then, remembering that the result of his exam must be out by now, recovered herself and asked, 'Charlie boy, tell me quickly, have you passed? But of course you have!'

'Yes,' he replied, 'I've passed.'

'I knew you would; but what does it mean exactly?'

'It means, Helen, that out of the dozen of us who entered for it I have come out top, and consequently I've got the job.'

Helen's eyes shone brightly and her whole face expressed what she could not find adequate words for.

'Oh, Charlie, I'm *so* glad – I do congratulate you, dear boy. Let me do it properly – bend down.'

Charles did as bid and Helen kissed him on the forehead. He put his arms round her and held her there. She did not object, for did she not love this friend more dearly than she could tell? – and he was gazing at her in such a way that she knew he loved her in the same way. Nor did she object when, having held her like this for a few minutes, he suddenly kissed her long and fervently.

It was at this moment that Penelope came in. She had been sent up by her mother to see why Helen, who had said she would come down and join them as soon as she was ready, had not done so. Having knocked twice, as Charles had done, and receiving no reply, she had also ventured to go in. The sight which met her eyes drew from her one suppressed exclamation:

'Christopher!'

She retreated rapidly and pondered outside the door what she should say to her mother. They none of them knew Charles was in the house, and she had the sense to see that this was not to be mentioned.

Having made up her mind, she returned to the lounge.

'Well?' said Mrs Wentworth.

'I – I don't think she'll be coming.'

'Why not? What is she doing?'

'She seemed very busy – I didn't like to disturb her.'

'Hmph! I'll go and see if *I* can bring her down.' Mrs Wentworth rose to her feet.

Penelope realized that something must be done, and quickly – Helen must be warned. They must not be surprised. She waited politely and discreetly until her mother had swept out of the room, then ran across the hall and dashed up the back staircase, which she knew emerged nearer to Helen's study than did the front one, and burst in without knocking in case her mother should hear her.

'Why, what on earth's the matter, Penny?' asked Charles, as the flustered Penelope hurried in, closing the door behind her.

'Sorry I couldn't knock, Helen – Mother's coming up to see why you don't go down. I told her you were busy – you'd better hide, Charlie. Quick, through the window, and I'll come too.'

No sooner said than done – and only just in time; for as Charles and Penelope escaped to the balcony and Helen seated herself in her chair once more, Mrs Wentworth knocked imperiously on the door and came in.

'What's this that Penelope tells me that you are too busy to come and sit with us in the lounge? What are you doing? Reading? Good heavens, child, why can't you do that downstairs?'

'I prefer to stay here until I have finished,' replied Helen. 'It's quieter.'

'Quieter! And why should it be quieter? *We* aren't making any noise!'

'No, I know you aren't, Mother dear, but I'm studying something important and I prefer to do that here.'

Helen looked at her mother in a clear, steadfast way which said as plainly as words, 'I don't wish to be rude, but I *am* nearly twenty-three and I have a right to decide for myself what I shall do.'

'There's a draught,' said Mrs Wentworth after a pause. Her eyes saw the French doors on to the verandah were not quite shut. Helen was immediately on her guard. There was a slight rustle outside (it was Penelope finishing her descent to the ground via the creeper-covered pillar so that she could be back in the lounge before her mother returned – she knew a convenient open window).

'What was that?' demanded Mrs Wentworth, moving towards the French doors. Helen was there before her.

'I don't know,' she said. 'I'll go and see.'

She slipped out and whispered to Charles,

'Get down into the garden – it's not safe yet. I'll bird-call when it's all clear.'

Charles silently obeyed and Helen returned to her room.

'There's nothing there,' she said (which was quite true by this time). 'It must have been your imagination, Mother. And now, if you don't mind, I'd like to finish what I'm doing or I shan't have time to come down at all.'

Mrs Wentworth grunted, and giving Helen a searching look, which her daughter returned without blinking, abruptly left the room. Helen waited until she heard the lounge door close, then she again passed through the French doors, careful to shut them after her. She leant on the balcony rail and gave a perfect imitation of an owl. Half a minute later Charles was standing beside her.

'It's all right now,' she said. 'Mother's gone. Thank heaven Penny came in.'

'Yes,' murmured Charles.

'What a beautiful evening it is!' exclaimed Helen. 'See how clear the down is tonight! Oh, Charlie, it is lovely here, isn't it?'

'Yes,' murmured Charles, 'it is.' There was a pause and then he went on in a tone of pent-up emotion, 'I must apologize for kissing you like that just now. It was very wrong of me, I know, but I just couldn't help it. I'm sorry.'

Helen was amazed.

'Apologize?' she exclaimed. 'Wrong? Whatever do you mean?'

'Well, you're engaged and I should have been able to control myself.'

Helen was even more amazed.

'Engaged?! But Charlie, I'm not engaged! Wherever did you get that idea from?'

'You're not?' Charles almost shouted.

'Hush! Not so loud! They'll hear you. No, I'm not engaged. What made you think I was?'

'I had a letter from Bristles a few days ago,' replied Charles. 'He told me. I simply couldn't believe it! I just had to come over as soon as I could to find out if it was true. That's why I came in this way. I wanted to see you alone, not with everyone else present.'

'But whom did Bristles say I was engaged to?'

'Bernard Robertson.'

'Oh-h-h-h, I see.' Helen turned away. 'No, I'm not engaged to Bernard – though I might have been.'

'So he did ask you?'
'Yes.'
'Why did you refuse?'
'Because I didn't love him the way he wanted.'
'I'm glad!'
Helen turned back again.
'Why?'
'Because, I'd be jealous. If you had got yourself engaged I shouldn't have been able to come and see you any more.'
'Of course you would! You dear, stupid old Charlie, did you really think it would make any difference to our friendship even if I had been engaged? You can't have a very good idea of my loyalty if you think that.'
Her tone was gently reproachful and Charles smiled as he answered,
'It would, Helen. It would be bound to, whatever you say.'
'Well, I'm not engaged to Bernard Robertson, so it's all right.'
'No,' said Charles. 'Funny, though. Bristles was definite about it. Here, wait a minute – I've got his letter in my pocket.'
He felt for it, unfolded it and ran his finger down the pages until he came to what he was looking for.
'Ah! Here we are. Listen. He says, "Now, I've got some surprising news for you. Helen is engaged! And whom do you think to? – Bernard Robertson!" '
Light dawned on Helen when she heard this.
'Oh, Charlie boy, you dear old stupid! I'm not the only girl called Helen that you know! It isn't I he's referring to – it's his sister!'
Charles let out a long sigh of understanding and then said,
'Of *course!* What an ass I've been! Of *course* it's his sister! Why on earth didn't I think of that? But I'll tell you why – you're the only Helen I can think of. But tell me' – as memory jogged his thought – 'when I saw you at their place in October I had the distinct feeling that Bernard had asked *you;* and now you say he did. There's been a pretty quick change, hasn't there?'
'Well, I don't know how quick it's been, actually,' replied Helen. 'I think I was only an infatuation and he knew Margaret would like it because I'm her best friend. I never could have made the right wife for Bernard. Helen Brisley will.'
'And to think I've been torturing myself all this time for nothing, thinking it was you!'
They both laughed then. Helen went to the balcony and leant on it.

Charles did likewise. For a while neither said anything. The stillness of the evening and the gathering dusk cast its spell over them and no sound, not even a slight breeze, disturbed the silence. Both were perfectly happy and realized more fully than ever before that it was only while in each other's company that this was so. Charles was the first to speak.

'Helen,' he said, 'do you remember that day when I left you after Penny's accident? You said to me then, "If there is ever anything you want, and it is in my power to give, you have only to come and ask, and you shall have it".'

'Yes. It still holds. Have you found anything yet?'

'Yes. I knew then what I wanted, but I was not sure, either of myself, or whether you could give it to me.'

'Are you sure now?'

'Yes. I'm sure of myself – and I hope – I would like to think – I was sure of you, too.'

'Good; then tell me quickly – what is it?'

Charles did not appear in a hurry to say. It was several seconds before he spoke. Then it was in a clear, steady way.

'Helen,' he said, 'we've always been good friends, haven't we?'

'Yes, Charlie boy, and we always shall be.'

'Always shall be,' repeated Charles, more to himself than to Helen. 'Do you think,' he added, gazing straight in front of him, 'that we could be a bit more than just good friends, Helen?'

'Well, aren't we?' she replied, wondering when he was going to get to the point.

'No, not what I want us to be. It's not all the time.' He still did not look at her.

'I'm afraid I don't understand,' said Helen. It was not true, but she wanted Charles to explain himself clearly.

Then he turned to face her, and gazing at her with eyes which plainly told what he wished to say, said quietly but sincerely,

'I'm asking you to marry me, Helen. That is what I want. I wanted it then and I want it even more now. I'm sure I don't need to tell you that I love you more than anything else on earth – you *must* know that. Will you, Helen?'

'Oh, Charlie boy, of course, of course! I love you too, with all my heart and I can't bear this separation any longer! These last seven months have been awful. I've missed you terribly and longed for you so much I have nearly burst sometimes! Oh, yes!'

*

Some time later they decided that they had better go and break the news to the family. As Helen said, after the recent incident with her mother, she couldn't go down to the lounge and sit with them as if nothing had happened – and why wait till tomorrow anyway?

Accordingly, they both came out of the room to go downstairs, but before they could go further, they met Penelope on her way to bed.

'Oh!' she exclaimed. 'Are you going down after all?'

'Yes,' replied Helen, 'we've got something to tell them.'

A thought had struck Charles when he saw Penelope. Remembering what she had said when she burst in on them in Helen's study, he asked,

'You came up to warn us about your mother, Penny. How did you know I was here? You didn't see me arrive, did you?'

'No,' replied Penelope. 'Well, you see, I had knocked before, because she sent me up, and you didn't answer, so I came in. You were – well, you know what you were doing – so I beat a hasty retreat and went back and told Mother you were – busy.'

'Oh, bless you, Penny! What it is to have such a considerate and understanding sister!' cried Helen, embracing her; and Charles added,

'Yes, indeed! Most kids of your age would have barged in and dropped bricks in all directions. Come here, Venus, and let me give you a hug too.'

'Oh, I say!' exclaimed Penelope, as Charles matched action to his words. 'You both look so happy – has anything happened? Have you got engaged, or something?'

Helen and Charles laughed.

'Is it *so* obvious?' asked Helen. 'Yes, we are engaged, and you're the first to know; and I think you deserve to be, after what you did.'

'Oh, I *am* so glad!' – giving her sister another hug – 'So I shall have you for a real brother now, Charlie, and won't that be grand!' – hugging him a second time as well, for in her own way she too loved Charles very much – 'Well, I'm going to bed – got to be up early tomorrow to go back to school, worse luck, but this'll be wonderful to go to bed on. I'm really thrilled! Goodnight!'

She departed to her bedroom and Charles and Helen descended to the lounge.

As she expected, both her parents were highly delighted with the news and when Helen explained her rather odd behaviour of earlier in the evening, Mrs Wentworth saw the funny side of it and they all laughed.

'Oh, dear, I did nearly put my foot in it, didn't I?' she said.

When the laughter had died down, which took a long time because they were all in an excited state, Mr Wentworth grasped Charles' hand and said,

'Seriously, my boy, I have hoped for many a long year that this would happen. You have known each other since you were children, so you are familiar with each other's faults as well as good points, and that's a great thing. You are absolutely right for each other and I'm delighted to welcome you into the family as another son. God bless you both.'

'Thank you, Sir,' Charles replied, much moved. 'I consider myself the luckiest man alive. I know I've known Helen since she was tiny but I still think she's the most wonderful girl in existence and I don't feel worthy of her at all. That she's prepared to be my wife in spite of knowing me so well is rather amazing – and believe me, Sir, I am very proud indeed to be welcomed as your son.'

'Do you have to go home tonight?' asked Mrs Wentworth. 'It's getting late and there's a bed made up in the spare room. You're very welcome to sleep in it.'

'That's very kind of you,' replied Charles, 'but I really think I ought to go home and break the good news to my parents. I could always come back again tomorrow.'

'Yes, that's quite right,' said Mr Wentworth, 'you must; but I'm sure they'll understand that you and Helen want to spend some time together after all these months of separation, so do come back tomorrow.'

'And stay for a few days,' interrupted Mrs Wentworth.

'Thank you very much, both of you,' said Charles, returning to stand beside Helen and pull her arm through his. 'I'll come over straight after breakfast and take her to Brighton to get a ring. That's the first thing to be done! And then we'll come back here and discuss wedding plans.'

After a few more things had been said, Charles said goodnight to Mr and Mrs Wentworth, with an embrace as well as a handshake, and took his leave. Outside in the porch he said goodnight to Helen in a more appropriate fashion, and strode off down the drive. It was now dark but there was enough light for Helen to see his final wave. Having locked the door inside for the night and bade sweet dreams to her parents ('No, Helen dear,' said her father, 'it's *we* should be saying that to *you!*') she went up to bed and was soon asleep.

Chapter LII

Charles appeared soon after breakfast next day, bearing his family's delight and felicitations on the engagement and saying they wanted to see Helen, so if it was all right, he would take her to his home for lunch and they would return later. This was agreed to very readily and he and Helen departed.

It did not take them very long to find a ring they liked and then they went on to Charles' home not far from Mereford, where Helen received more hugs and kisses from Mr and Mrs Mainwaring. They returned to Edmuston in time for supper, some decisions already made. Charles explained that as his new job started in September and as there was nothing to wait for, they had decided they would like to get married in August, in time to give them a month's honeymoon.

Mr and Mrs Wentworth thought that could be managed if they got down to arrangements immediately. Helen then said,

'I'd like to ask Len and Anne to be my bridesmaids, as well as Penny, of course, and Charles' sister Ursula. We don't need pages and neither of us has brothers or other relations young enough to fulfil that function anyway. And I'd really rather like to ask Mr Moore to marry us if you don't think Mr Ward would mind.' She had thought of this as a solution to what she foresaw could be an embarrassing situation otherwise. They would have to go and see the Rector about it in any case, because they would have to be married in the church. This would be bad enough, but to ask him to conduct the service as well, in view of what had happened, really would be like rubbing salt into the wound. 'Mr Moore has known me all my life and knows Charlie too, and I think Mr Ward would understand, don't you?'

Mr and Mrs Wentworth thought Mr Ward would probably raise no objections, but he would have to be invited to the wedding. Helen accepted this as unavoidable, and said she would go and see the Rector in the morning, if he could fit her in. She rang up to fix a time and came back to say he would see her at half past eleven the next day.

*

Accordingly, she went round to the Rectory at the appointed hour, her heart beating rather faster than usual; she was not looking forward to the interview. She found her hand was trembling slightly as she raised it to ring the bell. Mrs Smith let her in and showed her into the sitting room. Memories of the last time she was in it were painfully vivid and no amount of happiness over her engagement to Charles could efface the picture of Robert Ward's obvious acute suffering on that occasion. She had decided that it would be best not to refer to the conversation they had had that evening, and to introduce the subject as if it were a perfectly natural thing to be telling him. She prayed for calm and strength to carry through her mission without embarrassment. While waiting for the Rector to come in she stood by the window and looked out at the garden.

In a few minutes Mr Ward entered the room, apologizing for having kept her waiting – he had been on the phone. He bade her sit down and himself took a chair on the other side of the fireplace. She had her back to the window and so the light was all on his face rather than hers. The room was not dark, but it meant that she would be able to see his reactions better than she could have done if they had been sitting the other way round. After some enquiries about her family and what news they had of Philip's progress, the Rector asked,

'Now, Miss Wentworth, what did you want to see me about?'

Helen tried her hardest to keep calm as she answered, quietly and as gently as she could,

'I have come to tell you that I have just become engaged to be married.'

The reaction, if there was one, was so slight externally that Helen hardly noticed it; what the reaction was inside, when he received this final crushing blow to any lingering hopes he might have had, she could only guess at. A very slight pause before he answered, as if he were quickly setting his mind in order, was the only thing that betrayed the possible struggle he was having to keep calm himself. Then he said,

'Oh, have you? May I be the first to congratulate you. I am very happy for you.'

'Thank you.'

'Who is your fiancé? Do I know him?'

'No, he hasn't been here since you came. He has been up in Scotland for the past seven months. He is called Charles Mainwaring and we have known each other since I was two.'

'Oh, a childhood romance,' Mr Ward said, smiling. 'It is a good basis for a happy marriage to have known each other for so long. You will want to be married in the church, of course. When is the wedding to be?'

He took out his diary and began to turn the pages. Helen thought she could detect a slight tremble in his hands but he gave no other sign of inner turmoil.

'Well, we'd like to get married in August,' she said, 'and I thought – I hope you wouldn't mind – I'd rather like to ask Mr Moore to marry us. I've known him all my life and he knows Charlie too – and I thought – would you mind very much, Mr Ward? You wouldn't be offended?'

'No, not at all,' he replied quickly. 'I think that would be a very good idea. I'm sure my uncle would be delighted to officiate at your wedding.'

Whatever he might be feeling, the Reverend Ward gave nothing away and proceeded to discuss arrangements in a perfectly controlled and business-like manner. Helen mentioned their proposed date and Mr Ward wrote it down. He would have to see them both together, of course, and this was fixed for the following afternoon.

As Helen rose to leave, Mr Ward said in a voice that had a degree of tension in it, as if he had had to pluck up his courage to ask the question,

'Just one more thing before you go, Miss Wentworth – for my own peace of mind I must know this – you will understand – have you said anything to your fiancé about – ?'

'No, Mr Ward,' Helen hastened to assure him. 'I have not told a soul and I never shall. That is a secret between you and me and will remain so for ever.'

Mr Ward's expression cleared and he said,

'I am deeply grateful to you. Thank you. And you may be sure that *I* shall never refer to the matter again. God bless you.'

He saw her to the door and shook hands with her.

'I shall look forward to seeing you both tomorrow,' he said, 'and to meeting your fiancé. Goodbye for now.'

Helen walked home feeling considerably more light-hearted than when she set out. It was over – and he had been very nice about it. He, too, must have felt the wisdom of asking Mr Moore to conduct the service and had almost jumped at the suggestion. Going again with Charles would be much easier now.

Helen decided not to make her own wedding dress or Penelope's bridesmaid's dress but to have them made by a dressmaker in Mereford. There was so much to do and there really would not be time. Quite apart from arrangements for the wedding and arrangements for the honeymoon, they had to find somewhere to live. Charles would be starting his career in London and they had to make more than one trip to look for a house. Fortunately they found one in Hampstead without too much difficulty. Eleanor, Anne and Ursula accepted to be bridesmaids and everything went along smoothly.

In the middle of it all an airmail letter arrived from Mr Anderson saying he and Philip would be arriving at Northolt on June 24th. His wife, who was with the family in London, would meet him with their car, and he would bring Philip to Edmuston, having dropped her off en route. He hoped they would arrive sometime during the afternoon; he couldn't say exactly when.

> I should warn you, however (he went on) not to be too upset by Philip's appearance. It may come as a bit of a shock. He is very thin and somewhat haggard and he can't stand very much excitement yet. The journey home will be quite an ordeal for him and though he is longing to see you all, even that will be about as much as he can take to begin with. You would be well advised not to allow too many visitors at first, or let anybody stay with him too long. You should also ask your doctor to come and see him as soon as he gets home and then give him regular check-ups. He has been through a pretty dreadful experience and recovery will, I think, be slow. But he *will* recover, of that you can be absolutely certain. He has told me he would like to come with me on another expedition, if I'll have him, when he's fit enough. I have told him this should be an incentive to him to get better as fast as he can, and then we'll see!'

Chapter LIII

The days flew by and June 24th was upon them almost before they knew it. It was extremely difficult to settle down to anything. Helen had told the Headmistress of the village school that she would not be able to continue her work there after the end of June and had been very busy trying to complete things so that she would not leave any loose ends. On this particular day the Headmistress had told her to go home at lunch-time and stay at home for a few days over Philip's home-coming. She was grateful for such understanding.

At about four o'clock a shooting break turned into the drive, and Mr Wentworth, who was watching from the window, called out,

'They're here!'

Mrs Wentworth and Helen appeared at once. The front door was thrown open and the three of them descended the steps to greet the wanderer. Mr Anderson got out and approached them – a tall, broad, Norse god of a man, with a bronzed skin, fairish, bushy hair in profusion on his head and round his face and a pair of very bright blue eyes.

'Hullo!' he called out. 'I'm Edward Anderson. How do you do? I'm extremely pleased to meet you at last.'

They all took to him immediately and could well understand that Philip would like him on sight. 'Excuse me,' he said, 'I'll help Philip to get out.'

He went round to the other side of the break and opened the door. Slowly, slowly, the figure in the passenger seat swivelled round sideways and Mr Anderson helped him to get his feet on the ground. He held the crutches while Philip very gradually pulled himself up, took them and turned round. He came towards them and they towards him. Mr Anderson went round to the back of the break, opened the two doors and began to rummage amongst the items stored there. The first moments should be theirs alone. They didn't want him and he wasn't going to intrude.

Leaning heavily on his crutches, Philip slowly approached his parents. His black eyes seemed over-large in his thin and hollow-cheeked face. He was pale and dreadfully thin; but when he smiled they knew it was the same Philip.

'Hullo, Mother,' he said, without much energy, 'hullo, Father, hullo, Helen. It's *good* to see you.'

Making a supreme effort at self-control for her son's sake, Mrs Wentworth put her arms round as much of him as she could get at without overbalancing him, and kissed him.

'Oh, Philip!' she cried, 'Welcome home! Welcome home!'

Mr Wentworth then put his arm round Philip's shoulders and said,

'Thank God you are safely home, Philip.'

'I echo that!' responded his son. 'Now, Helen, come and give me a big kiss.' Helen did so, with suitable expressions of joy at seeing him. 'And I'm delighted with your news.'

They helped him up the steps and ushered him into the lounge and into an easy chair.

'Do you need a foot-rest?' asked Helen, as Philip flopped into the chair.

'No, I'm OK thanks,' he replied. 'Oh, this is wonderful! I've not sat in a chair like this for months!'

'I will get us all some tea,' said Mrs Wentworth. 'Go and ask Mr Anderson to join us, Helen.'

'Yes, indeed!' Helen went out to give the invitation and help Mr Anderson to bring Philip's luggage into the hall. Mr Anderson accepted gratefully and soon they were all enjoying an afternoon tea which had already been prepared and had only been waiting for their arrival to bring the kettle to the boil.

Philip said little. For one thing, he was too exhausted to have much energy for talking and also, he was content just to be home and sitting in a comfortable chair. He let the conversation flow over him and made very little effort to take part in it.

Mr Anderson said that he and his family would be in London for another three weeks and he would very much like to bring his wife and children down to meet them if they felt they could manage it amongst all the wedding arrangements. Mr Wentworth assured him they most certainly wanted to meet his wife and family, and Mrs Wentworth said of *course* they could find time to entertain the family which had been so kind to their son. It was arranged that they would come down for lunch in a couple of weeks' time, when everybody hoped Philip would be that much better and more ready to see his friends again. The date fixed, Mr Anderson bade them all adieu and drove away.

'Oh, Phil, what a marvellous man!' exclaimed Helen, when he had gone. 'No wonder you liked him.'

'Yes,' replied Philip, 'he's been a really good friend to me all these months. I admire him a lot; and I like his family, too. But Great Scott, I'm tired! We flew overnight, you know, and I didn't get much sleep.'

'I'm not surprised. Well, Doctor Kennedy is coming to have a look at you in about a quarter of an hour, and then we'll get you to bed, if you like'

'Oh, is he? Well, I can just about stand that, then I really shall be glad to get to bed; and when I'm feeling better, Helen, I want to have a long talk with you.'

'All right. I look forward to that; but try and get a little stronger first.'

Doctor Kennedy arrived, and having been informed of the details, refrained from his usual brusque banter and was gentleness itself as he examined Philip. When he had finished, he turned to Helen and said,

'Now, my dear, Philip is quite capable of getting upstairs to his bedroom himself, and I'll see him up there. I shall also help him with his washing – no don't argue, you know perfectly well that you and your mother *shouldn't* and your father *can't*, and who else is there, I should like to know? I'll get him into bed and then you can take over. Let him sleep on tomorrow as long as he wants but get him outside into the garden as much as possible. Feed him on good, nourishing food and see that he walks a bit every hour or so. I'll come and see him in a few days' time and I'll send the District Nurse in to attend to him. We'll have him thoroughly fit again in time for your wedding.'

'Oh, do you think so? That's wonderful!' said Helen, rising from her seat as Doctor Kennedy made to get Philip upstairs.

'And as for you, young man,' was his parting shot to Philip as the latter picked up his crutches, 'you do as you're told and behave yourself and make sure you get better in double quick time.'

Philip struggled to his feet – 'No, don't help me, Helen, I've got to do this by myself. I'm quite expert at it.'

He bade goodnight to his parents and left the room. Helen brought up the rear as they mounted the stairs, carrying the small haversack that contained his immediate needs, put it on a chair and took out the contents, placing them where they should go.

'I'll see you when I come down,' Doctor Kennedy told her. 'Don't worry, I shan't run away without speaking to you.'

Helen left him to it and returned to the lounge.

'That's very kind of Doctor Kennedy,' said Mr Wentworth. 'Doctors don't usually put their patients to bed!'

'He's a good doctor,' said Mrs Wentworth, ' and I think he saw that Philip needed a bit of help.'

'Yes,' agreed her husband, 'and it wouldn't surprise me if he wanted a quiet talk with him, too, on his own.'

'Possibly,' responded Mrs Wentworth. 'I just hope he won't tire him. The poor boy's quite worn out.'

'I don't think you need worry about that,' put in Helen. 'As you say, he's a good doctor and he knows what he's doing.'

In due course, Doctor Kennedy reappeared in the lounge and was offered a seat.

'Just a few minutes,' he said. 'I mustn't stay long. He's going to be all right, that I can state with certainty. Just let him recover at his own pace and don't try to force anything. He's been well patched up in the hospital and it sounds as if he's had good nursing care. They made him as comfortable as they could on the flight home and now all he needs is the kind of loving care I know he'll get in this house. It's a pity this had to be landed on your plate right at this moment, but there it is. We can't always arrange things the way we'd like.'

A few minutes' more conversation passed between them and then Doctor Kennedy took his leave, saying he would come in four days' time to see how his patient was progressing. Helen went upstairs to see if there were anything Philip wanted, but he was too tired to have any external need, so she said goodnight and was soon followed by her parents. He put his arms round his mother's neck and drew her face down to his, saying,

'I'm so glad to be home, Mother, you've no idea.'

Mrs Wentworth put her hands round his head and murmured,

'And you have no idea how glad and thankful we are to *have* you home. God bless you, my son, and goodnight.'

'Goodnight, Mother,' he replied, kissing her.

He grasped his father's two hands in both of his and they bade each other an affectionate goodnight.

A few minutes later he had fallen into an exhausted sleep.

Chapter LIV

Philip's recovery was steady. The weather was fine for most of the time and he was able to sit in the fresh air and take regular little walks about the garden on his crutches. His appetite slowly improved; he gradually began to lose his hollow look and put on weight. By the time the Andersons' visit was due he was considerably better and more like himself.

They arrived in the shooting-break about midday and were introduced to his parents and Helen by Philip, who was obviously extremely pleased to see them. Mrs Anderson was another 'fresh air' sort of person, and Stephen, Jane and Robert looked as though they enjoyed plenty of outdoor activity as well. They greeted Philip in a very friendly manner. Mr Anderson commented on his improved appearance and was delighted to hear that he was progressing so well.

After lunch they sat in the garden and chatted or were taken round it by Helen. At one point, Mr Wentworth took Mr Anderson aside under pretence of showing him a rare plant and when they were out of earshot of the others, he said,

'Mr Anderson, I want to tell you that my wife and I are more grateful than we can say for what you have done for Philip over these past few months. His membership of your expedition has been the making of him. That a chance meeting on a boat should have led to this is little short of a miracle. You don't know what Philip was like before, but we do, and I can tell you the change is remarkable. It leads me to think that perhaps that meeting was not just chance but was, in some way, meant.'

'It's very kind of you to say that, Mr Wentworth,' replied the explorer, 'but believe me, it has been a pleasure to know Philip and to have him on the trip. I was needing another member and up till the day I met him on the boat I had not found anybody suitable. I'd interviewed quite a few eager young men but none of them had been any good, for one reason or another. I had an immediate liking for Philip but the rigours and dangers of my work have taught me to be cautious. He was quite honest with me that he had no experience and in view of this I invited him to come and live with us for the month, so that I could assess him. My wife is quite used to being sprung on like this and wasn't at all perturbed when I brought a strange young man home with me and announced that he was going to stay with us! Had Philip not lived up to my expectations, I should have dismissed him, make no mistake about that. But he turned out well and I felt, in spite of the risk of taking someone who was totally green on such an expedition, I was going to trust my instincts and take him. I, too, feel our meeting was not coincidence, and if, when he is really fit enough to undertake another trip and he wants to come, I shall be only too pleased to have him. He is keen, learns quickly and does as he's told – and that's vitally important in the narrow confines of this kind of expedition.'

'That is very gratifying to know,' said Mr Wentworth warmly, thinking how different a picture of his son was presented in this description from the Philip who preferred *not* to do as he was told, 'and Augusta and I – and Helen – feel it is a great honour to meet you. We got your latest book out of the library in Mereford and couldn't put it down. It is *most* interesting.'

'Thank you. I'm glad you enjoyed it. You have said nothing of your own work – you are too modest – but I have read your books too and found them fascinating, though the Classics are not really my field.'

The day after the Andersons' visit, Helen was sewing in her study when there was a tap on the door and Philip put his head round it, saying,

'May I come in?'

'Of course.'

Philip negotiated the door, closing it behind him.

'I said when I came home that I wanted to talk to you,' he explained, 'but I hadn't the energy then. Now I feel ready and I'd like to tell you a few things, if you've got the time. Can you sew and listen at the same time?'

'Oh, yes, this is only routine sewing. Find yourself a comfortable seat.'

Philip did so and sat down, laying his crutches on the floor beside him.

'I hope I can be rid of these confounded things soon,' he remarked. 'Doctor Kennedy said he thought about another fortnight but I'd have to go and have an X-ray first.'

'Yes, you mustn't do anything rash. Be patient a bit longer, Phil. It won't be long now.'

'No.' He watched her in silence for a minute and then said, 'You say that's only routine sewing but it looks very pretty to me. What are you making?'

'I'm making my "torso" as Penny calls it. This is a blouse, and I'm only oversewing seams. I have to sew when I can. Now, Phil, I'm all ears.'

Philip nodded pleasantly, shifted his position and plunged in.

'Well, while I was in hospital I had a lot of time to think, once I recovered enough to think at all. To begin with it was enough just to realize that I wasn't dead, though there were times when I felt so awful that I thought it might have been better if I had been.'

Helen glanced up with sympathy but she did not speak. Philip was lost in his memories for a minute, but then continued,

'Well, I don't want to dwell on that. The point is that I did a lot of thinking – and praying, I might add, especially after the hospital chaplain came to see me; he was very helpful – and I realized in vivid colours, as you might say, just what a rotten, good-for-nothing scoundrel I had been – no, don't deny it, it's true; and nobody knows that better than you do. I really don't know how you all put up with me all those years.'

He shifted his position again. It was partly that he still became uncomfortable fairly quickly but it was more an expression of the tension he felt while telling Helen what he wanted to say. He was determined to go through with it but he did not find it easy.

'I thought back to my childhood,' he went on, ' and though I realized that the parents had perhaps not always understood me' (that, thought Helen, was an understatement if ever there was one!) 'and Mother tended to go from one extreme to the other in her dealings with me, that was no excuse, and by the time I was fifteen or so I should have known better. After all, we'd all had a religious upbringing and I'd listened to Mr Moore's sermons (or the school chaplain's) every week for years on end. I realized that my filthy temper had got me into trouble any number of times and I vowed there and then to make a real effort not to give way to it any more. I realized, too, that I was horribly selfish and wanted my own way all the time. There was no need to create so much trouble and unhappiness for everybody just because I couldn't have it. I began to feel thoroughly ashamed of myself.

'No, Helen, don't interrupt me, please. You can say anything you like when I've finished, but I want to get it off my chest first.'

Helen picked up her work again and bent her head over it, resolved to hear him out.

'I remembered particularly those last few months before I went to France the second time. Deep down I was ashamed of myself and of the distress I had caused, especially to Father, by being sent down. I behaved abominably and I'm heartily sorry now.

'Then there was your Charlie. I had no reason to go on being so beastly to him and I really don't know why I did. I suppose I was jealous of him, because he was such a fine character and I was so despicable. Then he got his relations to come and visit me and he wrote every week – did you know that? No, I daresay you didn't; it's like him not to have told you. He said if he could have found the time he would have come out to see me – and I believe he would, too. His relations came every few days instead. He's a very good chap, Helen, and I'm glad you're going to marry him and I can have him for a brother. Mind you,' he added, 'I always knew you would, one of these days!'

Helen smiled at him but said nothing.

'I've nearly finished. After coming home this time and everybody apparently going out of their way to be kind, I have felt even more of a worm; and I'm quite resolved, now, to be different – even with Alban!' He laughed. 'He used to annoy me so much! He always saw through me and didn't hesitate to let me know it, but heaven knows I gave him plenty of cause. I'm telling all this to you first, because you've always had faith in my better nature – though I'm sure there must have been times when even you wondered if I had one.' Then, leaning towards her and holding out his hand, he continued, 'Please forgive me, Helen, for anything I have done to upset you. I'm truly sorry.'

Helen put her work on to the table beside her, knelt down and took the proffered hand. She then put her arms round him, saying, very near to tears,

'Oh, Phil, *thank* you for telling me! I'm sorry you had to learn in such a hard way, but if you have, it's wonderful – wonderful!'

Philip hugged his sister and after a few moments he said,

'I'm going to apologize to Father and Mother and to Charles now I've talked to you – and Alban as well, when he comes home.'

'I'm sure you'll find they will all respond,' Helen told him. 'In fact, I know they will – and they will all be very pleased.'

'There's just one more thing I want to tell you,' said Philip, as Helen returned to her sewing, 'and that's about the Andersons. I can't explain it, but as soon as I met Mr Anderson I had a terrific feeling of understanding between us. As I got to know him better, I found him to be a person I could really admire and look up to – probably a bit of hero-worship going on! – but what I wrote about him in my letters to you is true, and everyone who works with him says the same. I owe him a heck of a lot – I can't ever repay it. I've come to the conclusion that that apparently chance meeting on the boat wasn't chance after all. You know,

Helen, though I'm sure even you find it hard to believe, I did pray for guidance, even in my worst periods, and to be shown what I might do with my life. I'm sure now that meeting Mr Anderson like that was the answer to my prayers. Funny, isn't it, that it seems you sometimes have to go through hell to find out about yourself? Didn't Oscar Wilde write a book called *De Profundis*? Well, that's what it feels like.'

'It's marvellous to hear you talk like that, Phil, and I'm sure you're right. Father and Mother think so too – that it wasn't just chance that brought you and Mr Anderson together.'

'Do they? I'm glad. The Andersons are a great family and I thoroughly enjoyed the month I spent with them. They made me feel so much at home – and I did feel at home, I can assure you.'

'Yes,' said Helen, 'we all liked them very much; and I hope your friendship with them will last a lifetime. It's grand for you to have found people with whom you have so much in common.'

'Yes, indeed!' There was a pause, then Philip said, 'I'd like to tell you a secret, Helen, but it's only for you, and I don't want anyone else to know – not yet, anyway.'

'You know you can trust me, Phil.'

'Yes, I do, and that's why I'm telling you.' There was another pause, then, 'I like Jane a lot – and I think she likes me.'

'Oh, Phil, that's wonderful!' Helen's face glowed.

'Don't jump to conclusions too soon. It's very early days yet! But she wrote me some super letters while we were away and when I saw her again yesterday, I – well, as I said, I like her a lot; more than any other girl I've ever met, anyway.'

Helen gave her brother a hug and said,

'If it does develop, I can't think of anything more wonderful for you than to be united permanently with the family you are so fond of. Jane's a lovely girl and I should be very happy to have her as a sister.'

Philip began to make a move to go.

'Mind you,' he warned, 'I can't be sure yet and you're not to breathe a word to anyone. If things do work out between us, I'll let you know straight away.' He adjusted his crutches and walked to the door. 'Thanks for listening to me. I'm glad to have told *somebody* and got it off my chest.'

Helen gave him a parting kiss and closed the door after him. She felt completely happy inside, and that from now on, it was going to be a totally different Philip whom they would see. What an incredible change finding the right kind of outlet for his energies had made – and would continue to make. All the friction caused by not fitting in to the setting in which he had been living all these years was dissipated; and if he could find with Jane the same kind of happiness that she had with Charles, that would surely crown it all and give him even more reason for persevering with his desire to overcome the faults in his character. She sat down again to continue her sewing but before taking it up, she closed her eyes and murmured,

'Thank you, God. Oh, *thank* you!'

Philip, Alban, Gerald, Penelope, Helen. Unfinished sketch (1946)

Chapter LV

True to his word, Philip had a heart-to-heart session with his parents, and when Charles came in later the same day he spent an hour or so with him. His genuine repentance for his past behaviour and his profound apologies for causing them all so much unhappiness were received, as Helen predicted they would be, with graciousness and appreciation. Mr and Mrs Wentworth were much moved, and Charles said that to have everything put right between them just before his wedding to Philip's sister was an extra bonus that he hadn't expected.

'Go in and win, old chap,' he said, 'and when you get to the top of Everest, send us a picture postcard!'

June drew to a close and after a visit to the surgery for an X-ray, Philip was pronounced well enough to progress to sticks. He was altogether stronger, and by the time Penelope and Gerald came home from school at the end of term halfway through July, he was sufficiently recovered to be recognizable as the Philip they remembered rather than the scarecrow he had been a month before.

'Hullo, sprat!' he said when he saw Penelope. Reverting to teasing helped to get him over some initial moments of awkwardness. 'And Gerry, little shrimp, how are you? Not so little now, are you? It'll be longs for you next term, I see!'

He kissed his sister and gave Gerald a slap on the back by way of greeting.

'It's good to see you both, anyway,' he went on. 'Thanks for all your letters and cards and things.'

'Oh, that's all right,' said Gerald. 'Thank you for *your* letter. I copied it out to show old Crocker at school. He was very impressed.'

'Good Lord! Is that old fossil still around?' asked Philip, and then, looking over the top of an imaginary pair of glasses, 'Carnaby-Smith, if you don't know where the Ganges is after all this time I shall have to keep you in after school until you do, eh? eh?'

Gerald burst out laughing at this imitation which he immediately recognized and the ice was broken. Philip then turned to Penelope and exclaimed, in a squeaky voice,

'Sister Penelope, I hope you have been behaving yourself since I last saw you. Beating everybody at tennis won't do, you know! What about us poor fellows? We don't stand a chance!'

Penelope grinned and replied,

'When you're better, I'll beat you hollow, Master Philip, just to teach you a lesson!'

'Done!' cried Philip. 'As soon as I can, I'll take you up on that and then we'll see who's best, young lady!'

'Oh, that won't be till next summer,' declared Penelope. 'Doctor Kennedy wouldn't let me do gym or games for a whole term after I broke my leg and that was only one bone. You broke heaps, so he will make you wait much longer than that!'

Alban was not due to come on leave until a few days before the wedding and by the time he did, Philip was able to walk without sticks. He went down to the square to meet the bus and the two brothers sauntered back to the house together. Nobody knew what passed between them but they came in laughing and joking as if nothing but such bonhomie had ever existed between them.

'Now let's have a final check on beds,' said Helen, the day after Penelope and Gerald arrived home. ' 'Len and Anne, Granny and the Lyndons are sleeping here the night before the wedding. Mr Moore is going to the Rectory and everyone else is either with the neighbours or in the Rose and Crown.'

'Who's "everyone else"?' asked Penelope.

'Bernard Robertson and the Brisleys are going next-door-but-one and we've managed to get the whole of the Herrick clan into the *Rose and Crown*. All our other friends and relations have had to make their own arrangements.'

'Oh, what a pity we can't have the Herricks here!' exclaimed Penelope. 'Then you could put Rupert in the coal house and give him black sheets, like he said.'

'I can't imagine anything worse,' said Helen. 'Imagine having to get him clean in time for the wedding. My nerves wouldn't stand it!'

The remaining three weeks passed rapidly. Helen had particularly asked that Margaret and Geoffrey might come two days before the wedding so that she could spend a little time with her friend before the

Great Day. The Lyndons accordingly arrived and Geoffrey was introduced. He was soon deep in conversation with Philip, turning over in his mind the possibility of making use of his adventures in the preparation of another book…

The following day Helen took Margaret up to the down behind the house and they sat down on a rock at the top where the view was good and the scent of the thyme was strong.

'Oh, Margaret!' she exclaimed, 'I'm so happy I could burst!'

'I know. It's wonderful. At one time I used to think you might make a wife for Bernard, but Charles is the man for you and always has been. I knew that, really, deep down.'

'Yes. Helen Brisley will make him a much better wife than I ever would. I'm very pleased for both of them. Now, as I've been far too busy to take in much except wedding for the past few weeks, tell me the news. When are they getting married and are your father and mother still with you?'

'At the moment, yes, but they're due back in India at the end of September. Bernard has been all right as long as they're at home but once they've gone he really would be lonely all by himself. He's off on a concert tour of Europe next week and that will keep him busy until the end of August, but then…In the end, it was decided that the wedding had better be as soon as possible after that. It's to be just a few days before Father and Mother leave. I've brought your invitation with me. We do hope you and Charles will be able to come.'

'Thank you. I'm sure we shall.'

They talked for some time longer and then got up and wandered on, only turning back when Helen looked at her watch and realized it was getting on for lunch-time. Before making the descent, Margaret paused, and taking Helen's arm, said,

'My dear, you are about to enter into the most wonderful and sacred relationship that there is and I wish you all the joy in the world. Geoffrey is the most kind and considerate husband anyone could wish for, and he is a good *friend* too. I'm sure you'll have the same with Charlie and I'm so glad we can share this experience in our lives too. There's nothing to equal it and before you have it you can't possibly imagine what it is like to be so completely and utterly happy.'

'In a few months' time I'm sure I shall agree with you,' replied Helen, 'and as I shared your last hours of spinsterhood with you, I wanted you to share mine with me. Thank you for coming. I really do appreciate it.'

'And I'm now going to ask you the same question as you asked me: am I allowed to know where you are going for your honeymoon?'

'And I'll tell you on the same conditions!' laughed Helen.

'Agreed.'

'All right, then. We're going to Scotland. Charlie loved it up there although it was winter and he wants to see it in summer. He says he wants us to bury ourselves in glens and romantic castles.'

'I'm going to do a repeat performance at bedtime, too,' said Margaret, as they picked their way carefully down the chalky, rutty track. 'I'm going to see that you get to bed early!'

The next day dawned bright and sunny and promised to be so all day. Eleanor and Anne were already in the house, of course, and John Mainwaring arrived in good time, bringing his sister Ursula. He 'saw her safely delivered', as he put it and then made his farewells. As best man he was conscious of his responsibilities and said he must see that Charles got dressed, didn't forget his notes and got to the church on time.

By half past eleven everyone except the bride and her parents had gone to the church and then the car came for Mrs Wentworth. Giving her daughter a final embrace, she turned abruptly and got into it.

As they waited for the bridal car, Helen took her father's arm and squeezed it.

'This has been quite a year, hasn't it?' she said.

'It has indeed,' replied Mr Wentworth, ' and now it's your wedding day and I need hardly wish you happiness because with Charlie I know you couldn't possibly have anything else.'

The car came and they got in.

It seemed to Helen, as she entered the church on her father's arm that the whole village had turned out to see her married – as indeed, with very few exceptions, it had. The Wentworths had many friends in and around Edmuston, and the school children, too, had come to support her; and as she slowly progressed towards the altar and saw Mr Moore standing there smiling, his white hair and saintly face caught in a ray of sunlight, she knew she was going to have a wonderful wedding.

Charles stepped out of the front pew and they stood together for the service.

The reception went off very well and guests were able to take their refreshments into the garden. Mr Ward was present, but once having been received and expressed his very best wishes to Helen and Charles, he receded into the background, and the only other time Helen saw him he seemed to be in earnest conversation with her cousin Anne. Later, Anne came up to her, when she was not talking to anybody else, and said, gravely but enthusiastically,

'That's a super Rector you've got, Helen! We had a fascinating conversation about St Paul just now.'

'Oh, yes, he's very nice,' replied Helen. 'He needs a good wife, though, then he'd be even better.'

'Yes,' said Anne, 'I thought that myself. By the way, did you know that I'm going to read Theology when I go to the university next year?'

'No, are you? That's interesting.'

'Yes, I'm looking forward to it very much. Mr Ward says he'll give me some advice if he can.'

'Oh, that's just like him. I should take him up on that offer, if I were you.'

'I shall, don't you worry!'

When she had gone, Helen thought to herself,

'I wonder. She's ten years younger than he is, but that doesn't matter. She's a very nice girl and if she's going to study Theology that would immediately give them something in common. It might work…I wonder…'

At last the time came to change and Charles and Helen departed to do so. Penelope had insisted on being the one to help her sister out of her dress and into her tavelling clothes, and performed her office with deftness and dispatch. Final goodbyes were said to all four parents inside and then they all came out on to the steps.

Outside in the garden everyone gathered to see them off and with the usual accompaniment of confetti, notices and old shoes affixed to the car, they smiled, waved, got in and drove off.

'Goodbye, Helen! Goodbye, Charlie! Safe journey! Goodbye!'